CRIMEUCOPIA

BOOMSHAKALAKiNG!

Modern Crimes for Modern Times

A Murderous Ink Press Anthology

****

CRIMEUCOPIA

BOOMSHAKALAKING!

Modern Crimes for Modern Times

First published by Murderous-Ink Press

Crowland

LINCOLNSHIRE

England

www.murderousinkpress.co.uk

Acknowledgements

To those writers and artists who helped make this anthology what it is,
I can only say a heartfelt Thank You!

Shrewd Women by Lynn Hesse, was first published by

Onyx Publications & Discovery Podcast 2022

And to Den, as always.

Contents

Listen Up Nickel Rats...

(An Editorial of Sorts)

[¿Que? Whatchamean that's **1950s Hipster slang?**]

So what's in a name? 'Boomshakalaking' is a variant of the expression 'Boomshakalaka' and is currently recognised as a boastful, teasingly hostile exclamation that follows a noteworthy achievement or pulling off an impressive stunt. Basically its meaning is similar to *in your face!*

Which is why this anthology is subtitled Modern Crimes for Modern Times, because most, if not all, are not your 'regular' crime fiction pieces — in fact some quite happily dance along the edges of multiple genres and styles, while others skew it like it is.

Of the 14 writers who appear in this anthology, eight of them are new Crimeucopians, and we open with **Scott Talbot Evans** and his **What's in a Name?** — a very modern crime of the times — before we head on into Off Centre City and let **Edward Sheehy** introduce us to **Lavender Diamond**.

Old hand **Robb T. White** brings us back onto a more steadier crooked path by talking about **Who Dips with the Devil**, and **Robert Petyo** pops up again to give an insight into a **Virtual Murder**.

From there, we take a very left field turn and let **Brian R. Quinn** recount his **Ode to the Papaya King**, which will help ease you into a wonderfully surrealesque piece from our 4th new Crimeucopian, **Orca Green**, as she tells us about **The Unity, Single-Minded**.

The Zoom Room from **Robert Parker** puts us into techno country by using post-COVID communications — while opening the door to another regular Crimeucopian, **Brandon Barrows** who rarely follows his title's advice, that of **Play it Safe**.

Two other seasoned Crimeucopians — **S.E. Bailey** with **So Clear it**

Burns, and *Edward St. Boniface* with his *Zero Points of Articulation* — make way for *Dan A. Cardoza*, who advises that we should *Never Disclose What You Bury*.

#HEIST (our first #-tagged title) sees the Crimeucopia debut of *Sean Marciniak*, our seventh new writer, who takes us into the humorous world of *Lynn Hesse* and her *Shrewd Women*.

And last, but not least, we are pleased to have *Hernán Salvarezza* within this anthology, as he recounts a tale set in Buenos Aries, and the events that occurred on *Burnt Tree Hill*.

And on a side note, in conversation with *Edward St. Boniface*, he assures us that Pyramid Ponzi is *not* the name of a 1960s female corporate assassin – but could be if the price is right....

As with all of these anthologies, we hope you'll find something that you immediately like, as well as something that takes you out of your comfort zone – and puts you into a completely new one.

In other words, in the spirit of the Murderous Ink Press motto:

You never know what you like until you read it.

What's in a Name?

Scott Talbot Evans

The voice on the other end of the phone was young and pretty. "There's no way my father commit suicide. Someone fake it. I want you to find real murderer." The number said *WITHHELD*, but she introduced herself as "Miss Knam."

I'd heard the story a millions times. Frankly, I was paying more attention to the sound of her voice. It was so high-pitched, it tickled my ear. She's young, probably in her twenties. If she's half as hot as I'm imagining her, I'm ready to propose marriage.

"Mr. Delgado, please help me."

"Call me Mark."

"And you can call me Faye." The way she said it, so sexy. *Is she coming on to me?* Oh course, I've been doing this far too long to even consider mixing business with pleasure, but that doesn't mean I can't enjoy it.

My fantasy was interrupted by a big *plunk!* The drip landing in the metal bucket in the center of my office floor. I look up at the ugly water stains disfiguring half the ceiling. I hope she is a paying customer. Just a few good days work and I'll have enough to fix that lousy pipe. I've had to put up with this water torture for over a month. Every two minutes. *Plunk!*

"My father was a happy man. He was in good health and ran a very successful business. He had everything in the world to live for." There was a pause, then I could tell she was crying. "He was a good man."

"He's at peace now."

She sniffles. "I want justice for him. I want you to find out who murder him."

There's something about her. Even when she's crying I'm turned on. Not that I would ever act on these impulses.

The last time I let a female get to me, I ended up living out of my car after the divorce settlement. Look at me, jumping to conclusions. I need to reel it in. Not every beautiful woman is a soul-sucking vortex of evil.

"My father had many important business dealing. There are many party who would gain by his death."

Oh, yes. I smell money. I look up at the ceiling and imagine what it's going to look like with a fresh coat of paint. "Don't worry, Miss Knam, I have a lot of experience with this sort of thing."

"Thank you, Mark. I had good feeling about you. Please, call me Faye."

"Well, if you want to come in, we can make the arrangements."

"That not possible. I am calling from Korea."

"Korea?" Nuts. There goes my ceiling. "I'm very sorry, but I…I don't take cases outside the US. Too many logistical problems."

"My father was murdered in San Francisco. That's where he live and work. That's part of the reason I chose you."

"Part of the reason?"

"There was another reason…"

My roguish good looks?

"Can I be honest with you, Mark?"

"Of course."

"Your name, Delgado… that is my mother's maiden name."

"Your mother is Italiana? Paisan."

"Yes. Call me foolish, but I thought it would be lucky."

"There's nothing foolish about believing in destiny."

"I'm willing to pay extra for the inconvenience of doing our business over phone."

Plonk! The sound isn't so bad when you know it's going to be fixed soon. Where did I put the plumber's number? I'm calling him as soon as I get off the phone. "I think I can help you, Faye, but just to be clear. I only work in the United States. If the case takes us to Korea, you're going to have to hire another agency for that."

"That ok."

"My fee is $300 per day and I would need a retainer of $5000 up front.

Does that sound acceptable?"

"Mark, my father was very wealthy. I wish to hire you to work only on his case. I want you to drop all your other cases. I'm willing to pay extra for this special service. I'm prepared to give you deposit now of $100,000, and more, for as long as necessary."

Ha! Other cases. "Of course, Faye," I say as I text her my account details so she can wire transfer the money. "I'll clear my entire calendar for you."

Plonk!

"Exactly what kind of business was your father in?"

"International currency exchange." She paused. I could hear her breath. Very sensuous. I could smell her perfume. She really was very beautiful.

"Faye, I will need access to your father's business records. I'll need to know the names of everyone he was in contact with."

"Of course. You will have full access. I'm sorry if my English is not very good."

"No. No. Just the opposite. I think your English is very good."

"My mother is American and my father Korea."

"That's sound like a good combination."

"Your mother and father are Italian?"

"No, actually my mother is Irish and German."

"That sound like good combination too. My mother's family name was Delgado."

"Mine was Ernst from the German side."

Plonk!

"Speaking of names, I'm going to need your father's full legal name?"

"Dae-Jung Knam."

"And his date of birth?"

"October 24, 1929"

"So he was 94?"

"Yes, he had a full life."

"Was he an American citizen?"

"He had dual citizenship for many years."

"And what was the date of his death?

"March 31."

"And he died in the city of San Francisco."

"Yes."

"I think I have enough to get started. Please make arrangements with his office about me getting access to his records."

"Yes, of course, and I will make transfer to your bank account as soon as we get off the phone."

"Very good then. Don't worry. We are going to get justice for your father, and please accept my condolences for your loss."

"Thank you. I think my family reputation is in good hand. Goodbye, Mark."

I call the plumber. He'll be here Friday. The San Francisco medical examiner happens to be a good friend, so this case is going to get a big head start.

Of course I don't want to solve the case too quickly, but that's never a problem. Things like this typically take a couple of months.

I get him on the phone. "Hey, Quince, I need some info on a deceased."

"Sure, buddy."

"Last name Knam, K-N-A-M. First name D-A-E-hyphen-J-U-N-G. Date of death March 31."

He works for a minute as I look up at the disgusting ceiling. The water has created a diseased drizzle pattern like varicose veins. The ceiling bulges down in the center and at the lowest point is the infamous drip.

"I'm not seeing it."

"It was ruled a suicide."

"I'm looking at the database now. If anyone died in the county I would know about it. Are you sure you have the right information?"

"I'm going to have to get back to you."

I check the bank to see if the deposit went through yet. It's going to be so sweet to see a one followed by six zeros. It's funny how fortune can change so quickly. *I'm rich. Filthy rich. Hee hee.*

The balance is 00.23. WTF? That can't be right. I know I have at least a thousand bucks in there.

I call customer service. Of course, it takes forever. Of course, we have to go through a whole rigmarole to prove who I am. The representative speaks in a professional, impersonal tone that gets on my nerves, and the whole time *plink, plonk, plunk.*

"It looks like there was a withdrawal at 3:15 this afternoon."

"I told you. I didn't withdraw any money."

"You've probably been hacked."

"Ripped off!"

"Whoever it was, they had your account information and your mother's maiden name."

Mother's maiden name? Ohhhh…that soul-sucking vortex of evil!

Lavender Diamond

Edward Sheehy

I'm done writing first-person point-of-view stories. My latest saga of a modern family stretching back several generations, voiced by 72 first-person characters including pet dogs and cats and a crow circling the narrative dispensing omniscient commentary, had been soundly rejected by dozens of publishers. My agent said first-person was overdone, mine in particular. Publishers didn't want them anymore. "Rewrite it in the third person. That's all I can tell ya." Estelle hung up before I could lodge an objection.

Rewrite? No way! To hell with what publishers wanted. What do they know? What I wanted now more than anything else was to rid my mind of all negativities. Breathing deeply and browsing the internet allowed my subconscious to roam and explore and bubble up a fresh concept. I clicked down one rabbit hole after another, an infinity mirror of celebrity gossip, horrifying crimes, and limitless trivia from the furthest corners of the metaverse.

A story about an armored car heist briefly caught my attention when I heard a crack. A dislodged chunk of writer's block landed square on my noggin and rendered me non compos mentis for twenty-four hours. When I regained my senses, I had a terrific idea for a third-person series. It was risky, but what the hell — what I'd been writing wasn't selling. Time to try something new.

The plot line needed background that could only be found in the Special Collections Archive at the downtown library—a glass and steel edifice designed by a famous architect whose name nobody could remember. As I entered the main floor reading room, my eyes locked on a striking woman in the Urban Street Lit section. Cream-colored silk blouse tucked into straight jeans and stilettos. Cascades of jet-black hair framed her lovely oval face and cheek bones so high they might require pulley ropes to properly survey.

Despite what I said earlier about swearing off first-person, there was no way I was going to allow an unreliable third-person to tell the story of what happened next. Besides, I'm the only person left alive who can tell it—so publishers be damned!

Read it and weep.

*****

The woman acknowledged my existence with a slight head nod and beckoned me toward the deserted stacks reserved for memoirs. Her eyes rolled in the direction of the next aisle over. A sultry whisper hissed from her red lips, "You see that man over there?"

A tall dude, six-feet-four with a shaved head, wore a gold chain over a tight turtleneck that showed off a thick musculature gained from years of pumping iron at Cumberland Correctional on a narcotics charge. Inside the joint, the dude known as Craz had been the leader of a brutal and murderous prison gang. Back on the streets, Craz was looking to even the score on the punks who set him up. A thug. A bad muthafucker. Call him what you want, just not to his face. I knew his backstory like the back of my hand. Craz pretended to scan the YA Romance shelves. I shrugged. "Yeah, so what?"

She shoved a package the size of a cigarette pack and a keycard in my direction. "Take this to my apartment at the Monarch. I'll meet you there. Don't let that man see you. Please, I beg you. My life is in danger."

Yeah, right. Damsel in Distress. The oldest ruse in the book. Talk about first-person being overdone. I wanted no part of this tired trope. "Why should I? I don't even know you."

She extended a well-manicured hand and whispered, "Lavender Diamond". And in the instant of our touch, I knew her backstory as well. Raised by a grandmother after her father was killed in a drive-by and her mother busted for crack, Lavender had to fight for everything she got in life. And the one thing she still craved, and would kill for if necessary, was custody of her daughter Vanessa, taken from her when she was 15. Only the bald-headed man in the YA aisle stood in her way

— the same thug who shot her father and the same punk who sold her baby for drugs. Revenge burned deep in Lavender's heart, and I felt the singe.

The pressure of her long nails dug into my palms and weakened my knees, and resolve. I grabbed the package and keycard and drifted over to the DVD bins, then made my way out the door. It had been a sunny and warm afternoon when I entered the library, but now the darkened sky, bruised with low hanging clouds, spat cold rain that left the street awash in neon reflections. The Monarch was three blocks away, overlooking the muddy river. I lowered the brim of my hat and made my way north.

*****

The Monarch rose above the mist-shrouded riverbank bathed in a rotating color palette by a sheath of LED sensors. As I entered the tower lobby, the color wash shifted from prince purple to blood red.

Lavender's keycard opened a private elevator and whisked me to the penthouse suite. Ceiling to floor glass windows wrapped around balconies on three sides. The skyline's twinkle accented the décor — gilt-edged simplicity for a cool 5 mil.

I didn't have much time. Who knew when Lavender or someone else might burst through the door. I walked to the kitchen and opened a cabinet. Inside, I found a bag of Fair Trade Peace Coffee. I poured half of the beans in the trash, then placed the small package in the coffee bag and placed it back in the cabinet. I don't why I hid it, maybe to protect Lavender, or me, if the deal went south. But why was I trusting someone I barely knew and had just met. None of it made sense.

Fortunately, I didn't have to wait long for the web of deceit that was bringing three characters together to reveal its true purpose. The elevator hissed open, and Lavender Diamond strode in like she owned the place, which she did ever since paying the 5 mil in cold hard cash.

Lavender faced me in the kitchen. "Great, you made it. I wasn't sure you would. But I had to take the chance. Where's the package?"

Before I could speak, the elevator opened again. Craz entered the room holding a Glock 17 with an eight-inch suppressor. He sized up the scene instantly. Total coolness. Motioned with the long barrel. "Both of you, over here. On the couch."

The couch was really a small sofa, but I didn't mention it. We sat very close together, knees against knees, facing an angry man with a large gun. The suppressor pointed at a spot on my forehead.

"I don't know who the fuck you are and I don't fucken care." The barrel swung over to Lavender. "Don't fuck with me, Lavender. Just give me the package."

"Then what," Lavender said, "you kill me anyway?" Her voice silky as silk.

"Last chance." His fingers grabbed the air. "The package."

Lavender and Craz locked eyes. An epic stare down of hate and betrayal. Lavender swore she'd kill Craz one of these days. Craz spat a vulgar slang, and off they went, a royal pissing contest with escalating threats and epithets. Lavender making it clear that she was the boss of the heist. The cursing was all distraction, however, as Lavender pressed my hand between the cushions until I felt the pebble-gripped butt of a 45 Colt Automatic M1911, the same military-issued model my old man carried in the Pacific and taught me how to shoot.

"Alright muthafucker, I gonna start with you." The barrel swung back to me as my hand raised the Colt and fired twice, one round catching him smack in the middle of two very wide and surprised eyes.

Lavender looked at the hole in Craz's face. "Nice shot. Now give me the gun."

I handed her the Colt. Lavender racked the slide, chambered a round, and pointed the barrel at my head. "Now give me the fucken package or I will blow your fucken brains out."

I raised my hands. "Easy, Lavender. I'm with you, remember?" I moved toward the kitchen. "But it involves coffee." I walked over to the cabinet, careful to show my hands at all times, and reached for the Fair Trade Peace Coffee bag. I spilled the contents on the marble counter. A small package slid out along with a scattering of finely ground Guatemalan beans that came from a sustainable grower cooperative and were roasted locally at a shop just a block from the Monarch. I was a huge fan.

Lavender's hand darted to the package just as a round hit her in the back and exploded out her chest, splattering me with blood. Craz not as dead as he looked. Another trope I'd have to work on. Lavender slid down the wall leaving a wet trail of blood. I yanked the Colt from her limp hand and pumped three more rounds into Craz's chest.

I lifted the package from the coffee beans and ripped it open. The paper wrap covered a polished blue box with an official seal of some kind involving an eagle. The hinged lid opened to a dark green velvet lining that encased the first and only United States minted platinum coin in the amount of one trillion-dollars headed for the US Treasury building in Washington, DC when a ruthless and highly sophisticated gang of thieves robbed the armored car on the day said coin was to be deposited in said Treasury.

The memories flooded back, before the writer's block. Of course! A daring heist in broad daylight! The trillion-dollar coin intended to bail out the country from financial collapse snatched away from right under the multiple noses of armed security guards, FBI agents, Treasury cops, and cybersecurity swat teams. Police worldwide were looking for any attempt to fence the coin, but no mention was made connecting Lavender Diamond to the biggest heist in history.

Global fixation on the theft skyrocketed. Who was behind it? In the absence of any firm leads, conspiracy theories abounded. One involved the NBA and China. All I knew was that I had a number of dangerous leads to follow in a limited amount of time and that I'd better get started.

Although news reports mentioned a shooting at the Monarch, interest faded by the time of the next shooting and the one after that. Still no word on the street about what had happened to Lavender or the coin. Nobody was talking. It was possible that only two people knew I was in her apartment the night of the shooting and they both were dead.

As the investigation dragged on, I pounded out the stories, while a few inches away, a small box used mostly as a paperweight, held the first and only one trillion-dollar coin minted by the United States Treasury—legal tender for all debts public and private. Right next to a postcard from my ex in Cabo. What was I going to do with a trillion-dollar coin? Turn it in and explain my role in two murders in Lavender Diamond's apartment? Including the one where I killed the same man, twice. No dice.

I finished a third-person take-no-prisoners survivor series set in gangsta world — Lavender Diamond, Monarch Queen. I moved the setting to Miami and quickly established a following. A niche market to be sure but it paid the bills. It was around this time that I started to suspect that someone was following me. Someone who hoped I could lead them to the trillion dollar coin. But I chalked the tingling sensation up as paranoia, right up until the moment one evening in front of my house while patting my pockets for a key I felt a hard poke in the ribs.

A silky voice said, "Don't turn around.

"Lavender Diamond! I thought you were dead."

"So did a lot of people."

I glanced over my shoulder. "Where have you been?"

She ignored my question. "And you been making a lot of money off my name, muthafucker"

I shrugged. "Not so much, really, after fees…"

"Shut up," Lavender snapped. Another poke. "And what's with all this third-person bullshit. It's my fucken story."

"Publishers," I said, "Not my idea."

"Move. Inside." Lavender stayed behind me as we entered the living room. When I turned, Lavender was dressed in a short-cropped red leather jacket, black jeans, and Timberlands. She pointed a Smith & Wesson Equalizer at my nose. "Now give me the fucken coin."

I motioned to the small box on my desk.

Lavender fingered the coin in disbelief. "You just fucken leave it out like that?"

"Why not. Nobody knows I have it."

Before Lavender could react, another voice spoke, "I do muthafucha." Craz stepped out of the shadows, behind Lavender, gripping a Baretta PX4, a lightweight model with a lot of stopping power.

I stared not believing my eyes. "Impossible!"

"The only thing impossible muthafucker is you walking outta here alive." Then to Lavender, "Drop the gun and hand it over."

Lavender let go the Equalizer, then thumb-flipped the coin to Craz. His eyes rolled upward, watching the trillion-dollar coin tumble and twirl, and in a blink Lavender slashed a razor across Craz's throat. He staggered backward, one hand grasping at the red tide gushing through his fingers, firing the Baretta wildly, nailing Lavender with a spray of hot lead.

The coin lay beneath a chair. A 9mm round had pierced the trillion-dollar coin, dead center, like a ragged bullseye.

*****

Three months later…

I was back at the desk working on the rewrite when my cell buzzed. 212 area code. I knew who it was. I tapped the phone. "Hello, Estelle. How are you?"

"I'm great, but the question is: how are you doing?"

"Making progress, half-way done."

"Excellent. And did you get rid of all the talking dogs and cats?"

"Done."

"And that stupid crow?"

"Gone."

"Fantastic. I wanna see some pages soon."

You will, don't worry. Gotta go, someone's at the door."

The girl standing on my doorstep figured to be about 15 or 16. She wore a shapeless gray hoodie, camouflage cargo pants, and black high top Converse All-Stars. Tall, with long black hair framing a lovely oval face. The same cheekbones. I was so taken by the angelic countenance that at first I didn't notice the Sig Sauer P938, a micro-compact designed for concealed carry, aimed at my gut. "You got something belonged to my mama," she snarled. "Give me the fucken coin or I will blow your fucken brains out."

And I remember thinking in that moment of a sequel series: Vanessa Diamond: Heiress to the Monarch Empire. I stepped back from the doorway, swept my arm inward, with a gracious welcome, "Absolutely I will give it to you. Please come in. I've been waiting for you."

Vanessa hesitated at the door, as if she'd overheard my interior thought for a sequel, then pressed the gun barrel to my eyeball, "My story better be first-person mutherfucker, or I'm gonna blow your fucken head off."

Who Dips with the Devil
Robb T. White

Part 1: The Plot

"Sorry to say this, Will, but I can't extend your credit line. You're up to thirty-five hundred. I'm sorry. I truly am."

"That's all right, Sam," Will replied. "I understand. Business is business."

"Business is business. I'm glad you see it that way."

The back of Will's neck burned, knowing the men back there chewing the cud in Sam's Feed Store were looking at him drive off, the bed of his pickup filled with nothing but Montana air.

Back at his house, he went to the fridge, grabbed a beer. *I ain't drinkin' my sorrows away. I'm thinking.* Will had discovered the time-honored stress reliever of talking to oneself. It didn't help much.

But he'd already done his thinking on the way back to the ranch, somewhere [past the neocortex and down where the reptile brain resides. He called his cousin's number and had one of the shortest phone conversations in his life. As soon as J.D. answered, Will said, "I'm in" and thumbed Off.

He fed his livestock with what was left, a mixture of grain and corn stalk he'd used to extend their feed.

Around six, J.D. drove up with the "friend" he'd mentioned the first time he proposed taking down the bank.

"William, this here's Pete Daniels."

Daniels had "shitbird convict" written all over him, even if Will didn't figure he was J.D.'s cellmate at Montana State Prison. Bigger than J.D. by three inches and thirty, forty pounds, he loomed over his cousin, car thief and family black sheep. Will shook the big man's hand, "Call me Will."

"Call me Dusty," the man said. "I was a guest of MSP along with J.D."

"What were in for?"

J.D. did a stutter-step. "Yo, cuz, that question would get you some stitches, you ask it around Deer Lodge."

"I'm askin' it here," Will said. "On my own property."

"No problem," Dusty replied. "This man has a right to know who he's partnering with."

"So what was it, Mister Daniels? You boosting cars like my cousin here, who's all nut sac and no brains like your boy who didn't realize they put trackers in car alarms nowadays?"

"You got no call to talk shit on me, Will—"

"Easy, J. D., easy."

The big man put a hand on J.D.'s chest without bothering to look back at him. Will thought of an alpha wolf pinning a rambunctious pup by its snout to hold it in the dirt, teach it discipline.

"MSP's got six levels of custody," Dusty said, his eyes took in Will with quiet assessment, a con's stare, belied by the friendly smile. "Three years in Medium Two, two more in Maximum for agg assault."

"That's honest," Will said.

"Fuckin-A, Will," J.D. piped in. "Dusty here, he took on three guys who jumped him in the showers. Put two of them in the hospital."

"What about the other one?" Will asked.

"Let's say he ain't spendin' his long summer nights splittin' the atom," Dusty laughed.

"You went in reverse then," Will said.

"Simple domestic got me jugged the first time. Shoulda been twelve months and out—more like six months with good time and weekend credit—but two weeks before my release date—"

"Yeah, he's doin' the short and shitty," J.D. said. "Guys find out, they try to fuck you up, get you time added when they know you're getting' out soon."

"Mister Daniels is doin' just fine, cousin. Why don't you let him say it?"

"What a prick you turned into, Willy. Not like I expected a fuckin' homecoming party."

"What was the beef?"

The smile on Dusty's face widened from razor-slit to toothy. "My wife— my soon-to-be ex-wife—was cheating on me with a Brand guy she met up at a NA meeting. He made a call to somebody at Deer Lodge—a guard the AB keeps on retainer. They told a probationer to start something with me in the chow line. It ended up with a promotion to Maximum and two more years."

"What happened to that guy?"

"Dusty caught him in the yard and broke his elbow," J.D. said. "You got any more of them beers around here, or does a man have to die of thirst waitin' for you to get done shootin' the shit?"

"Inside. Fridge."

Dusty continued despite the interruption. "Three guys were sent to discipline me for that one. Make sure the message got out. Shower's a good place for a demonstration. Warden wanted to put me in the SHU, what they call Closed Custody up there. I said I'd take my chances. I didn't want to give the Aryan Brotherhood that much opportunity to wreak havoc with my food."

"You on probation now?"

"Nope," Dusty answered. "Served my time. Fully restored to all citizenship rights and privileges. You mind if I get one of them beers?"

"Help yourself."

Dusty turned around on the top step to look down on him. "Your cousin's OK, a good man. This will go all right."

"I know J.D. all my life. He's been a cunt hair from trouble since he was fifteen. My aunt died broke-hearted because he let her down so much. It's you I'm not sure of."

"We'll have to see about that, won't we?"

Will watched him enter his house. The shadow of his back outlined against the screen door disappeared like a trick of the light. He didn't look bulked up from starchy prison food and slinging iron like J.D. He just looked big. Like a man who entered a room and tried to make himself look smaller so as not to frighten the women and children.

J.D.'s mother was a hard-drinking, chain-smoking, wild woman. J.D.'s father was her third husband. When lung cancer started to core her from the inside out like a rotten apple, she got religion and started reading the bible. J.D. wrote him from MSP, asking him to visit her before she passed. Will saw her before she died in her living room on a rental hospital bed with a hospice nurse and a Lutheran minister by her side. She was in and out of consciousness by then, often waking abruptly to shout some bible verse or chatter nonsense to people who weren't there, once talking to her three dead husbands all at once. She turned her head toward the place where Will was, and muttered, "He who sups with the Devil needs a long spoon."

Dusty Daniels appearance brought his aunt's words back. They seemed less crazy now.

He headed to the barn to work on his UTV's butterfly valve on the carburetor. He remembered Sam Butterfield's words denying him more credit that morning.

I hope business stays business, Mister Dusty Daniels...

*****

"Je-*sus* Ker-*ist*, Will, what do you got to know how the fuckin' thing come together for? All that matters is what we're going to do about it."

"Will's right to be concerned, J.D. Convicts talk a lot of shit. You know that."

"Sounds like he's sayin' his pussy hurts."

J.D. got up to go to the fridge for another beer. He was knocking back boilermakers like they were going to take the bottle on the kitchen table away.

Dusty could handle his booze. If his eyes took on a glitter as they drank and talked about the plan into the night, his smile and easy-going manner never altered. Will wondered if the two men he piped in the head back at Deer Lodge saw something besides that smile.

"See, the government opened up new leases so fast because of that bullshit overseas, so they're letting the oil companies hire, and believe me, they're coming like hogs when somebody bangs the swill bucket."

"Yeah," J.D. said, rejoining them; "companies are hiring roughnecks faster than rats can fuck, and they ain't getting' their panties in a twist over fracking like before. More oil coming down from Canada to the refineries in Great Falls and Billings."

"Your cousin's right. Bozeman's getting all kinds of extra cash to accommodate the growing population. A guy in our pod served in Afghanistan. He said it's like those days when the government flew in pallets of money, piles of it all shrink-wrapped and ready to be handed out."

"Your guy, what's he in for?"

"Fuckin' his dog," J.D. quipped. "Who gives a shit."

"Manslaughter," Dusty responded. "Point here, Will, is he drove for an armored car company that serviced that bank in Bozeman."

"You trust him to know?"

"I don't blame you for being skeptical. The convict grapevine's like a faucet on a country well. Lots of dirty water comes out sometimes. Sometimes it stinks of sulfur enough to where you could light it with a match. But sometimes, man, it's gold. This is gold, fourteen-carat."

"How come the papers don't report this sudden oil boom?"

"Fuck, cuz, when it's in the newspapers, it's over," J.D. snorted. "This is the time to strike. Right now, before the banks start backing up security. Things are loose. They ain't stayin' that way."

"Think of it like this," Dusty interjected. He reached down into his duffel bag for the state map, spread it out on the table. He took a pencil and drew an oblique rectangle connecting Havre and Wolf Point down to Great Falls and Billings. "Look at all these little shitburg towns. Right in the middle of the new leases going out like confetti. Plus, you got your pipefitters, contractors, caterers, every kind of spinoff business popping up. These suppliers need a steady cash outlay. The credit bullshit comes later."

J.D. swigged the last of his beer, burped noisily. "Dead soldier. How long Butterfield make you pay in cash before he let you draw a credit line?"

"Two years," Will said.

"There you go. I rest my case, your Honor."

"Let's go over it again," Will said.

J.D. groaned. Dusty's smile upped a notch, but not so you notice—more like a tic at the corners of his mouth before subsiding into that same fixed grin. He reached into his duffel bag again and brought out the lined notebook paper he'd showed them after supper.

He explained it again, same words, adding a caution here or a question there, talking to himself more than to either Will or J.D., as though absorbing their concerns into his recital. J.D. looked on rapt. Will figured Dusty had this worked out with his cellmate before the war vet got himself busted, which told him J.D. was a stopgap more than a partner. He spoke only to grumble about Will's questioning of a detail.

"Will, you keep interrupting the man, we're gonna be here all night. I've got some ladies I need to check out at the Red Dog Saloon over to Rock Springs."

"Whores, you mean."

"I don't pay for sex. I pay them to leave."

"When this is over, you can go wherever you want."

"Fuck that."

"Your cousin's right, J.D. We need to bunk down for the duration. No going to town. No going anywhere until the job's done."

"If this thing pans out," Will added, "and we got back with cash without a shitload of FBI agents surrounding the house with a bullhorn, I'm expecting you two to put a lot of distance between me and wherever you wind up."

J. D. stood up. "Hey, motherfucker. This job can be done with two guys, not three. So if I were you—"

"—and if I were you," Dusty said, standing to his full height without so much as scraping the chair legs. "I'd sit back down and show your cousin the courtesy he deserves for getting on board so fast."

If Will had turned his head a few degrees, he'd have missed it. Dusty was close enough to J.D.'s face to inhale the wash of fumy beer breath—an invasion of another man's space so fast that J.D. took an involuntary step backward into his own chair.

"For the record," Dusty said, looking at Will, "we need three. Two won't cut it. If I could do it with one, there'd be just me."

Looking over to J.D., he enunciated clearly. He poked an index finger into one of his sheets of paper where he'd drawn the interior of the Bozeman bank. "Two guys to put the guard and people on the floor—that's you, Will—one to get the manager or the cashier to open the vault. I can't do that alone, watch the tellers' hands for dropping in a dye pack or hitting the silent alarm buttons. That's why I need you back there with me as soon as you and Will have them secured out front."

He fixed J.D. with a look. "One motherfucking dye pack gets slipped in a bag and somebody's gonna answer to me. We clear on that, J.D.?"

"Got it...Clear, we're clear."

He motioned to his papers again. "Once I take the manager and the head cashier to the vault, we've got four minutes, not a second more. Will sings out the times so we both can hear."

To Will: "After the first one, count out the minutes. The tellers and the company officers need to understand we're professionals not to be fucked with. They think we're meth freaks who wandered in off the street we're in trouble from the git-go."

Dusty gave J.D. and Will exact positions, how to hold their weapons. Each command came with clipped, military precision. Will assumed his read on how tellers—young women mostly—behaved told him the man had seen the inside of banks as an uninvited guest before this. He drilled them separately, made them learn one another's roles at each interval of time. J.D. ceased carping. They practiced movements in the barn. Dusty drew chalk lines for the bank's dimensions.

Finally, weary of practicing, Will asked: "Why not the Billings bank? Bigger, way more money."

"Their security's state-of-the-art even with the influx of new people and businesses opening. Burglar bars, auto-lock doors, a CCTV system with high-resolution pixels that will count the pores in your nose."

J.D. laughed. "You think he didn't check it out, cuz?"

"Bozeman's smaller," Dusty continued, ignoring him. "Half the money—my armored car guy says three hundred thousand's a lowball figure. They never updated their security system when the pandemic hit."

"Better access to Interstate Ninety, cousin. No state police barracks a block away, no rapid-response SWAT team, no city cops on Main Street. It's *Mayberry R-F-Fucking-D.*, man."

Dusty left at six in the morning to drive into Bozeman "looking for anything out of baseline normal." He had them spend a day target practicing. By nine, Will and J.D. were shooting beer bottles at the treeline so they didn't spook the cattle.

"He sounds ex-military," Will said. Will took an exaggerated Weaver stance with the Taurus Will handed him.

"Fuck, this gun's a piece of shit. Let me have that Glock."

"Your aim's off," Will said. "When's the last time you went shooting."

"Probably with you down by the creek, as I do recall."

"Years ago. So what's Mister Daniels really doing in Bozeman? He doesn't want us leaving except for a beer run while he's hanging his face out near the bank we're going to rob tomorrow."

"The bank manager," J.D. said, firing off every bullet in the drum. The top of one bottle shattered. He reloaded, took aim at the bottles lining a tree branch they'd set up. "*You talkin' to me? You talkin' to me, motherfucker?*"

"You clown," Will said, looking at him in disgust. "Those gangsters at Deer Lodge train you to hold a gun like some TV asshole from Compton?"

J.D. blasted away, missed everything including the branch.

"What *about* the bank manager?"

"My bunkie wants to watch him. You know, get a feel for him. See if the guy's gonna act right when we put a gun in his face."

"What if he doesn't?"

J.D. cocked a finger gun, fired at Will, and blew imaginary smoke from the barrel.

"So he thinks observing him at work will tell him the man's character?"

"Beats me. He wants to see if he has a family. Is he gonna do a Rambo on us."

"The guns are for show, J.D. I made that clear to you and your asshole buddy."

"Whatever. I'm hittin' the Saloon tonight. Fuck him. Wanna go?"

"Not a good idea."

"Fine, chickenshit. Maybe I'll let you lick pussy juice from my dick when I get back."

*****

Part 2: The Heist

"Right there," Dusty ordered Will. "Turn left."

"I been coming here since I was ten," Will said. "I know where to turn."

They were on South Willson, a half-block from the First Third Bank on Main. Will simmered from the change in plans. Dusty's Nissan wouldn't start, so his truck was pressed into service—a change in plans big enough to demand postponing the job, Will said.

"No way, dude," J.D. snapped. "Now or never."

The closer to zero hour, the more J.D. began fidgeting.

"My truck, my ass," he complained. "CCTV cameras from here to Bozeman. Every house has a doorbell camera now. You think it won't be on video right down to the rusted tailpipe?"

"Stop whining, bitch. Dusty and me, we'll toss in a few bucks from our share. Buy you a Lambo."

It rankled Will that their mastermind, the stickler for every detail, was so casual about swapping vehicles. Hours ago, Will had to put himself between Dusty and J.D. yesterday morning to keep the big man from ripping J.D. a new asshole when he realized J.D.'s "allergy reaction" was a hangover.

Big thunderheads moved over the Rockies by noon. J. D. thought a big downpour would favor them. Will wasn't so sure. Fewer people and cars on the street; anybody speeding in the rain would get attention.

"Stop checking your watch," Dusty ordered J.D.

They parked in an abandoned lot behind the municipal building. The camera angle of the lens above the ATMs near the drive-through wouldn't cover them from that distance. The bank was located off the ground-level floor, but the lobby faced Main Street. A foyer with prints of the Rockies at sunrise and sunset led to a bank of elevators. "Lord, they designed it for a heist," J.D. said. "We'll be runnin' out that door with bags of cash like six-legged jackrabbits."

Two high-rises across the street behind the bank provided cover with pedestrian traffic.

"Look at these losers," J.D. mocked, watching the trickle of residents walking through the painted crosswalk to the back doors of the building. "First of the month. The welfare checks are in, boys and girls! Ha, lookie, that chick

22

in the sweat pants is already twitching."

"Pot calls kettle black," Will said. "You're awful damn antsy yourself bouncing around on that bench seat. What did you snort or smoke before we left the house?"

J.D.'s eyes were too bright in the rearview mirror; he kept wiping the sheen of perspiration from his upper lip with his cloth mask.

The Loomis armored truck went past ten minutes late. They couldn't see the delivery from their vantage. Dusty opposed J.D.'s suggestion he get out to watch from the street: "Forget it, moron. No phones pinging off cell towers, no eyewitnesses remembering some idiot standing on a street corner like a male hooker just before a bank gets robbed."

"Maybe they changed deliveries and pickup times since your guy was sent up."

"Maybe they didn't."

That ended that.

"Twenty minutes," Dusty said. "They're in and gone. Bags, gloves, masks, guns. Let's go."

"Yee-haw, time to quit fuckin' the dog, boys."

"Hang on, cowboy. Will, you get the guns."

Will had to be the armorer. Two cons newly released from MSP, one still on probation, made that logical. J.D. must have blabbed about him from his prison cell, said he had a cousin with guns, a base of operations, and now, the transport. J.D. was poor as a shithouse mouse. It explained why Will was included in the heist. J.D. wanted to saw off Will's 12-ga. shotgun and wear it on a sling inside his flannel shirt. "They hear me rack that baby, every fucker in the place will hit the deck," he crooned.

"It's a Browning over-under, idiot," Will explained. "I suppose the customers can stand around and watch you insert the shells while they scream."

"Knock it off, God damn it."

"Gee, Dad, sorry."

It was the only time Will saw Dusty Daniels come close to losing his temper. Will fetched the Glock, Taurus, and Browning .380 from the toolbox in the truck bed, a precaution in case they were stopped on the way by a curious or bored state trooper.

"Masks, left side pocket. Guns, right side, safeties off. Will, nylon cuffs. Don't let your hands show with that latex once we get out. Walk normal.

Cameras will pick us up inside with our masks, but let's not tell them ahead of time we're coming in to rob the place."

"Yeah, yeah, let's roll. Let's do this thing."

Will looked hard at his cousin. "Take your hand off it. It's in there, leave it alone."

"You keep fussing with it, dumbass, you'll shoot yourself in the balls and I'll leave you behind."

Dusty led, Will a step behind, J.D. bringing up the rear.

Inside the double doors, groups of people stood waiting for elevators. They followed some people heading left to the doors leading to the bank.

Will's eyes boxed the interior of the bank. Three customers wrote checks or did paperwork at the kiosks; the manager's and head cashier's offices were glassed cubicles side-by-side in the rear, just as they'd practiced in the barn. Three short lines of customers stood at the tellers' windows.

The plexiglass barriers were still in place from the pandemic, but the outsized footstep decals on the floor advising six-foot distances had been removed. About a third of the people in line wore masks, mainly the older ones, including an obese man in a wheelchair.

The mid-twenties, overweight security guard looked rumpled as an unmade bed. He didn't turn his head when the three assumed positions at the backs of the lines. A long fifteen seconds passed. From his place in the middle line, J.D. wouldn't take his eyes off Dusty despite the big man's lectures not to stare at him for the signal.

Dusty lifted his hand to scratch his right ear, J.D. and Will peeled off, guns out, yelling, "Get down! Get down!"

Will's first task was to disarm the guard—""Get that fat prick on the floor as soon as possible. I'm giving it to your older cousin here," Dusty explained, "because his blood's cooler."

"What the fuck does that mean?"

"It means it ain't running south of his belt every two hours from looking at porn on his cell phone and fucking up his brain like you."

The noise of shouts rose by decibels with every passing second. Will had the gun at the big kid's temple just as the guard's hand unstrapped the flap cover. Will clamped a hand on the guard's.

"Don't," he said in the boy's ear. Will put him on the ground with a leg sweep behind his knees and landed with his knees on his back. "Hands behind your back!"

To J.D. and Dusty, he shouted: "Thirty seconds!"

He kept the nylon cuffs in both side pockets and cinched them around his wrists. That was the one move he practiced on J.D. until his cousin refused to lie down for it one more time.

"Gonna be a big ruckus all around," Dusty told Will. "Things'll be moving fast. Keep your wits about you and don't let that guard think twice. Some of these rent-a-cops tuck a twenty-two or a four-shot Derringer in an ankle holster."

J.D. had the manager and head cashier out of their offices. He stuck his barrel in the back of the manager's neck and frog-marched both. Hands above their heads, they stumbled, following J.D.'s commands. Will flashed to a boyhood memory of primates at the Wildlife Zoo in Billings, the way bonobos ran through the grassy enclosure, hands dangling above heads like chopper riders, just like that.

"He won't give us no trouble," Dusty had pronounced on his return from his surveillance. "Got a family in a gated community who doesn't want to lose to protect the bank's money."

Will glanced up to see Dusty pointing a gun at the first teller's face, shouting through the veins in his neck. Frozen in place, she didn't comprehend his demand she open the small access door *RIGHT FUCKING NOW!*

Will bellowed above the tumult: "One minute!"

J.D., glistening with sweat from whatever drug he ingested, was bug-eyed, frenzied. He forced all the customers in the three lines down to the carpet, waving his gun and screaming. Only one old couple resisted; they pleaded, bent double by fear and age, but unable to drop to the floor. J.D. cursed, hurled the man to the carpet by his shirt front and slammed the butt of his Glock into the old woman's face. Teeth and blood flew from her mouth. She went down backwards in a heap and lay there motionless.

"Motherfucker! Motherfucker! Motherfucker!" J.D. bellowed, a savage mantra that terrified more than it becalmed the people on the floor.

Dusty hollered at him: "J.D., the door! Don't the rest of you fuckin' move!"

He pointed his gun at the other tellers.

Will heard a creaking noise and saw the wheelchair man heading for J.D. in a crazed act of bravura. J.D. shot him in the forehead. He pitched over his wheelchair, bringing it down on top of him.

Losing control, Will thought. *We're losing control...*

J.D. raced to the counter and hurdled it high-jumper style. Drugs or adrenalin enabled him to vault clear but his feet kicked a Plexiglas barrier, splintering it into shards that flew in all directions. One sliced open the cheek of the closest teller; a sheet of blood poured down her face.

Clusterfuck...clusterfuck... Will's stomach flipped with nausea. For a fraction of a second, he thought of bolting for the doors to escape before the rest of this house of cards collapsed. Instead, he refocused, stepping over to the prone bank officers and kicked the bottom of the manager's shoe so he'd know he was covered. His peripheral vision showed him J.D. opening the door for Dusty to rush through.

"Get them in here!"

Will hauled the manager and cashier to their feet and shoved them toward the open door. "Three minutes!" he said in a choking voice behind them.

Dusty grabbed the manager by the shoulder and hissed. "Open that vault!"

"I can't!" the man pleaded. "It's a timed lock."

Dusty shot him in the head.

Will re-entered the nightmare zone he'd left behind a moment—or a lifetime—ago. The man seemed to lean into the shot instead of backward, as though he were assisting his own murder. A geyser of red blood shot sideways. He dropped soundlessly to the floor. The middle teller erupted in high-pitched coyote yips. Another teller screamed, waved her bare right arm back and forth in a frenzied effort to shake off the manager's blood and a fragment of clotted brain.

As though God Himself were rendering judgment on the surreal grotesquerie, a clap of thunder crashed down from the skies, echoing ripples spread out like waves to make the walls reverberate; a deep, growling sound rumbled through the building. People on the floor who'd been silent began praying aloud, some wept.

Dusty howled into the head cashier's ears: "Open it! Now!"

She complied, her fingers deftly hitting the keypad and twirling the propeller handle. Dusty removed the vinyl bag from behind his windbreaker and began filling it. J.D. flung his at Dusty's feet while maintaining his guard-dog position. Will flung his over the counter, hitting Dusty in the backside. He didn't stop moving his hands. Wads of denominations flew off the shelves into all three bags. He tossed them over the counter. Despite his racing heart, Will admired the woman's calm. J.D., like a slavering dog at his master's feet, prowled up and down the line terrifying them, screaming unnecessarily, as though anyone in her right mind would resist at that point, with their boss bleeding out on the floor. The teller at the end of the row, the smallest and youngest of the women, slumped over in her chair and fell to the floor in a dead faint.

J.D. ran to her, wagged the gun in her face, threatening her to get up.

Will shouted: "She fainted, you idiot! ...Five minutes! Time, time!"

Somewhere an alarm clanged accompanied by shrill siren screams in three-second bursts. The hairs on Will's arms and neck stood up.

Idiotically, J.D. started scooping money from the drawers until Dusty barked, "Leave it!"

They bolted. Dusty burst through the access door, rocking it off its hinges, and tossed one of the bags at Will. J.D. caught a bag on the fly like a quick-pitch to a running back. Will followed them out, his back toward them—few were brave enough to look back at him. Gun in one hand, money bag in the other, he fled through the foyer doors. Dusty and J.D., legs pumping over the asphalt lot, raced ahead to the truck.

Will threw open the door, ripped off his mask, and heaved his bag at J.D. in back. Dusty sat stone-faced, still masked in the passenger seat.

With all the hooting from J.D. in back, Will couldn't think. He had the return route programmed in his head with contingencies like the silent alarm someone tripped that had already alerted cops. A mile to the entrance ramp for Interstate 90, he spotted the turquoise-cherry lights of three cruisers heading toward Main Street.

"Slow down, Will," Dusty said, clearing his throat of phlegm. "You mind asking your cousin back there to put a plug in it?"

Those were the first words Dusty spoke since they fled the bank.

"Whooee! Man, I can't breathe!" J.D. howled.

"You don't shut your trap, I'll do it for you."

"You shot a guy in a wheelchair," Will croaked, staring into the rearview. "Maybe that old couple, too."

The adrenalin rush subsided as the miles passed. His tunnel vision expanded, dissipated, dissolved. Will was left with a sour taste in his esophagus and a hot blob of grease in his stomach. His knuckles white on the steering wheel, he tried to relax the tension by staring at the landscape blurring past and realized it wasn't the same world he recognized that morning when he stepped off the porch.

J.D. broke the grim silence. "How 'bout some music, cousin?"

Murdered a man who couldn't walk...now he wants music—

Will relived the manager's surreal death scene. He opened his mouth to speak, but couldn't find the right words. Dusty reached over to punch the On button. Will's pre-programmed channels played in teasing sequence.

"That one," J.D. said when the third tune filled the interior. "Dolly. Love the hooters on that old hillbilly gal."

He lip-synced to "Jolene"; the barrel of the Glock his mic: *"I'm beggin' of you please don't take my man..."*

Without a word, Will hit the Off button.

"Dayyemm, you fellas are no fun. Hey, Dust, how much we got in here you think?"

"Enough, I reckon....Enough."

It was the way he muttered that final word that made Will uneasy. He made a noise that sounded like a sob which he tried to cover with a cough. Dusty turned slightly in his seat to regard him.

"You OK, partner?"

"Sure," Will replied. "I'm fine. We just killed people back there. Yeah, I'm fine."

He wasn't angry with the two men. He was furious with himself. He crossed a line he couldn't come back from. Discovering he didn't bring all of himself over that line disgusted him.

*****

Part 3: The Roundup

The money sat in three piles of banded denominations on the kitchen table with the Jim Beam and beer bottles. J.D. was polluted, drunk. The tiny kitchen reeked of marijuana smoke.

"Hey, how about some Texas Hold 'em? We got money to play."

"You two play," Will said. "I'm turning in."

J.D. had greasy slits for eyes for the last hour; once they got back, he hit the bottle hard and hadn't stopped.

"I'm turning in too," Dusty said. "Got a long way to go in the morning."

"What about your car?" Will asked.

"Probably the starter coil. I'll jump it in the morning. You got the cables in your truck. Give me your key, and I won't have to wake you. I'll leave it in the mailbox."

"You won't wake me. I'll be up to feed my stock."

"Suit yourself, partner."

J.D.'s head sank lower to the table as if someone were turning a valve. He blinked once, snapped his head up to ask a question: "Where we off to...morning...Dush—Dusty?"

They watched him pass out at the table.

"He can't hear you now."

"Don't matter," Dusty said. "He ain't traveling with me. You want some advice? Cut that fucker loose. He's headed back to the Graybar Hotel sure as shit."

"Thanks for your advice, Daniels. J.D.'s Momma used to say, 'Talk is cheap. It takes money to buy whiskey.'"

"Well, then, you got your money now. I'll say my goodbyes. So long, Will. Good luck with the ranch. My old man would say you're shoveling shit against the tide."

He said it with a smirk and went over to the couch to make up his bed.

Will hit the light switches, gripped J.D. under the arms and led him down the darkened hallway to the bedroom he and Maddy shared until the divorce. He had moved their bed into the smaller room in back where they kept boxes, mostly her sewing stuff and his hunting gear. He left the rest; from time to time, he thought about moving it all into the barn.

J.D. moaned, talked, and thrashed in his sleep. Will couldn't make anything out of the gibberish except that it sounded aggressive. It struck Will odd that his cousin might have demons plaguing him, but then, he didn't know what it was like to spend a couple years in a confined space with criminals, let alone cell with someone like Dusty Daniels.

Will knew the hours of the night as well as the scars on his hands. Shortly before false dawn, he heard another noise coming from J.D.'s room—a muffled noise, a loud groan. Will swung his legs over the bed, rubbing his eyes. He threw on pants, put on the snake boots he kept for hunting duck on the Gallatin River. The rest of what he'd worn for the heist as well as all their clothing and gear went into the fire pit, although J.D. refused to give up his own boots, claiming they were "lucky."

He avoiding stepping in the places where the boards creaked. He noted the bulky outline of Dusty on the couch barely illuminated from the window light.

Opening the door to his old bedroom, he made out the figure of J.D. lying on his stomach, one buttock cheek of his ass exposed to the saffron moonlight spilling through the window. One leg dangled off the bed. He thought of putting on the light but decided against it: *Let him sleep it off.*

The big man was right about his cousin and the likelihood of his return to prison—if they managed to evade the bank job, which he considered a catastrophe despite the three bags of cash totaling $98,000. His own sleeplessness was part guilt from seeing a killer staring back at him in the bathroom mirror, and part from severing a family tie he'd known since childhood. He was betraying his Aunt Winnie by kicking her son out, knowing it had to be. J.D. would drag him down; the boy had to go.

He'd turned around to return to his room when the door moved slightly. Will's neck hairs prickled—no draft tonight, just muggy heat. Last year, he'd been hit in the chest by his bull. It felt like that; he was knocked backward onto the bed on top of J.D., whose body moved from the force of Will landing on it. It told Will what his instincts failed to tell him when he detected the lumpy form outlined on his couch: *That's not him. He's in here*—Somewhere in his brain, below the neocortex, he knew from the phony goodbye hours earlier...

Dusty's arm swung in the dark but missed him. Whatever object he held in his fist when he swung raked the top of Will's head and knocked him off J.D.'s body but left him conscious. Will rolled to the end of the bed and dropped to the floor just as the object slammed into the bed where he'd been a moment before.

Trapped beside the bed and the wall, Will resisted the urge to raise himself up. Dusty was waiting for that—an easy finish. When Will's head failed to clear the edge of the bed, Dusty jumped onto the bed and brought the firewood in his hands down on the space where Will was tucked, knees and hands up to protect his face. The meat end of the log connected with the edge of the night table with such force that it splintered wood and ricocheted out of his hand.

"I don't need no fucking piece of wood to kill you," he grunted, calm as ever.

He pulled Will out by one of his boots. Will kicked him in the solar plexus with his other foot but couldn't get enough inertia behind it to do more than knock the big man backward. By the time Will got to his feet, using the mattress to brace himself, he failed to get leverage to set his feet for combat. His would-be killer had another advantage: Will was backlit by window light.

Dusty batted away Will's awkward swing as easily as swatting a pesky fly from his face. He hit Will in the nose, shattering cartilage. Will, blinded, took another clumsy swing that landed on Dusty's chin but did no damage. He was jerked off his feet by a pair of powerful hands around his neck in a vise grip. Will kicked at the big man's crotch; in that cramped space, however, it was like fighting in a closet. Blood from his nose flew, eye floaters multiplied like columns of gnats in shafts of light, turned reddish gold, and Will knew he was seconds from passing out.

Dusty's hands wanted to interlace fingers around Will's neck. Will gagged on blood choking him. He spewed a gob into Dusty's face. So unexpected, Dusty loosened his grip, jerked backwards, which allowed Will time to interlock his arms between Dusty's forearms and apply as much pressure on Dusty's elbows as he could muster in that weakened state. Like a swimmer fighting a rip tide, he held nothing back.

It worked—almost. Dusty threw him to the floor and kicked him in the head. The wall behind him threw off Dusty's aim and most of the momentum; still, his boot landed with enough force to bring Will to the edge of blacking out for good.

"Cocksucker, I'm going to break all your bones before I kill you."

The calm way he said it was a shot of adrenalin straight into Will's heart.

Dusty grabbed Will's head to slam it against the bed frame, smash it like a rotten cantaloupe. But Will's doubled-up, fetal position saved him once more. With his back leg tucked under him, he reached around for his boot and came out with it. Dusty leaned down to get a firmer grip.

The punch dagger went under Dusty's arm several inches deep into his armpit.

The big man jumped back as if bitten by a water moccasin.

"What the holy fuck—"

Will couldn't get up to fight. He was able to hold the knife in his fist in front of him.

Footsteps. The door slammed against the wall. Heavy footsteps in the hallway—Dusty in retreat.

Will was too stunned by the fight to know what happened. He realized the knife he held a moment before was not in his hand. He spread his palm on the floorboards feeling for it, knowing he'd die if Dusty returned with a knife or gun. That was all he remembered when the black vortex, a devil duster magically appeared in his bedroom to take him far from that place where he was snorting blood and pawing the floor for his knife.

*****

Light burned his eyes. His face was a throbbing bundle of exposed nerve endings. He tried several times to get up but couldn't manage. *Fuck it, I'll sleep for a bit and then try it again later.* There was something he had to do— something important—but he couldn't recall what that important thing was.

When he woke again, he knew the pain was spreading throughout his body. His limbs were numb from the cramped position he had lain in. Like a toddler, one foot in front of the other, he staggered out to the doorway. He cast a backward glance at J.D. knocked to the floor, lying on his back, eyes glazed like a dead bird's. The blood pooling around his head like a three-tiered halo exposed different shades: black at the perimeter, rust-brown below that, and a burgundy hue. Both nostrils, however, exposed candy-apple red plugs of snot.

Will moved toward him, changed his mind. He didn't think he had strength to spare.

"Sorry, D.J.," he croaked to the body on the floor.

He moved down the hall to his bedroom for his Browning shotgun and was grateful to see it still in his gun closet. In his confusion, he broke it, shucked out a perfectly good cartridge, fumbled on the floor to replace it in the chamber.

Making his way back down the hall, he hesitated at the entrance to the living room. If Dusty planned an ambush, it would be right there. The coverlet over the pillows mocked him for the ruse he'd bought that nearly cost him his life. Feebly, like an old man with severe arthritis in all his joints, Will swiveled his aching neck from one corner of the room to the other.

It seemed too good to be true that Dusty vamoosed. He spotted a pair of boots sticking out from the kitchen, toes up.

The man inside the boots was dead—bled out on the floor trying to stanch a fatal wound that had severed the axillary artery, a major vessel carrying blood to the brain. Blood-soaked towels lay about the body of Dusty Daniels; his expression in death was one of befuddled, grimly amused surprise.

Will sat on the floor beside the body and sobbed.

*****

"Ain't seen you much lately, Will," Sam Butterfield said. "Hope everything's OK."

"Everything's fine," Will replied. "I had this damn flu bug. Couldn't shake the damn thing off."

The raccoon eyes were cleared up, but his bent nose wasn't going anywhere.

"That your new pickup?"

"Bought it used at a lot in Three Forks." Which was true.

"You do look rode hard and put away wet. Lost some weight, too."

"Needed to." Will patted his belly, mindful of the healing ribs. "I figgered as I was back to getting on my feet, I might swing by to settle up my bill with you."

"Always glad to see money."

Will left Sam's small office in the back of the store with his receipt. One of Sam's nephews was loading up feed sacks in the truck.

Sam came out to shake Will's hand.

"I heard your cousin's out. Surprised he hasn't been around to the bars. He was a handful to your Aunt Winifred I recall."

"Maybe he'll be by. With D.J., you never know."

"So long, Will."

He had time to get home, replace some of the bandages that were sticky, and head for the Sheriff's auction at Jim Reece's farm on Bridger Creek Road. He needed the backhoe old Jim drove before his stroke. The putrid smell from the barn was getting so noxious he couldn't get within ten feet of it without disturbing the cloud of black flies hanging around. With $90,000 of cash left, he was beginning to see himself as the rancher his folks always wanted him to be.

Virtual Murder

Robert Petyo

Gunner didn't want me to kill him, just beat him up a little and make him reconsider his decision. Syd was hinting that he found another money-maker and was stepping away from the drugs. Gunner didn't like that since Syd was his dealer in the Black Mountain. I didn't like it either since running deliveries for Syd was my main source of income. I hadn't made a delivery in almost a month and my meager finances were drying up. I even had to hit Amy's corner store for a few bucks. It was hardly worth the risk, but I appreciated the few bucks it netted me.

I had spoken to Syd on the phone a few times, trolling for work, but all he said was that he was looking into some other options. That might be terrific for him, but not for me, or Gunner.

"I'm working on a new project," Syd told me. "I'm going to eliminate the middleman."

"You are the middleman," I said.

"Not any more. I'm going to go into business for myself. That's the way I'm looking at it. Big business. And I'm looking out for number one."

"Gunner's not going to like that."

"He could stand a little competition."

"Competition? You're staying in the drugs? Will you still have deliveries for me?"

"Different business, my friend. I'm moving on up. I won't need any deliveries. But don't worry. You can always work for Gunner. If he stays in business after I hit paydirt."

That wasn't what I wanted to hear. I didn't want to have to work directly for Gunner's organization. Too risky. I liked it better being a small, unobtrusive cog in the delivery machine. "So, what is this project you're working on?"

But he wouldn't tell me. I didn't think it could be drugs. Gunner controlled all of that in this county. I couldn't imagine that Syd would take him on directly. Maybe he was planning to go somewhere else.

I didn't really care about the details. All I wanted was for Syd to keep paying me to deliver.

I was still considering my options when I heard from Gunner a few days later. Well, not actually Gunner, but one of his underlings. Gunner sought me out because he knew I dealt directly with Syd. I didn't really want to play enforcer. Again, too risky. But at that moment I had little choice.

Syd lived in an upscale development about two miles from the river that separated the Black Mountain from the decrepit slum where I slept in Carla and her boyfriend's basement, payment for my acting as her occasional bodyguard. Syd's place wasn't a mansion, but running drugs had been good to him. Why he was looking into a "new project" and trashing a good thing was beyond me. But I do know Syd always considered himself a businessman first. A semi-legitimate businessman. Maybe he found another more successful business.

The houses on the sloped side of the development were widely spaced, each with immaculate lawns. A brick path ran about twenty yards up to Syd's front door. His paved driveway to the right led to the back of the house.

I had Carla's boyfriend drop me in front of the place and hurried up to the small front porch where I knocked on the door. A light flickered on the doorbell camera that was just to the left of the door. Leave it to Syd, the wannabe legitimate businessman, to have all the latest gizmos.

When there was no answer, I rang the doorbell. I heard heavy clanging of the bell like a funeral dirge from deep inside the house, but the door didn't open, nor did I hear anyone moving about. I waited another minute before leaving the porch and circling along the driveway to the back of the house. The two-car garage was open and the black Lexus parked inside told me somebody was home. There was a back door next to the garage, but it was locked.

I patted the inside pocket of my jacket, assuring myself that the gun was still there. It wasn't real, but it served its purpose, especially when I ushered Carla to and from her stripper gigs.

I walked into the garage and admired the Lexus before moving to the entrance to the house that was to the right between two large wooden cabinets that were padlocked. Syd kept some of his stash there, which made me wonder why he left the garage door open.

The narrow door was locked. I rattled the knob in frustration until I thought my hand would fall off. I rapped on the door but got only a hollow thump in response.

Hollow.

It wasn't a thick wooden door. I should be able to break it, if I could find something to use. I rooted around the back of the garage and found a big black crowbar. A few solid blows put a hole in the door that allowed me to reach in and unlock the knob. As soon as I pushed inside, crowbar still in my hand, fake gun in my pocket, I waited and listened.

The house was silent except for a harsh repetitive beeping, like a smoke alarm.

Alarm!

I should have known. Syd had an alarm system. If he was here, he would come running to see what was going on. If not, the cops would probably be here shortly.

Not much time.

But it didn't take me long to find Syd. He was in his basement entertainment room which included a sunken section in the center with a television screen and tons of computers. Syd lay on the floor in front of a larger TV screen that covered the right wall. He wore white goggles with solid opaque lenses that covered half his face, and there were two large white rings lying on the floor near his waist. One ring had two tiny joysticks poking out of the inner rim like a kid's video game. Multi colored lights on the sides of the goggles blinked.

"Syd," I shouted as I crossed the room toward him.

He didn't react, and as I drew nearer, I figured he was dead. Still, I crouched and felt for a pulse. Nothing. His cheeks were pale. I wanted to get a look at his eyes so I reached behind his neck and unhooked the goggles. It was a struggle getting them free, but I pulled them away and looked at his dead eyes, wide open, pupils dilated.

Heart attack?

Overdose? Syd rarely used his own merchandise, but I guess it was possible.

What now? Call an ambulance? The cops? Or get the hell out of there?

I chose the last option and grabbed the rings to go with the goggles as I hurried back to the garage. I heard the sirens as I neared the Lexus.

So soon?

I stepped out into the yard. The sirens were right in front of the house now, so I couldn't circle to the front of the house without being seen. Instead, I darted across the backyard toward a low fence that separated Syd's property from a neighbor's.

"Stop right there!"

I dove over the fence and somersaulted back to my feet. Still clutching the goggles, I ran to the right toward a row of bushes.

"Stop."

I heard the cop starting to run across the yard, but I had enough of a head start. I kept running along the fence into a second yard, then veered toward the house. If my sense of direction still worked, I would come down the back side of the hill to Fillmore Street, far from the cops who would be parked in front of Syd's house. I just hoped they didn't have anyone patrolling the area.

I raced down Fillmore Street to the entrance to the development, marked by two stone pillars, but no gate. A taxi was waiting near the entrance, its motor running as the driver leaned against the hood smoking a cigarette. When he saw me, he threw the cigarette down and stomped on it. "Are you Mr. Simonson?"

I smiled at him, said "hello," and knocked him on his ass, jumping behind the wheel while he was still rolling on the ground.

I only drove three blocks before banging the cab up onto the curb and dashing into Patrick Park, a large expanse of baseball fields and playgrounds surrounded by trees. All the time I kept listening for sirens.

Nothing.

Familiar with the park, I easily followed the hiking trail through the woods, finally coming out to the alley beside Four Tubs Creek.

Still no sirens. I took a few deep breaths and hustled to the bus stop on the corner.

*****

Sitting in Carla's basement I stared at the goggles that lay on the floor in front of me.

"I've got a gig in an hour," she called down the steps. "Are you going to be ready?"

"No problem." I heard her coming down the stairs.

"Hey, you know that guy Sydney Counsel, don't you?"

I stood up.

"I just saw it on the news. They found him dead in his house."

"What happened?" I asked, playing dumb as she appeared at the bottom of the stairs, ducking her head to get into the basement. Carla was— the term I would use is statuesque. It made her popular in the strip joints that don't have a lot of strippers over six feet tall. But it also made her too popular with some of the patrons. That's where I came in.

"They don't know for sure, but they think it was an overdose."

"Really? I thought it was a heart attack. I didn't think he used drugs."

"Just like you don't use them, huh?" She gave me a scolding look, her red lips curling in a sneer. "Wait a minute. You knew he was dead?"

Oops. "No. I just know he didn't lead a healthy life. Drinking and cigarettes. Anyone beat him up or anything?"

"Well, they did say someone broke into the place, but there were no marks of any kind on the body. Apparently, he just collapsed. Had to be drugs." She glanced at the floor at my feet. "Hey? What's that?"

I picked up the goggles. "I don't know. A friend of mine gave them to me."

She moved closer. "Yeah. I think they're one of those virtual reality things." She looked down and scooped up the two large white rings that were on the floor. "Yeah. My sister has one of these."

"What do they do?"

She checked the rings and pressed a few buttons. "Yeah. I guess this one's battery operated. Here. Let me see." She held out her hand for the goggles and when I handed them to her, she slipped them on me and snapped them shut in the back.

"Hey." I couldn't see anything, but I felt her hands running over the sides of the goggles until a light came on and the screen in front of me was a murky white, like a rain cloud.

"See anything?" she asked.

"No."

"Let me see if your friend left a program hooked up."

"Program?"

Suddenly, the light before me started to bubble like I was under water. Colors appeared. It firmed up into a picture of a park, a massive green field with a sunny blue sky above it. Not like a painting. More like a sophisticated cartoon. Animated. I saw some birds flying in the distance.

"What's going on?"

"See anything?" she asked.

"Yeah." I turned to the left and the picture before me rotated until I saw a small pavilion with a few benches on it. It was like I was in the cartoon. I reached out with my left hand and staggered to the side when I saw a hand appear on the screen. "Jesus."

"You okay?"

I looked toward the pavilion again and saw an animated figure stand and come toward me, one arm extended. "Take one," he said. I saw that he had a handful of white pills. "It's the best high you'll ever experience."

"What's happening?" I heard Carla ask.

Without even thinking I took one of the pills and slapped it toward my face. I swallowed, even though I knew that in the real world, there was nothing in my mouth.

After a few moments, the pusher returned to the pavilion. I turned and watched the birds. I felt like I had just awoken from a deep comforting sleep. The world was in front of me ready to be conquered.

I was in total control and unstoppable.

It was like my first hit of coke.

I took a deep breath and turned to the left to see that the pavilion was gone. Still, the birds swirled in the sky. So peaceful. I felt myself drifting upward. My arms spread like wings.

Suddenly, my vision started to blur like I had just had too many shots of vodka and I staggered back and felt my way into the chair. I slapped my hands to my chest where my heart pounded, trying to burst from its cage and surge through the fresh air.

"Murray, what's wrong?"

I barely heard her voice tickling my ears. Like I was flying at a high altitude, my ears suddenly blocked up and I swallowed, trying to clear them. My mouth was dry and I scratched my palate as I tried to swallow. I swung my mouth open, hoping to suck in some air, but I could barely breathe.

"Murray!"

The sides of my head screamed like someone had ripped some skin off when she tore off the goggles. For a few moments I still saw the birds circling the field, but gradually I saw the walls of the basement. I was still huffing, but I could feel my heartbeat returning to normal.

"What the hell was that?" Carla asked, staring down at the goggles that were on the floor.

I stood slowly, maintained my balance and reached toward her. "You say you've got a job, right? You better get moving then."

"But what about that?" She pointed toward goggles on the floor.

"Just get going," I said. Now I knew exactly what special project Syd had been working on, a million-dollar project that was now going to solve all my money problems, and there was only one person I wanted to discuss it with.

*****

The Manhole was a dank smoky bar in the basement of a building that housed a dollar store and a vape shop. It was one of Carla's main venues, but it was also my least favorite one because of the gang bangers, drug dealers, and gangsters who hung out there. There were probably more bouncers and security than there were patrons. It was a war waiting to break out. But people still flocked to the place, and occasionally I ran into people I'd rather avoid.

On this night, however, I was glad to be there. Carla had just started her routine near the metal pole in the center of the small wooden stage, about two feet off the floor, when I saw the Turtle, one of Gunner's henchmen. He was near the back wall talking to two women who looked like waitresses. I scanned the area around him, but there was no sign of Gunner. Too bad. He was the one I really wanted to see, but the Turtle would have to do.

As the music picked up and there were a few cheers as Carla removed her top, I headed toward Turtle. He saw me when I was about five feet away, and he nudged away the women.

"Hi," I said. "Where's your boss?"

He ignored me and looked toward the stage.

"Don't give me the silent treatment. I'm pretty sure he'll want to talk to me."

He gradually looked at me.

"About Syd Counsel." No reaction. "He was working for your boss." The stage lights highlighted a slight twitch of his eyes and I knew I was on the right track. "I think I have some information for Gunner. Something Syd was trying on his own. Something Gunner will want to know about."

Turtle made a big deal of shrugging his broad shoulders until he looked like a hunchback. "Don't mean nothing to me. Or the boss. Syd's dead."

I tried to move a bit closer but he tensed up, his arms raised to his chest, and I froze. "But he was working on a special project that might cut into your boss' profits."

Again, the shrug, this time his shoulders coming up to the middle of his red ears. "He was doing what he always did." He relaxed his shoulders and looked around as if suddenly concerned that we were being overheard. He grabbed my arm and yanked me closer to the wall. "He doled out the merchandise. That's all he ever did. We supplied it to him, and he used lugs like you to deliver it."

"No. This is something bigger." I was beginning to think that maybe Turtle wasn't in on what was going on. "I have to talk to Gunner."

"Ha." He shoved me away.

*****

I heard from Gunner the next day. I sat on the front steps of the brownstone just down the street from Carla's place. I was trying to figure out where I was going to keep the goggles. Carla's basement probably wasn't the safest place. I wondered if there was some way I could get myself one of those safe deposit boxes. Keep it locked up in a bank.

I stood up when I saw Gunner approaching, but immediately I focused on the guy walking beside him. It was Bart, Carla's boyfriend.

I waited until they were a few feet away before giving a friendly wave. Gunner was wearing a hoodie over a dinner jacket. The hood lay back, exposing his narrow skull that was topped by a fringe of yellowish hair.

But it was Bart I addressed. "What are you doing here?"

He tilted his head toward Gunner. "I'm just here accompanying my friend Mr. Guntherson, just to make sure there isn't any kind of trouble."

"You work for Gunner?"

"Mr. Guntherson," he said loudly, "is a friend of mine."

I looked at Gunner who said, "An employee of mine said you wanted to talk to me."

"That's right." I looked at Bart again, trying to figure out what he was doing here. He had his arms folded and looked aside as if he was allowing us to have a private conversation. He moved slightly to let a woman pass on the sidewalk. He bowed slightly and tapped an imaginary hat.

"I have something you could use," I told Gunner.

"Is that so? I'll have to have some of my collection agents check it out. See if it's worth my time."

"Oh, it's worth your time all right. But before I let you see it, I request a small fee. A finder's fee. And the chance to work directly for you, taking Syd's place."

Gunner said, "I need some more details before I can make such a decision."

"It's a new drug."

He smiled. "In my business I keep up on all the latest drugs. I don't need your help for that."

"Not this one." He winced like I had slapped him, and Bart started tapping his foot on the pavement and flexing his fists. "Syd was trying to go out on his own," I said, hoping to calm everybody down. "He was developing a new kind of virtual reality drug."

Gunner twisted his face in an attempt to act surprised, but it was more of a mocking smile. And that smile told me that he already knew what was going on. Like he had said, he kept up with all the latest drugs. And Bart's mocking pose told me I had fallen into a trap. It was Gunner's men who tampered with Syd's programming so he ended up overdosing, just like I would have done if Carla wasn't there to save me. They wanted him gone for trying to go out on his own.

"I can show you the technology," I said, hoping to salvage something from all this. I still had one chance. "I have the device."

"No, you don't." Gunner shook his head like a mourner at a funeral. "I already have everything I need."

I glanced at Bart and saw him struggling to hide a grin.

Carla's basement.

I had left the goggles there.

And Bart worked for Gunner. What a fool I was.

"I actually came here to warn you," Gunner said.

"Warn me?"

"The police are about to take you in for questioning."

"For what?"

"Syd's death. They have video of you breaking into the house. The ME has determined the cause of death was a drug overdose, and you are a known drug dealer."

"No. No."

Gunner tilted his head slightly to the left. "In fact, I think a few detectives are approaching now."

I looked to his left and saw a car parked across the street. Two men got out, buttoned their coats, and crossed the street.

"I think Mr. Guntherson and I should be leaving now and let the police do their duty," Bart said. He touched Gunner's arm and winked at me. "Good luck with the detectives. Considering your record, you're going to need it."

"Did you kill Syd? Are you the one who tampered with his programming?"

He and Gunner were walking away. "I know nothing about virtual reality."

"You didn't want him going out on his own. You didn't want him cutting into your business. You set me up. That's why you sent me to his house." I felt a hand on my arm and I turned to see Detective Labar smiling at me. My heart started to pound like I was overdosing on Syd's virtual reality goggles. Labar was basically an employee of Gunner's organization. I was screwed.

Ode to the Papaya King

Brian R. Quinn

Winks and me gotta go underground. We usually hang on Eighty-Sixth Street. No more. Eighty-Sixth was a good spot, The *King* got a special, two hot dogs and a juice, five-twenty-five, which means every man, woman, and child come outta that joint got seventy-five cents in change. Them quarters is *ripe* for the pickin'.

Winks and me set a cup down on the sidewalk, a big one, don't gotta say a word, just try ta'look kinda fucked up and collect all them *sweet sweet* quarters.

Me and Winks.

Winks's ain't lookin' so good. His skin's all yella' and dirt's collectin' in the hollowed-out parts'a his chest, between his ribs, and in that big divot at the base'a his neck. I keep tellin' him he's gotta get more to eat. He tells me I gotta do the same.

I ain't so skinny.

Osiel works at the King grillin' dogs. Osiel don't need no quarters 'cause he got da brown. He got dime bags wit' purple papayas stamped on'em. Papayas's supposed 'ta be yella'. What he doin' wit' *purple* papayas…I just don'know.

Winks and me grab the cup, go inside. We don't order no dogs. Osiel know what we want.

Osiel lives Upper East, on the Drive. He got a place near the water, more like, *in* the water. It's concrete, some sort'a pumpin' station, at least it used ta'be. You gotta lift the manhole cover on top and climb inside.

"This my crib," Osiel says, all proud'a hissef.

He don't got no furniture, just some nasty blankets on the floor. They's damp. The place stinks from the bucket in the corner. Osiel ain't got no toilet. He do got a ol'fashion coal lamp though, carries it around lookin' like some kinda' spooky-ass train conductor or somphin'.

"Where'd you get dat'coal oil?" I said.

"Coal oil? Man that shit ain't coal oil!" Osiel said, sticking the lamp under my nose. "What'szat smell like?"

I don't got much smell.

"Dat shit is *lilac!*" Osiel said, laughing. "I got it at da'bodega on'a'undred and twef. Where da'guy got one eye. You been dare? He gots it. Got some *bad ass* sammiches too. Ham, an'roast beef. Chicken salad too."

Winks and me, we been there. It ain't bad ass.

"You wants'a dog?" Osiel said. He got a big plastic bag full of 'em.

"Naah," I said.

"Winks? You hongrey?" he said, rattlin' the big bag.

"Naah," I said, lookin' at Winks, knowin' he got it bad. He ain't listenin' to nothin' we say, just rockin' back and forth on his heels, pullin'at that flap'a skin on his elbow. He get *real bad,* he start moanin', rockin'n moanin'. Dat shit gets on my nerves.

"Winks don't want no hot dog," I said.

*****

I never tasted no junk 'till Winks skin popped me.

"Arch," he said, "you gotta try this."

Winks had a crib back then on Avenue A, had a dog too, a big German Shepherd. Me and him'd sit out on the stoop wit'dat dog and smoke us some fat blunts. Three o'clock come, we'd talk to the kids on their way home, tell'em ta'stay in school, listen to their mammas, shit like that.

"No," I told 'em, "dat shit scares me."

So Winks, he up and pops me. *BAM!* Right in da'shoulder.

"Don't worry," he said, "you gonna love it."

That smack ran through me like wildfire, raced down my arm, into my chest, my head. It was like a magnifying glass. I could see, and feel, everyting. Every cell in my damn body, every goddamn hair on my arm. It all stood up, screamin'.

Skin pop.

From then on I was hooked, junked, jonesin' for more.

*****

Osiel had a ol'fashion strong box. It was black wiff gold trim. Had one'a them floppy handles on top and a keyhole in front. Looked like somphin' he stoled from his grandma.

"You'd better have cash this time," Osiel said.

"We got cash," I tol'im.

"Well it better not be no bag'a quarters. Last time you brung them quarters…" Osiel said, shaking his head, "pain in *my* ass."

Me and Winks got trouble that way. Nobody wants no damn quarters. We gotta go to the *Bank'a America.* They got a machine. We dump our quarters in and the thing spits out dollars.

I gave Osiel our dollars. He gimme a dime bag wiff 'da purple papaya on it.

"What da'hell Osiel?" I said. "Papayas supposed'ta be yella', not no damned *purple!*"

Osiel laughed. "Dat's my brand," he said, thumbing through our singles, "part'a my street cred. Buy da'papaya, you *know* you gettin' good shit!"

I do all the cookin'. Keep the dose clean. Dirty needle? Shit in da'water? You in trouble. Get some'a dat hepatitis shit. I always rinse out my tub. It ain't a bathtub, it's a measuring bowl, like from the kitchen, only it's tiny, a toy, got *Mattel* stamped on the bottom and a pink plastic handle so it don't get too hot to hold.

I open the envelope, shake the brown flakes into the tub, add some fresh, clean, water. Osiel got bakin' soda. Da' soda smooves out da'load. Wit'out'it the junk burn all the way up your arm. I use the corner of the silicon bag like a baby shovel, dig into the soda, drop a bit into the cook.

Winks is startin' to chill. Just knowin' it's comin' makes him chill.

I fire up my lighter, melt the brown, watch it bubble up. It don't take long. Then I suck it up into the syringe through a bit of cotton. Clean. Everything got's to be *clean.*

Needles is all about the gauge. I got a blue tip. Blue tip, that's my bitch.

Me and Winks are gunna share the dose.

I tie him off, slap his arm, wait for the vein to pop up. He's breathin' fast, dying for the hit, that freight train that sets everything right. I point the syringe toward the ceiling, tap it, squirt it, make sure there ain't no air.

I pierce the vein, slide the needle in, and raise the point to make sure I'm in. I pull the plunger back and suck some blood into the mix, watch it swirl, then hit it. The vein swells. It's just a little pocket of juice now, held back, building up, until I untie the knot and let the junk flow.

"This shit's gunna' waste ya," Osiel said smiling, until he heard footsteps on top'a the pumpin' station.

We freeze.

Listen.

More steps.

The manhole cover flips open. A beam of light shines into the hole and sweeps across the room. Looks like one'a them prison movies. Stalag 13 or some shit.

Osiel drops to the floor, real quick, like he's trying to disappear or somphin'. An arm reaches in holdin' a flashlight. A man's head appears all upside down.

"Osiel?" the head says, shining the light around some more, pointing the damn thing in my face. "That you?"

I raise my arm to shade the light outta my eyes. "It ain't," I said.

Winks, he's noddin' out. It's those first moments, right after the hit, so warm, and sweet, make you feel like you gunna live forever.

Osiel was right. Strong shit.

"Po Po! That you?" Osiel said. "Come on down here Po Po! Lemme get a look at you!"

"Oh I'm comin'," Po Po said, climbing down with the flashlight in one hand and a nasty lookin' Glock in the other. "I'm comin' down all right."

Osiel kicked a blanket over his stash box and stood up real slow.

"Where's my damn money?" Po Po said, leveling the gun at Osiel.

"Money…well," Osiel said, "I got *some'* a ya'money…."

Po Po didn't wanna hear none'a that shit. He reached out wit'dat gun, *real fast,* and smacked Osiel on the side a'his head.

Osiel went down *hard.* I never seen nothin' like it. Most guys, they get hit, they go down like a sack'a nails. Osiel, he go down, he *runnin'!* Legs pumpin' and scissorin'! Looked like he was tryin'ta get away only he couldn't, 'cause he was stuck layin'on his side and couldn't get no traction.

Next thing I know the gun go off.

Now a gun go off that shit is *loud!* But a gun go off inside a concrete box? Shit's so loud you think you gunna *die!*

I trew myself on the floor.

Da' lead bounced off da wall and hit Osiel in the chest. Now he runnin' *an'* bleedin'! Blood pumpin' outta his chest like a fuckin' garden hose.

Po Po, *he* falls down, right on top'a me, and he got blood runnin' down *his* face!

I look over Po Po's shoulder. Winks is standin' over us. He got a crazy look in his eyes and a lead pipe in his hand. He's breathin' fast, and hard.

"Get the box," Winks said.

*****

Winks and me need a place to lay low 'cause Po Po knows we got his dope, and he ain't gunna let it rest. Winks says we should head to Saint James Church on Madison. "They got soup," he says, pickin' through a trash can on the corner of Seventy-Second and First, "and needles."

There's a fat guy sittin' on a milk crate next to the garbage can paintin' little watercolor pictures. People pay him for that shit. Go figure.

"I ain't goin' back to that fuckin' church," I say.

Winks finds half'a slice'a cheesecake, sniffs at it, throws it back in the can.

"We gotta go to Mumphie's," I tell him. Mumphie's Momma, she got a place. We gotta ride the Q crosst the river, but she got a place.

"His momma's crazy," Winks says, "last time we was there she tried to stab a knife into my heart."

"That's 'cause we runned outta dope," I tell him. "She OK. Long as you got's a taste, she OK. And that ain't a problem now is it?"

Mumphie's Momma live in the Queensbridge Projects. It ain't bad. Con Ed got a plant right near there. Big smoke stacks. She'a skinny-assed bitch.

"What you two want?" she says, hardly openin' the door, jammin' her skinny-assed bitch face through the crack.

"Me and Winks need ta'crash," I say.

"Crash? *Here?*" she said, eyein' us.

"We got dope."

Mumphie's Momma open that door like we was long lost cousins.

I get out my tub and cook. Got so much smack we don't leave the crib for days. Mumphie's Momma says she wants'a Italian Ice, says she's gunna go down to the bodega and get us all a ice.

A shifty little Puerto Rican bastard named Pedro runs the place. He knows Mumphie's Momma, sees her all the time, her rail thin arms, and her dry, cacklin' laugh.

"Four ices?" he says, eyein' her.

"Yeah! What's da'matter wit'jew?" Mumphie's Momma' says. "You deaf or somphin? *Four!* Four ices! Now. Gimme!"

Mumphie's Momma get high she talk too much. She tell dat son of 'a bitch her son's friends stayin' wiff dem for a while. "Ooh…they havin' a *high old time!*" she says. "Only they needs a ice 'cause my boy Mumphie, he got it. Got it in my place. More dope'n you *ever* did see!"

Now this little Puerto Rican, he ain't stupid. Woman come in like dat, talk shit, OK. But she wasted. *Days* wasted. He knows somethin' ain't right.

"Where they get all this dope?" he says.

"Day stoled it," she tells him.

✶✶✶✶✶

Winks takes one look at his ice and he ain't happy, says he needs a dog, a *Papaya dog!* Says he's gunna hop the Q and head back to the King.

"We can't go to the damn King," I tell him. "Po Po be lookin' for us.

Da King ain't safe."

Winks don't wanna hear it, tells me he don't give a shit. Says he gunna get hissef a King dog.

I let him go. I never should'a, but I let him go.

There's times, ya do shit ya just know is wrong.

I let Winks go without me.

*****

Two days later no Winks.

Now, middle of the fuckin' afternoon, *I* gotta ride the Q. Find him.

The King ain't busy. There's only a ol' woman pushin' a dog in a stroller out front. Dog look like it half dead.

I spot Winks right off. He under the red'n yellow neon. He ain't alone. There's cops, four of 'em. Wink's got his cup out. He lyin' down. We don't never lie down. Lie down, people think you passed out. People don't give no quarters to no passed out junkies.

I'm cool, move slow. Figure Po Po be on the lookout, got somebody watchin' for us. I walk over lookin' like I don't got a care in the world. Them cops, they ain't botherin' Winks. One of 'ems writin' in his fold over notebook, another's talkin' on his radio.

I step closer.

Winks is lying down all right, lyin' in'a pool'a blood.

My knees give out. I can't breath, reach out, real herky-jerky, try'ta steady myself on a parkin' meter but my hand slips and I can't stay up.

The cop writin' in his book sees me, walks over.

I'm looking at Winks, my brotha', lyin' dead on the ground. There's a long nasty gash acrosst his neck, looks like lips, all red and puffy. The skin on the edge of the slash is dryin' out, turnin' brown. I can see some sorta' white shit that looks like gristle poking outta the slit.

"What are you doin'?" the cop says.

My stomach heaves, tries ta'jump outta my mouth.

The cop jumps back just as my puke spews all over the sidewalk.

"Fuck!" the cop says.

I look at 'im. This ain't good. This cop watchin' me cryin' and pukin'. It's Po Po. Po Po done this. *Po Po kilt my boy Winks.*

The cop takes my pichta' wit' his phone. That ain't good. Why this cop be takin' my pichta'?

"Who the hell are you?" the cop says.

My body goes cold, starts to shake.

"I said who the hell are you?" the cop says again, grabbing me by the shirt, pulling me up.

I can't speak.

The cop shakes me, looks into my cold, dead eyes, then lets me go.

I slide, face down, on the sidewalk.

The cop nudges me with the toe of his boot. He got them heavy *poh-lice* boots.

"Arthee," I say, usin' the sidewalk like a filter. "Arthee."

"What?" the cop says.

I blink. Inhale.

The cop grinds his boot inta' my collar bone, really leans into it.

"Archie," I say, liftin' my head just enough to be heard.

"Archie!" The cop says, excited, motioning his buddy over.

The two'a them pick me up, throw me in the back of a police car.

*****

We drive crosst town. Stop near the West Side Highway. Seventy-Ninth Street exit. There's construction. The street's all torn up. The exit is closed.

The cops drag me down a gravel path lined with bare bulbs and a chain link fence. One of them slides a plywood door open and shoves me into a big open chamber. There's hundreds'a columns in the chamber, temporary columns, with big twisty screws that keep the ceiling from cavin' in. Cars be zingin' by on the highway overhead.

The other cop slams a chair down. "Sit!" he says, like I'm a fuckin' dog or somfin'.

But what do I care? Winks's dead, flat out on the ground, dead.

I sit.

The cop, with the chair, he got a stick. A bamboo stick. He hauls off, hits me wiff dat stick. It hurts real bad. Then again. He hits me again, the prick. He don't say nothin', just hits me wiff dat stick.

I jump up, go for him, try to scratch his eyes out.

The other cop he grabs me, punches me in the back'a the head. Two quick shots, then slams be back down on the chair.

"Wo!" the first cop says, "You dangerous! A real killer!" Then starts in again, laughin' like hell, playing stick ball with my cranium.

I slump over. My ears is ringin' and blood's runnin' down my neck.

"*Please!*" I say, "*Please!*" It comes out all high pitched. Sounds bad. I know it, but I can't help it."*Please Stop! No more!*"

Somfin' hits me on the side'a my face. Somfin' soft. I can't place it. It don't hurt, it just felt kinda' lumpy.

A line of stringy saliva runs outta my mouth. I try to focus, follow the string down its long path to a red and yellow *Papaya King* take-out bag on the floor.

"Dat's for you," a voice says.

I raise my head.

It's Po Po.

Last time I seed Po Po he was lyin' on top'a me unconscious, and Winks was standin' over us wiff dat lead pipe. Now he got a bandage wrapped 'round his head.

Po Po jerks his chin at the cop wiff da stick. The cop hits me, in the mouth.

"It's Papaya King," Po Po says, steppin' closer, pickin'up the bag. He ain't walkin' so good. His knees don't bend right no more. "Pedro says it's your favorite."

"*Paith...ro?*" I say with a mouth full'a blood and busted teeth. "Who's *Paith...ro?*"

"Pedro," Po Po says, plain and simple, like that explains everything. "You know him. He runs that rathole bodega in Queensbridge. He's a friend'a Mumphies' loudmouth junkie mother."

"*Paith...ro,*" I say again, putting it all together. Mumphie's Momma told Pedro all about Osiel's dope.

"Your man Winks loved that papaya dope didn't he?" Po Po said, folding the brown paper bag, slowly, carefully, into quarters. "Me too. Only my dope don't come in no brown paper bags."

I didn't say nothin', just dropped my head on my chest, my skinny-assed chest.

"You stoled my shit!" Po Po screamed, real loud, in my face. *"Where's my shit?"*

I shake my head, close my eyes.

The cop come'round in front'a me, Po Po give him the nod. The cop draws back and slams me in the mouth.

I'm bleedin'. Bleedin' and chokin'. The warm blood's runnin' down my chin on'ta my chest.

The cop chops me in the throat.

I can't breath, lurch forward, try to suck in some air. There is no air, only blood. It's like drownin'. I ain't never gunna take another breath.

"Dat hurt?" Po Po says. "No worries. I'm gunna take care a'ya. Gunna take da'pain away."

The chamber, under the highway, with its high ceiling and countless columns condenses and shrinks. The world goes small.

Po Po gunna take my pain away.

"You stold my dope," Po Po says, "think you're the damn Papaya King now, right, fuck head? Well let me tell ya, you steelin' my shit don't mean *shit! You still shit!*"

The cop grabs me by the hair, raises my head, and punches me in the eye.

"Get his damn works," Po Po says.

The cop digs through my clothes, finds my works, passes'em over to Po Po.

Po Po, he got some bags, some'a them dime bags with the purple papaya stamped on'em. He tears three'a them bags open and shakes the flake into my tub.

My tub. The one Winks and me found in the trash when he still had that place on Ave A.

Po Po got a bottle'a water, takes a drink, pours some into the tub.

"Clean," I say, only I can't talk so good with so much blood comin' in my mouth, "gotta be qween."

"Clean, yeah," Po Po says, spittin' into the tub. "I'll be sure to do that."

I think about my first dose, that time Winks skin popped me. I was so mad. Now here I am, gettin' the shit beat outta me, and still, as bad as it is, I'm jones'in for this next hit. I know what's comin'. Can't fuckin' wait. That papaya shit be strong, and Po Po got three dime bags.

The brown melts and bubbles up. It don't take long. Po Po, dat fool, he don't hold the pink handle, gets his fingers burnt. He don't use no filter either, just sucks the shit up with the blue tip, my blue tip. He squirts a bit at the ceiling. "Don't won't no bubbles rushin' to your heart now do we?" he says.

The cop ties me off wiff his belt.

Me and Winks used to share the dose. Not this time. This one be all mine.

Po Po slaps my arm. Waits. Stares. Nothin'. "Damn," he says, "you got any blood left in that arm?"

My arm. I look. He's right. It's skinny as hell, almost translucent. There's a faint blue vein, but it ain't plumpin' up.

"Do it," I tell him, "just do it."

"Damn junkies all the same," Po Po says, shakin' his head. He laughs a bit, but not really, it's just that sound, when air comes rushin' outta ya'nose. He pinches my skin, right below the damn cop's belt.

I'm happy now, knowin' it's comin'. The dose. Let it come. Po Po and this damn cop beatin' on me. Winks dead. Just let it come.

I feel the needle pierce my skin, watch the blood swirl in the mix, welcome the pressure as Po Po pushes the plunger down. The vein plumps, swells. It's just a beautiful little pocket of juice now, held back, building up, waiting to flow.

The Unity, Single-Minded

Orca Green

I have witnessed the great preacher who waved the holy water in his hands and sprinkled it on those who prayed; I have seen the great preacher who wiped the blood from her hands, who dismembered the devil with her own hands, who made us purify that devil with the acid of our mouths, she is the great preacher.

1

They called me Milligan, though I did not think it was my name. The nurse spoke in a dissonant voice before my eyes, and I watched as her tear ink zoomed in and out, the colour gradually blurred, and in the blink of an eye, it was the stage of emptiness, and my thoughts ran away again until I realised it had become the black and white floor beneath my feet. I imagined myself running helplessly, and frankly, I didn't think I was sick. But no one believes it, just as no one knows that normal is a word that mixes concepts, imagination and delusion, like the freedom of the air, unseen sound waves and the data of life that is taken away.

睬

She placed the cylindrical tablet in her hand on my desk, and the sound of those waves forced me to look at him. My ears heard the clacking of the tablets as they smiled at me and told me not to kill them. Then the nurse's nails hit the glass table and bang, and she forced her attention back to herself.

"Did you hear that? Michigan."
I nodded.

The nurse turned around and poured a few feet of water into the glass, water again being a fluctuating, fluid substance or element. No one should question the potential of water, its plasticities like dissolved glass, and metal, its ability to resist external forces, its natural fluidity, its ability to take on any shape, depending on its environment, depending on itself, and no one would argue with that physical phenomenon, that fact. To be honest, even if you oppose it, it doesn't change its potential. She pushed the glass towards me, perhaps she was one of those cautious people who needed me to take the cloudy pill before her eyes before letting me go. I wasted some time staring at the water, I didn't like the way it swam, I hated the white foam, or the microorganisms in the water. Few people notice these, but do you ever think that it's life?

I took the pill, held the glass of water in my hand, put my head back, and with a gulp, I swallowed the pill. The nurse's hand told me to stick out my tongue for her to check, and then under my tongue too. I laughed at this weak trust.

眯

Another morning.

The annoying alarm clock went off and I watched the count stop at five o'clock. As it was still light, I decided to let the alarm clock keep ringing, listening to the regular sound, the regular melody, until the time finally reached '5.4 minutes and 59 seconds'. I felt myself dying little by little and then waiting for the next day to be reborn. I barely opened my sleepy eyes and then accidentally closed them again in a blur. The second alarm sounded before I decided to get up.

I searched the kitchen counter for my mother's psychiatric pills, ground them up and poured them over my breakfast, a mechanical act, but not enough to allow me to just let go.

"Good morning, how are you?" I said.

I don't remember knocking on the door, but if the action becomes habitual, it can be done without giving and receiving signals, and memory is a wasteful act, provided, of course, that we can learn from the past, an act that not everyone can do. I went to their room and took my mother out and put her in a wheelchair for easy mobility. Perhaps time has long since stolen her vitality, or perhaps we are just vessels of memory, a funnel that keeps counting down.

I could hear her soul yearning to sing, her hands thirsting for the lights of the stage as if they were aimless, or maybe she wanted to let out one last roar and then disappear. My thoughts drifted off again to who knows where. I pass the food to her dry lips, and I can't resist sharing something with her, "Do you remember the girl I mentioned once?

I think my mother still remembers because those memories are still there. I was one of the pieces of her memory, I was a part of her life. I used to hate growing up, and now I just want to count down to death.

"Yes, I've got a date with her at the restaurant tonight," I responded.

"No, you're wrong," I responded.

"I went to a follow-up appointment yesterday, I'm going to a party tomorrow," I lied.

2

I remembered my first meeting with Megan.

It was just a normal meeting, where lost groups choose to share their stories, and the community centre was a charming haven for us. I chose to sit near Mary, who suffers from bipolar disorder because she was more interesting now. She took the centre's biscuits and drinks and put her feet on Leda's table, and Mary felt that Leda wouldn't object, although, of course, she didn't have time to react. Mary always likes to drink while people are talking, even through a drinking tube, and the sound of gurgling fills the room, but only because she hates dull conversations.

She feels younger than she seems, and her thoughts are so direct and emotional that she can't remember why she developed bipolar disorder, whether it was parental discipline, emotional problems, or a broken relationship. She doesn't know, but she feels fine now. She's not the most annoying person here.

"So you think I'm gay because I was invaded as a child?"

Mary suddenly leaned on my shoulder, before I knew whether her invasion was a metaphor or a physical act.

"This is Freud's theory, you know, another clever Jew who was also the founder of psychoanalysis." He argued, for example, that the Oedipus complex is universal, that dreams are a subconscious activity, and that the human being's psychological defences suppress his or her own desires. And psychosexual development is saying, for example, that a baby may become a cunnilingus or anal sex lover if it doesn't suck enough breast milk during the 0-18 month oral period. I sometimes automatically ignore what she says, even her sexist gestures. I chose to ignore what he was doing like any normal person would, which is the best way to deal with a crazy person.

And Megan was the volunteer of the day. I looked at her with her brown hair and her lovely bangs, and she reminded me of the ocean, maybe because we only met once in high school. All I could think of was that she was even more beautiful than before, like that moment when everything suddenly concentrated in half a minute, and I hoped she would remember me. "It's hard to believe," I responded with a sigh, and Mary realised I wasn't responding to her.

"You really are too easily distracted."
Mary looked in the direction I was staring at and smiled.
I nodded to Megan.

眯

"So it seems like you're really good at being late?" She digressed, carefully avoiding Peter's gaze, and grabbed a paint roller from a nearby tool basket. "Interesting information, I don't trust people that easily, so unless I see it for myself? I wouldn't believe that fact unless I saw it myself." Gabrielle waved her hands as if praying that the awkwardness would end soon.

"Sorry." Peter scratched his head, messing up his perfectly styled hair. Gabrielle dared to stare at the man for just a moment before continuing to stain the walls back to white. "So what's on today?" Peter held the paint roller and leaned against the wooden stick. He dared to look directly at Gabriel, and she realised she was now being forced to explain the day's activities to the late Peter.

"We're cleaning graffiti off the wall." She frowned at Peter.

"Is there anything I can do to help?" Peter twirled the roller around in his hands.

"Haha…you won't believe this? We've left all the hard parts to you." Gabriel pointed towards the higher ground where the other uncles were helping. "So it's a good thing I like to take on the hard stuff?" he could only laugh to himself. He could only laugh to himself, then touched Gabriel's head. "Go on, help! My friendly neighbour." Her eyes glistened with the sun's rays and she nudged Peter. "Yes, yes, miss," he laughed, then pretended he was taking off his hat and saluting like one of those Englishmen.

"I thought you might need a hand?" Peter's hair was flying up in a tangled mess. Everyone had deliberately covered their ears and noses with fabric to avoid smelling paint for long periods. His jeans had a little paint on them too. "It's not even close," she responded.

They sat like that for a while, Gabriel waving his legs in the corner of the terrace, both of them silent. Even if they had something to say, they were silent again at that moment, looking at the lights of the city. "So what do you think of today?" Peter unpacked his clothes and wondered why it was so cold in New York. Gabrielle watched Peter put on his coat as she waited for him to finish before speaking.

"I …What do you think we're doing?" Gabrielle shifted a little and tried to make a place for Peter to sit.

"You mean clean?" Peter didn't mind sitting next to her, but he was surprised by the question and could only look at Gabrielle. She laughed at his awkward smile and said, "Haha … Do you think we're destroying the past?" She watched his reaction and then began to try to explain the feeling. "I mean I don't know what the story or symbolism of all the paintings here is, but it's my job to just clean it all up?" Gabrielle notices this silence again. She had a tendency to do a lot of little things when she was insecure, so she saw that he didn't respond. Again, she absently lifted her hair behind her ear: "Sorry, my aunt likes art and stuff, so …."

"Nothing, I just didn't think you'd think that."

"Oh, really?" They lapsed into silence again. They sat outside on the terrace, which was actually quite cold, but they sat in the corner of it. Knees and arms just touching, and then just staring at the lights of the city.

Before Peter had time to think about his next response, Gabrielle spoke again. She pointed to the white wall outside.

"What do you think will be painted behind this wall?"

"Hip-hop? A tribute to a celebrity, or maybe …." Peter thinks of the art teacher discussing the origins of graffiti, hip-hop, anti-social, political, and current affairs, a representation of the voice of the people of the time? But most graffiti walls are most often about sexual organs.

"I hope it's a hero, an object of hope and righteousness, or a symbol of remembrance," Gabriel said, laughing. They laughed as they remembered the remarkable painting they had just seen. Gabrielle curled her feet and then rested her head on her knees as she gazed at Peter.

"I think the most beautiful thing about art is that it's inherited and innovative, it's constantly being redefined, but it's not wrong or right." Her eyelashes are like butterflies, her eyes are like jewels, and the living presence of a human being is an art. And so we talked, about the present and the future, about life, about art, as if we had a lifetime to talk about, until the next morning. No one wanted to stop, no one wanted to end, we just wanted to cherish the present.

I said to her, "See you next time?" I stood there shyly waiting for her response, her sunny smile, and she said to me, "Are you free on Tuesday?"

I immediately responded, "Sure."

But no, no, I still want to be your favourite boy, I still want to be your best day.

I remembered some melody, she reminded me of the meaning of a smile.

眯

I looked for her at her workplace, I parked my car at her building, I stopped at her door until she saw me. I smiled and waved my hand, and she came out to me.

"You're early," she said. Her red lips chewed on the words.

"God, how on earth did I ever agree to go crazy with you!

"Catch me!" Amy screamed from the back of Lance's motorbike! She couldn't help but close her eyes while Lance gripped the handlebars of the motorbike and pressed the button, and the extra parts of the motorbike shape-shifted to form a windscreen for them. And Amy opened her eyes at Lance's prompting. In front of her was the city of Degama, where the shadows of skyscrapers enveloped the intricate streets, where neon glow illuminated the stage where flesh and metal played together, and where searchlights and giant screens lit up the sky where floating vehicles roamed. This is the heart of the world and the place where everyone's dreams become reality.

Even if Degama is a city with a high crime rate, even if you don't know if you'll be killed by a tear gas canister on the road, this city is for those who don't want to be ordinary. "Do you want to die a quiet nobody, or do you want to make a name for yourself? The big signs on the advertisements tell you every moment that anyone can be the talk of the world, that this is the place where dreams come true! And you will become a legend in the city of Degama.

"Lance! Where are we going?"

"The east coast of Degama City! The scene of the crime!"

Lance flew Amy to the east coast, and the moment Amy stood on the ground, she was drawn to the place just beyond the coastline. Such is the magic of the city of Degama, the enchantment that keeps every spectator and explorer in the city for the rest of their lives.

"It would be a good place to meet if there weren't a few metres of parapet." Amy noticed that there were many rocks and fences close to the waterfront, and if you didn't look closely you'd think they were piles of rubbish. Although there are more waterfalls in Olga, anyone who walks past one is worth stopping to enjoy the scenery that is part of the city of Degama. Amy took a bird-like device out of her pocket and dropped it on the beach, and the gears in it worked as if it were alive.

Lance is looking for a parking space, and everyone here seems to know Lance. He was greeted by an older man who was fishing by the sea, and a child next to him handed him a fish he had just caught; they chatted enthusiastically until Lance remembered that Amy was still waiting for him near the shore.

"There are so many people fishing here, I almost couldn't find a place to park? Are you seeing anything?" Lance saw Amy looking through the telescope, the metal with the brass screws and glass shaping the gorgeousness.

"The sun," Amy replied perfunctorily to Lance.

"Have you ever heard of Ackles?"

"The clothing brand?"

"No, Ackles? It's recently announced plans to build a satellite base in space, something called the Crystal Palace?" Lance's mechanical eye was also a joint invention of Ackles and another corporation, famously able to watch Orion's shoulder end burn and a thousand beams of light flash in the darkness near the gates of Tannhäuser.

"I'm pretty sure we're talking about the same enterprise, Zululand's ambitions are too big. It's a good thing she's not so arrogant as to expand her technology in the city of Orica, or she'd be written up and stored by us. Zululand is the president of Akeris.

"Orica, classic."

"What's your idea of a 'Lambton'?"

"Jumping into the sea maybe, but the body drifting to the Devil's Peak area? Hardly. Unless she's a rock climber, there's no way her hands are unmarked." Lance is looking out, the sea is almost a metre from the breakwater, the bay is being reclaimed, there's a lot of stagnant water everywhere, there's a lot of construction boats in the bay, and there are usually passers-by on the east coast in the morning and at night, so it's hard not to be noticed.

"There is no way the deceased could have made it that far out to sea with all the road construction and blockades around here. To be honest, if you're going to kill yourself, you might as well go to Graber House and jump off a building." Amy nodded her head as the gears of the telescope pushed. Through a method unique to the city of Olga, her eyes were able to see the angle of view that the bird saw.

"Ha ha." Lance loved Amy's humour, her eyes showing a blue picture. The West End and Brooke districts are the main development areas of the East End, with the eastern shore of Degama City close by.

"What are you looking at?"

"The Westminster and Brook areas are not far apart, but the waves alone will not bring the bodies to shore."

"What?"

"Your telescope." Lance took Amy's binoculars from behind her back and told her to focus on the view in them. The Westminster area is where we are now, and the Brooke area is eight kilometres to the right. The victim was found near the surface of Devil's Peak, and the east end has been windless for several days.

No. Lance thought to himself. We don't know that for sure yet, we only know the scene and the circumstances of the crime for now, but Christie's relationship with other people or what happened before she died are also important clues, we need more.

眛

”Oh my God, you're taking someone to the crime scene on a date?" Mary chewed her gum, still resting her feet on Leda's desk. "I just thought she'd like it, too," I responded.

"So it's … The idea." Mary curled her fingers as if the comment was sarcastic.

And I remember this was the first date. We went to the Moondance Diner, which I don't know if you've been there before, people in my head? The diner had a 1950s feel to it, but my mind was still playing with the glitz and glamour of the 1920s, and I was more into the drunkenness of the Lost Generation or the colourful Roaring Twenties. Maybe Megan is more into the Beat Generation, and she comes into the restaurant with an endless stream of great things to say.

"Have you seen Naked Lunch?" she continues. She goes on to say what the story is about. An addict of heroin, morphine and opium, a refugee from the US, Mexico and Tangier, Morocco. The story is a remarkable depiction of the addict's mental world and abnormal state of consciousness. The work is a non-linear narrative that expresses the experience of fragmentation. "I have heard that his work even influenced William Gibson." I look at her cigarette butt, the smoke from the woman's mouth scattering to every corner of the city.

"Dull."

I didn't even realise the words were coming out between my lips. Megan crumpled her face with such sensitivity. I couldn't see who it was, or maybe it was just me, and I should have objected to the rudeness, but at the same time, the rational me was tired of the words existing in the woman in front of me. I saw a man, a figure, whose fist punched me, and the next moment I felt a sharp pain, and the next moment after that I found I was on my way home.

"I'm sorry." I see this text message on my phone, but I still don't know what's happening.

3

I realised it was a dream. Because they weren't me, it was like I was watching a story unfold.

"So how did I die?" Leda finally found the courage to ask Anteros.

I found the story unfolding like a script.

"Wow, do you really want to know? You know it will definitely change the way you see things around here. They forbid it, they want you to really enjoy the concept of 'eternal happiness'.

Only the man called Anteros responded to her.

"Yes, I want to know how I came to be here?

You watch their conversation, and gradually you have to sit down on that plane. Because you could not find your way out.

"On 23 July, you cried late at night, unable to accept that you had failed your exams and that you would not be able to go to university. You felt you had failed the world, you felt you had failed everyone who had taught you and believed in you, you felt you didn't deserve…"

"I never thought that way … But it does seem like something I would do." Leda listened to Anteros' tone like he was reading aloud, and although it was telling his story, it sounded like it was just something someone in the world did at one point.

"You let the tears fall, you try to sleep, try to believe that maybe the universe will tell you that it's just a wonderful prank. But before sunrise, you kill yourself before the world is in a hurry to wake up." Anteros closed the booklet on Leda's life in his hands. Although Leda hadn't seen it herself, the editor had put a year's worth of events on the same sheet of paper, and her life was shorter than many, but I have to say it was beautifully written.

"Wow, is this why I'm in hell?" Leda leaned back in her chair and crossed her legs. "Just for committing suicide?"

I realised I had never seen Leda like this before.

"What?" Anteros didn't seem to understand what Leda was talking about. "The fifth commandment: don't kill? We must value and preserve our own lives and the lives of others?" To be honest, Rita didn't really understand them either, she had never been that faithful.

"You think you're in hell because you killed yourself?" Anteros frowned as if the words were too foreign or incomprehensible to her.

And Leda could only be embarrassed, she couldn't think of anything she had done that was so bad that she had to go to hell?

"Suicide is not the main reason you are here. There are millions of people in the world who have come here by accident or by natural causes, and suicide is the most complicated way to die. Suicide, as the name suggests, is the act of one person, but the causes and effects of it are more horrific than any other death. Of course, none of the deaths is more regrettable. You can blame an event, a substance or even a concept for murder, accidental and natural death. It is too easy for human beings to blame something else for an incomprehensible event; suicide is not why you are here, and of course, it is wrong to lay down your life or to take it away from someone else, but suicide is not the main reason why you are here." Anteros tried to explain the apparent strangeness of this, but again she could not explain it directly.

"But isn't that a sin?"

"Suicide is a consequence, like the consequence behind all actions, and its rightness or wrongness comes from the reason behind the action. Suicide is not a sin, because it is a choice. What can be said is that there are many people who have failed, many who have suffered; some who have come through safely, some who pretend they are fine, some who … Some are safe, some pretend to be good, some are…"

"Like you said they were too good to be loved, and the world didn't deserve them, so they left."

"But do you think it's true?" Those who die tragically are angels from heaven because God loves them.

"Not so much. Because it is a gift to have an end, and eternity is just a suffocating curse."

"As J. R. R. Tolkien said." Leda thought of humans and elves who could only reach the so-called paradise if they died fighting. Anteros didn't seem to have heard these stories, and Leda wasn't quite sure what era Anteros was from.

"That's because it's a choice. There are so many choices in a person's life that you can't know what is right or what will fail. The point is that suicide is a choice, you can try harder, you can … Maybe tomorrow will be better? But you chose … You stop choosing, you stop taking responsibility for every experience in your life, and you stop enjoying every failure and loss. You gave up all the unknown possibilities, you gave up the future and the past, you gave up, and that was the end." Anteros spreads his hands dramatically.

"Would you consider suicide cowardice?" Leda frowned, pondering for a moment.

"No, it takes more courage than one might think. Sure, they gave up on their future, they ran away from their problems, they let someone they cared about hurt their feelings, but suicide is … We only need one reason to persevere, but too many events happen, too many things beyond our control, too many reasons to give up, and it just takes a leap of faith."

"What do you think of … What happens after that?"

"Your family? Your story's over. You'll have to read their booklet to find out what they think. Anyone who thinks of suicide in Anteros wants to know what happens to the people around them after they die."

As soon as she thought of it, she had a few pamphlets in her hand that were still being filled in with quill pens.

"No, I guessed that. I mean, what happens to the world afterwards? I know it's silly, but aren't you curious? Maybe the world has changed a little because of my death, maybe it has inspired others, or maybe someone will improve the future because of me?" Leda stopped Anteros as she tried to describe her thoughts in a simpler way.

"Yes, but not like this. The second outcome is not necessarily the best, or better than the last, but it is a choice, and we cannot control all the outcomes, but we can control our thoughts. The world does get worse after you die. If you want to say that I think it's everyone's fault, you never wanted to make the world a better place. It doesn't matter if you kill yourself or not, there will still be people in the world who are unhappy, people who will still be killed or treated unfairly, and of course you can grow up and change this slowly, but you will definitely have setbacks, you will definitely be opposed and questioned, because the people of this world don't want to be changed by anyone who has new ideas.

"Can't we avoid it? Or is pain and frustration just a test?

"Nietzsche once said that he who cannot kill me will make me stronger. Yet Nietzsche also thought that God was dead, that man should transcend God's power and become superhuman, and that the superior man should have more resources; don't be silly, can pain bring growth? It is we who choose to grow, we who survive setbacks and despair, not failures that make us strong."

"Is the world hopeless?" Leda doesn't understand how Anteros can state an end so easily.

"But, oh, man has never been the master of this world? What will the world be like afterwards? You are all too selfish to think that you are important." Anteros looked at Leda and sighed.

"But the truth is that people are important because of numbers."

"Numbers?"

"Solidarity, to be precise. One man does not have much influence, but one tyrant, one leader, one representative, one man's power is magnified, and one man's actions are imitated and admired by others. Meaning is no longer confined to an individual's point of view, but rather it symbolises an entire society or even an entire system. Thus man can become the master of the world, he can talk about religion and the dead, he can use history to determine the future thousands of years later, he can even manipulate and kill a soul."

"Manipulate and kill?" Leda could not understand what this meant in a literal sense.

"I quite believe in this. Everyone is different, but there are limits to what one person can do. Maybe it's because we have the same idea? We can be united. One person is a small force, but if there are a hundred of us? A thousand or ten thousand, we can conquer the earth and rebel against the system."

"Like the French Revolution?"

"An overturn? The overthrow or replacement of a system? Exactly."

"So you recognise violence?" Isn't a revolution a form of violence? But when is resistance ever an option?

"My people have chosen violence, and in its place, misfortune and subjugation. In this way, if only the world were like a game of chess." Anteros' hand mimicked the action of holding the pieces and then placing them on the table. She smiled a little, knowing that Leda needed time to digest it, that it was no longer her duty.

"So you recognise destiny?" That was her last question.

"No." Because it's a question of how many people believed that Apollo's bow would hit Achilles' heel, and how many people let their dreams and passions fall into the River Lethe of the Underworld.

The story ends with a kind of sudden discernment.

You discover a keyword, Leda's suicide. You try to force yourself to wake up, but the man called Anteros comes back to talk to you.

"You're here, it looks like Hypnos brought you back."

You cannot tell what kind of being he is, for a moment you cannot see his face, nor can you distinguish his voice. "The next time you come here it won't be us, the monster called Antle will come for you and stop you from doing something stupid." She restrains your breathing, and for a moment you feel yourself stiffen as if you're being held against your will. You can't get out of his grip, you can only look at his pale face, black with tears and no eyes.

"Believe me, he has no intentions."

Anteros showed me the monster, the black figure spreading into the antlers on his head, nine feet tall, who would eventually find me and kill everyone.

"You are a murderer, Milligan."

A million voices surround that phrase, and I don't think it's my name. It can't be my name, it's the wrong word, it shouldn't exist.

In my awakening, I realised that I suddenly found the glorious side of life hovering in my mind. And if I had done nothing, I would have regretted it so much, and the feeling would have been too heavy for life to bear.

"Mary, do you have Leda's number?"

"You better have a good reason or Hannah will kill me."

Hannah is her girlfriend, they met in high school but I don't know much about their story either, oh well, none of us are unless we've been there and experienced it, let alone I understand you or it doesn't hurt, I've been there before and it hurts more. In Mary's description of Hannah, she was the best ballet dancer Mary had ever seen, the future doctor who always got high marks in biology, the way I'd seen people fall in love and discuss love, always so touching like they were shining. They think about the people they like.

"Leda, I feel something's wrong with her."

"Come on, we're all crazy, no one's normal!"

I heard a cut from Mary's side, I couldn't actually imagine what Hannah looked like.

"Mary … Do you have Leda's number?" I said again several times.

"That's stupid!" My memory suddenly returned to Mary's words.

"It's the 21st century and we're still living in a patriarchal world! Equality, a word that existed at the end of the 18th century, is still racist and sexist all over the world, not to mention the tampon tax in foreign countries where condoms and lubricants are tax-free, which is obviously pro-gay! I don't care if some women don't think it hurts, they scream when I punch a man in the balls, it can be a workplace injury, a physical pain! What I like to eat, my lifestyle, what hands I use to go to the toilet, whether I put my tissues in front of me or behind me, it doesn't make any sense. To be honest, everyone deserves a few days off for no reason, that's freedom in itself! It's a freedom to not choose. Fuck those self-righteous politicians! When you're called a woman and a feminist for everything you wear and do, hey, I thought you were a female boxer, oh, what's the fucking problem with being yourself and choosing your own comfortable way of life?

The coach told us not to respond to others because the discussion is controversial, and this is the place to share. We don't need to comment, but it's really strange to see such one-sided absorption.

"I sent it to you, what happened?"
I turned off the call with Mary and called Leda: "Leda?

睬

"It's early in the morning?" The young woman's voice came out. I didn't know how to talk to her for a while, we probably didn't know each other as well as I thought, I hardly knew her.

"Are you coming to the party tomorrow?" I said, and after a moment I continued as if I had made up my mind: "I suddenly had a dream about you, with a man called Anwortros.

All I could hear was her breathing.

"Because you were talking about suicide, and I … Anteros, in Greek mythology, is the god of reciprocal love — literally, love in return, or counter-love," Leda suddenly responded, carefully saying the Greek and English words.
"Counter-love?" I questioned, unconsciously.

"Robert Frost's poem 'The Most of It', He would cry out for life, that what it wants
"Is not its own love back in copy speech, But counter-love, original response. Anteros is the punisher of contempt for love and the avenger of those who stand in the way of others' progress."
"Max Ellmann's Desiderata, You are a child of the universe, no less than the trees and the stars; you have a right to be here.

"Why?" I heard her cries, transmitted here, in my head, through the fluctuations of the telephone. Why, why are there a thousand reasons to live and a thousand reasons to die, why do we exist and seem not to exist, why do we breathe and suffocate, what if our choices are insignificant, what if death ends in nothingness, why? "I may not know exactly how you feel, but I know I want to … " I don't want anyone to die because we didn't try, I don't want anyone to die because of what I said, but I'm just a piece of dust in time, I don't have the power to control other people's souls, I'm just an ordinary person. There are no heroes who fall from the sky, only mortals who stand up for themselves.

"I'll be fine, just like they say. Why can't you be more optimistic? There are people in the world who are more miserable than you are.

"Why, they don't call a cancer patient, don't be so sick, you're really in trouble, have you thought about your family? Can you give me some health back soon? I'm just sick, not crazy."

"Leda?" I suddenly couldn't hear if she was still there.

"But I have a feeling it's going to be cloudy tomorrow."

I didn't know how to go on. I don't think I need to convince her that maybe tomorrow will be better, I don't think she needs these assumptions, she doesn't need convincing, she doesn't need it, maybe what she needs more than anything is empathy, understanding, she needs to know that she has some connection in the world.

"I don't want to lose you."

"I think you make the world … It's not that shit."

We were both silent — then…

"Thank you, Milligan. It means a lot to me." Leda took a deep breath and cried, but also felt better.

<h2 style="text-align:center">4</h2>

A butterfly flapping its wings in Brazil could cause a tornado in Texas a month later.

I began to dream and lose track of time.

睞

The man in the suit, wearing those weird glasses like one of those professional psychiatrists, was holding a patient report in his hand and somehow I could see it clearly.

"So I think if you need a leader to lead people to express themselves and fight for the rights we deserve, you need someone who is not more silent, I believe that as a candidate you should not be flattered, that effort and justice should be proven by action, not by false promises and promises. I believe in justice and equality, and I believe that my ideas will resonate. "Ask yourselves whether you want a humble servant who works or a revolutionary who leads the people to the glory of humanity? "I am radical because I am anxious to plan for the next generation, because I am aware of the role that our generation of young people will bear, will symbolise, will represent, and we will reject the bread and circuses, the uptown people who are so happy with the people, and refuse to question the past because now we are creating the future.

I remember that he was a liberal candidate, he had less experience in politics than the other conservatives, but his art of speech was very attractive, his tone, his accent and his knowledge of words, his feeling of speaking were very impressive, but he had no respect for the people of the last parliament, and the fact that nobody liked the last parliament is a fact, basically nobody likes politics. Basically, no one likes politics as a representative. It is easy to blame society and our problems on one thing, and coincidentally this is the responsibility of the people's public servants.

I thought the public would like this new hope until I saw another group of people putting the blame for bribery on him.

Noel was a man of his word, a man who sought efficiency, a man who gave benefits in the name of a candidate and was eventually convicted of fraud because he lost the election. Perhaps it is because the people themselves have no right to defend their own interests and fight for their own welfare, or perhaps that is why no one is brave enough to speak out anymore because it has never been our game. I've never understood what politics means, it's always controlled by the people above, the uncrowned kings, the best people who think they're the best.

"No, in fact, they ended up convicting me of invasion of privacy.

I don't know why he's here, but I hate the sound of him eating his biscuit.

"They're just afraid that someone else is getting the data because technology is power. Every breath we take, every second we're on the internet, we're using our data for society's resources, but we're giving our consent, our hand-pressed consent, even if we don't know what we're doing. Noel accused him angrily, but no one wanted to pay attention to his words. "They were just another one of those who took the banner of justice and then socially killed a man in an inhumane way. All great men are mad, otherwise, how can they bear this ugly humanity? Do you know what they said when I found out the truth? It's because you're too stupid to think the world can change. With that, Noel put his pistol gesture to the side of his head, and with one click, he could say goodbye to this awful world. We are all in the gutter, but some of us are looking at the stars.

Mary would discuss it with me later: "To be honest I didn't like him very much, how can I put it, he was too serious and always said a lot of serious, serious things, and that was too boring. To be honest, I think they're the same person in a way, but I'm also reminded of what Wilde said in The Picture of Dorian Gray: "None of us can stand people who have the same problems as we do. (None of us can stand people with the same faults as us.)

睬

The restaurant has a 1950s feel to it, but there's still the glitz and glamour of the 1920s playing in my head, and I'm more into the drunkenness of the Lost Generation, or the colourful Roaring Twenties. Maybe Megan is more into the Beat Generation, and she comes into the restaurant with an endless stream of great things to say.

"So how are you doing?"

Megan was sitting opposite me in the booth, I don't know what time it is? I don't know what time it is, but it's like we're back at the Moondance Diner. It's like a bit of déjà vu, but I don't know why. I didn't realise I was looking at the side and I realised that the characters were like characters I'd seen in comic books and they were playing the same story.

"Are you home late enough?" Mr Andrews said.

Witt didn't really see Archie until the morning, and as an exchange student Witt actually needed instructions on how to get used to living in Riverdale. But now?

He is home on time for breakfast every day and wonders why Mr Andrews is the only one here. *Oh my God, am I being someone's son?* Witt thought to himself.

"Music practice?" Archie had spent the summer working at his dad's company and then was torn between his interest in music, his dad's desire to continue with the family business and the rugby tournament. "But what about me being a music exchange student?" Witt was just getting up, witnessing a cold war and almost setting himself on fire, but in the end, he decided to ignore a family war that had nothing to do with him, and Witt was simply useless in Italy.

"You might as well be playing rugby." Witt ate his breakfast cereal, he should have given some reaction when he had to, to lighten the mood or something. "So you're on the rugby team, huh?"

"Do you have a partner for the ball tomorrow?" Archie suddenly asked, remembering that Veronica and Betty had just agreed to go together yesterday and that he had the responsibility of looking after the newcomers anyway, so he could just invite Witt along?

"Tomorrow? Too bad I don't like parties." Witt just nodded and didn't make any eye contact at all.

Witt covered his face with his hoodie and ran out with his gym backpack. He sat down at the only restaurant in town to play with his mobile phone, and when he got tired of waiting he just laid down on a chair.

Someone suddenly appeared in front of Witt, so he had to put down his mobile phone, *please, I am definitely a polite person*. It was then that he realised Witt was wearing smoky make-up, black cross earrings, a dead eye compared to his usual flirty smile, plus he was wearing a blue plaid jacket, black vest and green army trousers.

"First you take my seat."

Seriously? Witt frowned at the strange man with the eyes.

"What do you think of Kelvin Krall?" Witt said suddenly, and it felt like a hallucination. "Why would a handsome exchange student care so much about a country's openly gay guy?" Dilton asked, sensing that there was an indescribable thread to the statement.

"I'm just curious." Witt looked back at his phone, clearly not feeling obliged to answer that question.

"Maybe it's like how Hannibal feels about Will," Witt added, a beautiful thought in his head.

"Actually, I just like strawberries."

Witt reached straight for the fruit on top of his milkshake. Witt especially likes strawberries and strawberries. Whether the restaurant has a fruit platter or a dessert, he can always find a strawberry to eat. Witt slapped the man on the shoulder and left. Because he knew that everything he wished for, he never failed to get.

"Gago, have you seen Betty?" Archie just brushed past Witt.

睬

"You're gawking again," Megan said.

I found her drinking a cherry milkshake, her hand was holding a strawberry. Maybe I'm still dreaming, I smacked myself in the face at the thought. "What are you doing?" Megan looked at me in surprise.

"Nothing, what were you saying?"

Megan seemed surprised by my condition. "It's just Leda ... I'm so worried about her."

"You know she tried to kill herself, right?" Megan continued. She held her drink in her hand, which was melting. "I knew all along that she was depressed, and if I'd known she was prepared for this, this plan ... I should have paid more attention to her."

"No, you can't," I responded.

I've heard some mental health talks about suicide prevention and the attention we can give to things like TOOL, THOUGHT, PLAN. it's a good standard, but depression is often suffering from a transition, from light to medium, medium to severe, a thought can bring rebirth and a fall, can I heal? Do I hate myself? Do I want to make peace with this self? I don't know what they think.

"I don't want anyone to die because I didn't try harder, I just don't want anyone to die because I didn't do a good enough job." I suddenly heard the hiss of a monster as I finished speaking. The environment became so cold that I couldn't help but shudder. I could see the monster's thin, withered surface, the harsh hiss of its breath through jagged teeth, and the sharp claws of its hands leaving long, deep scrapes in the corridor. I could no longer hear Megan's words. The monster's body reeked of blood and decay as if it had just crawled out of a tomb. Long white hair covered its face and my eyes were filled with fear.

"What is this?" I had to speak in a lower voice.

Antle, the monster's name. A black figure spreads into a head of antlers, nine feet tall. He was outside this restaurant, his body structure deformed, his seemingly rapid and overgrown bones tearing at the skin, and somehow he had to bend his body to move forward. There was a poem read over and over again that rang in my ears:

There was a crooked man, and he went a crooked mile.
There was a crooked man, and he went a crooked mile,
He found a crooked sixpence against a crooked stile.
He bought a crooked cat, which caught a crooked mouse.
And they all lived together in a little crooked house.

"Don't you ignore me? Michigan, I'm still talking." Megan frowned, and I could only wonder why she couldn't see the monster outside the window. Then they called me by that name again. "That's not my name! It's the name of a murderer." I had to get out of here before the monsters noticed me. Maybe it was just a dream, maybe it was just a memory, but either way, I had to try to get out of there. Megan grabbed my wrist tightly, it was the only way I could get out of there. "And who are you? Who did Milligan kill? What do you remember?"

I have seen the great preacher who waved the holy water in his hands and sprinkled it on the praying people; I have seen the great preacher who wiped the blood from her hands, who dismembered the demon with her own hands, who made us purify that demon with the acid in our mouths, she was the great preacher. That memory forcibly invaded my mind and an unclear fear spread through my body that the creature had found me.

For a moment you look into the monster's eyes and you realise that they are human eyes. Maybe he's panicking, maybe he's scared, these emotions mingle until the piercing scream can only be pulled from your throat.

眯

You feel human again, thank goodness. It's easy to forget who you are in those days of being a Wendigo, but now you finally have time to remember what's happened.

You are Josh.

You have two sisters, Betty and Hannah, both of whom disappeared in 2014, and a year later you arrive at the scene of the case, in the woods, but after that happens, you become a monster too. The most important thing is that this time you choose to end up either dead or a monster.

You're not sure if you've really become a monster, or if you still have something rational in you? Who are you now? What should you do next? These are all questions. Your head is full of questions, and then you see her, and the only thing she says to you is that her name is Adolfo Kelsa. She saved your life, but you didn't know her either.

That day you decided to go to the highest point of the forest to watch the sunset.

There were two options: you could invite her along, or you could find your own way through the forest on your own.

Josh felt he didn't want to find his way through the scary forest alone, so he chose to invite Kelsa along. Not to mention that she seems to be the only human you can see in the forest.

"So you'd like to wander?" you ask. You realise that this is the first time you've looked directly at Kelsa.

"Yes." She doesn't look so sure, maybe it's just because we're not used to talking like this.

Josh and Kelsa gradually made their way deeper into the forest.

Kelsa seemed to feel uncomfortable. She could run fast, but now she was forced to slow down, and looking around, the forest always felt dead and lifeless. When they finally reached the top of the tallest tree, where Josh should have seen the sunset, Kelsa suddenly decided to stay in the shadow of the leaves.

"If you need me, I'll be here." Kelsa felt uncomfortable all over, like a sudden itchy feeling in her body. Her body reacts by sensing danger, and it scares her. Once again you see two options before you: you can invite her to join you, or you can ignore it.

Josh chooses to ask her. "Do you want to come up? Please."

Even if Kelsa is uncomfortable, she will go with you, and she will choose to watch the sunset with you.

When I finally reached the tree, all I could feel was the searing light, the sunlight melting my surface, and gradually I watched my hands, rapidly drying, cracking, withering, one wound after another ripped open by the insects moving through my body, worms emerging from between the chunks of flesh that would pierce my bones and crawl out of my eyeholes. I saw myself die.

"Kelsa?" Josh shouted.

睬

You've just come to your senses, you realise that what you've just seen isn't real, but there's no doubt that you're sick too.

"I used to love climbing, but my sisters would never go with me." You just listen to him and you are quiet because the sun still burns you.

"Are you all right?" Josh asks. Maybe he knows the answer to that question. "Can we leave?" Kelsa asks. You don't understand why looking at the sun turns Josh on. I hate the sun. You think so.

"Kelsey, what do you think we are? What kind of monster am I now?" Josh felt lost, he used to be able to know for sure that he was human, physically, sensationally and intellectually, of course, he knew he was human, but now he wasn't so sure, staring at the sunset, watching the amber sun gradually being swallowed by the sea, it could be romantic and it could be carelessly lost in his own thoughts.

"You don't need to know what you are, you just need to know that this is where we belong," says Kelsa. Kelsa says. Pure white hair and skin, even her eyelashes are as white as snowflakes, she is one of the children of the moonlight. You can see yourself through your pale red eyes, you are a real person, and nothing will change this visible fact. This place is for monsters, that's the word they use, monsters.

"The most important thing is what you want to be."

"… I don't know."

"Well, I just want to tell you that whatever you think you are, I want you to feel at home here, that you can be whatever you want to be, that no one will stop you, that no one will think you're scary or weird or different from anyone else, just like home."

Kelsa was reminded of Genesis 9, where God created the rainbow and promised that the water would never again become a flood to destroy all life. Whenever I make a cloud over the earth and a rainbow appears in it, I will remember the covenant I made with you and with every living thing. As God says, the rainbow is a sign between man, creatures and God, a promise to all the animals that came out of the ark, every animal that lives on earth, until the end of mankind.

"God said to Noah, "This is the sign of my covenant with every flesh and blood creature on earth.

"Are you a Christian?"

"No, I'm a Catholic." Kelsa realised that there were many people who did not know the difference and she could only try to explain what she did know.

We believe that when you end a human life, what you do is important to where you go after you die. We have Purgatory, where people will pray for a second chance to return to heaven. And living humans will pray for the dead and pray for the saints. We believe in the Trinity and they only pray for God.

We read and learn how to sing or say our prayers and every day is a day of celebration and prayer. They put so much effort into their singing that you have no idea why. Being a priest, or a nun means not being married, being dedicated to God, they often represent the word of God and they are meant to be a single-minded role.

"Do you remember your family?"

"Maybe, but most of them are forgotten."

What I see before me is a new life, a whole new story. After all, now we're in the middle of an empty forest, feeling sorry for ourselves. Do you really believe in God in this world?

Belief is a choice.

I believe it was just a choice I made when I was young, or maybe it was because of my family that I became a Catholic, I didn't have any other choice then, but I still choose to believe it now, not because I hope I will be saved when I die, but because those who believe make me choose to believe. Kelsa only remembers part of being human, but deep down, what she can't forget is what her family taught her about sharing and loving.

眯

Saoirse suddenly sensed something and her eyes suddenly moved somewhere. She was much more alert and capable than the average person, not only could she see things in the distance with her wide vision, she could feel many things in detail, and she could feel gravitational forces and fluctuations that slowly affected the ocean and the sky, perhaps unaware that there was someone out there who was watching them, something that was hostile to them. Once again, her mind was ringing with sounds that made it impossible to think clearly. Different voices reverberate in the mind, and perhaps the only way to resolve this pain is to go forward, perhaps to face it. Everything is so visible, but only with eyes closed.

"Can we go now? It's getting dark."
It took a moment for Josh to respond:
"Sure."

By the time we left the moon was already in the sky and night had fallen, which spread an atmosphere of terror throughout the forest. Even if we are part of the forest, even if we are the monsters that humans think we are, it's just the way the universe works. Kelsa sat on the ground, watching the Wendigo wander around without meaning to, just as Josh did.

"Don't you think they're scary? I mean … What do you see?" Josh asked the question.

"…They look like humans to me."
The place suddenly got colder as Kelsa finished.

There is always a reason why you are who you are, everything is interconnected, and every part of the past forms the present, and everything comes together to make you who you are.

Josh remembers coming here again to prove that he has moved on from the tragedy of the past, the death of Betty and Hannah. But this experience has caused a part of me to become abnormal, and I can't pretend that it never happened after this nightmare. I could never go back to being normal, and another part of me longed to know what had happened. Maybe deep down I wanted to believe they were still alive, just ....

Then the doctor told me I was suffering from severe depression.

"You've been through a lot, but it's not your fault," Kelsa said. "It's a good thing you didn't try ECT. It's a physical therapy for severe depression and schizophrenia. No one knows why this sounds so funny," Kelsa says, laughing.

睬

"What the hell is happening now!" Megan shook me once more. My consciousness was back in the restaurant, the monster had walked in and we were forced to hide behind the service counter. If she had been the character in the story, she could have killed me easily, but for some reason, she hadn't found me yet.

"What if we've always been like this? What if this is really who we are?"

I know that's my voice, but I don't know why I'm saying it. These stories force me to think, who defines what is normal and what should be? And who gave humans the ability to define anything in this way?

"You know, the theory that people are constantly trying to understand this theory, this fairy tale, about whether equality is a myth or a reality. Some people think that this mythology, this belief in equality, comes from the Abrahamic mythology, that all humans should be equal in the eyes of God and that the so-called inequality is due to the devil; in fact, it also influences Greek mythology, that all heroes have to pay a price, that they go out of their way to be extraordinary, to try to sit on the throne of the gods, or at least to get a place in the land of bliss."

"His arrogance believed he could fly here and touch the Olympic sunlight on a pair of candle wings alone." His hand hid the light from his face.

"The last melted candle made him fall and he fell into the sea and drowned." He wiped the non-existent dust off the bed to the floor, telling the story as if it were a deliberate allusion to something that was to be said about not flying into the sun, about not being too ambitious or greedy.

"Icarus," I said in reply.

When he heard it, it was as if I had hit on something complicated, and he immediately stood up happily and walked over to me: "So you know! I was beginning to hate the way the gods were always glowing, and I couldn't keep my eyes open because of his overly blinding smile, and then suddenly he said, with some regret, "I just hope you don't turn into him. His hand touched my face and he tried to push my loose hair back behind my ear. "But this quest for freedom from mediocrity was seen as 'arrogance', which angered the gods and brought many heroes to Tartarus, the hero of Greek mythology. They believed that everyone needed to know their place in the universe, whether low or high."

"So death is your answer?" Megan was so used to my crazy talk that she had to shrink into a ball to keep the monster from seeing her. But it was all in vain, the beast could see everything without using his eyes, his height, and his breath drew everyone's attention, and I could see that his bones were made of crystal and ice, I had heard this myth linked to the story before, that maybe the only way to defeat him was to cut out his heart, and for some reason I was still connected to his thoughts deep inside, maybe… Maybe he wasn't a bad guy, or maybe he was just the monster that others thought he was.

Naturally, this is just my imagination.

His antlers pierced my torso, tearing my flesh with his claws and teeth, and the pain was so intense in every part of my body that I could imagine that the next moment he would eat my brain and slowly kill me.

5

I gradually regained my composure, and although my body still felt a sharp pain, I woke up in a blank room.

At first, I heard a familiar voice: "You want to draw a card?"

She must have been Kelsa, and she didn't seem to have noticed me yet. "Or should I ask you to think about a question first? If it helps you to think clearly, then the cards will answer your question."

I realised that she didn't look white, except for the fact that she had lighter pupils, which felt really strange, but I said her name first because she didn't look like the beast anymore.

"You're Saoirse?"

"I'm Kelsa Graham."

I realised the image was familiar, because she was sitting in the nurse's chair, and I looked like a former mental patient being restrained in that chair.

"So I'm dead?"

"No, I would call this a memory palace, but your memory is not quite solid like there are many different parts of you scattered all over the place. Our brain is a very powerful memory bank of what we have experienced and what we have absorbed, and you have somehow managed to mix it all up, like a cherry milkshake! Kelsa placed the drink on a table that looked like a chessboard.

"What does that mean?" I realised that what she was saying was starting to confuse me.

"We want you to know what's misinformation and what's real and what you've really experienced."

Kelsa turned around and grabbed a stack of tarot cards from somewhere. "Come on, draw a card, will you?"

I had to blink as if my mind was creating images of parallel universes — *universii*? I could be Peter, Mary, Lance, Anteros or Noel, I could see the world as they see it through their eyes. I felt I was experiencing everything they were experiencing, I could be Kelsa or even the nurse.

I drew three cards.

"The Hanged Man, for sacrifice, new perspectives, suspension, conformity," Kelsa said of the cards in my hand.

"In other legends, the Hanged Man is a depiction of the Norse god Odin, who hung himself from a tree in order to gain knowledge. She flipped the card over and over again with great skill, and the pattern on the card changed. The hanging man is bound by a yellow cable, and the figure no longer has a halo around his head; spiritual power and enlightenment come from the cable that controls him. The figure is surrounded by four men with righteous eyes, three with red eyes and one with yellow eyes, who are the group that controls the world, and the boy's cable is wrapped around the yellow-eyed men, who control it. The cable in the boy's body is also wrapped around the yellow-eyed men who control it. "The hanging man also means that to gain, one must pay. The sacrifice of the Hanged Man opens the way to a new life, but this path will be strewn with pain sealed in time, and your choice will lead to death or rebirth."

Lance imagines himself swimming in the endless sea.

The silvery metal legs of a prostitute were making blistering shapes in the water. She emerged from the surface, her short, dark blue hair and neck — the black mechanical surface, her feet glowing green. With a single breath, she dived into the depths of the ocean, the machine at her neck forming gills — cracks in a row on either side — and then she was able to move freely in the deep like any other sea creature.

"Lance!"

There she heard her name called from the bottom of the sea, and she headed to the bottomless depths; the only light in the entire ocean was the green glow of Lance's righteous leg, but there was something about the depths that drew Lance in. Even though the sea is full of waste plastic and factory waste, she can't stop herself from diving deeper.

睬

Kelsa's hand pulled me back.

"Listen to Milligan, you have to save this, put everything back the way it was before." Saoirse took my hand and walked down the white corridor, which was lined with room after room of memories. It wasn't a very long corridor, but it almost took longer for Kelsa to figure out which door we should go to.

"What does this mean?"

"We're going home." Kelsa pushed open the familiar door. The whole place suddenly stirs up memories, the wooden staircase in front of you, the white fence, the building that has always given you a feeling you can't quite put your finger on. At least you begin to remember that you were not so popular here, that your father was The Emperor of the cards, in his armour and red robes, that his exuberant gaze was always the rule in your life, and that I always felt the uncontrollable shaking of the board standing on that canoe, that the joys of my life were not determined by me, but by his hands.

For a moment it was like I was back in my childhood, my horizons had become limited, the paths I walked on were filled with that nameless curiosity, everything was big and small, and I thought I would never find my way to that room, but in any case, the spirit of my childhood led me to experience this nightmare once again.

I saw the relic he had given me, a Webley .455 Mk VI revolver.

My father had told me time and time again about the horrors of war, the struggle he had lived through, how previous generations had thought that only those who lived through war were brave, that it was an honour to die on the battlefield, but no one could understand that we did not face the war itself, nor did we face the so-called fear, but those who survived the place where humanity was obliterated. Some people say: "We don't choose the war, the war chooses us". I have seen fathers pointing to this phrase and cursing the heavens. They accuse those who are foolish because everyone knows that when war comes, no one can stay away because it is the idea of the weak, because they want to blame the myth of Ares, the heretic and the outsider, for all the bad behaviour that is involved in endless struggles, confrontations and disagreements. Perhaps it was the high and mighty who wanted to blame the soldiers for all these sins, for their hands were not stained with real blood, but it was obvious to all that their thrones were strewn with the souls of the people.

My father was born into a world where showing one's heart was seen as a weakness, living in a time when the only way to breathe was to satisfy society's so-called normalcy.

This sound was the origin of my nightmares.

The bullet's calibre was .455 Webley. I watched my father, who had let the silent Sonatos take his life when I wasn't looking. Father held the muzzle of the gun in his mouth, towards his palate, like a gipsy's curse, the bullets already marked with a price. I watched the tears on my father's face, why I never noticed his pain when I thought I would never forget it.

"Good morning, how are you?" I said.

I don't remember knocking on the door, but if the action becomes habitual, it can be done without giving and receiving signals. I went to their room and took my mother out and put her in a wheelchair for easy mobility. Perhaps time has long since stolen her vitality, or perhaps we are just vessels of memory, a funnel that keeps counting down.

I could hear her soul yearning to sing, her hands thirsting for the lights of the stage as if they were aimless, or maybe she wanted to let out one last roar and then disappear. My thoughts drifted off again to who knows where. I pass the food to her dry lips, and I can't help but share something with her and say, "Do you remember the girl I mentioned once?"

眯

I suddenly saw my mother's roar, the way she was suddenly pulled back, now thin as a scarecrow, her skin already grey and her teeth long gone. Yet now she is tearing her aged body apart, as if waiting for another rebirth, just to destroy everything, to kill her broken self in order to welcome a new one. Her skinless flesh and blood, her fierce gaze seeking to pierce my childhood, the corridors filled with her screams of pain, from which I could never escape as long as I remained a child.

"You are the devil, Milligan! Son of the preacher of Satan!"

In a letter to Maya, I read my mother's regrets.

I don't know how she met my father in the end, but that smile, which I can only see in those frames, may have been a time when she too had hope when she too found the so-called purpose of life when her eyes too witnessed that bright flash of light. Perhaps her eyes had seen the bright flashing lights until her feet were broken and her hands bound until her dreams were clipped just as she was about to take off until one expectation after another came down on her and one responsibility after another killed her flight.

Through these clues, perhaps I can understand where her hatred comes from.

"Yes, I've got a date with her tonight at the restaurant," I responded.

I thought you had killed them.

"No, you're wrong," I responded.

You're sick, Milligan, just like me. All good people are crazy.

"I went to a follow-up appointment yesterday, I'm going to a party tomorrow." I lied.

睬

I went back to my room and slammed the door behind me. Kelsa appeared in front of me, and I wasn't sure what her role was here, whether she was a character I had created or a real person. Why was she here?

"We have to fix this and go back to the way things were before! she said, glaring at me, hissing like a mother.

"Kelsa, but the past isn't better! It's still as bad as shit!" I accused her of thinking that the past was good, that obsessing over it wouldn't change it!

Kelsa just exhaled when she heard this, forcing herself to calm down and try to return to a professional tone:

"All emotions are meaningful, all experiences affect your life and form you into who you are now. Only when we face it, only when we understand what it means, can we grow and we can ultimately become a better version of ourselves."

Kelsa said the official phrases, repeating lines I was already tired of.

"So who the fuck am I?" I shouted, almost helplessly.

睬

I went back to that moment, the night I killed my mother.

The annoying alarm clock went off and I watched the count stop at five o'clock. As it was light, I decided to let the alarm clock keep ringing, listening to the constant sound, the constant melody, until the time finally reached '5.4 minutes and 59 seconds'. I felt myself dying little by little and then waiting for the next day to be reborn. I barely opened my sleepy eyes and then accidentally closed them again in a blur. It was only after the second alarm that I decided to get up.

Michigan, my mother kept repeating the surname vaguely.

Milliken Milliken Milliken Milliken Milliken Milliken Milliken

Milliken Milliken.

I had to ignore this mental abuse and had to put up with the ridicule brought on by my mother, who was the only family I had. I had to put up with her outbursts, I needed to look after her and I knew the responsibility. I can only assume that if she were me, she would do the same. I still wonder why.

眯

"Why can't you do it right even if you're dead." He punched the tutor again, hitting him on the head like he never knew how it would hurt someone's pride.

I poured hot water over his body as soon as I was angry, and it gave me great pleasure to see his look of discontent. He didn't stop hitting me on the head, he hit me again. "If he had a weapon, he would have killed me." The thought came into my head that he would have killed me if he hadn't done so.

"I wish you were never born."

"I hate you!" I hissed, "I'm going to be a monster like her. I would become a self-righteous adult, and when I looked in the mirror, I could only see myself becoming one of those shameless adults. They accuse me of being useless, questioning the value of every action, are you useful? Is your existence really meaningful to the world? Looking at the silence, that place of indifference, I had had enough.

"I hate you so much, I wish you were dead."

I reached out and pressed my hand against her throat, all I wanted to do at that moment was to see her in pain, all I wanted was to see her say to me that she was sorry. But her old, withered hands just smacked me on the shoulder, her eyes saying something I couldn't tell. I wished it was forgiveness, I wished someone would give me closure, but there was none, just me and my nightmares.

"You're cursed, Milligan." She whispered her last words in my ear, and then the cloudy eyes faded to a blank. It was all over.

6

Another morning. I didn't pay attention to the numbers on the electronic alarm clock, I just saw the light of the sun falling on my hands, a wonderful but warm feeling. The alarm clock kept ringing, listening to the regular sound, the regular melody, but I hadn't yet found the courage to get up.

The sandalwood fireplace was still calm and elegant, and the smell of wood was coming from the old-fashioned tea cups, followed by the smell of the coffee I had poured out. I searched the upper cupboard in the kitchen for cereal and milk and watched the news play in a strange language as I placed the cups and dishes on the table in the centre of the living room. I suddenly remembered Megan, my girlfriend.

I opened the door and knocked on it towards her place. I saw her and hugged her, and for a moment she seemed unable to respond, remaining stiff and unenthusiastic in her embrace. "Who are you?" Her voice was slightly frightened, and I saw that her smile made the freckles on her face look like glittering galaxies, the sound of saddle shoes on her feet, and her long hair like a forest fire. She was a beautiful woman, but she was not the Megan I had in mind. I didn't say a word, only daring to stare at the woman's clothes, the plain collared shirt, the thin belt and the plain trousers, the cheap red lips chewing on words.

"You're Megan?" I couldn't quite put my finger on what was wrong here, but she didn't have that familiarity with me.

"I remember … I've seen you at the community centre." Megan slowly walked away from me and I realised her face frowned with that scared and frightened look. "You followed me, and then my friends found you."

She said this without stopping, and then I pulled her arm sensitively: "What the hell are you talking about!"

"I don't know what's going on with you, but I want you to calm down. Especially because we don't know how it is, we don't know how to face or understand you, I don't know what's happening to you, and I want you to stay calm … Stay kind." Megan kept trying to step back and include the words calm, kind and real in her own meaningless sentences. Megan tries to loosen my grip and convince me to calm down one step at a time: "You need help, then you can come back."

"What if this is me, what if I'm willing to be like this?"

眯

Michigan returned to the cottage of his childhood, as if impatiently moving away from the wooden staircase in front of him and towards the white walls, and saw Kelsa sitting near the glass table again. "Here you are again, Milligan," he said. Kelsa smiled pleasantly. She pointed to the tarot cards still on the table: "Would you like to see the other two cards?"

One card was the Death in reverse, and the other was the Emperor in the square. The Emperor's card is the figure of great Michigan, wrapped in a mummy-like wrapping, but the restrained patient is seated on a throne wearing a crown, a red robe and metal boots. The throne still bears four white ram's heads in relief, with wave after wave of mountains in the background, waiting perhaps for the light of the bright blood moon; and beside Death is the white warhorse as described in the biblical Revelation, with the black banner behind it. It was only with a sudden shock that Milligan saw that Death looked like Kelsa. The woman who represented Death, whose look could be described as cold-blooded or calm as she looked down on the living on earth, strangely held her hand out before the eyes of the king who resisted death, like an incomprehensible hatred for each other.

"Who are you?"

Milligan, startled, dropped the card from his hand immediately. Kelsa's smile inexplicably deepened in horror.

"Death is the most misunderstood card in the Great Arcana. The number thirteen has always been seen as being associated with death — as is the case with the Tarot." Kelsa put the cards back in the pile and began to use her tarot cards to describe her reasoning. "Death rides in armour on a white horse, showing his irresistible power. Death is an irresistible natural phenomenon from which there is no escape, and from which there is no need to escape. The white horse of Death is also a symbol of purity, of washing everything away and starting anew in order to be reborn. Kelsa finally scattered all the cards of the Tarot on the floor, only by starting over, only by choosing, can we be reborn."

For a moment Milligan is back in his psychotic corset, the emperor of the cards, with helpless eyes staring at death: "Isn't it obvious, you killed our mother?"

Everything will return to normal.

Milligan realised that this was the only way, he saw the truth, he saw everything and it was left to him to make a choice. Kelsa sat across from Milligan, a glass table between them, with the same familiar chessboard. The difference is that instead of glasses of water, pills, milkshakes or tarot cards, they are looking at their father's belongings. A Webley .455 Mk VI revolver with bullets marked and engraved with their names, now it was up to the gods of fate to judge us by death, depending on who Pussys favoured.

Kelsa was always the fearless one, she loaded the bullets herself, loaded them and pulled the face guard, and Milligan had to follow her lead until Milligan realised they were going in different directions, Kelsa had never seen a gun swallowed properly, she could only aim for the head, that place at the temple. And Milligan wondered about his father's methods, he wondered why everyone could face fear without being afraid, he wondered why his father preferred death to survival.

"God, I just don't want to be forgotten," Michigan sighed.
"And abandoned." Kelsa smiled genuinely.

They pulled the trigger.

Tomorrow would come … and everything would be a new beginning.

The Zoom Room

Robert Parker

Evie had so much to do—two loads of laundry, her monthly newsletter to write, three guest-blogger deadlines—and now she had to answer that nasty email from her new agent. The agent had ghosted Evie's last four emails and now, all of a sudden, she expected Evie to get back to her just like that (Evie snapped her fingers). But Evie was all wrapped up in writing her next novel, so she couldn't resist the tempting pleasures of her monthly write-in, sponsored by Sisters in Crime Chicagoland. Since the COVID-19 pandemic began, they had started meeting over Zoom. She loved Sisters in Crime, the mystery and crime writers organization. Most members of her Chicago-area chapter didn't go to the write-ins, but there were five regulars. She felt like a hypocrite for the way she told the other writers in the group that she found their work *just fascinating* and *so intriguing*. Gag me, she thought, remembering the tripe she spoke into her laptop over Zoom when she praised their story ideas, but she knew they'd never see through the buttering up. Writers were suckers for flattery. Even so, just getting together with other mystery and crime-fiction writers helped her get her words out. Plus she loved to show off to them, to crow about her latest pubs and her new big-shot agent, but she made a point of dialing it back a little so they didn't get jealous.

In fact, she was so eager that she logged in a few minutes early. The others must have shared her enthusiasm, because she was the last one to arrive, and her four sisters in crime writing were already chatting away. Evie eyed the five Zoom rectangles. She saw Agatha Lightfoot rubbing her nose as if no one were looking. Behind Agatha, Evie saw the same crowded bookshelf as always, with Agatha's two books face forward to the camera. In the next rectangle, Barbie Braddock's peroxide waves glared out from the shadows of her bad lighting. Cleo Messenger's rectangle came next. Cleo looked as Goth as ever, with her raven hair and her black top and her maroon lipstick. She'd stuck "(she, her, hers)" next to her name, as if they didn't already know, Evie thought. In the fourth rectangle Evie was no more pleased than ever to see the tiresomely histrionic Delilah Caligari. Delilah was still pre-published, as they said in Sisters in Crime, and—Evie was convinced—she would stay that way, even if she finally managed to finish something, which she never would. Delilah liked playing the part of a writer, Evie thought, joining Sisters in Crime and all that, but Evie didn't think Delilah had the butt-in-the-seat stuff to grind it out to the end of a story. And of course Evie saw her own rectangle: Evie Desrosiers. Her lighting was perfect, she thought, as she dragged her rectangle to the middle of the top row so that she could look at herself comfortably, and so that everyone else would see her straight on at her best angle, looking right at the camera, even before they saw the plaques and posters behind her. (She loved those posters of her book covers. Who wouldn't?)

Soon they'd chat for fifteen minutes about what they wanted to write today. Then they'd turn off their audio and video and write for sixty minutes. Then, after a break, they'd chat about what they had written. But first, each month, one of them would talk about a mystery or crime-fiction topic that she loved. Two months ago, when it was Evie's turn, she talked about revenge stories, from *The Spanish Tragedy* and *Hamlet* to Michael Connelly and Stieg Larsson. Today's topic was locked-room mysteries. Evie didn't like them herself—they seemed so artificial, so dependent on cleverness—but Agatha liked them, and it was Agatha's turn to present. Last month, Cleo had opened the meeting by talking about poisons. That was good, Evie remembered. Evie had never used poison, and sometimes she worried that she was running out of ways to kill people, so maybe poison was a good way to go.

"Hi Evie," Barbie said, with her insincere, toothy grin shining out from the shadows of her misplaced lamp. Agatha waved. How could that birdbrain Barbie not have figured out, Evie wondered, that she should put the light in front of her, not behind her? Didn't she ever Google anything? Cleo nodded her usual understated, wordless greeting, and Delilah typed "So good to see you, Evie!" in the chat. Evie hated exclamation marks.

"Shall we get started?" Agatha said. "Does everybody have their tea?" She held a delicate pink teacup up to the camera and took a sip.

Cleo, Delilah, and Evie held up their teacups.

"Wait," Barbie said, laughing, as a cat climbed onto her lap. "I'm sorry," she said.

Barbie *would* have a cat jump on her, Evie thought. She wrote about them enough, in those insipid cozies, when she wasn't writing about recipes. Evie saw Cleo rolling her eyes, and not for the first time she felt a kinship with Cleo.

For a time, they'd even had the same agent. Cleo's writing was dark, like Evie's, even noir, and Cleo had a way with a cynical simile that Evie had to admit she envied.

Barbie stroked the black cat. "There you go, Edgar," she said. "There you go." Edgar turned his neck and leaned into her hand, and then she settled him on her lap. "All set now, girls," she said, and she giggled. Then she gave a thumbs up and took a sip of her tea.

"Okay," Agatha said. "I'll hit the record button."

"Recording in progress," announced the Zoom software.

"As you know, I'm going to talk about locked rooms," Agatha began. "Edgar Allan Poe, the founder of detective fiction, also wrote the first locked-room mystery in his great story 'The Murders in the Rue Morgue.'" Then Agatha's face froze, and then her eyes twisted, and then, with a thud, her head fell forward and her laptop shook, shaking her rectangle on Evie's screen, and then they all saw the top of Agatha's chestnut-dyed head lying like a smashed deer on the highway in front of her suddenly silent laptop.

Barbie gasped. Hardly a moment later, they all gasped. The cat leapt off Barbie's lap, and several of their laptops shook, as if Agatha had bumped into them when she fell. Evie heard a suppressed scream, or was it two screams, or three, counting her own—had she screamed too?

"Agatha!" Barbie said.

"Agatha, can you hear?" Delilah said. "Agatha!"

"Is she okay?" Barbie said, looking from rectangle to rectangle.

"Does it look like she's okay?" Cleo said.

"She looks—" Delilah couldn't complete the sentence.

"She looks dead," Cleo said.

"Oh no!" Barbie said.

"What—what should we do?" Evie said.

"We should help her," Barbie said, horrified, with her hand over her mouth. She coughed in confusion and fear.

"Sure," Cleo said. "You do that, Barbie. Help her."

"Does anybody know where she is?" Barbie asked.

"She's in hell," Cleo said.

Barbie's face twisted with agony. She was starting to cry. "Doesn't anybody know where she lives?" She had trouble just getting the words out to ask the question.

"I don't know where any of you live," Delilah said. "I've only seen you on

Zoom.”

“Me too,” Evie said. “This is horrible!”

“Horrible!” Delilah said. “Didn’t Agatha say she lives in Rogers Park?”

“I think she said Highland Park,” Evie said.

“No,” Cleo said, “Wasn’t it Park Forest. Or was it Forest Park?”

“We’re hopeless!” Barbie said, her voice straining. “We don’t know anything!”

“What should we do?” Evie said, staring at Agatha’s motionless head sprawled in front of her laptop.

“Does she live alone?” Delilah said, and, at the same time, Evie said “Is she married?”

They all stared aghast at Agatha’s rectangle. Barbie was shaking. She looked ready to vomit.

“Married?” Cleo said. “Hell no, she’s lesbian.”

“She’s lesbian?” Evie said. “How can you tell?”

“I’ve never seen her except on Zoom,” Delilah said, “and—and—over email.”

“Me too,” Evie said.

Then Barbie collapsed in front of her laptop. Her head made a thud as it slammed onto the table, almost the same as the sound they heard when Agatha fell.

“Barbie!” Delilah said.

“Oh no!” Evie said.

“No!” Cleo said. “Barbie! Can you hear?” Then Cleo said “I’m scared!” Her face had changed. She’d smudged her eye liner under one eye and smeared her lipstick around her mouth like a sick clown. The others saw her get up from her chair and race to the door behind her, shake at the door handle, and then turn around, her hands in the air. She yelled at her laptop: “It’s locked!”

“Locked?” Delilah yelled back.

“Barbie!” Evie screamed. “Are you there? Are you okay?”

“Somebody call her!” Delilah said. “Does anybody have her number? Barbie! Agatha!”

“I feel so helpless!” Cleo screamed. She disappeared in a panic off to the side and then reappeared holding furiously to a startled, uncooperative cat, black like Barbie’s cat but nothing like Barbie’s in temperament, at least not now amid Cleo’s spiraling panic.

“I’ll Google Agatha’s address,” Delilah said. She started typing. “Someone else Google Barbie's address while I look up Agatha's."

"On it," Evie said.

Cleo coughed and started to shake with fear until finally she could hold the irritated cat no longer and it jumped out of her arms.

"I'm not finding anything," Delilah said. "It's like she didn't exist."

"Barbie Braddock, Barbara, Barb," Evie said, "there's a million of them. I'll never find her fast enough to help."

Then Evie, staring at her screen, saw Cleo collapse on the floor between her laptop and the locked door. "Cleo!" Evie yelled. Delilah looked up. They could see Cleo lying on a black rug, her body jerking in spasms.

"No!" Delilah said.

"No!" Evie said. "It's not possible. Agatha! Barbie! And now Cleo!"

There was a silence, and Evie saw Delilah turning to stare at her with a new intensity.

"You did this!" Delilah said.

"It's terrible!" Evie said.

"You did this!" Delilah said.

"What are you talking about?"

"You know exactly what I'm talking about," Delilah said.

They stared at each other, glaring at the rectangles on their screens.

"A locked-room murder spree?" Delilah said. Then she said "Wait," and she disappeared off to the side.

Then she came back, her face awash in panic.

"You did this!" Delilah screamed.

"Are you crazy?" Evie said, panicking now even more.

"My door is locked too!" Delilah said. "A locked-room mystery! A locked-*Zoom* mystery! It had to be you! There's no one else! You're a monster!"

"You're lying!" Evie said. "I didn't do anything! It must be *you!* You did it! It wasn't me. There's no one else! You did this!"

"Agatha!" Delilah said. "Barbie! It's like Cleo said, last month. The poison! Remember when she told that story about how you could poison a keyboard? Put the poison on the E key, the M key, and the space bar, she said, if you want to kill them fast, so when they rub their hands, their poisoned fingers, against their face, against their mouth, they're done for, and put it on the Q key if you want to kill them ever so slowly. Agatha, Barbie, Cleo! Is that how you did it, Evie?"

"You're crazy," Evie said. "I write novels." She gestured toward the posters for her novels on the wall behind her. "I don't kill people. I write about killing people. So do you. It's not the same thing."

"It sure as hell isn't the same thing. Agatha, Barbie, Cleo," Delilah said, this time slowly. "Oh no. A-B-C—damn you Evie! Damn you! Am I next? A-B-C and then D?"

Evie's eyes bulged. "Are you alone?" she said. "Call the police! Call 911! Tell them where you are! I can't help you! I don't know where you are."

"I hate you!" Delilah said. "You betrayed us! You betrayed us all!"

"I didn't do anything!" Evie said. "How do you feel? Do you feel anything yet?"

"Is that what you want?" Delilah said. "Do you want me to writhe and choke until I shrivel up and die like the others? Why did you do it, Evie? Why? What do you have against me, against Agatha, against Barbie? I get it—nobody likes Barbie—but what did you have against Agatha, against Cleo? What do you have against me?"

They stared at their rectangles.

Evie shook her head. "I hate you," Evie said. "I hate all of you. I can say it now. Now that you're about to die."

"So you admit it! Now that you know we can't do anything about it, you admit it."

"I don't admit anything. I had nothing to do with it. Maybe I'm next, after you."

"Really? Is your door locked?"

Evie looked to her side, the panic distorting her perfectly made-up face. Then she started to get up.

"Wait," Delilah said. She was choking on her words. "I feel it now." She shivered. "I feel that damn poison. It's my turn! Why did you do it, Evie? Why do you hate us? Have you ever killed anybody before? I mean, really killed anybody, not just in your books?"

"You bet I have," Evie said.

"Did you really?" Delilah said. "Did you? Tell me, Evie." Delilah squeezed at her neck and squinched her eyes. "I don't have much time left. Maybe it wasn't the keyboard." She coughed, and her eyes seemed to bulge. "Maybe it was the tea. How did you do it, Evie? I need to know before I die. Who did you kill before? Why did you do it?"

Evie coughed. She could feel the fear and the poison too. She was sure of it. She could feel the poison making her shiver, because surely if Delilah was about to keel over, then Evie's turn could not be far behind.

"You want to know who I killed? I'll tell you who! For starters, I killed that terrible man with the evil eye. Cleo knew him! He was her agent too! I stabbed him, and I loved doing it. He never responded to my emails on time! He jerked me around on the marketing for my books. I don't think he ever really tried to land me with the Big Five. Oh, he saved that for Cleo! He didn't have time for me! But he had lots of time for Cleo! What makes her so much better than me? It doesn't matter anymore. Somebody's gunning for us all. You'll be dead soon like Cleo and the rest of them, and"—she shivered—"I'm next." She coughed at the thought of the grim death that awaited her.

"Now!" Delilah said, with recovered energy. "Now—" and then all at once Agatha, Barbie, and Cleo's corpses rose from the dead. "We have it all recorded," Agatha said.

"And you're going to fry for it," Cleo said. She bent down again and then stood back up, holding the black cat. "Would you like to meet my roommate?" she said, looking into the camera at Evie. Barbie had disappeared from her screen, and now she came on camera with Cleo. "Meet my wife, Barbie Braddock," Cleo said, and handed the cat to her.

"Hi Evie," Barbie said.

"We got her," Agatha said. She lifted her pink teacup and held it to the camera.

"We sure did," said Delilah, and she too lifted her teacup to the camera.

"Evie," Cleo said, raising her cup, "your story is over."

Play It Safe
Brandon Barrows

New York broiled under a heatwave, but the interior of my office was dim and cool, tucked in the back of the ground floor of the Village Film House. It was my second office, actually — I have one in each of the two movie-theaters I own, and each has a private entrance so I can come and go as I please without anyone the wiser. Each theater also has a competent manager, so I rarely handle day to day stuff, but never knowing if I'm in my office or not keeps them honest and on their toes. In truth, I'm rarely in either office, so for all intents and purposes, I'm not really part of the machine at all, but the system still works: I've never had problems with either of them.

Which is good, because aside from handling cash, I don't know a thing about running a theater. I bought both the Village Film House and the Metro 9 as-is, and all I really know is that they're the perfect way to make money I'd rather not explain come out looking nice and clean. On their own, the theaters provide a small income, but the IRS believes them both to be very successful, and as long as they get their cut, they'll stay happy. It took thought and planning to put the process in place, but the layers of protection it provides are well worth the effort. I value my peace of mind more than just about anything.

The pay-as-you-go cellphone on the desk rang. It was the only reason I was in the office and I'd been waiting nearly an hour, so it was a relief. I'm a patient person, but waiting makes me worry, makes my imagination conjure worst-cases, adds to my stress.

"Ezra?" the voice from the speaker asked, making me wince.

"No names, Seaver, you know that." Since I'd never used this phone, the risk was minimal, but now it was split between us. I imagined Marcus Seaver's irritated expression. He didn't like being corrected; the rich rarely do.

Any annoyance was kept to himself, though. "Been a minute, huh?"

"Almost a year. There's a new project, I assume."

"Uh huh. Short-term, but it needs doing fast. The client's ready to move on."

"Where are you now?" I asked.

"My usual place."

Even if I hadn't met with Seaver in ages, we'd been seen together before in the "usual place". I didn't like that, but he wouldn't change his plans on my say-so. I did some mental math, weighing my options, and in the end, the fact that Marcus Seaver was generally willing to pay very well tilted the scales against the risks.

I told him, "I'll see you in thirty," and cut the connection. I broke the phone in half and put the pieces in my pocket to later be tossed into the first public trashcan I saw. It was no great waste; I had a desk drawer full of them.

*****

Marcus Seaver inherited an empire, and for as long as I knew him—almost seven years—he struggled to hold onto it. He was rich, he was ruthless when he needed to be, he could be clever on occasion, but none of it was ever enough. Somehow, he never learned from past experiences and kept making the same mistakes. Because of that, it seemed like there was always someone crossing him, or a business rival he couldn't outsmart, or an employee caught with their hand in the till. Most of his troubles he handled within his organization. Anything out of the ordinary, he came to me.

Seaver perched on the edge of an uncomfortable-looking wooden chair at a postage-stamp-sized table in one of the thousands of small, interchangeable coffee shops that dot Manhattan. He rose when he saw me, met me halfway, said his hellos, shook my hand, and returned to his table.

He sat, but I looked around. The décor was different from last time we met there. Probably an ownership change, a frequent occurrence with that type of place. That was good, less chance of anyone remembering me. Except for a bored barista at the end of the room and a blond, too-tanned guy I recognized as one of Seaver's, we were alone.

I sat. Seaver snapped his fingers at the blond guy, who jumped to his feet, hustled to the counter, and a moment later brought us two massive cups of steaming foamy stuff pretending to be coffee.

After the blond returned to his seat, Seaver began, "How you been, Ezra?"

"Fine. Who's the client?" I'm patient, but I don't like small-talk and I don't pretend to be friends with my own clients. Keeping my distance is another kind of self-protection.

Seaver looked a little hurt—another of his mistakes; his emotions were always plain on his face—but he recovered, blew on his cup, and tried a sip. "Carl Green," he finally said. "You know him?"

"No." I didn't know the man, but I knew the name, and I'd seen him from a distance once or twice. Carl Green was a gnome of an accountant who had to be seventy if he was a day. He worked for Seaver's father and Marcus inherited him along with everything else. I heard somewhere that Green was retired, though, so what could Seaver have against him now?

"Why Green?"

Marcus shifted uncomfortably on the wooden seat. "You really gotta ask?"

"Retired, isn't he?"

"Yeah." Seaver nodded. "But listen — he knows stuff. Like, *everything.*"

"Your father trusted him," I reminded Seaver.

"Yeah," he said again. "I did, too, and when he asked to retire, I didn't worry much. So I say okay, and then — poof!" He made an exploding gesture with his hands, flicking all ten fingers open at once. "Gone. Disappeared. Guy's lived in the city his whole life and I figured if I knew where he was, nothing to worry about. I could keep an eye on him. But then he's just gone, and it makes me nervous. Guy vanishes, who knows where he'll turn up or what he'll get into?" He sighed heavily. "I'm sick of gettin' the short end of the stick, man. I'm tryin' to wise up, and loose ends ain't wise. You know what I mean?"

I made a sound that might have been agreement. Was Marcus Seaver finally becoming just the slightest bit self-aware?

"Anyway, it took eight months to find him," Seaver was saying. "But we got him. He's living in a podunk in Ohio, name of Carrollton. Using the name 'Ken Gaines' and keeping to himself from what I been told."

"So where's the harm?" I asked, already knowing. Someone who knew the ins and outs of any organization, running around unchecked, without any way to keep tabs on them, could be worrisome. I wanted to hear it from Seaver himself, though, to make sure he really understood. I had no problem killing, but not if it wasn't necessary. I was a contractor, not an employee, and if this was just some whim, rather than something he reasoned through, if this was only Marcus lashing out because Green didn't follow his unwritten script, I'd walk away. Impulses are dangerous and I wanted no part of Seaver's, if that's what this was.

Seaver's face darkened. "The shit in his head? And him walking around? Who the fuck knows what he's thinking? Maybe he's got good intentions, but maybe someday he finds himself in a jam. What's the first thing he thinks of? A get out of jail free card. That's a complication I can't afford, Ezra."

I pushed. "He's stayed quiet for years. Seems like a safe bet to me."

"Maybe," Marcus admitted. "But let's just say I want to hedge my bets — you know, play it safe. Something I learned recently and I plan to live by it."

Sure, when he thought of it he would. Mentally, I shrugged. Maybe Seaver would break his bad habits, maybe not, but he still had a point. Green knew where the bodies were buried, figuratively if not literally. I worked for Marcus often enough that I couldn't be sure that I wasn't in danger myself.

"All right, Marcus. I'll do it."

We talked money, an envelope changed hands, and then I got some more details. Seaver wanted to shake hands again afterwards, and then he actually told me to "have a good one". He really was in the wrong business.

*****

Four hours later, I was heading west on I-80 in a car rented under an assumed ID used solely for travel. I could take 80 all the way from the city to the Ohio state-line, a straight shot of about seven hours if traffic wasn't bad. I hated driving in the city, but I liked the interstate because I could see far ahead, plan out moves in advance. The sense of control was almost relaxing, and before long, I was enjoying the novelty of the open road.

Cruising at seventy miles an hour, a safe five miles over the speed-limit, I pulled into the left lane to pass a tractor-trailer. As I did, a compact, blazing white in the bright afternoon sun, pulled out of line several cars back. The brilliant shine of the car caught my eye in the rearview mirror and I wondered why people with those crappy little hatchbacks took such pride in them, and if it cost more to insure a souped-up version than it did the factory standard. Shifting back into the right lane ahead of the semi, though, the other car was hidden again, and I forgot about it almost instantly.

I reached Carrollton, Ohio around eight o'clock. It was smaller than I expected — just a village, really, and it looked like its best days were long gone. I had Green's—or rather "Ken Gaines's"—address, but I was in no rush. The drive was exhausting, and it was so much cooler out here than back in the city, that all I could think of was a pleasant night's sleep. Being well-rested lowered the risk of mistakes and Carl Green behaved himself this long, so another day couldn't hurt anything.

I spent forty minutes more in the car, getting a feel for the layout of the town, planning possible exit strategies if anything untoward happened, then ate at a roadside diner and checked into a motel near the highway for the night.

In the morning, I showered and shaved, dressed, then cleaned the little .380 automatic I brought for the job. It was already clean, and I'd used several like it before, but never this particular gun, so I wanted to familiarize myself with the weapon, even if I would only use it once. I never used a gun more than a single time, in fact, and when I was through with it, a little work with a rat-tail file would change the rifling of the barrel just enough that for all practical purposes, the gun that killed the target would cease to exist. That done, I could sell it to any firearms-dealer and make it disappear forever. It may sound complicated, but I sleep well at night so it's worth the trouble. After all, it's the little things that trip you up — but only if you let them.

When I left the room, the motel's lot was fuller than the night before, but there were no cars parked in front of the units to either side of mine. Two spaces to the left, however, there was a bright-white compact hatchback. For just an instant, I felt a tingle of warning, of danger, and I couldn't think why — then I remembered the car I saw on the interstate, blazing in the afternoon sun somewhere back in the wilds of Pennsylvania. As quickly as the feeling came, it disappeared, and I laughed to myself. There are cheap cars everywhere; I was making too much of a coincidence.

Just the same, I walked down the concrete strip in front of the rooms, gave the car a surreptitious once-over, and satisfied myself that nothing was out of the ordinary. Ohio plates, gleaming, gold-colored rims, giant stereo-speakers sitting on the backseats, and odds and ends scattered in the foot-wells. A young man's car, like thousands of others across the country. Feeling both better and a little ridiculous, I found a place to have breakfast and put it out of my mind.

*****

A plump, balding man was down on his knees in the front yard of the small, light-blue bungalow, digging in the dirt of what might once have been a flowerbed. Now, it seemed to be mostly weeds. He was wearing a sweatshirt, and ratty blue-jeans, and had less hair and more wrinkles than I remembered, but it was Carl Green. Even without Seaver's photo of Green, I would have recognized him. I was sure that he was doing his best to fit into this quiet hamlet on the edge of the Midwest, but something about him still said Manhattan.

"Mr. Bellows?" I called out as I walked across the stubby grass, picking a name at random.

The smaller man looked up, turned in my direction, and then looked away and back again, as if wondering whether there was someone else in his yard I might be addressing. So far as could be seen, though, we were the only ones on the entire block at the moment. "Me?" Green asked.

I stopped several paces away, smiling, sensing even as I did that it was having the opposite effect: Green's guard was up and even on his knees, he was tensed, as if prepared to spring up and bolt at an instant's notice.

"You're Edward Bellows, aren't you, sir?" I asked. I turned the smile up a few watts, shifting the empty document case in my right hand to my left. I held out the freed up hand as if to shake. "I'm Harvey Roberts, from Midwestern Mutual? We spoke on the phone yesterday afternoon, and—"

"My name is Gaines," Green said. He seemed to grip the trowel in his hand a little tighter, and though he was polite, there was a firmness in his voice that almost made me want to believe I really was wrong. "Ken Gaines."

I put on an exaggerated frown, as if I couldn't understand what was happening. "This is 416 Poplar Street, isn't it?"

"No, 416 Cedar. Poplar is a street up."

"Oh. I'm sorry, Mr. Gaines. My mistake." Of course, it wasn't any such thing. I just wanted to confirm for myself that "Ken Gaines" really was Carl Green. Now, despite his dedication to the act, there wasn't the slightest doubt in my mind. Everything from his reactions to his body-language told me that this man was afraid of being noticed, of being found out, that he was hiding. Marcus Seaver had a reasonable fear about Carl Green's knowledge being exposed to the world, but seeing and speaking to Green now, I didn't agree at all that he was dangerous or think for a second that he might get himself into trouble. Clearly, all he wanted was to be left alone, and if it was up to me, I would have. But it wasn't up to me; I agreed to do a job and I'd already taken partial payment.

"No trouble," Green said, his tone different now. He couldn't hide the relief as the tension flowed out of him, though he was trying. He pointed with the trowel. "Down to the end of the street, take your right, and then it'll be your next right."

"Thank you, Mr. Gaines. Sorry again to bother you."

"Gaines" turned back to his bed of weeds and waved the trowel without otherwise responding.

*****

I had an early, fast-food lunch and then drove back to the motel. Pulling into the parking lot, I noticed the white compact was gone, and felt silly for worrying myself over nothing. Prudence was a byword in my profession and the core value I lived by, but I was still too young to be fretting like an old man over shadows and reflections.

I napped a full eight hours. I preferred not to drive at night if I could help it, but I didn't plan to stick around Carrollton after the job was done. Counting on light overnight traffic, I could be back in New York before morning. Seaver would be happy, and I could collect the balance of what I was owed and go back to loafing for a few months.

Around seven-thirty, I showered and shaved again, dressed, and went in search of a good dinner. The steakhouse I found was adequate, but would never compare to Gallagher's back home.

Returning to the motel, I inspected my gun one final time, then retrieved my things, checked out of the motel, and made my way back to 416 Cedar Street. I saw only a handful of cars on my way there.

The evening was soft and hushed and dark, but there was light from Green's house. Across the street and a couple of houses down, I sat behind the wheel and watched for several minutes, but there was no movement aside from a faint breeze. Carrollton really was the quietest town I'd ever been in. I very much hoped that Green enjoyed his retirement, short as it was.

Slipping from the car, careful to avoid the spill of light from the few streetlamps, I crossed to Green's lawn. A big, orange-glowing picture window at the front of the building was draped, but a smaller window at the corner of the house was uncovered and wide open. Through it, I saw Carl Green shuffle from the front room into a cubicle-sized kitchen and move to the refrigerator, where he ducked behind the open door and came back up holding a can of beer. He pressed the cold aluminum against his forehead for a moment, let out a sigh of pleasure, and then popped the top. As he lifted the can to drink, my bullet smashed into the base of his skull, pushing him forward in a shower of blood and beer to slump against the refrigerator and crumple to the floor.

I turned and walked slowly back towards my rental car — along the sidewalk this time, just a man taking an evening stroll. I didn't check to make sure Green was dead—I knew he was—and I wasn't worried about anyone hearing the shot. Even without a suppressor, small-caliber guns make relatively little noise, and almost no one thinks a single gunshot *is* a gunshot, so I was in no hurry.

I turned the car in the direction of the state highway that connected to I-80, keeping exactly to the speed-limit. No headlights trailed me and cars from the other direction were few. I was safe, in the clear. It was obvious that Green lived alone, and he probably wouldn't be discovered for days. There was no danger to me, and Seaver could rest easy knowing that there was none to him — at least not from this particular former employee. Despite what he said, I knew him well enough that I was sure that bad habits would return and that his troubles would never really be over.

I felt good, relaxed. My work wasn't difficult, it paid well, and with all proper precautions taken, there really wasn't much risk involved. I rarely worked more than twice a year, and I enjoyed long periods of time off in between, but I always felt a sense of satisfaction when a job was done. This time around, I also enjoyed seeing some of the country I ordinarily wouldn't. I was city-bred, but maybe a vacation somewhere in the heartland would be nice. Not Ohio, of course.

For the first time in a very long while, my mind must have been wandering as I thought of vacation spots, because a split-second's flash of headlights from a side-road was the only warning I had. I braked hard and jerked the steering wheel, but it was too late. The lights smashed into me and I was spinning, spinning, as the outside world tilted crazily — and then pain exploded, jolting through my body as the car came to a stop.

I passed out, at least for a few seconds. When I opened my eyes, I realized I was hanging sideways, that the rental car was suspended on the edge of a steep ditch, half in and half out of it. I tried to move and felt metal creak and shudder with the shifting of my weight, but that was all I accomplished. One of my arms was broken and useless and I couldn't feel my legs at all.

Panic screamed through me. The identity I was traveling under—Harvey Roberts—was rock-solid, but I had no excuse for being in the area in a car with New York plates, and more than that, I still had the gun with me. There would be questions, and I had no answers that authorities would accept, because this was nothing I ever planned for. I was so concerned with wild scenarios that could make the job go sour, or lead trouble back to me, that something this mundane happening never occurred to me.

The car's engine was still running, but over its noise, I heard another engine. I didn't think it was the car that hit me.

With the way the rental was perched on the side of the ditch, the high-beams shone upwards like a spotlight and in their glare, a third car appeared — a bright-white compact. This time I knew it wasn't coincidence. It just couldn't be.

The compact's door opened and heavy-booted feet stepped out. "Help!" I croaked, hoping against all evidence. It was more than a hope, that one word was almost a prayer.

The boots clambered down the edge of the ditch and a face appeared, backlit by the headlights of the little white car. Even shadowed by the bright lights, I recognized it: Kelleher, a member of my particular fraternity. It was several years since I last saw him, but he hardly looked to have aged at all. He was still a young man, still in the right age range for a tricked-up little hatchback.

I heard he left the city a while ago, but I had no idea where he ended up. I didn't need to ask what he was doing here now. It was obvious that he was still working in the same field.

"Bad luck," Kelleher said, looking over his shoulder. "Lady came out of nowhere, like a bat out of hell. Probably drunk. Whole front end's crushed; she's had it." He turned to me. "Thought this was gonna be easy money, just Seaver's back-up plan. No work for me at all, and you'd never even know I was here, but… well." He shrugged. "Sorry, Foley, but Seaver says no loose ends and you know he pays pretty good."

The job went fine, but because of one freak instant, now cops would be involved and Kelleher couldn't be sure what would happen next, so Seaver's plan B kicked in. I knew what was going to happen, though. I knew it all too well.

Absurdly, I wondered how long my theaters would hum along before someone realized I was never coming home. Cautious as I was, I never put a plan in place for this possibility. All along the line, I played the game as safely as I knew how to, and in the end, I still lost out. I set the system up so that it didn't need me and maybe that was my first mistake.

"'Playing it safe,' Seaver said. He really is learning." I tried to force a laugh, but it came out a strangled sob.

"Sure," Kelleher agreed. His fist came up, filled with a gun much bigger than the one I used on Green.

So Clear it Burns

S.E. Bailey

Maggs came down to the kitchen a quarter after 3a.m and fixed a cup of instant.

She'd slept some; a few hardscrabble hours of hard-won dozing and fretful dreams was all she managed these days, since that letter arrived two weeks back.

Terrell's letter had done the impossible - left her hurting worse than after Kenny died; even worse, maybe, than after the thing with Charlie.

Well … maybe not quite.

She was older now and didn't bounce back like she used to … hit anything hard enough, it breaks. That goes for people too; no matter what Kenny preached or things the Bible claimed.

She looked at that old photograph hanging over the range, the one of her and Kenny, with Charlie as a little kid.

Happiest time of her life.

She felt a surge of shame for feeling such hate for Terrell. Kenny wouldn't have wanted that.

Her hands shook as she swigged the coffee — low caffeine but she shouldn't be drinking it, not with sleep the way it was.

Still, her shaking eased after the first mouthful.

Caffeine was the strongest non-prescription thing she took in near-on forty years, since Kenny had gotten her clean. She made a mental note to go back to plain water once all this was over.

She'd decided to burn Terrell's letter and let that be the end of it.

Except … she was going to read it one last time.

She knew she shouldn't, but she took the letter from the shelf where it now lay, trespassing next to Kenny's dog-eared Bible and the pictures Charlie drew when he was little.

She felt her chest flutter.

Terrell's letter had come in an official envelope with a bar-code sticker, identifying that it came from Angola — not the African country but the other Angola … the nickname of Louisiana's Maximum Security State Penitentiary.

A certified stamp confirmed that correspondence from an inmate lay within.

When it'd arrived Maggs had felt her breath knocked out of her. She'd already known it was from Terrell but that hadn't made receiving it any easier.

Maggs had half expected the letter because she'd ignored that Ansara woman twice.

The first time she'd written had been introducing herself, signposting Maggs to the bestseller she'd written and that PBS documentary about her; the one where she'd gotten tribe people with lopped-off limbs to sing in a choir alongside of folks from the other tribe that'd done it to them.

The whole thing was posted up on Ansara's YouTube account.

It had two million views and a heap of warm comments below — made, no doubt, by people who'd never lost a fingernail on account of anyone else.

Maggs ignored that letter but Ansara had written again.

Next time she bit harder; told her what she wanted, in a roundabout way.

It was clear she'd done research about her.

Maggs wondered exactly how she'd found her address and all the other stuff out. She'd not given interviews at the time of Charlie's death, nor did she put herself out there on-the-line.

Had Ansara come snooping around Vacherie by herself or did she have people who did that for her?

However she'd found out, Ansara made a big thing in her letter about Kenny being a man of God and how Maggs had supported him in his ministry.

She didn't mention Charlie directly, nor what'd happened to him.

What had happened … meaning what Terrell had done.

How he'd beat her son to death; took his life for no other reason than to look tough in front of the low-rent criminals that Charlie had taken to hanging with.

Instead of retelling all that, Ansara served up some crock about how hurt was like fire, how it'd burn you up inside if you weren't careful. It was fire only you could put out, though only if you had the right help.

Ansara had been a Carmelite Nun in Indonesia who'd quit that gig and now spent her life travelling the globe, following her new calling — spreading the message of forgiveness and its healing power.

Her letter told Maggs that all the praise she'd gotten for doing this didn't belong to her but was really down to those people themselves … the victims of all the bad shit. All she'd done was help them find that power to forgive that they'd always had within.

She finished by telling how she'd come to know Irvin Terrell; at first just from reading the articles that'd appeared about him down the years. Ansara claimed she'd expected some monster or, worse still, a dissembler; a born liar and master manipulator as smooth as Satan himself.

But, apparently, he was nothing like that — not since he'd found the Lord.

Ansara asked Maggs if she'd be open to receiving a letter from Terrell.

She didn't outright ask her to forgive him, leastways not yet. She was asking if, as a Christian, she'd take that first step of being open to hearing a soul in pain. The ex-nun said she knew a man like Terrell was something a person of Maggs's background had no experience of but she told her not to be afraid.

But that, like so much in her letter, was something Ansara had got dead wrong.

In a different life, Maggs had known animals like Irvin Terrell all too well.

In fact, way before seeing him at the trial, she'd even once been in a room where Terrell himself had been present; though in the courtroom he'd only given her a brief glance, with no hint of recognition.

It hadn't surprised her because she hadn't known Terrell well. After her time at the Legion compound ended and her true life had really begun ... the family years with Kenny and Charlie ... she'd dramatically changed the way she styled herself.

She'd looked totally different. Being loved and kicking the drugs had taken care of that.

By the time of Terrell's trial, she'd long been a new person ... born again, not on account of Kenny's religion but more just down to his love for her and, later, Charlie's love too.

Those were the things that'd helped her build her new life ... before Kenny's cancer, and Irvin Terrell's brutal violence, had destroyed it all.

A woman of Maggs's 'background' ... for all her snooping and her cast-iron certainties Ansara hadn't the first clue about what Maggs's background had been or who she really was.

That bitch didn't have the first goddam clue who she was fucking with.

*****

Maggs took a breath and another gulp of coffee, then poured a glass of water.

Though she'd ignored Ansara's request to allow Terrell's contact, the ex-nun and the psychopathic ex-biker gang leader had gone ahead anyway.

They must've figured silence indicated consent, a misguided viewpoint that was probably common amongst Angola's inmates.

Her hands still shook as she laid out her pills ... the one for her joints, the one meant for sleeping, the ones for her heart.

She looked at his letter like it was an accusation.

She'd felt she had to read it one more time before burning it. Now she knew she couldn't even stand to see his handwriting again — the neat, surprisingly delicate print in which he'd framed his plea, which managed to ask forgiveness without mentioning anything he'd done wrong.

She crossed to the stove quickly, so as not to change her mind. She lit it, dropping Terrell's letter inside and watched it burn.

The relief only lasted a moment.

*****

She'd also burned Ansara's letters but bits kept returning to her. The woman had a way with words. Also, some things she'd written about Terrell were accurate.

For instance, Ansara correctly said Terrell was real smart. Maggs hated his guts but knew that was true. He'd studied a law degree in his first ten years and got it with honours, although his appeals all still got denied.

Maggs had followed whatever snippets she could find about Terrell's incarceration over the years. She couldn't help it.

During the early years his huge size, ultra-viciousness and shot-caller status in LLMC - The Legion - had all made him feared; a real big dog inside Angola's walls.

Then, twelve years into his sentence, something big changed.

Maggs recalled when she first heard that Terrell had been moved into protective custody within the prison. It'd been the same month Kenny had his final round of chemo, just over eight years back.

One of Kenny's parishioners was an ex-cop. He hadn't dealt with Charlie's murder but, like everyone in Vacherie, he knew the story.

He'd come by on the day Kenny returned from hospital and told them Irvin Terrell had been moved out of the general population — which meant there was an on-going, credible threat to his life from somebody, or more likely some group, within the prison.

Kenny had thanked the man but Maggs knew he didn't mean it.

Kenny hadn't even been able to stand hearing Terrell's name. But Maggs hadn't been able to stop thinking on what the ex-cop parishioner had told them … not just who'd want Terrell dead, but also who might have the juice to make it happen.

She knew Angola's inmates were mostly black and The Legion were as crazy-violent a group of white-power peckerwoods as you'd find anywhere outside of a Klan rally. Even so, Maggs hadn't figured some black inmate gang as being responsible for Terrell's move out of gen pop.

He'd been there too long, so they already knew who and what he was. Also, the LLMC's whole 'white hate on wheels' shtick was strictly to frighten non-biker civilians and motivate their more gullible foot soldiers. Maggs knew for a fact they'd make behind the scenes deals with black gangs, or Mexicans, or whoever else helped them turn a dishonest buck on the outside; so she guessed it was probably the same inside Angola's walls.

When it really came to it, the only color the Legion cared about was green; so whatever caused Terrell's move into protective custody was something different from race hate.

From the moment she realised that, Maggs started paying special attention to the news.

The whole thing coincided with the end of Kenny's treatment so it hadn't been the main thing on her mind. Even so, news items seemed to jump out of the t.v at her during that time.

Like that big drugs bust in Lafayette — the Legion hadn't been mentioned but she knew they'd run that scene back in the day. No reason to think that'd changed any — so that meant LLMC had taken a four million dollar hit when State police and the FBI raided their secret distribution warehouse.

Then, a few weeks later, the Department of Homeland Security stopped a boat heading into Baton Rouge with a bunch of young Honduran girls as cargo — frightened, doped up kids who'd been tried out and broken-in already; all pre-hurt into readiness for their new lives, turning tricks for the pleasure and profit of vicious men.

Again, the t.v news hadn't mentioned The Legion but she remembered well enough they'd always had a stake in that business.

There wasn't anybody in the whole state who sold girls without a slice of that action going to LLMC … nobody had better reason to remember that than Maggs.

That second story had proved her suspicion. No matter how unlikely it seemed that anyone would dare, it was clear someone was ratting out the Legion; a big someone with enough juice to know all the little details of all the big projects.

Terrell.

That was why he'd gone into protective custody.

And the cold realisation of exactly why he'd done it started growing inside of her, as slow and nasty as Kenny's tumour … Irvin Terrell intended to walk free one day, by whatever means necessary.

Killing Charlie hadn't been the only serious crime they'd got him on but it was the only one where they had him red handed.

Red with her child's blood.

Maggs knew for a fact it wasn't the only time Terrell had taken someone's life but she didn't know names, dates, or where the bodies were buried.

Even making that accusation would've opened up a whole can of worms about her past — exactly how the middle aged, goody-two-shoes wife of a Baptist preacher knew anything about Terrell or the world he inhabited.

It hadn't been her reputation or notions of respectability that'd ensured her silence. It'd been the certain knowledge that her past coming out would hurt Kenny that'd kept her quiet.

Kenny had hurt enough for one lifetime. So had she.

Besides, nothing she said would've meant Terrell would serve as much as an extra day. And, by the time his trial was over, she'd had every reason to think Terrell would never be a free man again.

He'd beaten Charlie to death at a rendezvous with the guys that Charlie had taken to hanging out with — a crew of small time, wannabe criminals; one of whom had set up the meeting with Lucifer's Legion Motorcycle Club.

They were trying to sell them crates of bourbon one of the guys pilfered from his warehouse job but the bikers just took it off of them without paying — laughing at the teenage pretend tough guys.

Terrell had been there and he'd beat Charlie to death on a whim, off the back of some smart comment the kid made … that and the fact he'd referred to them as 'Hell's Angels' when just about everybody knew the LLMC once had a decade long war with the Angels.

Nobody there knew that one of the boys Charlie was hanging with had a ten-year prison sentence hanging over him and was working his way out from under it by being a Confidential Informer, wired for sound by the Feds building a case against the Legion.

The whole meeting had been their idea but they'd never expected LLMC's top lieutenant to even be there, let alone get him on tape beating someone to death. But by the time they'd realised what they were hearing and stormed the freight yard where it all went down, it was too late.

Charlie's whole body had been mangled in Terrell's crazed onslaught and his brain so pulped the pathologist said in court he'd never have walked or talked normal again, even if he'd lived.

And even that would've been better than how it ended up; Maggs would've looked after him her whole life.

But he hadn't lived.

Terrell stood trial for murder — pleading out to second degree on account of saying it'd only been an ass-kicking that'd gone wrong; though the Feds still had him as accessory to other stuff — extortion, distribution, pimping …

Maggs knew they didn't have the half of it.

Even so, the judge gave Terrell 147 years with no possibility of parole — a tiny piece of human justice in response to God's colossal, cosmic insult to her and Kenny.

She didn't know if Kenny stopped believing after that — he stayed on as a minister but something inside him died for sure.

Still … Irvin Terrell would never see another day as a free man, he'd be locked away with all the other animals that couldn't be trusted around normal humans.

She was sure of that much.

Or, at least, she had been — until that day twelve years later when Kenny's ex-cop parishioner told them about Terrell's move out of the prison population … until all those TV stories of big law enforcement triumphs that followed close behind, then just kept on coming one after the other.

Instinctively, Maggs knew what was happening.

The knowledge was always there, like tooth ache — even as she watched Kenny fight the cancer in the year that followed his parishioner's visit.

She just knew it.

That smart-ass college law degree had been a bust for Terrell. All that studying nights in his cell got him a fancy certificate but hadn't taken a day off his 147 years.

But spilling the Legion's biggest secrets just might.

If it didn't get him killed first … which Maggs found herself hoping it would.

She'd decided, after weeks of obsessing over which tv news items were Legion related, to focus instead on Kenny — the good man who'd given her everything and who'd lost as much as she had.

As well as cancer he was fighting his guilt over his arguments with Charlie. He wondered if the kid's wild nature had been his fault all along; some reaction to the white picket fence, church going childhood they'd put him through.

Maggs told him that was plain wrong but felt her own guilt, for different reasons.

Charlie had lived free, no matter what anyone said. He'd been that way since he was little, and it'd gotten worse in his teenage years. He never learned life's one big lesson — that there's always a price for how you live.

Or rather, learning that lesson had been the very thing that'd killed him.

Maggs felt guilt because that's how she'd also been when she was young. She'd always put that down to her having been an orphan, an inmate in the worst kind of children's home. She'd explained away her own delight in rule breaking as down to all that early abuse and the fact that, after she'd run out of there at fifteen, she'd ended up with one no-good, dead-beat guy after another — trading her young flesh; first for food and a roof, later for money and drugs.

It was a life that'd led to a dirt road that wasn't on any maps, a place outside of Morgan City — to the secret compound of Lucifer's Legion Motorcycle Club; a one-percenter biker gang so insanely vicious that all the other outlaw bikers nationwide left Louisiana to them.

Young Maggs … strung out, barely able to read or write, so used to being abused. But she'd had a young, firm body and looked good enough for them to make use of. Her only aspiration had been to maybe get noticed by a full patch member; dreaming perhaps one of their top guys might ask her to be his alone, his 'old lady'.

Thinking of her younger self made Maggs almost cry.

But, in those months when Kenny was dying and blaming himself, it also made her feel guilty.

Explaining away her flaws as a result of her horror-show childhood was too easy.

Charlie had the best Dad and the best upbringing any kid could have. And Maggs had been a great Mom, even if she did think so herself — she'd loved that kid in ways she'd never known she had inside her.

So, the only reason Charlie had been so off the rails had to be her — it stood to reason … something genetic … bad blood.

Old Ma Crawford — Kenny's Bible-thumping bitch of a mom had as good as said so on the day Kenny told her he was going to make Maggs his wife.

Ma Crawford passed a year after Charlie's birth, having lived to see Maggs become the perfect wife and mom.

Maggs had nursed her in her final months.

But she'd never fully felt her trust; and, after Kenny died, she thought that maybe Ma Crawford had it right all along.

*****

Ma Crawford, Kenny and Charlie were buried next to each other at the tree-lined edge of a small graveyard, just outside of Vacherie.

Maggs went to lay flowers and speak to them after the service every Sunday afternoon.

She went there on the Sunday after she'd burned Terrell's letter. It was where she first came face to face with Ansara.

*****

She'd put down the flowers then plucked the wild crabgrass off the graves like normal. It'd been two weeks from hell, or a different kind of hell from her normal weeks.

She touched Charlie's gravestone; closing her eyes and trying to see his face and wondered, yet again, if all that God stuff was just some story people tell. Maybe all she was doing was touching stone and talking to herself.

Leastways, it was over now. She'd burned his goddam letter and was going to evict that monster from her head. The thought raised a weak smile, at the exact moment she saw the woman standing a few yards distant.

On the documentary and in the letters Ansara was forthright and certain. But this woman seemed nervy and looked around, as if trying to find some chance to not speak with her. Ansara looked delicate; small boned and real pretty with smooth, gold-brown skin her new friend Terrell would've hated her for a few short years ago.

Their eyes met.

Ansara stepped forward.

'Mrs Crawford … I'm …'

'I know who you are.'

'I came to offer help … I feel so sorry about ….'

Maggs felt her face contort. Her heart went fast and hard; she tried to speak, or scream, or make any noise to tell Ansara to get the hell away from her.

But she had nothing. Everything span and her legs gave out.

'Mrs Crawford … are you ….'

But Maggs heard no more words, just jumbled sounds from far away. A kaleidoscope of sky, trees, then grass and grave-bed passed before her. She was on the ground, someone was talking but it sounded like another language.

Things came back in focus. Ansara's face loomed into view. Her voice was soft.

'I wanted only to talk …'

'Pills.'

She only managed a whisper but Ansara found the pills in a side pocket of Charlie's old hoodie that Maggs always wore for grave-tending. She helped her to sit up and take the pills, a flask that Ansara hadn't seemed to be holding appeared from somewhere.

Maggs was shaking, big tears rolling down her face.

'I'm ... not cryin'.'

'Of course ... of course, Mrs Crawford.'

*****

In spite of herself, Maggs ended up sitting opposite Ansara in the diner that lay a short walk from Charlie and Kenny's final resting place.

Ansara had weak tea with lemon. Maggs resisted coffee for a glass of water.

'It's all I'm safe to drink ... my health.'

'I am sorry. Do you often ...'

'Wig out? Like just now? No, but my health sucks. It has for years. Got worse after Charlie's murder.'

Maggs looked at her hard when she said it. Ansara's big brown eyes met hers, her pretty face didn't flinch.

'I don't fear that word. I understand the magnitude of what Irvin did.'

'Do you?'

Ansara looked through the diner's grimy window at garbage-scraps moving in the breeze through the empty backstreet.

'My brother died when I was small ... leukaemia. Before you say that's not something another person did ... it was curable, if you were rich. My family was poor.'

Maggs blinked. It was Ansara who finally broke the silence.

'What was he like, your son?'

Maggs couldn't resist answering, as if talking to someone who'd never met him brought a part of Charlie back alive.

'He annoyed the hell out of Kenny, me too sometimes. He wanted to be a rebel but it was just a phase. The thing was, Charlie was more like Kenny than either of them knew ... Charlie didn't have an ounce of mean inside him. It was just the style he wanted ... being something different from Mom and Pop. He didn't understand authentic badness, had no idea how to hang with real bad men. Men like Irvin Terrell.'

Ansara looked suddenly more assured. Maggs guessed she must consider questions of right-and-wrong to be her turf.

'I believe there's good in everyone.'

She glanced away and seemed to ponder before adding,

'… and I know there's enormous good in Irvin Terrell. I've heard him speak about his past and his hopes for the future.'

'His hopes for the future!'

Maggs couldn't keep bitterness from her voice. She was shaking again.

'Listen, do you think you're the first pretty little good girl to have a thing for some good-looking thug? Kids like Charlie want to be bad boys, and girls like you want to be with bad boys. But it's all just outlaw aftershave, Honey. The real bad boys are creatures you don't even want to drive past in the street — believe me.'

The slightest flicker on Ansara's face showed Maggs she'd said something that'd hit home. But it lasted a second then Ansara was serenely gazing back at her again, matching her in the stare-out with those big eyes.

'You're so angry Mrs Crawford. I am worried you will have another episode. What is it that you want? Do you wish for me to leave?'

Maggs wanted to yell that she'd never wanted to speak with her in the first place. But she found herself saying quietly, to her own surprise,

'I want to … to be able to laugh again someday.'

They sat in silence for a full half minute.

Maggs felt her heart slowly resume its normal rhythm. Finally, Ansara got up, took a card from her purse and placed it on the table.

'It's my contact details. I am working at the State Penitentiary for a month, not just with Irvin. I would welcome the chance to… to begin a dialogue. I know that Irvin would welcome this, also. To heal, and perhaps to offer you a chance to heal also. Will you consider this Mrs Crawford?'

Maggs said nothing but she took the card.

Ansara smiled, nodded briefly and left without another word.

*****

Night brought dreams unlike anything she'd experienced before — even in the days after losing Charlie.

'Mommie, Mommie, look at the witch …' five year old Charlie shrieks with laughter, points at the melting witch after Dorothy's thrown the water on her.

Next, a jumble of images race by … holding him that first time as a baby … the day of his funeral … the most raw memory she dreams is the day of that god-awful fight he'd had with Kenny, when she'd gone to him outside, pretending not to notice his red eyes from tears he'd wiped just moments earlier.

'Hey … why so hard on Dad?'

'Sanctimonious asshole.'

'He's a good man … he's your Dad.'

'He's not like you Mom … you've got my back … always … Right or Wrong.'

*****

And now she lay fully awake, sweat drenched, heart racing and fighting for breath.

She got up and staggered to the kitchen, poured water and downed yet more pills.

She sat, focused on her breathing. Tears pricked her eyes. She felt shamed by the memories and how she'd meekly taken that bitch's card, like she might actually forgive that animal one day.

In her sleep some things had come together — all the thoughts that'd swirled round for years since Charlie, then since Kenny … stuff about the universe and the way things really were, once you strip away the bullshit.

The God stuff was all hogwash.

She saw it now — saw it so clear it burned.

There are those who take, and those who get taken — that's what life is and what it always was.

She'd understood it just fine when she was a kid, then she'd started thinking things were different during her years with Kenny.

But she'd been wrong, and so had he.

The currency might change but the transaction stays the same.

Take Irvin Terrell, for instance. Muscle and meanness had got him all he'd ever wanted, until it hadn't any more. But he'd found a different way to take.

If you can't make everyone in the room afraid, then make them cry instead; make them believe some inner journey's turned you good.

Because everyone wants to believe good men exist.

She saw it now, how it would all play out.

One day there'd be another documentary, this one about how Ansara had saved Irvin Terrell, or maybe there'd even be a Hollywood movie. Charlie would be some bit-part actor's role but Maggs herself might even be worth a scene if she played her part in the scenario they were setting up; if she went to Angola and forgave him.

They'd make it the feel-good ending.

But that wouldn't be the story's end.

Terrell and Ansara were lining it up that he'd be released one day. The courts would buy it if they lobbied hard enough and got the right publicity. They'd relent on parole; on account the busts from all his snitching, his newfound piety and the fact his victim's mother had forgiven him.

The takers and the taken, how it always had been and always would be.

She'd started her life as the latter.

Having her young body used and her self-respect taken by men like Terrell. Now they'd set her up for the take all over again. Except now they wanted so much more; wanted her to lick up all the pain with a shit-eating grin on her face … *kill my son Irvin, really, it's o.k … we were only ever bit players in your story, after all.*

Maggs was shaking harder now but for a different reason.

Something else had slid into place; alongside of all the big notions about life and the universe, a different kind of answer had come to her — a plan so simple and yet so huge it took her breath away.

Maggs was going to kill Terrell.

And now she knew just how to do it.

*****

Mid-morning found Maggs watching strip malls and bean-fields roll by, her mind racing as she rode the slow bus into Morgan City; a journey of an hour, taking her back nearly four decades.

Travelling this road had been her greatest fear for years. It'd given her nightmares in the early days with Kenny, that decade before Charlie … amongst other things, like groups of raucous men or the unexpected roar of motorbikes.

But today, she didn't feel afraid.

She disembarked on the other side of the Atchafalaya by noon then made her way to the little travelled back-roads on foot.

It took another hour to get there. She ignored the trespass signs that got more lurid and less legal the nearer she approached the compound.

Finally, she stood in plain view in front of main gate. Thick woods on three sides, the dirt track she'd walked up on the other. The compound itself was a couple of acres but only fully visible from the air. She stood before the razor wire topped mesh gate. The CCTV camera's red light blinked, like the eye of some demon guarding Hell.

Maggs eyeballed it right back, stony faced.

They sent one of the old ladies out; some bikers' moll in her twenties with a cute body and a nasty face.

She stood the other side of the gate, looking Maggs up and down.

'Lady, you ain't gonna sell no cookies for the library fundraiser here.'

Maggs stared at her.

The girl sneered and pointed down the road.

'Listen, you got lost in these woods. Turn round and walk; you'll hit the interstate with foot blisters and a big story for the knittin' circle.'

She kicked the gate, vicious eyes glinting.

'Now … Scram out of here grandma, before I beat your scrawny ass.'

Maggs spoke quietly.

'I came to see The Hogg.'

She spoke to the camera, 'does this thing do sound? I came for Hogg. No-one else.'

Maggs turned back to the open-mouthed girl.

'I'm going to kill Irvin Terrell and he's going to help me, go and tell him that, girl — or he'll know you're the one kept it from him.'

The girl blinked.

'I said go tell him, bitch.'

Her look was poison, but she walked away.

Maggs faced the camera again, so cold she didn't even need to flip off whoever was watching.

Next, they sent one of the soldiers out to see if they could make grandma blink. A mean looking mess of hair, leather and race-hate tattoos stared hard at her for a cold minute but Maggs just rolled her eyes.

He opened the gate and turned, still silent. Maggs followed him inside the compound.

She followed him to Hogg's place — passing all the old landmarks on the way. To the left was The Hard Yard, the no-rules fight ring where beefs got settled; she remembered the gouged-out eye and the brain damage she'd seen inflicted, cheered on by a hundred screaming Legion guys, on the night they'd made her the ring-card girl.

A little further on were The Boneyards — the place the Legion buried its dead … meaning the ones they'd made dead.

The compound had a hundred such buildings and dedicated areas, all with their own names and disgusting legends attached. But none was more dangerous than where she was headed now - Hogg's Pen.

The walk brought back that memory of Irvin Terrell — that time he'd roared into the garage block with the small crew Hogg had given him. Maggs had been there with the guy she'd been with at the time, passing him tools as he fixed his ride. She recalled the awed hush as Terrell came in. He'd been new to the Legion but everyone had known he was something special. They'd said Hogg had taken such a liking to him he might even let him take it all over one day.

On that long ago afternoon she recalled now how Terrell's eyes slid over her and, with shame, how it'd given her a buzz.

But Terrell was new to The Legion and the asshole she'd been handing tools to had started beating her soon after. It was why she'd lit out of there in the end. Terrell's first weeks with The Legion had been her last.

*****

They stopped in front of a tumbledown cabin at the compound's edges, a few feet from the back fence.

Hogg's Pen was a shithole but now she felt her first moment of fear.

More people had died in there than anywhere in the whole evil place. Women had been raped while Hogg sat watching — guys too, sometimes. She wasn't afraid on account of herself but more in case this was the end of the road. She needed to achieve what she'd come back here to do.

It all hung on the next ten minutes. She had to sell it to The Hogg … make him believe in it like she did.

If he sensed one ounce of fear she was dead.

*****

Her guide opened The Pen's door and pointed her to go inside. Then he walked away, glancing back with almost sympathy.

Maggs stood in a gloomy hallway, light blazed from the room at the end.

The place stank of farts, greasy food and engine oil.

'Come on in, Honey. I'm waiting.'

The voice bellowed from up ahead.

Maggs walked inside.

Hogarth 'Hogg' Prosser lay open legged on a recliner, wearing a string vest and dirty underwear.

She kept her face impassive.

The last surviving founder of Lucifer's Legion might've looked like young Brando in biker leathers once but now came over more like the big slug character in that spaceships movie that Charlie had liked so much as a kid — the one that had the princess on a chain.

But Prosser wasn't some fantasy villain.

The black eyes that crawled all over Maggs looked dead, but the rest of his bloated face twitched with vibrant, agitated life. She met his stare,

136

returning that dead-eye vibe with interest, until Prosser threw his head back and cackled hard.

'You got stones, Honey.'

Then his voice got harder, '… but you spoke the forbidden name out there … we don't never say his name here … How come you know the traitor?'

'He killed my son.'

Prosser blinked, glanced out of the grimy window, then looked at her again.

'You that preacher's wife … Crawford? Why ain't he here? Why's he send his woman?'

'My husband passed … eight years this Fall.'

Prosser made a sound in his throat that could've meant anything — though Maggs thought sympathy was unlikely.

He looked sharp at her and blinked. She sensed his sudden recognition with dismay.

Prosser could smell out someone's secrets like a pig snorting after truffles.

'Hey … it can't be … are you Red Lynx?'

Prosser had always given the women pet names … Sweet Cheeks … Wildcat … Honey Tits … anything but a real human name.

Maggs had been Red Lynx during her years here; on account of her hair and also, he'd said, her fierce and sneaky nature.

'Well … I'll be …'

His wistful moment lasted a second, then Prosser was all business again.

'So, you're gonna kill the traitor … you. All a hundred and ten pounds of you. Let me tell you something, Honey. Two of our guys in Angola tried already, that's why he got put in protective. One of them boys is in the morgue, an' the other can't walk no more. The so-called law didn't add a day on his time neither, on account of his snitchin'. That son-of-a-bitch bears a charmed life …'

His rage suddenly pivoted her way.

'But you're gonna kill him. How's that, Honey? Enlighten me … You one of them Charlie's Angels? You gonna kung-fu his ass? He's quick, mean, smart and weighs near on three hundred pounds. You're lucky I don't plant you in The Boneyards, Red …'

Prosser leered, '… but you're gonna dance for me again, like back in the day.'

He drooled and grinned, showing teeth that could bite through planks.

'That's never happening and you're wasting my time,' she said it calm and slow.

'It's on me … believing you were still hard-core, like when I was a kid. So, listen good, this is your last chance. I can fix it so I'm in a room with that thing by this month's end and I'm going to kill him there. I know just how. It'll be easier if you help, then you get to be part of it too. So, help me, or don't - but he's a dead man either way. I will kill Irvin Terrell.'

Prosser glared harder still, so Maggs held his stare some more.

Finally he said, 'Tell me … an' it'd better be good.'

So she did.

And by the time she'd finished, Prosser wasn't sneering.

'That could work,' he said quietly, '… the right guard … a little luck, it could …'

'Can you handle your side? It has to look real … like it's store bought.'

He cackled and leered again, an even darker glint shining in his black eyes.

'Can we handle it? That's why you came here. When it comes to hurtin', the Legion are the Ivy League.'

*****

He gave her a burner with one pre-loaded number, then pressed some hidden buzzer and the hard-faced chick who'd met her at the gate was waiting outside.

Prosser bellowed out the window, 'hey, Candy Snatch. See Mrs Crawford out … and respect your elder, girl. That there's a special lady.'

They walked to the gate in silence. After the girl unlocked it Maggs said, 'what's your name, Honey? Your real name.'

Candy looked surly but murmured, 'Delores … ma'am.'

Maggs stepped outside.

'You've got a good body and you're tough, Delores. If you got any brains alongside those things, then start living better. Get as far from here as you can.'

Then she set off down the track without looking back.

*****

She started the next phase reading Ansara's book twice over, then carefully watching that crap she'd put on YouTube .

Maggs knew she had to understand the stuff that victims she'd chosen to highlight were saying, had to make sure that what she said herself was the same, without sounding rote learnt and rehearsed.

Ansara wasn't stupid, arrogance was her weakness — like most all religious folks she thought her own epiphanies applied to everyone; though, of course, she was still the special one for dishing out all that wisdom.

Ansara and her kind just didn't get it, that others might have seen a different light.

A few days after returning from the compound she called the number from that card she'd been given. She'd prepared carefully but selling a lie's as much about tone and pace as what you say.

Maggs didn't overplay things, she let Ansara think she was leading. The forgiveness guru wanted it to be true and, Maggs knew, wanting's half way to believing. She'd seen enough desperate folks inside of Kenny's church to understand that much.

Ansara made her go to meetings, like those long-ago addiction cures she'd done for Kenny, sitting with folks in a circle. The others were victims, or victims' families, too - people raped, murdered or maimed by guys doing time in Angola.

Maggs became the star turn, saying all the right stuff.

She said how her son had told her what to do in a dream; which was true, though she left out exactly what that was.

After that session, it was time to push Ansara.

*****

'I'm ready now, to meet with Mr Terrell. Strange, calling him that …'

'It shows how far you've come, but I'm not sure …'

'Time's the enemy here. I'm unwell. I've got to do this soon, or it'll be too late.'

She stopped talking, let Ansara join those dots herself.

Ansara's work at Angola was wrapping up. In a few weeks she'd be flying out to some war-torn hell-hole to add her own special insult to whatever injuries she found there.

Maggs could see her calculating if could she bring her schedule forward and get it all wrapped up — in case Maggs dropped dead before fulfilling her function; providing something she and her boyfriend could one day wave under a parole boards' noses.

After the meeting, she texted the agreed emoji to that number on The Hogg's burner. By the time she got home a package had already been put on the porch. She opened it right there, not even waiting to get inside.

When she saw what was inside, it made her heart race but not like when she got sick.

Nobody would doubt it was real … It was perfect.

*****

There were a few more calls that week then one more in-person meeting but she knew the whole thing was fast tracked; like things always are when they're not for your benefit.

Saturday found her at Angola's gate, met by two guards who drove her in.

Angola wasn't a one building kind of prison. It'd been a plantation where slaves picked cotton in antebellum days. The site covered acres, as big as a town. Maggs was driven past the main bloc and a variety of scattered buildings. Men ambled, and some worked out, inside a caged yard just yonder.

The guard driving her said nothing and she focused on the sweat running down his bull-neck.

They were headed to a bloc at the estate's remoter edges, a small building adjacent to the isolation unit where they kept the bully magnets, imprisoned ex-cops, freaks who'd harmed children and the man who'd killed her son. It was some kind of cottage she guessed they used for conjugal visits, she was taken to a meeting room inside of it.

The guards and Ansara would also be present.

She wondered which guard was The Hogg's guy but neither gave any sign.

They made a per functionary search. One of them carefully handled her keys, feeling for signs they'd been sharpened. She held her breath but, when he looked at the other guard, the guy just shrugged.

Finally, she was sat and at table with an empty chair opposite, the guards sat in different corners.

She nervously got out her pills and her brown-bagged lunch and asked one of them for a plate and a cup. When he got back, she took out her sandwich then counted out her pills. Nearly time, her hands shook a little taking the cellophane off and breaking the water bottle's seal.

Then Ansara came in. Irvin Terrell was right behind her.

*****

Terrell was only a little younger than her but seemed more vibrant; trimmed down but still enormous, his long hair styled shorter and flecked with grey. He looked strong and moved fluently but seemed reigned in; the lurid jailhouse tats the only thing stopping him passing as some demobbed war hero or retired cop.

He sat down opposite, had no problem meeting her eye but he arranged his face to look kind of sympathetic.

'I want to thank you, Mrs Crawford … for agreeing to see me today.'

Maggs indicated Ansara, sitting now with one of the guards. 'Thank her,' she said.

Speaking to Ansara directly now, she added, 'I want you to know it's down to you. This whole thing here and now … everything that happens from now. I was lost, but you gave me this chance and I just don't have the words. Thank you isn't enough.'

Ansara smiled. Terrell was nodding.

'It's you too Mrs Crawford, taking those first steps … after what I did…'

141

'After you murdered my child … For fun.'

He blinked but didn't flinch.

'Worst thing I ever did. I was a different kind of man back then.'

Maggs nodded.

'We both need a chance to show our real selves, here. I need hope to…to laugh again. Could you provide that?'

'I want to Mrs Crawford, you've learned about restorative justice now…'

'But you can't restore what you took away, if you were halfway normal you'd understand. But you're not a normal man, Irvin. You're an animal — a dangerous one that needs putting down.'

Ansara started to interrupt, trying to bring things to a halt but Terrell waved her off; his body language saying it's o.k, I got this.

He turned back now to Maggs and he'd kept his cool.

'I'm real sorry, truly … but you've wasted this chance if this is what you really came for, to tell me I'm beyond redemption.'

Again, Ansara tried to interrupt but they were locked on each other and both ignored her now.

'The only restorative justice I'll take is seeing you scream, Irvin. But I don't believe in heaven or hell anymore, so the reason I came here's to make it happen for myself, in this world.'

Now he couldn't help but sneer, a guy who sees the thing he's best at in this world coming right for him but this time in a form that outright made him laugh.

Ansara's bleating reached a pitch now and Terrell told her to shut her mouth before he said real quietly to Maggs,

'I see where that pencil-necked kid got his big mouth from. So, what you gonna do to me, little woman? Enlighten me.'

She looked down meekly, kept silent for a long moment and fiddled with her pills, getting a better grip on her cup.

'Hogg said hi,' she whispered.

Terrell's eyes widened. It was true he was real quick — moving across the table at her before the guards even stood. But none of them were quick enough, she'd practiced this part hard.

She threw the liquid and all of it landed, she got a real good spread right across his face.

She got all his right eye for sure, some in the left one too. Also, like she'd hoped he'd been snarling so that a good amount went in his mouth.

His skin got livid red almost at once and he staggered backwards.

Only Ansara looked confused but when he screamed, even she realised.

He bellowed like a beast in a slaughterhouse, trying to speak even as the liquid from that pretend store-bought water bottle she'd gotten the Legion to fake-up was burning out his lying tongue and running down his throat. Like the others, Maggs watched in silence in the first seconds.

Terrell was carnival-freak horror-show ugly now. His right eye was a burst blister; he was kind of vomiting blood and some solid bits from his insides, all whilst trying to breathe at the same time. He smashed his head on that table over and over, then staggered up and did the same thing on the walls. They spoke to him. But Terrell was alone now; lost in a world of agony so intense the only answer that burned clearly was plain crazy … more pain to block it out.

Welcome into my world, Irvin — the one you created then made me live in.

Ansara was screaming, as one guard grabbed at Terrell's flailing body the other came right at her.

Terrell's gasping told her it'd be over soon; but for him that could never be soon enough. His last minutes in this world were a long and lonely walk across a continent of pain.

And, all of a sudden, Maggs found that she was laughing. It wasn't that she found any of this funny, but she finally laughed again.

She threw back her head and laughed like she'd never stop, even as the guard dragged her from the room.

Maggs was still laughing even hours later, in the cell where they'd taken her to await the cops' arrival.

Zero Points of Articulation
Edward St. Boniface

Timeline: September-October, 1975.

To distort later investigations, every political homicide needs at least two or three plausible explanations and alibis for those involved.

(Gary Banomena in his concluding remarks for 'The Practical Economics And Business Model Methodology Of Organised Political Homicide', withdrawn term paper, 1964.)

Transcript-excerpt from *Black Hand Incorporated* personal confidential archives, categorised *Strictly Classified* at highest security designation, company president's eyes only. Decision to release to company archivist pending. Original spoken recording and subsequent audio dialogues captured using replica micro-miniaturised tape recording device once the property of the Central Intelligence Agency. Locations vary as indicated. First recording made 23:07–23:52 in review of appropriate referred events evening of 13.06.1975 and prior. Recording made by company president Gary Banomena privately, transcripts executed unofficially as indicated. Site of initial recording is the original company headquarters building, Blackwell's Island, New York City, in company president's designated office, other company officers in attendance.

COMPANY PRESIDENT GARY BANOMENA (*summarising*): "…which is still problematic, to say the least. So we're going to leave this one entirely off the record. In closing I'd say the scenario is, for me, essentially identical to that of *Rashomon*. But with Styrofoam."

(*Murmurs of agreement, then an audible* click *ending recording as company president switches off device.*)

*****

From *Black Hand Incorporated* company confidential archives, press cutting in Media Related To Operations (tangential) file. Item is an arts and leisure review piece for the *Manhattan Globe And Mail* newspaper, New York City, special arts correspondent and senior editor Michael Tumesne writes (dated 10.06.1975):

'Generally speaking, this dedicated grizzled hack sees himself very much as a *"Shoeleather"* journalist, one habitually out pounding the mean pavements rain or shine in search of a current story against the deadline and payday. The hard street and ugly gutter is where this reporter likes to find his stories.

As opposed to *"Parlour Maid"* journalists as we call them, more accustomed to waiting on the wealthy and powerful and celebrated. That's a beat normally spent waiting in comfortable corporate lounges outside their boardrooms. Well-heated lobbies in public offices. Plush sofas in fancy hotels waiting to join press conferences and time-managed interviews, often being courtesy-fed and watered if your customers are the smarter kinds.

Taking down scripted statements and announcements. A few brief questions and answers off the cuff, a telling gaffe or two if you're lucky. Hack work doesn't wear out the shoeleather quite so fast that way.

Personally I prefer those other quixotic, unglamorous places from where what we eventually call The News oozes up. Because often it's a dirty story. You can never tell where the real thing will come from next.

All too often it's the most unlikely place and you have to be tuned to it. My chosen beat is normally the harsher underbelly of this great city. Occasionally further across this great, imperfect nation we inhabit.

History is always being made and demonstrated in the most improbable corners and byways. A good Shoeleather has to be ready to run after and catch it. Now and then, run *for* it if history catches them in the wrong place at the wrong time.

Art and its self-absorbed pretensions seldom capture and compel my dirty-story imagination. Newshounds like me habitually occupy a distinctly seedy and frequently dreary world. Among other things of flyblown bars, dubious moth-eaten informants, boring loitering with intent and too many grubby police and public records departments in assiduous search of the pieces in my puzzle of the moment.

Vaguely vagrant trenchcoat men like me are usually turned quickly and smartly away from the swank kinds of uptown galleries and art-houses and miscellaneous haunts of the counter-culture where the creative scene hang out. I confess to philistinism when regarding a self-proclaimed 'artist' like Andy Warhol and that anomalous menagerie he calls his 'Factory', for example. His garish silk screen productions look only like the work of a bitter and belligerent infant to me.

I see little or nothing substantial emerging from those kinds of self-promoting clubs of the pretentious. Emphatically I prefer the dustier and more solid Old Masters like Rembrandt and Michelangelo and Raphael and Da Vinci and Jacques-Louis David. Pop Art can eat itself, as far as I'm concerned.

That said, now and then I do see something that genuinely captures the spirit of the future-shocked age we live through. All too frequently I don't like it. Which tends to paradoxically grab and reel me in nearer despite myself with a kind of horrified voyeurism.

Zero Points Of Articulation ('assorted works in ultramodern materials' according to the lavishly illustrated and meticulously item-priced limited printing signed catalogue: $45.00), is brought to you by increasingly famous sculptor Gerd Gold. Now on Technicolor exhibit in newly opened permanent gallery space at the notorious communist and liberal bookstore *Kerry's Kuomintang* down in Greenwich Village.

One million illegal fly-posters throughout Manhattan and an unsolicited press invitation reeled me in more-or-less willingly at its gala premiere on Sunday night. I didn't like it. But it is admittedly the current epitome of our deranged and Future-traumatised age.

Former mannequin-maker for assorted downtown (and a few lesser uptown) department stores and whizz-kid plastics chemist Gold presents us with a range of statues, cruel caricatures and highly imaginative less classifiable objects cast with a satirical edge. Thermoplastic and Styrofoam and Polyvinyl Chloride and other exotic synthetic materials are the only ones you'll see here. Moulded with an admittedly wild and deft and sometimes seriously weird multi-chromatic flair.

Gold is controversial. He's been on the fringes of the art and celebrity scene for years, cropping up in the tabloids at least weekly over some peccadillo or offbeat remark. Dismissed by many commentators as just another gadfly creating a little media buzz for himself, it would seem he has proved himself to be far more.

Kerry's Kuomintang is a radical bookstore and notoriously hard-left-wing intellectual hub I know well. It's the go-to first stop for your wannabe revolutionary zealot. You can get both *Pravda* and *Izvestia* the Soviet state newspapers, that day's issue (25 cents separately or 45 cents for both), but get to the store early because they sell out fast down there.

Tele-printed copies of each are delivered direct from the Soviet Union's smart New York consulate each morning by special arrangement, the only commercial one I know of in America. You can also get current printings of That Little Red Book. A whole shelf of *Toward Soviet America* by William Z Foster, vintage 1961 HUAC edition. If it's vaguely Red or Pinko, you'll find it.

Hoover tried to have the place shut down repeatedly through the Sixties. That is, until a class action brought by a coalition of like-minded bookstore owners across the country went to the Supreme Court. They forced him to back off with distinctly ill grace. One of the many very funny stories in the owner's memoirs which became an unexpected number one bestseller a few years ago.

Now Crawford Kerry, likeably flamboyant and well-known proprietor of said subversive nest of intellectual insurrection, is hawking the iconoclast visual arts *Zeitgeist* too. And with an entertainingly provoking panache. A giant reproduction of Warhol's humorous portrait of Mao Tse Tung, author of the aforementioned Little Red Book, grins down rather creepily as you enter. Che Guevarra in his various iconic incarnations glares sullenly from everywhere else.

Classic Soviet propaganda posters crowd the walls and there are busts of Lenin and Stalin and Trotsky. Lithographs and unflattering photographic portraits and vintage police mugshots of all the noted anarchists and political terrorists of the nineteenth century. There's even a smaller scale replica of Karl Marx's tomb from Highgate cemetery in London from whose front shelves you can pick up his complete works and those of Frederich Engels.

Last year the place got a makeover, largely funded through Crawford himself and a coalition of New York's left wing scene. Once a pleasantly down and dirty kind of scuffed-heel dive in the best counterculture tradition it's now smarter and savvier than all but the best uptown bookstores you can find. But the message is still defiantly and courageously seditious.

New gallery space, and this exhibition is its own debut, is smart and simple with modular partitions. A ramped one-way three sided balcony for smaller works and prints with a built-in lift makes for a cool multilevel balance. Movable lighting on tracks and rows of suspension hooks installed in the ceiling maximise display versatility. The joint is right up to the minute in advanced avant-garde presentation shtick.

This I liked. Care and thought and consideration and professionalism have been liberally lavished. Crawford's gone into the radical revolutionary *chic* patronage market now, and it doesn't feel even in the least corpulent-capitalist in tone.

Selling socialism and ideological Marxism is one thing. *Kerry's Kuomintang* is practically next to the viper's lair of Wall Street so it cain't be too hard. But Gerd Gold was already selling out his catalogue before I got there. Crawford himself told me more than half the *objets d'art plastique* to be seen were sold before hitting premiere hour.

I believe it. Gold has a barbed and wicked sense of humour, especially in his portraiture. The works that give the exhibition their name are especially outrageous, block-lining the walls and uncomfortably surprising you each time. There's unquiet talk of litigation from some of the subjects. Inventive statues and mannequins like the best of which first made Gold's name crowd the centre.

All cleverly placed so you have to navigate through them like a milling crowd. Carefully contrived, it looks offhand and nonchalant but ain't no such thing. Like the elevated rampway there's only one path to follow, but it's so efficiently well-crafted you don't notice.

A fun show, whether you're a True Believer of the Revolution or a capitalist pig slumming it or looking to bet on polypropylene futures...'

*****

Notation and dialogue following excerpted from ad hoc personal review recording by company president immediately following ZPOA pre-show viewing by invitation (07.06.1975):

GB: "Note for personal record: formaldehyde's too good for this mutant Gerd Gold, whoever or whatever he is..."

Went to *Kerry's Kuomintang* on a whim one Saturday morning when we'd had a quiet week apart from that staged 'remorse suicide' of a debt-ridden chairman at the prestigious Daroquefort Centre. It had been difficult to get an effective hanging rope long enough to loop through the chandelier ring at the apex of its famous pastorally themed Art Deco interior auditorium dome, and also reach near enough the floor for said late chairman to be properly visible for the horror-pix photographers. In the end we used adapted bungee cord.

Hadn't been back to the bookstore for years. I'd originally found a job there not long after making my way to New York essentially as a runaway. Worked the less popular night shifts, and it just kept me during a lean time.

Crawford Kerry and his notorious self-proclaimed Bolshevik Emporium were still going strong. By the mid-70's lot of the more idealistic and experimental counter-culture had been forced out of Greenwich Village. It was what would later be called 'gentrification' in the newspapers.

Now a lot of The Village was less of a village community. More of an easy commuter option for newly minted young urban professionals. Most of them visibly regarded the deteriorating Beatnik population as akin to extraterrestrials.

Wasn't expecting to meet Crawford either. That was a big part of the reason I felt safe heading over there. I'd read in the society pages of the *Manhattan Globe and Mail* that he'd been in hospital for a few days following some undescribed accident or injury. Naturally I assumed he'd be at home quietly recovering.

But here he was, energetically the demagogue-huckster at the centre of things as usual. Sarcastically haranguing his customers to become devoted fanatical acolytes of the now-stalling New Left in the recent era of *Détente* between the Soviet Union and the western powers. Heard him long before I saw him, but something stopped me at the doorway from turning back and propelled me into line of sight.

I thought it would be good to say hi first.

(*From company president's private recording, sounds of a bustling* Kerry's Kuomintang *bookstore in audio background.*)

GARY BANOMENA: "Hi, Crawford."

CRAWFORD KERRY: "Gary, my dear God's own original angry and aggrieved child intellectual! Something uncomfortably pertinent reminded me of you just the other day. You're looking rather gaunt and determined and presumably in need of some light lefty reading material. Howabout Sergei Eisenstein's gloriously tedious *Film Form: Essays in Film Theory* with all the quotes from Lenin to keep himself alive with Boffo Boss Stalin? I have a beautiful new illustrated reissue just in."

GB: "I need the new copy of Michael Tumesne's *Necrobiz Trilogy*. He just released an updated Volume III and I'm keen to read the extra chapters. Especially the one on legitimate manacle manufacturers and torture chamber surgical suppliers here at home. The ones who also do business with the private hospital trade domestically and internationally."

CK: "Why so, pray?"

GB: "I was thinking of upgrading my current investment strategies."

CK: "*Snark, snark*! Still fiendishly sardonic, my favourite infantoid. You're in luck, my first consignment of them was delivered just this morning. Hardbacks all, the updated paperback version isn't due out for a month yet. Still in the store room boxes, but we'll go back there and dig one out. And if you decide to drop in this Sunday evening or before, I could get Michael himself to sign it. I'm sure he'd be enthralled to meet you. He'll be here for the Gerd Gold premiere."

GB: "I read about that. It sounds grotesque. Good to see you, Crawford."

CK: "Likewise, my swarthy almost pretty boy. I'm hoping the show will be a positive *phantasmagoria* and provoke legal action. Monster movies are making an inglorious comeback, so monstrous grotesque art made by a real living monster should be a fertile gro-bag area."

(Company president and Crawford Kerry pause and laugh.)

CK: "Enough of this mad awkward banter. We're old fellow travellers in this desolate money-mad wilderness of Gotham. The book is on me, and I'll show you Gerd's hideous ductile multi-coloured nightmares in advance of the advance showing tomorrow night. The exhibit's almost ready apart from a few details and late deliveries. Come along."

*****

And so I saw *Zero Points of Articulation* practically before anyone else in New York. Reading Michael Tumesne's typically avuncular but surprisingly approving newspaper review later in the week I was surprised how much it chimed in with my own first impression of Gerd Gold. Against my will I had to admit the guy was abrasively talented.

Somehow I couldn't seem to quite avoid the insightful and intuitive and appallingly dangerous investigative journalist Michael Tumesne, no matter how I strategized that. He'd latched onto our operations and been shadow-tracking us for years. Gotten way too close to us in his inferences of how *Black Hand Incorporated* did its business.

Partly that was the reason I wanted Tumesne's new updated *Necrobiz Trilogy* omnibus. It was a comprehensive academic and anecdotal study of death industries and arms manufacture and trading and mercenary sourcing and recruitment and supply activity in America and Europe. Frighteningly accurate, methodically insider-informed and comprehensive with hundreds of interviewees in those fields.

Tumesne even devoted a chapter to us. Or rather possible firms like us, in a special long speculative chapter right at the end. He'd even cleverly deduced a list of likely cover business categories that included our own of private communications contracting.

Crawford got and generously gifted me a copy of the *Necrobiz* omnibus, just as he'd promised, and then we went out and around back to the service entrance I knew so well from my days working for him. Then into the brilliantly lit big new gallery space, which seriously did impress me. *Kerry's Kuomintang* really had changed in the last few years.

Piled-high merchandise in higgledy-piggledy order had been the norm. New publications sat alongside second-hand stock and privately published polemical tracts with rough uncut pages and uneven hand-stapled bindings. I'd even had one there myself.

Communist aesthetic was right in your face. It emitted a distinctly dangerous vibe, and you kept expecting some kind of police raid which never happened. When I worked there I was always wondering if I was being photographed and followed by plain-suited federal cops.

Now the shelves were ruler-straight painted steel, never fell over, and the place was ventilated and pleasantly airy with a strict no-smoking rule. Cleaners went through once a day instead of every six months and the ceiling was a mass of low-key lights instead of dripping with nicotine residue. Not a trace of mould or mildew anywhere.

A state of the art eight-track player on an intercom system piped out a continual loop of *The Internationale*. Stirring patriotic war songs from the Soviet Army male choir. Assorted other strident insane-sounding political hymns from communist nations otherwise through a series of powerful hundred-watt speakers all through the store.

It was like the Greatest Hits of the Warsaw Pact and the Working People's Paradise on *Radio Young Apparatchik* or something.

Ultramodern gallery Crawford showed me to was incendiary in yet another incongruously updated form. Designed by a well-known avant garde architect, it was a brilliant synthesis of up-to-the-minute 1970s Brutalism and classic Soviet Constructivist totalitarian monumentality. It reminded me of a spanking new corporate headquarters lobby in Seattle we'd once dynamited for late payment reassigning their treasurer and half his senior accounting team.

Perfect setting for a surprisingly numerous series of garishly coloured massive plastic monoliths set against the long curving walls. Cyclopean polychrome slabs with three-foot wide faces looming out of them at different angles like maniacal death masks. Demanded your attention the same way as an unpaid mid-town taxi fare.

These surrounded an even more numerous crowd of surreally variegated mannequins in the centre. Some were only vaguely blockily anthropoid, and seemed to wander around each other in a subtle and finely-judged placing. These were all solid figures as well, cleverly designed and weighted and balanced.

You followed an intricate pathway of artificial footprints through them. Somehow it adroitly threw you off-balance. Just like being in an actual living street mob.

(From company president's private recording, occasional construction sounds of a gallery show setup.)

CK: "Positively *hallucinatory*, isn't it, my dear? Take a look at the assorted famous faces round the circumference left to right. That's old LBJ on the imperial purple one, Richard Nixon on the incandescent pink, Queen J Edgar on the chequered, Carl Gustav Jung on the mysterious black cinematic one, Gerald Ford on the prismatic spectrum and Andy Warhol on the boring grey. Now he really is plastic like he wanted. I particularly like that barbed touch. I myself am portrayed on the fluorescent cadmium yellow one. Very particularly, I do *not* like that iteration. Between you and me he's visually accusing me of trying to poison him with some rather unusually powerful opium we once shared."

GB: "Not that overpriced venom all those tennis shoe-smoking Beatniks flippantly call *Rangoon Swoon*, by any chance?"

CK (*pause*): "The child is full of surprises, as he always was back in the day. It was indeed that, and do tell?"

GB: "My company installed some phone security equipment for Warhol a few years ago in that zoo of his called The Factory. He invited us to a degenerate party there the same night. I saw what Laotian highlands-cultivated *Papaver Somniferum Omni* did to some of his more prominent cohorts. Trucker said you have to get it from Golden Triangle nation diplomats or some special super-creepy senior supercreep Triad outfit who have the sole non-governmental sales franchise."

CK: "I was given some by just such a beneficent consular gentleman in gratitude for a substantial discount on a few crates of the collected works of Eduard Bernstein for their political education schools. It was old stock I was going to donate free to libraries anyway, so I only asked for a nominal sum. You walk in many interesting *milieux*, Gary."

GB: "Don't fool around with that stuff, Crawford. It'll turn you into *Doctor Strangelove*. More spaced-out than Skylab. Extreme suggestibility is one of its effects. Trucker said Kerouac, Ginsberg and Capote all woke up thinking they were penguins. Hunter Thompson had to shepherd them outside and then stop them getting run over. They thought Union Square was Antarctica and the taxis were yellow honking walruses."

CK (*chuckling*): "Well, I was advised on careful use for novices and my experience was rather enjoyably fabulist. Communing with all the carbon atoms in me from the hearts of diverse stars across the universe. Merging my spirit with the original light of those ancient and vanished suns still in them. All of it was gratifying and fulfilling in a hard to describe way. Gerd however seemed to…recoil from it. After we both recovered he winced and wouldn't tell me what he saw. He was very upset with me for quite a while. My diplomatic benefactor had said something cryptic to the effect that the true character of the soul was the prism by which you would imagine the Swoon's visionary potential. I guess it all sounds pretty Out There."

GB: "I limit myself to the strictly Square. It keeps peacenik madness like that at bay. Jest telling you a freak-out will inescapably see more freaked-out things. From the look of this Gerd Gold's stuff, he's one hundred and ninety-nine percent certifiable."

CK (*laughing softly*): "That mordant to-the-point humour of yours. I'd forgotten it too. And how much I enjoyed having your caustic verbal inventiveness around the store. Well, you've summed up Gerd all too accurately. And as you can see he's not shy of applying that unflattering perspective to himself. This is his self-portrait monolith here. "

GB: "He's done himself with little horns in sky blue with cloud patches. That sure draws the eye. He's doing the exact opposite of applying the same unflattering treatment to himself, Crawford. Gold's an obvious obsessive egomaniac. Not one of these other blocks has the same peeper-grab impact, and it's intentional."

CK: "If there was a Holy Inquisition operating today, you'd be perfect for them."

GB: "Now this one next door actually is interesting. Sean Beatty here on this marbleised replica Bakelite thang. He's a favourite actor of mine. I think that's meant to be his character in *Cold Dialogue*. One of my favourite paranoid surveillance thrillers. So the guy has a little taste well-hidden somewhere. Is this white one meant to be Medusa?"

CK: "With the face of Bette Davis from *Whatever Happened To Baby Jane?*. I think Gerd was also going to put Joan Crawford on this one just below on a black bottom half which would have been optically stunning, but she threatened to sue. Mommie Dearest, like life, is a bitch; my sweet."

*****

Unsettled best describes how I left Greenwich Village later that afternoon, far longer a time than I'd anticipated. Not content with giving me a rather expensive updated *Necrobiz Trilogy*, Crawford insisted on taking me to lunch at an almost infinitely more expensive private supper club, one of the most exclusive in the city owned by the current dowager of the Vanderfeller dynasty herself. It booked months in advance but he had not the slightest trouble getting us a table and we had the best service there I'd ever known in any restaurant.

Crawford seemed to know everyone in New York society, the disreputable radical politics world, metropolitan arts and letters and broadcasting and of course the gay subculture, regaling me for the next few hours with hilarious anecdotes from all of them. At the same time I could tell he was pumping me for information about something, but it stayed equivocal. Despite myself and my guarded way given my actual working commitments, I gradually unwound and enjoyed his *bon viveur* company, which became an alarming intuition that he somehow wanted something that had a nebulous connection with my real job.

But that wasn't it either.

What unsettled me was being unexpectedly enlivened with a kind of implacable fury I'd forgotten since the assassination death of my benefactor and mentor Achille Kolobo Entebbe ten years previously when I'd worked briefly for him at the United Nations. Frigid rage at the injustice and cruelty of his death, provoking a bleak determination in me to inflict it back. Impetus which had originally launched *Black Hand Incorporated* itself suddenly rekindled and terrified me with its diabolical power.

Crawford Kerry, the only other person who had showed kindness and care to me in New York apart from three trusted colleagues and my lost hero, nursed and unsuccessfully concealed with thick white cosmetic two very black eyes. Walked a bit unsteadily, and to my practiced eye after years of professional brutality clearly had sustained a severe beating or assault recently. And from the few hints he seemingly reluctantly gave it was clear that the perpetrator was Gerd Gold.

*****

(From company president's private recording, sounds of gallery show held in Kerry's Kuomintang *bookstore in audio background, voice of Crawford Kerry giving a raconteur's description of exhibits, 18:08-19:01,*

11.07.1975. All four company officers present at location.)

SURVIND JUGGERGHAZI, COMPANY DEPUTY PRESIDENT AND OFFICIAL ARCHIVIST: "Are you quite sure this is entirely prudent, Gary?"

GB: "Not completely Trucker, but I still want a look at this creep. He should be here any minute, he's been making return appearances all week since Sunday to keep up the buzz."

S('T)J: "The exhibits are certainly remarkable. Most of the mannequins are caricatures of the artists' patrons over the years. Some of them quite damning and vicious."

GB: "Crawford said he's actually just turning up hoping someone will serve a writ on him for the extra publicity. He's got some of his own photographers here just in case."

S('T)J: "But he scarcely needs it. Almost the entire exhibition contents have been sold, some were even being bid on at the last minute and went for several times original asking price. It's all been spectacularly successful. Gerd Gold is unquestionably a millionaire now and the press are fawning over him."

GB: "Dirty laundry always makes the biggest splash, Trucker."

(Both laugh as two sets of footsteps rapidly approach, faint commotion in audio background.)

WARKENTIN WESTGATE: "Guys, I think we should hop back into the bookstore part pronto and do a little intervention."

DAG ULKÖLN: "As in riot control. Our notorious artist just came in, started making a lot of loaded remarks to the crowd at the free show-buffet and there's a full-blown tantrum going on between him and some of his former boyfriends."

GB: "Angry rich ugly lover-*patrones*, right?"

WW: "Right. It's the exploding fruit salad inevitable in there."

DU: "They're chasing him through the aisles, and he's leading them. Two display shelves gone crashing over already and more on the way."

GB: "Hokay; let's go pacify things. I hate those types who don't respect a legitimate odeum."

S('T')J: "Typical culture-vulture New York. We're just lucky Gore Vidal and Norman Mailer aren't here tonight too…"

GB (*humorously imitating the gruff voice of Norman Mailer*): "Gore, I don't like your tie. It's too long. Like your sissy-boy novels…"

(*Chuckling from all four company officers as they audibly rapidly run off towards increased sounds of commotion and falling objects, shouts now rising from bookstore area.*)

*****

(*Same location, approximately half an hour later.*)

CRAWFORD KERRY: "Thanks for all your help, my loves. That was quick thinking, using the fire extinguisher on those brawling yahoos. Even they couldn't help laughing at themselves."

WW: "Made sure to get those photographers first. They were following around snapping everything so I bulls-eyed them. Unloaded their cameras fast while they had the foam in their eyes and dropped 'em back. I don't think they even noticed in all the confusion."

DU: "I checked and made sure there weren't any other shutterbugs, like amateurs with Kodak Brownies or Leica's or something. Nothing, so apart from the actual damage it'll all be hearsay."

GB: "Good work. Kee-rikey, does that Goldie-boy have one *creative* vocabulary. I could barely hold him, seriously wiry and wired at the same time. Swearing like Ladybird's parrot, he was."

WW: "That dude must have a copy of *The Professional Profaner's Thesaurus* or something."

S('T')J: "Hah, hah. At least a pursuit turned on the pursuers defused the situation. They were too surprised to think or react. We made sure to funnel them into the cafeteria area so the book stock wouldn't be further damaged."

CK: "Yes, that was very…professional."

DU: "Scenarios like that you improvise on the run, sir. We temporarily shored up those shelves they pushed over, but you'll need to replace them."

CK: "Gentlemen, I'm in your debt and in more ways than one. Howsoever might I reciprocate?"

GB: "Put on more boring exhibitions, Crawford. '*History of Commie-Themed Samovars*', or '*Triple-X-Classified Lonely Hearts Ads In* Pravda' or sumpin'."

(*Uproarious laughter.*)

*****

Likeability is one of those factors that can make a typical job difficult. Most of the time, any necessity of switching off empathy for a reassignment task subject didn't even arise. Unexpectedly though, despite a shockingly vile lexicon of threatening abuse and psychotic tendencies when provoked into a temper, there was something I liked about Gerd Gold.

Inexplicably pretty much against my instincts and will. Hard to effectively restrain, he almost gave me a black eye as well. Took both me and Warkentin to fully subdue him in the end at the gallery bust-up he intentionally baited.

Frighteningly strong and agile he almost got away from us several times but then clearly gave up and shifted into a friendly composed mode without missing a beat. Impeccably behaved for the rest of the evening, although of course we watched him closely. Startlingly well-disciplined for an obvious psychopath.

Yet persuasively cleverly charming when he wanted to be, and undeniably talented, entertaining when describing his remarkable work. Charisma has an occultary quality that defies easy categorising with most of those who really have it. Crawford was clearly infatuated with him despite mingling that with noticeable wariness.

As the presumed victim he would say nothing definitive to me. Naturally I couldn't interrogate either of them. Gerd Gold himself, entirely unprompted, offhandedly confessed his violent attack on Crawford to me when we found ourselves temporarily alone in the gallery later.

Without a trace of conscience or embarrassment or remorse. It amused him that a sad and stupidly romantically obsessed old man would put up with his abuse, so he took it as far as he could get away with. Gold was just having a laugh.

He actually said that.

Glacid rage took hold of me again. But helplessly I couldn't do anything and too much risk of exposure was implicit if I did. Certainly I couldn't involve the guys again, we'd done too much so effectually containing the bust-up crowd already.

So I gave something back to Crawford. At least take some of the anguish he was subjecting himself to away. I owed him.

*****

(*Private recording resumes, 09:43-09:48, location* Kerry's Kuomintang *bookstore, 12.07.1975*)

CK (*audibly surprised*): "*Four* ampoules of Rangoon Swoon? How in the pink blazes did you acquire these little treasures, Gary? Do you have any idea how valuable these are?"

GB: "About this year's model Cadillac, yeah. With enough left over for the posh customised seat covers."

CK: "Conservatively. Why me?"

GB: "Thank Warhol. We still maintain and periodically upgrade the phones at his new place. I had his setup replaced for free as a courtesy three months ago and he gave me this when I went around to verify the work with one of my colleagues you met. I don't know how to offload them. Frankly, I'm too scared and square to take them either. So I thought you might be able to enjoy 'em better."

CK: "Darling boy, I don't know what to babble in thanks. You hardly know what you're giving away."

GB: "If you see Buddha, say a big *Hi* to the Fat Guy In The Sky for me. See you on Friday night."

*

Trucker was against it. Our company pharmacy naturally had a stash of

Papaver Somniferum Omni. We'd made sure to have some in stock ever since Survind discovered its existence at Warhol's original Factory in the Decker building. The suggestibility I described was real and potent, but it was far too expensive to use regularly.

Keeping the supply current was also tricky, it only kept efficacy for about a year or so. In fact our latest cache had come from ripping off some of those senior Triads I'd mentioned, actually Burmese military officers. Cleverly they were posing as gangsters posing as Chinese government officials out of Peking making the deals Kissinger and Nixon had paved the way for a couple of years earlier.

Blackmailing yet another late-payer corporate chairman, we'd intercepted a personal delivery bound for someone he knew. Information had just slipped out of the creep when he panicked and blabbed after only a little rough pressure when we cornered him in a Seventh Avenue sauna. He made me laugh so I waived half the due fee.

Couriers were intercepted in broad daylight on Madison Avenue in front of the spanking new high-rise Vanderfeller Centre complex. Just as they were going in to get the elevator to the appropriate corporate offices and make their drop-off as an official business appointment. That's how they did things, right in the open above legitimate suspicion.

Warkentin ducked apologetically in behind them as they went into the big brass revolving doors. Forcibly took their briefcases off them before they could react and shoved them hard against the thick glass. Doors went full circle back to the street where we were waiting, then me and Dag walloped both the dupes harder with knuckledusters before they could get their guns out.

Survind was waiting in an unmarked car idling at the curb. We piled in fast and drove off leisurely before anyone could think. Took less than a minute.

Survind had quietly eliminated their armed contingency spotter across the street just beforehand. One of Trucker's smart and silent throwing star turns did the job before he unhurriedly crossed the street back and into our getaway. An inconspicuous lookout dressed as a tourist with camera, but he was Burmese too and one of them, so easily identifiable if you knew his face.

We'd made certain of their *modus operandi* beforehand, observing a prior drop at the same spot for the same corporate customer. Photographing everything meticulously from multiple angles to be sure, particularly the spotter and his surveillance movements. Extremely risky, but we prepared carefully and they had no idea who literally hit them.

Forty ampoules. Price of a small fleet of Cadillacs. Four was at least one of that fleet, but it was how much I felt I owed Crawford.

*****

(*From company president's private recording, sounds of continuing gallery show 'Zero Points Of Articulation' held in Kerry's Kuomintang bookstore in audio background, unknown voice listlessly giving a half-hearted description of exhibits, 20:38-20:51, 13.07.1975. Noises are noticeably quieter than previous gallery show recordings and no sounds of bustle. Company president and deputy president are at location, in outer open doorway audibly smoking as customer footsteps enter and exit.*)

SURVIND ('TRUCKER') JUGGERGHAZI: "Gary, I am worried about Crawford Kerry."

GARY BANOMENA: "Me too, Trucker. He hasn't shown up and neither has pretty bully-boy Goldie. Crawford gave me the word tonight was going to be some big capstone kind of publicity stunt to round off the show, but I can't get a home phone answer from him. Normally he'd be here or there."

S('T')J: "My feeling about this is grim. Instinct tells me something has happened. I also think we should not be here and too easily identifiable."

GB: "What if they suddenly spring up together and that publicity stunt is on?"

S('T')J: "No journalists have showed up tonight. They would have been told to make sure of maximum coverage. The young man in the gallery doing the exhibition commentary is a bookstore assistant filling in as best he can. Not very well, as you can hear. He told me himself none of the staff or night manager have heard from Kerry. No instructions have been issued to be ready for a surprise arrival or event, which would surely have been the case. It's very atypical behaviour from a usually responsible boss."

GB: "And they both have big stakes in a final night's performance going well."

S('T')J: "As you might say Gary: '*Zackly*. This is lacklustre and uncharacteristic. Something is clearly wrong, but not just for Crawford Kerry."

GB: "How so?"

S('T')J: "With him. Your friend has not been quite straight with us. He described his black eyes and injuries to Warkentin and Dag as a combined street mugging and homophobic attack. I believe the term is 'queer bashing'. For myself he said it had been some unspecified domestic accident in his apartment building and a fall downstairs. You said Gerd Gold confessed to it."

GB: "Anyone would be embarrassed and evasive about something like that, Trucker."

S('T')J: "Agreed. Kerry gave too much detail and specifics. To me the stories sounded pre-rehearsed for our benefit. I think it's deliberate. There is an important missing factor here I can't quite envision."

GB: "Maybe Gerd Gold is the missing factor and we should hit him up for some answers. So to speak."

S('T')J: "Ha, Ha. I think that would be our best course. His studio is in a converted warehouse down in Greenwich Village. I heard Gold mention he'd had new locks fitted recently. A custom-built Master Lock system, one they send experts up from their Milwaukee plant to install."

GB: "Warkentin got the current configuration plans from his contact there? I saw the payment in our operating expenses ledger review."

S('T')J: "A simple modulated electromagnetic field will trip the electric tumblers. And Warkentin has adapted his excellent portable device for the new settings."

GB: "Okay, let's call the guys and do this mob-handed..."

*****

It was too easy. I got that same grim feeling as Trucker less than an hour later once we were inside Gerd Gold's silent and darkened sanctum sanctorum. Just as Warkentin almost effortlessly opened the doors I thought I heard the faint distant clank of an industrial door closing deeper inside, but couldn't be sure.

Eerie hardly began to do it justice. The place was a miniaturised industrial workshop for producing plastics, complete with chemical mixing vats, separators, processing units and high-temperature crucibles. There were even heat insulation suits and several kinds of breathing apparatus like you'd find in a steel mill for being near superheated metals or a car factory for applying toxic paint finishes.

Rails in the ceiling held articulated small cranes and light armatures to manoeuvre and pour mixtures into moulds, state of the art equipment. What looked like surgical platforms with tumescent bodies on them, but were actually workshop tables with alarming experimental objects in progress. A whole rack of frightening saws for fiberglass and other tough-to-work materials.

Right in centre stage there stood an exhibition all on its own. Single glittering humanoid figure of natural proportions with its arms raised in some kind of ecstatic benediction or supplication. Petrified and silent and haunted as the motionless studio around it.

We found and hit the lights.

Got the message.

My *God*.

*****

(*Private recording resumes, 21:49-21:59, location Gerd Gold's private studio, Mollitia Buildings, Baekeland Street, Greenwich Village, New York City, 13.07.1975*)

WW: "Oh. My. *God*."

S('T')J: "Vishnu and Shiva and Nemesis and Juggernaut come to mind."

DU: "My old-country mum would have invoked Balder and

Freya and Odin for something like this."

GB (*long pause*): "Crazy; man."

*****

Gerd Gold stood before us entombed in thermoplastic with an ultra-hard Styrofoam finish. It had dried so smoothly over his body he was indistinguishable from one of his own sculptures. He had put on weighted boots that went up past the knees, a brace normally used for mannequin treatment.

These clearly kept him upright, the brace was too heavy to topple over. So he had been rooted to the spot while the liquid polypropylene enveloped him. Residue ran down into a steel drainage grille on which the brace stood, and a visible chemical pool underneath gradually dissolved the runoff.

Clearly from his posture he had angled a container of presumably boiling liquefied synthetic polymer precursors to envelope himself. The automated armature set immediately above was designed to lay down two layers by quick-pouring inundation. Normally that would be over a plaster or fiberglass or metal figurine.

After the thick fast-drying base, liquescent polystyrene foam had clearly been quickly applied the same way from another container as the mechanism rotated. The artist/subject was famous as a plastics chemist. He'd clearly invented an easy way to apply Styrofoam that would set with the same kind of solid patina as polyvinyl chloride or acrylic.

Inert figure of the late Gerd Gold was absolutely solid and cold and gleaming. Almost no chemical smell in the air, so he must have been like that for many hours. Waiting for his first audience.

Hideously detailed plastic death-mask face was composed and practically beatific. Clearly Gerd Gold had smothered and probably scalded to death horribly as the high-temperature shell around him formed. But there was not the slightest visual indication he was suffering while it happened.

Knew only one credible explanation for that.

*****

(*Private recording resumes, 22:02-22:05, location Gerd Gold's private studio, Mollitia Buildings, Baekeland Street, Greenwich Village, New York City, 13.07.1975)*

S('T')J: "Clearly we are going to have to go to Crawford Kerry for our answers now."

DU: "Guy's made himself into the ultimate collector's item."

WW: "Warhol should do the same thing, he's been losing it for years. Last good print he did was that cartoon commie Chairman Meow-Meow. I think he did a couple of hundred or something. Not exactly imaginative."

S('T')J: "…Gary?"

GB (*longer pause*): "Far out. That really is zero points of articulation. Guys, I think I hear sirens out there coming our way."

S('T')J: "I suggest we kill the lights and exit swiftly by the fire door exit at the back. It leads into an alley where we can quickly get to Seventh Avenue unseen."

DU: "How do you know about that, Trucker?"

S('T')J: "Crawford Kerry."

*****

Just as Trucker said we found the fire exit and got safely to Seventh Avenue as the sirens rose behind us, clearly converging on the workshop. Splitting up we got taxis separately back to Blackwell's Island where we reassembled to debrief. Pretty much shell-shocked, so to speak, there wasn't much to discuss except the actual known facts.

And how to get all the remaining facts.

*****

From *Black Hand Incorporated* company confidential archives, press cutting in Media Related To Operations (tangential) file. Item is excerpted from a six page special obituary and post-career profile piece for the *Manhattan Globe And Mail* newspaper, New York City, Sunday morning edition. Special arts correspondent and senior editor Michael Tumesne writes the foreword (dated 15.06.1975):

'Shoeleather or Parlour Maid, every journalist is assigned sooner or later with contributing to the more unenviable beats of the typical reportage agency or newspaper or magazine. These include ones personally unengaging to me like Human Interest, Food and Health, Weather and Local Notices. Subjects best left to the specialists and enthusiasts of those also very useful pertinent fields of newsy record.

And then there are the Dead Files.

Obituaries are a unique written form. All newspapers local and national have their files of the prominent and interesting and controversial to mark passing when their time comes. Once I had the strangely cathartic task of commemorating in print a much-loved friend and patron, the redoubtable Cressida Rosemary Vanderfeller-Daroquefort who was murdered in Central Park in 1967 by person or persons unknown.

Writing a memorial to a friend tempts you away from the strict objectivity and detachment a journalist should normally command in all their pieces. So I wrote as honest an elegy as I could. Gerd Gold, subject of the following obit since I reviewed his premiere exhibition only a week ago and it was a personal request from the managing editor, was emphatically not a friend of mine.

I didn't react particularly well to meeting him. Or much like his seemingly good-humoured brash demeanour, which looked to me more like unstably conceited self-absorption and impunity. But maybe great art requires that.

Bizarre suicide of this undeniably talented young man discovered last Friday night in his own studio has been followed up by an even more outrageous sequel. According to a typed and signed note found with his body, Gerd Gold's last stated wish was that his self-laminated remains be put on public display with his first and last exhibition. This very unusual request has been successfully expedited by his friend and patron and named artistic and legal executor Crawford Kerry.

Only a fortnight has been granted by concerned city authorities before formal burial is required and conducted in the usual manner. Kerry is also arranging this and will host a special press conference and memorial ceremony on the night of final closure, which will be the first of August. Continuing exhibition *Zero Points Of Articulation* has been similarly extended in duration for the public to have an additional chance to view and pay their respects to the artist, who has now joined his own work as a centrepiece.

A book of condolence is available to leave signatures and observations in the lobby of *Kerry's Kuomintang*.'

*****

(*Private recording resumes, 13:26-13:44, location* Kerry's Kuomintang *bookstore, 19.07.1975*)

GB: "Hi, Crawford."

CK: "Ah, Gary. I've been expecting you these several days past."

GB: "Turning up at the wrong time for the right reasons in certain ambiguous places is usually a bad idea."

CK: "Would you like to view Gerd's final work for a second time privately? The gallery is closed lunchtime and we can talk it through if you like."

GB: "No thanks, I know what he looks like. So you *were* there. I heard the fire door in back close as you left. Called the cops on us from a booth?"

CK: "No my friend, I promise you I didn't set you up. I'd tipped off the police more than half an hour before you all let yourselves in. In fact I used Gerd's own telephone in the studio. They took their sweet Fatty Arbuckle time arriving. I could hardly be found there, could I? And I wasn't really expecting visitors."

GB: "You intentionally told Trucker about the rear exit to plant the idea, though."

CK: "Guilty. But not to entrap you. Like Gerd, I guess I wanted an audience."

GB: "How did you get him to take Rangoon Swoon again?"

CK: "I told him it was synthetic mescalin, a particular variety he had been keen to try. Convincing Gerd I was still in love with him despite everything wasn't difficult. Sadistic narcissists are often like that."

GB: "And once he was suggestible enough, you also told Gold to glaze himself alive."

CK: "To be fair, it was his mad idea in the first place under the influence. I merely encouraged it. Everything else he did himself. Gerd had a brutal imagination in all things. Finally applied it to his own quite voluntary demise. I stayed there for hours in vigil after he made his terminal gesture and finally called the police. I only realised the time when you four paladins arrived."

GB: "Crawford, I can understand you wanting revenge for what Gerd Gold did to you. But I didn't give over that Rangoon Swoon as a manipulation and murder weapon."

CK: "Didn't you, old friend?"

GB: "Let's just say there would be cheaper alternatives available if you wanted them."

CK: "And I appreciate that more than you know. But it was a very personal matter and had to be handled that way. Certainly I didn't know how it would go. He could very easily have turned on me again. The scenario could have been my own quietus and I was prepared either way for the justice of fate."

GB: "Outright poisoning and induced mesmerism is what it was, and I think you know that."

CK: "Doubtless an ancient kind of vengeance. That's what made it so bitterly satisfying and genuinely traumatic. I had to sacrifice a small part of myself to do and see it through. A private rather than a *political* kind of homicide; Gary."

*****

Every single nerve in me instantaneously goes hyperborean cold when he says that.

*****

GB: "Don't rightly know what you mean, Crawford."

CK: "Of course you do. What you don't know is that when you left my employ ten years ago, several of your photocopied epistles '*The Practical Economics And Business Model Methodology Of Organised Political Homicide*' remained behind in the store. One afternoon

Michael Tumesne came in and idly picked up and read through a copy as we talked about this and that and the other. I'd already known him for years previously and he regularly dropped in then as now."

GB: "…?…"

CK: "You have a very practiced composure, my dear boy. I admire that kind of remarkable *sang froid*, it's difficult to achieve convincingly. Don't worry, Michael didn't buy a copy. They never sold otherwise so I eventually took them off the shelf. But I think Mike vaguely recalled the work when he later started to suspect the existence of and investigate your organisation. You reminded him of it yourself in advance, you see."

GB: "I run a private phone installation outfit."

CK: "You and your friends demonstrated with the utmost capability exactly what you are when you expertly broke up that brawl here. It amazed me. I'd only suspected before, but I knew then. And that undoubtedly you were the people Michael has deduced and been looking for all these years."

GB: "No one respects Michael Tumesne more than me. Look at the man's investigative record, he's a crusader. But to be honest with you Crawford, the man's a raving lunatic about this privatised assassination bureau thing of his. Murder Incorporated is straight crime fiction fantasy stuff."

CK: "A couple of years ago I was invited to a charity event promoting libertarian literature with some rather high-powered corporate sponsors. Afterwards I took some of the senior executives to the same private dinner club I took you. They were astonished I could get us a table just by walking in and later opened up to me. Rather oddly the subject of occupational hazard came up. I mentioned fear of federal prosecution. Several of them mentioned corporate assassination without a trace of irony. Not politically or ideologically motivated. Their own colleagues conspiring to have them, I believe the vulgar term is 'bumped off' to avert scandal or put a rival out of the way. Purely as a business methodology."

GB: "I doubt they used that word."

CK: "No, indeed. I'm quoting from your paper, of course. They were describing exactly what that paper set out as a business plan. Your business plan. One of them quietly mentioned the name *Black Hand Incorporated* in a low voice. I had to strain to hear it. Two of the others immediately recognised the name and told him to be quiet in no uncertain terms. They changed the subject and wouldn't mention it again."

GB: "Sounds like a TV movie title. They must have seen a rerun of that one *The Periphery* from, I think it was 1970. Frank Gorshin and Angie Dickinson and Burgess Meredith. Surprisingly good, totally bonkers, and wasn't Tumesne an advisor on that?"

CK: "He was, and also told me he kept his name off the credits. Deliberately, so as not to alert the real perpetrators he suspected and helped write into the teleplay. You must have noticed and done some quite thorough research on what's an obscure and forgotten television pilot movie."

GB: "Nothing more than paranoid conspiracy thriller crapola, Crawford. Just another stupid Friday night movie entertainment genre for the crowd. It's been going since *The Manchurian Candidate*. All you do is replace the commies with multinationals, then let subsequent mania and gratuitous corporate cabalism rip. It's exactly the same plot-and-counterplot template. Pakula's raking in a cinematic fortune off it. So are the Sids' Lumet and Pollack and Frank Coppola and Stan Kramer and Don Siegel. They're all cashing in on the new evil Big Biz franchise. I'm waiting for *The Three Stooges Join Parallax Corporation*."

CK (*chuckling*): "That quick wit and intelligence is the reason you've survived, Gary. Clearly you're their leader. Harshly pragmatic and fearsomely proficient in a way I never anticipated you could make yourself. I admire that too."

GB: "Nothing to admire about hit men. Whatever kind of take they put on it. They're gangsters and mercenaries and lower life forms."

CK: "And you still have that awe-inspiring conscience. I can't imagine the reconciliations you must have to endure. How you all became professional assassins or why I don't know. But I instinctively sensed you could bring me what I needed. My means to punish Gerd Gold. Condemn and cut him down to size as he deserved. Avenge the spiteful and vicious way he accepted my generosity and love, then savagely beat up on me out of his own twisted guilt and self-loathing."

GB: "You surely did that. With my innocently meant purely medicinal gift. So what makes you better than him, Crawford?"

CK: "Nothing at all. I sincerely regret what I did. Robbing the world of an artist with the makings of real greatness and a younger man of his rightful success is a crime just as ugly. But he hurt me too much to forgive it."

GB: "Well, I'm not going to report you. Guess that makes us even." (*Rustling paper noise.*)

CK: "Thank you, my friend. And in return, here is the sole surviving copy of your highly original *magnum opus* and business plan in all its poorly mimeographed and badly stapled glory. Apart of course from my own private high quality photocopies of same. Along with detailed accounts of my knowledge of you and your friends which reside in several safe and trustworthy places. Ones staffed and inhabited with equally principled and entrusted people. Michael Tumesne need never know. All those years ago I told him I'd disposed of the remaining copies. He *did* remember later you see, and came here looking. Luckily for you I would never inform on a friend, whatever their possible crimes. I don't neglect my insurances, however."

GB: "You don't need any, Crawford. I'm grateful."

CK: "And along with the epistle you'll find four permanent membership cards to the store giving each of you a 15% discount on all purchases. This will be our own rather peculiar kind of *Détente.*"

GB: "Call it incentivization. Works for me, anyways. Always knew you were a bloated capitalist hog at heart, Crawford."

(*Both laugh softly.*)

*****

And that was that. A few days later a detailed interview with Crawford about events was front-page of the *Manhattan Globe and Mail.* A few months after that a new edition of his memoirs was published. Naturally with a long updated chapter about him and Gerd Gold, and it became a bestseller all over again.

Michael Tumesne conducted both the interview and ghost-wrote the updated memoirs chapter for Crawford. Both then cashed in again by rushing out a deluxe collaborative photo-illustrated biography of Gold and his work. Another bestseller, and they jointly cleaned up that year.

Interview and additional chapter both pointedly mentioned Gold as having been claimed by a *'mysterious dark hand of Fate'*, Crawford's clear warning to me. Uncomfortably I knew that Survind would certainly wonder over it. He never said anything but I knew how his brilliant mind worked, and it would always be on mental file.

Black Hand Incorporated itself was left with a degree of risk-exposure that I'd never anticipated, and couldn't share with the guys for my own safety. Four ampoules of Rangoon Swoon opium and a little anonymous public intimidation visibility were nothing. Michael Tumesne was something else again.

He had read me. *Read* me. All those years ago, just about at the time I seriously decided to create *Black Hand Incorporated* on the basis of that half-jokester's pamphlet.

From the beginning he had dogged our steps, remembered the original source. We were known directly through Crawford Kerry. I myself had been the catalyst to place us inextricably next to our most persistent and dedicated enemy.

Realised also, with surprise, I hadn't actually read the original paper after drafting our company charter and constitution and operating rules. Ten years had passed and a lifetime of murderous adventures and demented episodes and capital crimes. I could hardly remember who and what I'd been beforehand.

So I reread the entire thing, again in solitude at Blackwell's Island, the only place I felt really safe; thinking back to our first days.

*****

From *Black Hand Incorporated* confidential archives, company history section, excerpted from Chapter Nine: 'Managing the Aftermath', 1964 end of term graduate paper *The Practical Economics And Business*

Model Methodology Of Organised Political Homicide by Batchelor Degree course scholarship student Gary Banomena (current company president), then at the Central University of Indiana:

(Subsection *Collateral Damage Opportunism*): 'Depending on their size, sophistication and frequently the personal quirks and specific motives of those involved in political homicide scenarios, collateral damage to bystanders and unintended victims and/or property is almost inevitable. Despite the most careful planning, unforeseen consequential death and injury and miscellaneous destruction are inherent. Therefore, all operational protocols must allow and provide contingency for capitalising on the unexpected. These include inconvenient survivors, potentially unfavourable investigative attention and cost overruns.

Media manipulation, where possible, is a key tool in continually enhancing the company profile and professional image to customers. A perception of infallibility in execution is essential to maintain. Liabilities are best presented as assets and traded on accordingly.'

*****

To my surprise, almost every kind of obstruction and problem and unforeseen complication of our many operations had been foreseen in a general sense by my paper. In retrospect, and simply letting my imagination run wild for fun, I had anticipated almost everything significant.

'Political Homicide' had segued almost effortlessly into 'Executive Reassignment.' The Business plan had proven basically sound for a decade. But somehow I knew that wouldn't last.

With any business, any pioneering endeavour, you have to advance the frontier. Something more daring, with greater scope of vision is needed to take that original vision and impetus and conquer new territory. I had to conceive of and prepare us for something bigger than we had ever contemplated.

Something historic and revolutionary and truly fearsome.

Back at Albany operational headquarters and manning the switchboard on a morning shift, my very next received coded telephone enquiry is about arranging an induced corporate chair suicide. They want the reassignment subject to dig his own grave first in a hypnotic trance. A clincher I also found problematic.

'We heard that could be done on the *Plastic Fantastic* grapevine'; they said.

Never Disclose What You Bury

Dan A. Cardoza

I was the lead producer on this stellar Podcast, Crime Ghosts. We worked out of San Francisco until Joey relocated to Austin, Texas.

Hi, my name is Tommy 2-Tone. I use the handle to pay homage to the 1981 Rock Band by the same name. The band Tommy Tutone rocked — *867-5309 / Jenny, Jenny, who can I turn to?*

How can I ever forget the year? I was in 1981, the time when dinosaurs roamed the earth. It was the year they almost jailed the crooked San Francisco District Attorney, Bentley Cummings?

At Crime Ghosts, I prepped the shows and scheduled the guests.

We'd rented an abandoned flat across from Golden Gate Park. The building is haunted. It's more vandalized than gentrified. F

A few years back, Joey and I were seated at our favorite sleaze bar called the Last Rites. It's the one on 14th Street.

We'd finished watching some big screen T.V. That's when I brought up Jack S. Sorenson. Sorenson's story is convoluted. He'd done some exciting work since he'd left the San Francisco Police Department.

"Okay, Joey, let's go back to 2017. We are in Iowa. It's early February."

"I love Iowa. I killed a buck there once," says Joey.

"Chill, Joey, I'm just starting my story," I say.

I explained how this grave digger arrived late to work one morning hung over and how he'd jumped on a golf cart to make his rounds at the Woodland Cemetery in Des Moines, Iowa. What he'd discovered was extraordinary.

I'd seen some of the crime photos online. The pictures were creepy as hell, especially in the grayness of winter.

"You got my attention, Tommy, so what did the grave digger discover?" Joey asks.

"Well, his name was Bumble, the cemetery worker who'd made the grisly discovery. He'd stumbled upon a grave exhumation. The grave's anatomy had been emptied of dirt." I say.

"Okay! I like the story so far." Joey's eyes turn into pinwheels.

"Well, this guy, Bumble Jenkins, discovered a skeleton without a head. The skull had been displayed next to the hole on this piss-yellow patch of lawn next to the grave. You can't make this shit up, Joey."

"Holy shit!" says Joey, excited.

"Joey, inside the cadaver's dirty eye socket was a wad of cash."

I'll never forget that night at the bar, the way Joey blew snot bubbles. We both gave it up until our guts hurt.

"So, that's some crazy shit, Tommy?"

Joey demands more drinks.

"Barkeeps, put these on Tommy's tab!"

Joey had a bad habit of leaning into me, even though he made much more money on our podcast than me.

"This pile of bones and the skull had been put to rest the previous year, Joey."

"Wow!" Joey blurts out.

"So, Joey, it took days for everything to unfold. From what I've learned, cops guarded the crime scene while the Des Moines Police sought out the corpse's family.

Eventually, they reached Kevin. He flew out to Des Moines from San Francisco. Kevin was the dead man's oldest grandson, who'd appointed himself the spokesperson for the entire family.

"He'd been asked to inspect the chaotic upheaval, the bones, and the skull."

"I'm with you," said Joey as he reached for the pig's feet jar.

"Okay, so Kevin Bennington is this wealthy, young insurance executive. He and most of the family live in Marin County in California. The only thing that appeared to be missing was the dead man's war medals.

"So, what's the big deal, Tommy? They will just rebury everything that remains, right? Get out of the way and let the police investigate the crime scene."

"Not so fast, Joey, there's more. Apparently, the dead man was a family patriarch. He was adored and practically worshiped because of his lifetime of generosity.

"Here's some of the back story, Joey. Melvin Bennington headed west in the early '60s to make his fortune in San Francisco. In short order, he made a killing in the insurance industry. He was so wealthy that he'd purchased a mansion in Pacific Heights."

"Cool!" says Joey.

"Listen up? We're talking Ivy League schools here. The elder Melvin Bennington paid to educate every single younger Bennington.

"From what Google told me, the only thing he asked in return was to be buried with his cherished medals.

"The medals meant so much to him. And so the family honored his request. After the Benningtons learned how the medals had been stolen, the family suffered what can only be described as a co-dependent case of depression.

"Jesus, stuff happens, Tommy. What's the big deal, war medals?"

"Joey, apparently, the Bennington's had done the Tango with religion since it was invented? To them, a person's faith and wishes had to be honored. Senior Bennington must have been some kind of Moses?"

Grandson Kevin took things the hardest. He vowed to get his grandfather's medals back, come hell or high water.

After Kevin returned to San Francisco, he hired a private dick. His name is Jack Sorenson. Jack had recently retired from the San Francisco Police Department. Since he was still young, he opened up a P.I. firm. He named it–Gotcha, Inc.!

Since being commissioned to solve the cemetery crime, Jack has been a rat terrier on the two grave exhumations. However, he's gone down a lot of empty rabbit holes. But remember, detectives are like taxi cabs? The further you go, the more you pay.

"For the right amount of cash Detective Sorenson committed to solving both mysteries, one in Des Moines and one near San Francisco."

"Wait, did I hear you right, two graveyard crimes, Tommy?"

"Joey, you are going to kill me. I have to get home early tonight. I've got a date with a beautiful bong I purchased down in Chinatown. Let's continue our conversation at a later date?"

"Tommy, I won't forget this, asshole. You cock-blocked me at the end of the story. Get this detective Sorenson on the show again as soon as possible."

In truth, Joey and I were not even close to the end of the story.

*****

Joey Morrison is the infamous cock rooster every successful rock band fronts. He started the Crime Ghost Podcast several years back. He boasts two-million subscribers.

Joey opens up episode 255.

"So detective Jack Sorenson–by the way, listeners, the detective runs a successful P.I. operation out of the Tenderloin. He's getting rich?"

"Well, Joey, you are the goat here," says Jack Sorenson.

"Okay, Jack, we don't have much time. So let's get to it."

Following Joey and Jack Sorenson's conversation, I jump on Google and scroll through some of the detective's most infamous cases.

"See there." Joey pointed at my rolling computer monitor. "Slow down the scroll, Tommy, damn it!"

I smile, nod in submission, and look at the projection screen.

Joey continues, "Jesus, look at all the cases you've solved. Well, Jack, let's return to the cemetery case's beginning. I understand two well-known families are paying you a lot to solve a pair of Cemetery crimes?

"I can't discuss details, but yes, I am working both cases in Iowa and here in the Bay Area."

"Okay, detective, walk us through what you have."

Joey is a master of the dramatic. He's delivered for us for the past two years.

But in truth, I'm the one who got us on Spotify. He underestimates me.

I'm the one who makes sure we capture every demographic God

invented. Show sponsors chase us like lines of cocaine.

At the Crime Ghost Podcast, I toss Joey the easy layups too often at my own expense.

He's a great host, don't get me wrong. But I'm the one who makes the podcast fire on all cylinders.

*****

Camero Blanko paid cash to transport the Kubota Backhoe to Des Moines, Iowa. He did the same for the Colma, California, grave exhumation. Cam is a genius when it comes to leaving zero evidence. His crew includes a backhoe wizard and two Sumo wrestler sized laborers. Camero pays them handsomely.

The three are professional fixers.

They'd timed their arrival at the Woodland Cemetery in Des Moines at exactly 12:30 A.M. That's when security goes home.

They'd worked like muscular ghosts until 4:30 A.M., until their last bucket sweep. Once done, they headed back to New Jersey.

As soon as Camero Blanko received the stolen property, he inspected it. It had been placed in a hospital bio bag. Later, he placed the Iowa dead man's war medals in the safe.

Narciso Blanko had been Cam's grandfather.

He'd practically raised the young Camero, his parents having stayed behind in Italy.

Narciso had been horribly wronged by a corrupt San Francisco District Attorney. Cam's grandfather had died an untimely death. Cam sought revenge.

*****

Joey and I were headed to Austin, Texas. He'd leased a jet. We were discussing how rich we would be and the tax perks Joey would get in Austin, Texas. We were shit-faced and loving life.

"Okay, Tommy, how about finishing your story. You know the one you cock-blocked me on at the Last Rites bar, the Iowa exhumation, and now the Colma dig?"

"Right, of course, I owe you that. But, Joey, like you say, always hold something back, right?"

181

"Whatever, let's get after it!"

"Let me think. I need to get this right, Joey.

Firstly, I know more about the connection between the two grave exhumations than Detective Sorenson? That man can't find his ass with both hands."

We toasted and laughed, throwing down those tiny bottles of whiskey.

Next thing you know, I'm telling Joey how I'd visited this grave groupie named Looney at the Colma Cemetery, just south of San Francisco. This is the site of the second related cemetery digging.

"It was cold, December 27th, 2021, just before nightfall, Joey. I'd caught up with the groundskeeper. I introduced myself. The man said to call him Looney, so I honored that.

"What's with the stack of rotting bones the police discovered out here, Looney?" I ask.

Looney appears suspicious in the building fog. His eyes move around, lizard-like.

"We did some small talk. I warm him up to a conversation.

"Looney eventually blurted out the name Joe DiMaggio. He'd been buried at the Colma Cemetery, Looney disclosed. Before I could wrap my head around what the hell he was referring to, he moved on.

'Hell, we got us, Wyatt Earp, out here, son. Only, he's in Eternity."

"Eternity," I ask.

"Yes, Eternity is the name of the designated Jewish resting section at the Colma Cemetery.'

Joey chugged around another tiny bottle of liquor and leaned in closer.

After mentioning the Eternity section, the grave digger disclosed more demographics.

"The population of Colma is under 1,600, but we count the dead and buried. We have over a million in total," says Looney.

You'd think he was the graveyard's mayor the way his chest stuck out, Joey?"

"Enough chit-chat, Tommy, get to the story," says Joey, now looking impatient.

"Okay, Joey, basically, what I discovered was that Colma had a grave robbery nearly identical to the one that occurred at the Woodland Cemetery in Des Moines, Iowa.

"Regarding the exhumation out here, this older guy, Frederick Zimmerman, had been buried in the Jewish section. Apparently, he'd lived a storied life. He was well loved."

"How are the two grave robberies related, Tommy?" asks Joey.

"This guy Zimmerman, well, his wife's precious ashes had been buried with him in an urn. Now the precious urn is missing."

"Wow! Tommy, keep rocking it. Joey's excited once again. We got us some real mysteries here, two grave exhumations involving precious things stolen?"

"We got us a real who-done-it, Joey."

"That's some sick shit, Tommy."

"Check this out, according to Looney, the Zimmerman family committed to pay anything to get their cherished patriarch Nellie's urn ashes back."

"Oh shit, Joey, did you feel that, the turbulence?"

"No, but I'm drunk."

"Let's buckle up," I say.

"Tommy, don't do this to me again? What is the connection to both the grave robberies?"

"We can revisit this after we land, Joey. Safety first." I say.

Our landing turned out to be rougher than expected.

*****

Joey had grown impatient with me over time and angrier. He needed the entire story about the two grave robberies. In truth, I couldn't solve the puzzle, at least not all of it.

A week later, I got my last check. "Sorry, pal, I have to let you go. I've outgrown you," says Joey.

"But Joey, we both came from nothing. We are just getting noticed?"

"Well, I'm somebody now," says Joey.

I was forced to leave the studio the same day.

I grew depressed over time.

After I was fired, I stumbled around the Bay Area, getting canned from a rat's nest of entry level jobs.

By mid-2022, Joey and I quit speaking. Well, in truth, he wouldn't take my calls.

It was like when Joe Rogan dropped Brian Redban from his podcast.

Brian is such a good soul. He'd never taken his firing personally the way I do.

Looking back, I had a hunch but didn't know who'd committed the graveyard robberies. And more importantly, what were the related motives.

*****

"Hello, Tommy, Tommy 2-Tone, right? I'm calling from Tuscan Italy."

"What, who the hell is this? It's 2:00 in the morning, for God's sake."

"Tommy, you don't know me, but my name is Camero Blanko. I'm a big fan of yours."

"Camero Blanko, who in the hell is Camero Blanko?"

"Call me Cam, Tommy. I feel like I already know you."

"Ah, okay, what do you want, Cam?"

"Dude, it's not what I want. It's all about what I'm going to give you."

"Really, what would that be, sir?"

"Well, I need you to fly over here to Italy. Here we can discuss all the details."

"What, when?"

"As soon as possible, Tommy. I hate what that egomaniac did to your career. I intend to make things right. I have more money than God. I did well in the Frisco high tech boom in the '90s. I did even better with all my investments."

"Okay, count me in, Cam."

"I'll FedEx the airfare to Lazio tomorrow, Tommy."

"Deal, Cam."

*****

So I jetted into Rome's Ciampino Airport. It's about 26 Kilometers from Cam's estate near Lazio.

Cam's driver was waiting for me.

On the way to the estate, the beautiful countryside got me thinking. So many people seemed happy. I watched as they waved. I thought how much Cam must be loved.

After I got to the mansion, this Salvador Dali character escorted me to my personal quarters. He said to freshen up. After, he'd arrange to bring a sumptuous dinner to my room.

"In the morning, you will be having brunch on the patio with Mr. Blanko," Salvador says.

"Thank you, sir. Can I leave a tip?"

Salvador glares at me like Tony Soprano.

That night, I slept like a baby.

Around noon, Salvador knocks on the door. He escorts me to the expansive patio.

As I walk toward the table, I notice Camero. He appears to be in his mid-forties. He seems a little pale, but that doesn't detract from his handsome, rugged good looks. A confident look that shows he hasn't lost many battles.

Over espresso and Belgium Waffles, we discussed the vastness of his vineyards. They seemed to stretch to where the sun intended to go down.

After more small talk and a few mimosas, we wade into a deep conversation.

"You see, Tommy, as I've aged, I've mellowed. I've learned to cherish and embrace the calmness over here. Don't get me wrong, I miss many things about the States."

"Thanks for sharing, Cam," I say.

We both chuckle. What I said sounded awkward.

Going forward, things got less formal.

"As I said, Tommy, your partner did you wrong by dropping you from the Crime Ghost Podcast."

"I agree," I say.

"I'll get right to the point, Tommy. I know a lot about you. You are good people."

"Well, thank you, Cam."

"We have much in common, Tommy, although I hope you don't have terminal cancer. My mind is sharp, but my body is failing. But before I go, I want to do something for you, like I have for my loyal staff."

"Sorry to hear about the cancer, so there's no hope?" I say.

"Zero, my man. I've been given six months, max. But I'm okay with that."

A soft breeze grooms the garden, chasing songbirds off the branches of trees.

"I don't know what to say, Cam."

"You don't have to say anything. Shit happens. Like Jim Morrison once said, Tommy, no one here gets out alive anyway.

"This is what I propose. I intend to gift you five million dollars. I'll place it in two offshore banks in the Caymans. Use the money as you wish."

"What the hell?" I say.

"Listen, Tommy! I know what passion really feels like. Hell, I helped build Silicon Valley. It's obvious that I have passion, right?"

Cam waves his hand over the prime grape fields that stretch to where the sun will end up in the evening.

"I would like you to pursue *your* passion, Tommy. I want you to start a new podcast. You can use some of your gifted money."

"How do you know I won't mooch away all the money, Cam?"

"Well, that's fine, too. But you see, Tommy, I know a lot about ambition."

We laugh. Cam catches his breath and coughs into his fist.

"I'll do what you ask, Cam. And yes, I am ambitious. I do have a lot of ideas."

"I love ideas, Tommy. My mind is a carousel of ideas. By the way, I have an ending to your story that might work on your first podcast."

"Really, lay it on me, Cam."

Cam extracts a notepad with a pen from the briefcase he'd placed on a spare patio seat. He asks that I take notes. What I will hear is pure genius.

That early afternoon we waded into the tall weeds of the two graveyard exhumation mysteries. It takes nearly three hours.

First of all, as you know, Tommy, both of the deceased that had their graves exhumed, made a life in San Francisco.

Secondly, each victim had been a juror on a well-known fraud trial in the city."

"Yes, Cam, I know all that. What I don't know is the, *why*?"

"Okay, Tommy, I'll take you back to the fabulous 80s in San Francisco. This hotshot District Attorney named Bentley Cummings had been running the city. He was well known and accomplished, a graduate of Cal Berkeley, Bolt Haul, top of his class. Though brilliant, he wasn't wise.

"Well, to summarize, Tommy, he'd bribed two critical jurors who made sure my grandfather Narciso Blanko and the person he supported to challenge the D.A. got convicted of campaign fraud.

"At the time, my respected grandfather had backed another candidate, a rank and file police officer with a good chance of defeating the corrupt incumbent Bentley. To eliminate his competition, police officer Jenkins and my grandfather were arrested on trumped charges."

"I'm with you so far, Cam." I stop writing and fox my ears.

"Well, Tommy, the bottom line is that the D.A.'s bribery scheme worked. Ultimately, my grandfather and Officer Jenkins were convicted and imprisoned."

"Damn, Cam, that's some evil shit."

"It gets worse, Tommy. While in prison, my grandfather hung himself with his bed sheets. So much for the American Dream, right?"

"OMG, that's so messed up. I can see how that would poison your mind, Cam."

"I was enraged."

"I bet," I say.

"I wanted revenge in the worst way. Since the two jurors had died and were buried, once I decided to take action, I decided to take what the two dead jurors valued most in life," says Cam.

"Cam, I almost hate to ask, but how did you know what precious cargo the two men placed in their caskets?"

"Good question, Tommy, through the two separate obituaries. Mostly, sharing your last wishes rarely turns out well."

I listened to Cam and all the details, his instructions. I promise myself not to be judgmental, and I'm not. Each one of us has sipped the poison.

Cam explained how horribly the corrupt D.A. Bentley Cummings had died. It was sometime in the nineties. There'd been a single car accident in the Oakland Hills. The accident reconstructionist determined that Cummings accelerator must have gotten stuck in auto-drive.

*****

What Cam told me proved to be correct? Putting the entire story out there got my new podcast off the ground. I call the podcast, Never Disclose What You Bury. It's a smash hit based on any standard.

In one sweet year, I passed up my old partner, Joey, leaving him in the dust.

I also make sure to carefully follow Cam's instructions.

I returned the two well deserved war medals and the polished urn with Nellie's ashes to the respective families.

We all agreed to keep things out of the press.

As 2022 anemically limps into 2023, I got terrible news. Cam had passed away.

Yet I smiled upon hearing the news.

He would have wanted that.

Later that evening, alone at the Last Rites watering hole, I toasted Camero.

The barkeep looked at me funny. He must have thought I was toasting a ghost.

I'd say out loud, "Here's to you, Cam."

The following week, I learned how Cam was buried on a hillside overlooking his Promised Land.

I plan to visit his grave someday.

#HEIST
Sean Marciniak

Dahlia was goddamned if she knew why her father, the famous Marty Farr, texted her at 2:23 am on a Tuesday morning after so many years of low-grade estrangement. The message came as always from an unknown number, but the all caps was a giveaway:

> KIDDO, NEED TO HUDDLE ASAP.
> SERIOUS STUFF.

> What? Are you safe?

> IT'S ME, YOUR DAD. ALL OKAY.
> TOMORROW? DON'T TELL THE
> OTHERS.
> NAMASTE.

Dahlia full-well knew that TMZ was reporting Marty as 'missing', and that he'd been AWOL for months. The most viral rumor saw him being elder-abused by his manager (also his lover), and not even Dahlia's baby half-sister, the favorite child, had a lock on the situation. But *no*, Dahlia told herself, *do not engage*, her belly already heating up with the usual stew of morbid curiosity, abandonment trauma and sibling rivalry.

That should've been that, except she dropped her phone. The *thwack* echoed through the house, waking the baby she'd put down five minutes ago, and if she had to feed and reset her daughter in the crib one more time she'd seriously have to question the surgeon general's warning against shaking babies. So she woke her husband and let him know what was what and went to bed.

Come next morning, as sunshine burned off the fog over her Noe Valley home, she confirmed the "where" and "when" with her father. Then she hopped in her Prius and drove the four hundred miles south from San

Francisco, through the soupy haze of the Central Valley, to see him in Los Angeles.

Marty watched her park, sitting in the window of a neighborhood bar. He didn't wave or smile and she wondered how much weirder this would get. The bar was called *Marty's Place*, owned and operated by a fanboy, and the idea such a thing could exist curdled the *In-N-Out* burger in Dahlia's stomach — making her regret getting a double-double.

He wore a Panama hat woven of toquilla straw and a shirt crowded with palm trees. She pulled out a seat opposite him, a mismatched chair. Photos of him adorned the walls and, at the end of the bar, a life-sized wax figure of Marty in the role that had brought him acclaim — that of a Harvard plumber who anchored the end of a Boston bar in a successful early 1980s sitcom.

So many of her father's eyes, those round hazel eyes, tracking her.

Dahlia lost her footing and fell into the seat.

"Prius jokes are dead," he said, "but those Teslas and the nerds that drive them … now that's fertile." He picked up the Boulevardier that'd been resting near his fingertips and drained it. "Speaking of which," he said, and tipped his glass toward the pregnant waitress leaning against the bar. The waitress gave him an Army-perfect salute and Marty toasted her, mouthing the word "captain."

Dahlia hated these little games he'd play with people, routines seemingly tailored and special. "She's not fertile if she's already pregnant," she said.

Her father's eyes dimmed; she read his thoughts. How could she be so smart but unfunny? When would she grasp the rules of improv, starting with the first commandment: *Never* shut your partner down? An unimaginative, desk-ridden attorney, all the charisma of a potted plant.

"I'm funny," she said. She eyed her Prius by the curb and wondered if she could make it back to San Francisco by dinner.

"Nobody said you weren't."

The waitress returned with his fresh Boulevardier — a hint of citrus from the orange zest — and Marty winked at her.

Behind him, in a corner near the ceiling, a boxy old-school Zenith television played one of his films — *Dios Mío, the Ice Burrito,* the story of a failed Canadian bobsledder who plunged south of the Rio Grande and assembled the first Mexican bobsled team.

She hated that movie. Dahlia looked down and picked desiccated baby vomit from the wool of her sleeve.

What was it that had brought her here? Ah, yes, the text. "Serious stuff," he wrote.

Dahlia decided to do what she came to do: check on him. She scanned his face for trauma.

"Do you have a black eye?" she asked. Something was definitely up. An eggplant-colored blotch under his right eye, distanced from notice by concealer.

He saw where her eyes stuck. "I'm playing a down-on-his-luck boxing coach for a Tijuana fighter," he said. "Ed Norton is directing." He took a sip of his drink.

She wasn't sure she believed him. But the rest of his face? It looked fine. Just wrinkles in echo of a lifetime of laughter, a peppering of freckles on the forehead. Tan skin, the everyman's nose, the rested hazel eyes. So despite the metastasizing rumors, she decided she could leave in good conscience, and she picked her phone off the table and planted her puffy sneakers on the floor.

"How's your husband?" he asked.

Dahlia paused. She and her husband were at the point of asking one another questions but caring little for the answers. "I have a new daughter, you know," she said. "Your new granddaughter?"

Picturing her baby sent an ache through her breasts, now distended and tender, and her thoughts skipped to the breast pump in the trunk of the Prius.

Marty eyes were still, tepid pools, glossy with senility or self-absorption. Which was why, so very often, she wished to be fatherless. Excising him from the picture, her life was worthy. She, a respected criminal appellate lawyer, with articles in the *Harvard Law Review*. A darling at parties where Berkeley scholars swirled their Napa wines with notes of blackberry, while she walked them through her habeas corpus work.

But she was a paper lawyer, not a courtroom lawyer, and if you googled her name the algorithm returned a handful of pleadings with her name embedded in a block-letter captions. Those results? But grains of sand of a beach on which her father sunbathed.

Dahlia blinked for composure. To him, she was what, just another audience member?

"Why?" she asked.

He squinted.

"Why —" her voice broke and she could only whisper the last of it, and it wasn't even what she truly meant to say "— am I not shiny enough?"

The question hung in the air between them. Her stomach buzzed.

Her father took his hands from the table, then looked into his lap where he polished a thumbnail with a paper napkin. "I wasn't good, you know kid? I didn't learn to be a good father until later."

"Until later" meant his time with Sammie, his youngest, who now had comedy specials on multiple platforms. The apple of his pouchy eye. The girl wasn't even born of love, but from a weird experiment involving a sperm donation and a female comic.

Dahlia's chest ached and her eyes flitted to her car. A breast pump in the trunk of a Prius, how delighted he'd be to know this, perfect for a comedy bit.

"Excuse me." It was a stranger, a middle-aged female fan, mumbling about a picture and brandishing an iPhone.

Marty turned. "No pictures," he said. "Let's make a memory instead." He stood and hugged her.

Dahlia pushed back her chair. The ball footings groaned against the wooden floor.

Her father, still in mid-hug, reached down and placed a hand on her arm. It was a weighty hand, enough tendon and bone to overspill a salad plate. He said goodbye to the stranger and sat down and waited for the woman to leave before he spoke again. "I need legal advice," he said.

Dahlia pulled her arm away. "Unbelievable" — she inhaled — "transactional, of course it is." Why, she thought, did she ache for a place in his life?

"I need you to help me get out of something," he said, sitting back down. "You're the only person I trust." He picked up his glass and drained it with a single swallow.

"Marty," she sighed. But a patch of neurons murmured somewhere in the lifeless coils of her gray matter and her core muscles tightened, pulling her from a post-partum slouch. Returning now was the other Dahlia, the strategic thinker, the woman who graduated first in her class at Berkeley law, who knew that embedded in every need was the possibility of exploitation. And, as her mind sped through these thoughts, she wondered: If her father wouldn't give her what she needed, what was she willing to take?

She folded her hands on the table, and asked, "What've you got?"

His whole face changed and he took another drink but found only ice in the glass.

"Kid, this is serious," he said.

"Your text made that clear."

"It involves Hadassah."

Dahlia bit her lip. Hadassah was the lover-manager the world was buzzing about.

"She suddenly decided we're married," he said. "Under something called the Common Law. You ever heard of that?" He didn't wait for an answer but blundered into a monologue littered with the misuse of legal terms. Dahlia picked out the remaining crumbs of baby vomit from her sleeve and let him ramble.

"And," he said, "She's decided she's taking half."

"She's divorcing you?"

"Am I married?"

"My God, didn't you learn the first time?" At seventeen Dahlia had helped her mother outsmart a daisy chain of Hollywood lawyers and pry fifteen million dollars from Marty, after they'd learned he had a second family.

"I need to protect what belongs to the kids."

"Which kids? You know, I'm one of those kids."

He covered his mouth. "I have obligations to Ray-Ray."

Dahlia's eyes flitted to the movie on the TV. Her half-brother was part of that second family, conceived when Marty filmed *Dios Mío, the Ice Burrito* in South Texas. What it'd taught her was that Marty had never been a father, but a man. A man who enjoyed grotty sex with strangers.

"Really?" she said.

"Yes, really."

"I thought Sammie was your favorite."

"Dahlia."

She shook her head, staring at her lap, tears germinating.

"Honey …"

She decided there and then she'd fuck him over, and immediately snapped wholly into that bittersweet role — the attorney. Hated, needed, dominant.

"Enough." She looked up, her focus recalibrated. "Tell me what we're dealing with."

His finger traced the rim of his glass. "It's actually because of Sammie. You know that bit in her HBO comedy special, where she imitates Hadassah?"

Dahlia smiled, she couldn't help it. Sammie did a dead-on impression of their father's somewhat-famous girlfriend, everything from the Eastern European accent to her sneer.

"Hadassah said to make her stop," Marty said, "and I wouldn't. So I got the ultimatum: her or Sammie. She doesn't get it — you gotta laugh at yourself."

"Well," Dahlia said, "We don't have Common Law marriage in California. Where are your other homes?" Electricity coursed her brain, synapses firing in familiar rhythms.

"Key West, of course."

Dahlia scanned her father's palm-tree print and his stupid straw hat. He'd started a movement among his fans, ready to pick up the narrative when Jimmy Buffet died. "No Common Law marriage there either," she said. "Where else?"

"The family estate in Toronto."

Dahlia waved it off. "What else?"

"We have a home in the Texas Hill Country."

"Uh-huh."

Marty stopped fiddling with his glass. "Uh-huh doesn't sound good."

Dahlia pinched her nose. "Why don't you hire a lawyer?"

"It gotta be *incognito*." He threw in useless air quotes. "She monitors all the bank stuff, the credit cards."

"She has access?"

"She's my manager."

Dahlia put her face in her palms. "I'll have to look into this."

"Will you?"

His eyes were open, watery. Was it practiced? He'd been a good funnyman, but not an especially good actor.

She nodded her head. "I've got you," she lied. "Did you drive here?"

"I don't drive anymore, I'll take an Uber."

"Seriously?"

"I like meeting strangers." He checked his watch. "Can we meet again tomorrow? Can you learn something by then?"

She raised her chin and looked at him through her lashes. In the end, she had nothing to say, so she kissed him on the forehead and walked out.

*****

The audience at the *Comedy Store* knew Sammie had come to her favorite part of the set by her gap-toothed grin. Washable markers sat atop the stool, next to her glass of water, and she uncapped the orange one and drew contour lines beneath her cheek bones, then deep creases over her brow, transforming her open-eyed anime face into a severe caricature of her father's girlfriend.

She narrowed her eyes and looked into the audience, into their eyes, and affected an unplaceable Eastern European accent. "In Bulgaria, we have four food groups," she said, wrinkling her nose. ""Turnips, cabbage" — she ticked off fingers as she listed them — "pigeons, ash."

Hadassah wasn't in fact Bulgarian but a refugee from a Hasidic sect in Brooklyn. Her accent was born of Yiddish, not the Black Sea, and months earlier Sammie had found herself in the crosshairs of the Anti-Defamation League until she reminded the world on Twitter she was Jewish, claiming her attack on her own people was merely introspection and self-hatred, a tradition dating to the Talmud. Besides, she tweeted, could they really believe Hadassah's origin story? Wasn't Hollywood built on bullshit narratives?

Sammie crossed the stage and looked into the face of a man with hands clasped over his belly. "In America, there is fifth food group. Here, I feed on Marty Farr."

No one laughed. Their faces had blued in the glow of their phones, lips murmuring, eyes flicking at her, then away.

She broke character. "Are you all fucking serious?" She was trying out new material, sure, but it wasn't that bad.

Radio silence, still.

The club manager beckoned from the wings. Sammie took a last glance at the audience and met him.

"So." He looked at his pattering foot. "Your father died."

"What?"

"In an Uber car crash."

She blinked. "You made me come to *you* for this?"

In the bathroom she fumbled through her phone for a news story but push notifications blotted her screen, dozens of them. Text strings and emails crying for attention, so she turned off the device. A pipe dribbled water behind the drywall. The muffled blather of another comedian murmured through the door. Sammie put her face in her hands and cried.

She'd been the baby. Her father was many different things to many different people but he was hers, and she was his. They could trade entire conversations through glances. Even Hadassah barely dented the glossy finish of their relationship. When Sammie first started impersonating her, the woman's lawyers served her with a cease-and-desist letter. Her dad asked her only one question, "Is it funny?"

Sammie washed the orange marker from her face and hands and left through the club's backdoor. Once home at her apartment off Sunset she swallowed fifty milligrams of cannabis gummies and buried her face in a seam between couch cushions. She woke up once in the night, transposed to her childhood bedroom where her father stood in the doorway, backlit by amber light, watching over her. She felt herself within his all-enveloping hug, a real hug, a most excellent hug.

She awoke in her adult bed somehow, her mouth open on the sheets, a saliva stain on the thread count in the shape of an empty speech bubble. Never had she felt more alone. When Sammie's mother passed away from breast cancer, Sammie felt her spirit accompanying her in the following months, whether in third-tier comedy clubs or Carolines on Broadway. Ghosts—she believed in them, and extra dimensions of the universe, including one made wholly of love. But her father's spirit … it was absent. Her eyes landed on an unused chess board on her nightstand, one of the castles tipped over.

She wanted to see her half-brother Ray-Ray, the bastard son. Caramel, high-resolution skin instead of pitted, capillary-infused cheeks, but the same face shape, the same hazel eyes.

Marty had three kids by three different women and her half-brother bloomed into her life a year ago, attending each of her shows and afterward partaking in the Adderall-fueled banter she traded with other comics about the dipshits in the club, dipshits who ran the club, and dipshits who loitered after shows to see if they could make a comic laugh. Mostly she found office funnymen hanging around the alley where she vaped with her peers, water-cooler champs who never realized they weren't, and never would be funny without an HR straight man nearby. Stand-up was an art. It was hard work. But Ray-Ray — he was funny as hell, without even trying. He came with endless, stream-of-consciousness stories of bizarro shit. Adult booger collections, a heart-breaking tale of a horse that choked to death in the New Mexican desert on Arby's meat sandwiches. More than once she brooded over his raw talent.

But he reassured her. "You've got it wrong," he said one night, intuiting a thought behind her micro-expression. "I'm not funny. Doing weird shit and making people laugh like you do — getting up there, under those lights, those high expectations — that's a whole other special thing."

She was struck by this, grateful even. But one night a fellow comic suffered a similar jealous twinge, and told her brother he was full of shit.

Ray-Ray hit him in the face.

In the nose, precisely, out of nowhere. The thing was, comics used their words, not their fists, and she sat in disbelief. Nor could she process the seconds that followed, sitting in witness of his shining eyes, cheeks prickled with heat, almost a smile as her colleague tried to stop the bleeding with pages from someone's joke diary.

She wondered how much DNA they shared.

A few days later she met her father in a neighborhood bar to check in on Ray-Ray — what she saw, what he knew. Because Sammie didn't grow up with the others; she wasn't even supposed to be part of the family. She was an experiment, a test tube baby, the upshot of Marty donating his seed to an old friend — a fellow comic at the end of her child-bearing years who then carried her and birthed her and raised her on an opposite coast. But from day one she'd been funny, and the gravity of her bright eyes and imperfect smile drew Marty into her orbit. Entire chapters, then, in the Farr family lore remained sealed in pages unavailable to her.

The day after Ray-Ray's nose punch she sat with her dad at "his" bar with that hilarious wax-figure they always laughed about. "Look bub," she'd said, and told him what happened. Then she pushed her forefinger into his shoulder. "What do I need to know?"

Marty took her hand and looked in her eye and told her that at least once a generation, the Farr family produced such a creature. Violence and humor, born of the same hatreds, were closer cousins than people imagined. His own little brother, he told her, had spent two years incarcerated for stabbing a man in the kidney after a pool hustle. From his wallet he pulled a photo of him and her uncle, standing under winter twilight in the concrete parking lot of the kielbasa factory where they worked in their twenties. Cracked lips grinning against a polar vortex. "Love them all you can," he said, "but they'll disappoint you."

It was prescient. Two weeks later, just after they found her apartment burgled, Ray-Ray vanished. No call, no note, nada — and she hadn't heard from him in months. She'd ruminated on that, on what she'd done wrong.

They hadn't fought. Not once. Had she made too big a deal of things in a quieter way?

Sammie sat up in bed and rubbed her eyes. The knock on her door, sharp, sent a flutter in her chest. It was him, she knew it, and she yanked open the door.

Dahlia held out her arms for a hug. Sammie bit her lip and followed protocol but the embrace clicked as well as mismatched puzzle pieces. She tried to succumb to it, to surrender, but her sister's back wouldn't yield. This was Dahlia distilled to an essence, refined through adherence to an ordered life. Sammie inhaled and her stomach hit a blockage, rectangular and hard between their bellies, about the size of a coffee maker.

Dahlia looked down. "Oh, that's my breast pump."

Ordinarily this would've delighted Sammie. She would've grabbed her Moleskine notebook and jotted down "hug DENIED by breast milk pumper." She smiled at Dahlia, an offer to share in the absurdity. She found no return volley.

"You have a baby?" Sammie asked. Dahlia had been born in a different decade, and they only saw each other every few Thanksgivings.

Her sister nodded. "Three months. Her name is Gray."

"Gray? Like the color?" She remembered her sister had grown up in a hippie commune north of San Francisco.

Dahlia picked at her neckline.

"It's a nice name," Sammie said, but she'd told enough bad jokes to know you can't take certain things back.

Dahlia closed her eyes, reset. "We've got a problem,"

"What?"

It came in a machine-gun torrent of words, heated explanations laced with strange terms like *intestate succession* and *caveats* — which Sammie gathered had something to do with either IBS or inheritance. She stepped back and appraised her sister. What the hell was she talking about? How was it she didn't feel the same way? How had her heartbeat not slowed?

"I'm not interested in fighting," she said. "Whatever you decide."

Dahlia was eyeballing the dead plants on her windowsill. "We can't ignore this, Samantha. Hadassah is a monster."

"This isn't my fight," Sammie said.

"I'm surprised you'd say that."

"Why?"

"You don't know, do you," Dahlia said. "She's already cremated him."

"What?"

"We're not even invited to the memorial."

Sammie's attention skipped to her darkened phone, swollen with unread messages and alerts. "Cremated?" She'd absorbed that much, and her earth began spinning on a different axis. She sat herself on the floor. "Fuck that bitch," she said.

Dahlia knelt beside her. "The service is in three days, in Key West. But there are things we can do," she said. "Temporary restraining orders…" She began outlining legal strategy, building sentences about civil procedure and the ownership of ashes.

The hinges of the front door whined; a man stood in the doorway. "That's a coward's way out."

Saltwater blurred Sammie's vision but the shape was unmistakably Ray-Ray's. His bigger-than-average head, his square shoulders. Sammie once told him he had a butcher's stance.

"We ain't fucking doing any of that," he said.

Dahlia winced.

Ray-Ray paid her no mind. He lifted Sammie to her feet and pulled her into an embrace, all enveloping and warm. "Hermanita," he said into her ear, "you shouldn't leave your door open like this. En serio."

Sammie inhaled. The smell of nicotine. His neck bore a tattoo of a chess piece, a dark knight. Tears welled and broke over her eyelids. "I missed you Ray-Ray," she said. "Where've you been?" He'd lost weight, his shoulder blades sharp against her hands. His hair, grazing her cheek, had thinned.

"The question is, where are we going? The answer: Key West."

Dahlia stood up. "We're not invited."

He gave her a dark look. "We're crashing. It's been arranged." He separated from Sammie and fished a phone from his pocket and tipped the screen toward them. It framed Hadassah's Twitter account, acknowledging the funeral would be held in Key West, but asking for privacy. Below that, Ray-Ray's response:

> *Thx Hadassah for welcoming Marty's*
> *bastard Chicano son and his sister to the*
> *festivities. #Healing.*

His post was likeable — 84,000 hearts, 5,700 comments. Ray-Ray grinned. "A liberal Hollywood agent's got no choice here, does she?"

But Sammie was fixated on Dahlia's face, papery and blue, as she scrutinized the message. Perhaps noting it referred to just one sister.

"Also," he said, "we're going to take the ashes."

"That's stealing," Dahlia said.

"You can't steal what's already yours."

Sammie shook her head "Wait, what? The ashes?" She tossed that idea around, breaking it down. A smile crept into her jaw.

Her brother scrolled through Hadassah's feed to another photo, framing an engraved, stainless steel flask containing their father's cremated remains. "I've ordered a duplicate. It's the old switcheroo." From the inside pocket of his canvas jacket he fished a vessel with a mirrored finish, their father's name engraved.

Sammie fist-pumped. "Nice," she said.

Dahlia was shaking her head. "This," she said, her voice sharp, "is not how we do things. And you," she rounded on her brother "You're not involving Sammie in this world of yours — you should know better."

"Maybe you should know better," Ray-Ray said and took a step towards her, a flash in his eyes, a window into a purity of intention, which was to hurt her. He filled the room suddenly, his chest swelling, the air faint with sweat and something bitter underneath. Sammie looked back at her sister and in the black dilating pools of Dahlia's pupils was a trembling recognition of something she knew that Sammie didn't.

The strap of the breast pump bag snapped from her sister's shoulder, the machine skidding down her leg. Sammie began to cry. She couldn't help it, didn't want to help it. "Stop it," she yelled. She slapped Ray-Ray's chest with her palm. "Why would you do that?"

Whatever it was between her brother and sister, this ancient blood feud, it was that unquestioned blind spot on Sammie's proverbial field of vision, the dead patch where the optic nerve met the retina.

Her two siblings stood in her foyer, a room too small for three people, the remnants of a snarl still on her brother's lips, her sister's hands clasped, knuckles white, looking at the toppled breast machine. Sammie stood in their orbit and closed her eyes and sobbed into her hands.

Ray-Ray dragged the heel of his boot against the tile. "It's not really stealing when it's already yours," he mumbled. He squatted and retrieved the fallen bag, then stood and presented it to Dahlia. "But you owe this family," he told her, a lingering tightness in his voice.

And Dahlia nodded. She closed her eyes, then nodded again. "I'm in," she said. "But we do this legally. Deal?"

With their heartbeats in downshift, the room in détente, Sammie felt something stirring in her chest. The three of them stood on the cold tiles of her foyer, under dishwater-green fluorescent lights, each being seemingly broken, but they'd do this together. And wasn't Sammie still young enough to believe something was possible simply because she could imagine it?

✳✳✳✳✳

Thirty years earlier Marty Farr had walked into a bordertown in Starr County, Texas, hungover but primed to start filming a movie. And on the second day of shooting, he'd fallen in love with a young woman — honey-colored skin and hair the color of ink — who'd sat behind the desk of the only hotel in town. He decided he loved her, he later told people, during the longer minutes of a Saturday afternoon while sharing a cold Modelo Especial under the feathery shade of mesquite. They'd been sitting atop bluffs overlooking the languid Rio Grande, and he'd slowly picked the gold foil off the sweating glass of the bottle.

Ramiro was conceived a few weeks later but when filming wrapped, Marty split. He returned a few times a year, a family reunion of sorts in a McAllen hotel, and called the boy Ray-Ray.

Decades later Ray-Ray remembered these visits with high-definition clarity. The only other memories he kept: him and his mother in their home by the river with the shades drawn — seemingly always drawn — while she lead him gently through the steps of salsa and cumbia,. The music, set low, underlain with touches of static from the phonograph she kept in the corner, a keepsake from a previous life in Zacatecas. The rest of his life he preferred to forget.

In school Ray-Ray was gordito and paler-skinned than his classmates. His parentage was a family secret but whispered rumors spread fast through the bordertown of six hundred. The kids noticed his hazel eyes and his thin nose and they called him Martito.

Martito gordito, they sang, *se traiga burritos.*

As he aged into middle school, some of them rubbed their knuckles while they chanted it.

Each afternoon he would spend hiding in the town's one-room museum where the bobsled from *Dios mío, the Ice Burrito* sat in the corner on a small platform. It had been a real, working bobsled, with steering cables and brakes, but it was a contraption the rest of the town avoided. Radioactive almost.

Ray-Ray spent hours inside the sled. To him it was no different than an alien spaceship, proof there were other worlds where perhaps he fit in, and he'd tell himself stories that it was just a matter of time before his father would pluck him from this place and take him to those other worlds.

Then one day he heard shouts and war cries and the clop of many feet crowd into the room and he stayed very still in the bobsled, willing himself not to breath. It was futile. The sled lifted into the air, a dozen boys hoisting its runners onto their shoulders, and they carried him toward the door. He turned to exit out the sleigh's back end, and found himself staring into the square face of a boy twice his size, who they called *El Oso* — The Bear.

"We saw the movie," he said. "Diego's parents had a copy, you know. We saw it. They laugh at us."

The boys had carried him through the low door and into the street, then along the downslope of the plaza toward the river. The plaza sat thirty feet above the Rio Grande, the drop sheer and ending in the poky bramble of carrizo. They chanted as they walked, "Dios mío, el fin al río."

Ray-Ray had turned and scrambled toward the back of the sled, but *El Oso* punched him in the nose. He tried to stand and throw himself over the sides but boys had begun shaking the bobsled, the pitch and yaw plummeting and rising, and Ray-Ray had fallen deep into the nose of the sleigh. He clambered again toward the back of the bobsled and his face met with the palm of *El Oso*.

The other boys stepped onto the gravel apron beyond the plaza — loose stones scoring the dirt under the twists of their shoes. When he'd heard the crunching he'd started crying. The bluffs of the Rio Grande were rocky, unforgiving, the fall three stories high.

"Mira!" *El Oso* said. "Martito está llorando." And it was true, his face was awash with tears.

They laughed and carried on.

But aside from his looks, Ray-Ray had inherited something else from his father. Marty Farr might've fit the image of an assembly line worker at a Chicago kielbasa factory but he could take a sledgehammer in one hand, his fingers curled around the very end of the handle, and touch the stone to his nose. Ray-Ray had discovered this inheritance then, at that moment. He grabbed the boy's hand and corkscrewed his wrist. *El Oso* cried out in pain and his arm fell away. But behind this first guard there had been others awaiting.

Ray-Ray pulled on *El Oso's* arms, pulling the boy halfway into the rocking sled, then wrestled him into a headlock. If they wouldn't let Ray-Ray off the sleigh, he'd take one of them down with him. The biggest one.

There was a shout, then murmurs. "Chingou," he heard, "bájalo." The bobsled was lowered to the ground and Ray-Ray stood immediately, still holding *El Oso's* dazed and lolling head. He dragged the boy with him from the sled, a ragdoll hostage, and looked straight into other boys' eyes. It had previously been something he'd always been afraid to do, and to his relief he'd found many unwilling to meet his gaze..

One of the boys had spat into the dirt. Looking back up, the he'd said: "That's fine … But the sleigh still goes."

After that day, nobody called him Martito. Nor did anyone speak again of the bobsled or that bullshit film.

At home Ray-Ray remained tender. Each night he and his mamá would watch telenovelas with the windows open, in the hope that a breeze would move the 110-degree air. In the distant honks of old cars motoring through the Mexican town across the river. They numbed their lips with icy raspas and mocked the TV characters and — oh — he could make her laugh. Her teeth, so white, her eyes dark and shining.

When he was sixteen, his mother had succumbed to the deadliest disease on the border: Diabetes. The upshot of a lifetime of starch.

With the small amount of money he'd inherited, Ray-Ray hitchhiked to Hebbronville. There he'd bought a Gerring Streaker, a baby-blue van with a bar of flames down the side. He'd then stopped by his uncle's house at the edge of town and found the man sitting on a bucket of drywall in a dirt-floored garage, his *tío* surrounded by tools and detritus. The man listened and pursed his lips as he then pried a flake of packed loam from the ground with a flathead screwdriver and dropped it in a Ziploc bag. With less certainty he'd reached under his workbench and retrieved a snub-nosed handgun held there by duct tape. He handed both to the boy, saying, "Ten cuidado 'ijo," — Be careful son.

Ray-Ray's eyes widened. His uncle was a religious man.

"La verdad?" the older man said, "There are places in this world where even Jesús cannot protect us. Only for defense, me entiendes?"

Ray-Ray had nodded.

"Good." The old man pressed himself up from the bucket. "Now let's go out back, and I'll show you how to use it."

Come next morning Ray-Ray drove toward Big Bend, then El Paso, and on another two thousand miles. Eventually he reached the golden hills of California — the clouds overspilling them like water — and then into the misty coastal towns north of San Francisco, where a magazine said his father had taken up residence in a town without a name. His mother had promised him that his father loved him, that only "complications" had kept them apart, and he believed in her promise, it was enough. But whatever shot he and Marty Farr had of reconnecting, Dahlia had destroyed with a single, duplicitous phone call, such was his truth.

Thirty years later, enduring the assault of noise inside a twin prop plane,

Ray-Ray soared over the waters between Fort Meyers and Key West, watching Dahlia read a legal memorandum she'd prepared. It was just the three Farr siblings in the six-seat plane, and Dahlia read aloud how one could legally steal a flask of ashes.

Her reedy voice made his skin itch so he read the document over her shoulder. She'd written: *Are ashes "property" under Florida law?*

Likely. The flask definitely was.

Is petty theft a crime in federal waters?

Hadassah had planned a sunset cruise, departing Key West and traveling seventy miles southwest to the Dry Tortugas islands where a 200-year-old island fort decayed. Between Key West and the Dry Tortugas was the Strait of Anian, a ribbon of water outside of Florida's jurisdictional waters.

Therefore, Dahlia, wrote, *there exists a viable argument one could possess the flask without incurring criminal liability as theft is only a state crime and not a federal crime.*

Ray-Ray held in his lap a replica of the flask, its convex belly a carnival mirror, warping his mouth into a sneer that bothered even him. But Dahlia's little sentences, they were so misleadingly delicate. She'd set him up before with this kind of trickery, and had ruined his relationship with their dad by twisting the law against him. Her dog-eared memo rested on her little annoying breast pump bag, a monstrosity woven from hemp. It'd done nothing but draw stares since they'd left Los Angeles, and caused a still-unexplained, thirty-minute delay at airport security. "Why bring it?" he'd asked her. "Your baby's at home."

Sammie had swatted him. "World's authority on boobs, ladies and gentlemen."

In Key West's slow-motion streets they were swarmed by bicycles, their spokes threaded with glow strings. Ray-Ray strolled through the wash of afternoon laughter, the noise of inebriated crowds roosting in open-air bars, seduced by the illusion of a world without problems.

And then, a few blocks east of Duvall, there a catamaran. Three stories tall, a minimalist design incorporating only white-enameled carbon fiber and vantablack glass. More like a BMW dealership, not at all their father's jam.

Ray-Ray and his sisters stood in line for the sunset cruise amid a loose assortment of powerful people who never stood in line, and who looked downright uncomfortable in the tropical prints and straw hats they'd donned to blend with the natives. Some faces they recognized, but most were strangers, almost certainly Team Hadassah. His sisters hid behind sunglass lenses eclipsing half their faces, yet the crowd marked them immediately. A throng of paparazzi leaning against an outdoor bar uncapped their cameras.

Ray-Ray eyeballed Dahlia's saddlebag, embroidered across the flap with *Liquid Gold*. "C'mon," he said, and pulled Sammie by her elbow. "Let's do recon."

At the front of the line, guests dropped cell-phones into gray neoprene pouches with magnetic locks, then squinted over paper forms. Security guards proffered pens, insisting on signatures, and peered into purses and travel bags. Ray-Ray readjusted the straps of the olive, canvas bag on his back where he'd stashed the replica flask. He'd the sense of being watched.

Hadassah stared down from an upper level of the catamaran. She wore a shirt without a collar, framing a corded neck, overhung by a severe chin. At her hip the stainless steel flask — the top of it flashing in the sunlight — the remainder occluded in the loose sleeves of her dotted Swiss sundress.

She stared at him, staring until he met her gaze.

Ray-Ray respected her but it wasn't mutual. She held his gaze but words pearled from the side of her mouth, meant for a companion, and Ray-Ray read his name on her lips. Then she laughed, her stomach fluttering under the nearly sheer cotton. And why shouldn't she laugh? Hadassah had a team behind her, well-oiled, unified. Ray-Ray had a broken confederacy of half-siblings. But there was the flask, within sight. Saliva welled beneath his tongue.

Sammie poked him in the shoulder. "Enough, weirdo."

Back in line he glanced at Dahlia's breast pump bag, ferreting a place to smuggle his replica flask. "We're putting the dummy flask in there," he said. "I'll buy you a new pump." He nodded at the emerald water burbling between the boat's hull and the dock. "Dump it."

"No," she snapped. "I've done my part."

"You owe me."

A tug at the corner of her mouth. "I said no."

Ray-Ray wiped his jaw. "Don't pretend like this is beneath you." He'd leaned in close, hissing through his lower teeth. "You're already deep in this conspiracy."

Dahlia's lip trembled. "Get away," she whisper-shouted. "Get the fuck away from my breast pump bag."

Those in line began to turn and Ray-Ray tipped his forehead into a hand, his fingertips dancing on his skin.

"Sammie," he said.

"Yes boss."

"El Cheapo."

Sammie saluted. "Ay yay," she said. Her hand snapped to her pocket where she fished out lipstick, uncapped it, and plowed her face with lines of wine-colored wax. Crow's feet appeared. Frown lines on the brow.

"Achtung," she shouted. Those in line turned, and the paparazzi surrendered their beers to the bar and raised their cameras. They all knew who Sammie was, knew immediately who she was imitating, and they fixed every last graviton of attention on her clowned face, understanding its deliciousness, understanding Hadassah stood not forty feet from their heads. Ray-Ray bit his lip, worried she'd go too far, that they'd never even get on the boat.

"Listen," Sammie said, raising her chin, surveying everyone through her lashes.

One beat.

Two beats.

But there was no talk of turnips. She returned the lipstick to her face and drew a moustache beneath her nose, then hiked her pants above her waistline and waddled around like Charlie Chaplin in a lopsided circle, her duck-footed steps veering dangerously close to the edge of the dock.

Ray-Ray exhaled, of course a pro like his sister would find the line and merely toe it. Outside the spectacle she'd created, he eased the canvas backpack from his shoulder and tossed it across the two-foot gap onto the catamaran's gunwale where it landed in a frayed nest of mooring rope. The toss was fluid, almost gentle, not a ripple left in the universe.

Dahlia stared, her nostrils dilated. Ray-Ray could feel her jealousy, its energy. At the fact he could succeed without overthinking things, at his camaraderie with Sammie.

"El Cheapo, huh?" she said. "What's that, some code word between you two? Some shoplifting ruse?"

"It's a chess move cabrona."

In the days when he'd palled around with Sammie, they'd spent long stretches in the middle of the day playing chess. The cheapo was a trap, a cheap trick, designed to reverse a fortune. But, he decided, Dahlia didn't deserve to know.

"It's too small," Dahlia said.

"What?" He didn't understand, didn't think he heard right.

"The flask. You ordered the wrong size." She threw her chin toward the top of the catamaran where Hadassah stood eyeballing Sammie, trying to burn holes into her.

Ray-Ray took a second look up at the catamaran but the flask wasn't visible. "You're full of it," he said. But inside, in his gut, a cold edge twisted. He didn't disbelieve her.

*****

An hour into the sunset cruise the catamaran crossed the eighty-second meridian and entered the Strait of Anian. The crowd had sorted itself into two: Marty's more feeble-minded acquaintances, elderly and draped in linens and printed tropical shirts, and those in service of Hadassah, younger and physically stronger, their muscles pronounced in fitted apparel and their gazes occluded under the reflective coatings of Maui Jim and D&G lenses. Waitstaff flitted between them with trays of mahi-mahi hors d'oeuvres.

Dahlia checked her GPS watch. By her calculations they had seventeen minutes to steal with impunity.

Hadassah swayed on the far side of the deck holding the flask like a baby. Ray-Ray wouldn't look at it, wouldn't acknowledge the possibility Dahlia had been right, until Hadassah pulled a power move and strode close enough to Ray-Ray for her dress to graze his calf.

Dahlia saw him see it, then digest the truth — the real flask was monstrous.

It dwarfed the hip flask Ray-Ray had squirreled into his canvas bag, which now hung again off his shoulder, uselessly. Who knew human ash needed so much space? She caught up with Ray-Ray near a gurgling aquarium in the galley on the first level of the catamaran. "Admit it," she said.

Her brother rounded on her. "We'll do it anyway." He looked west through a window into the yellowing sky, working his lip, soothing himself with heated mumbles. An omen of recklessness.

Dahlia watched him, a sense of déjà vu in the uncanniness of it, an echo of that first day so long ago when he'd shown up in her California village. He'd been a stranger, framed against the aqua panels of a van, its engine ticking as it cooled. Muttering, chewing the inside of his lower lip.

It was a strange sight because strangers didn't visit *Skara Brae*. They never found it. The townfolk had removed all highway and street signs announcing its existence and left them rusting in a cove. The village itself spanned five blocks, homes and shops nestled in the mists of the Pacific groves. Shopkeepers accepted no money, preferring a barter economy. Home-baked flax bread for patchouli oil.

Dahlia had been seventeen then, and in that gray morning she spilled from the front door with her thumb in a law book — a hornbook on habeas corpus and unlawful searches and seizures. Her mother oversaw a death row law project, a partnership of UC Berkeley and San Quentin, and under home-school tutelage Dahlia had immersed herself in cases. Minutes before she'd broken one wide open with a realization about a warrantless search of a broom closet. It was the first for her, proof she could do adult things, and with buzzing skin she'd set off for the local café to tell her mother. She would free a man, a real person, using only her mind. A gain in the war between underdogs and oppressors.

But this strange teenager arrested her. Roving the edges of their property, whispering to himself. With her mother down the street and her father in the back tending beehives, she took a breath and told herself to be unafraid. She grabbed a hive scraper Marty had left on a rocker, a tidy iron tool with an unpolished blade.

Ray-Ray's eyes flitted to the scraper. "I need to see Marty Farr," the boy said. "He live here?"

She didn't have to answer. Marty rounded the house in a mesh helmet, a solitary bee lazing behind his shoulder. "Hey kiddo, what —" He stopped, removed the veil from the helmet. His irises were spinning, but he blinked them still.

"Ray-Ray?"

The boy nodded.

Marty wetted his lips with his tongue and said, "Let's all be pessimists for their destiny is filled with pleasant surprises."

She recognized that from a paper slip in a Chinese fortune cookie and looked at her father who surveyed both children, his mind cogitating, working out who to comfort first.

He turned to Ray-Ray and opened up his arms. "My boy, bring it here."

Dahlia never forgot this.

Inside the house Marty showed off the machine gun prop he'd wielded during a Cold War spoof that somehow stitched together boot camp, mud wrestling, blonde KGB bombshells, and nuclear weapons. Dahlia's attention danced between them, seeing past their different hues, the differences in their stature, and zeroed in on traces of their common pedigree. The thin nose with the bulbous tip, the large hazel eyes.

"You keep the AK," her father told the boy, handing him the plastic gun. The boy seemed to understand he'd received something — that it meant something — but the skin around his eyes never slackened. That evening he refused to sleep in the house, choosing the mattress in the back of his van. But the toy rifle went with him and Dahlia contemplated the now-blank space on the wall where it'd hung for years.

She'd known her father wasn't happy here, tending bees, feigning anonymity. For the first dozen years of her life he'd lived a world away in Hollywood, stopping in now and then, joyous occasions for her, those visits brimming with energy and laughter. But then the American public lost its appetite for bawdy comedies and the name Marty Farr lost its flavor. He was old news, his jokes predictable, and for the past three years he'd returned to his family. The second coming of his career was still years off — that boom of quirky, reflective comedies populated with eccentric characters, dressed in limited color palettes, moving through rooms arranged with eerie symmetry, absorbed in ruminations on the loss of innocence. This intermission in Skara Brae marked the doldrums of Marty's career.

And this town in the coastal fog belt was a place without fun, its citizens absorbed in social responsibility. There was no Sunday church but Dahlia and Marty nevertheless lived with severe commandments, prohibitions against ingesting chemicals (no frosting!), mobile phones (brain cancer!), and buying just about anything from a store (no corporations!). But in the evenings, outside her mom's earshot, Marty told her bedtime stories from his hey-day in the larger world: Taking mushrooms with famous actors, visiting subterranean bowling alleys in Beverly Hills mansions, embarking on spontaneous road trips lasting days, climbing working oil derricks and riding them like mechanical bulls. These whispered indulgences were their shared secret and the plastic AK-47 was part of that small world. And now, almost casually, Marty had given it away. And to who? Somebody from a different universe in her father's multi-verse, populated with people he loved the same as her, maybe more. She was replaceable.

Early the next morning she trudged to the beach. The waves were choppy, the sand littered with the husks of dead crabs and awash in pewter water.

How, she thought, had she been so stupid? How could she have expected a man so desperate for attention would be happy in a town with no street signs? She teared up. She thought she'd been enough.

Her introspection was her undoing.

"If it isn't little Dahlia, our own baby movie star." The town delinquent, Posy Sayles, stepped from the grove onto the beach. She held a bag of chips — not gluten free — and blew a traffic-orange crumb from her lip. Her cousin Shane emerged too and rested his hip against the twisted trunk of a Monterey cypress.

They were transplants from back east, both tall, fair-haired and limby, with seawater eyes. Most nights they spent smoking weed inside the coastal blackberry bushes; most mornings they warded off strangers who dared surf the local waters with fistfights and slashed tires. Insolent youth grown strong in their pursuit of dominance and territory, unhindered because the local cabal of adults denied such impulses existed. Dahlia turned to go but Posy closed the distance and grabbed her shoulder.

She was a full foot taller than Dahlia. Her hand felt like a claw. "She's pretty, don't you think Shane?" Posy's grin was easy, her eyes glassy, her smell a blend of seaweed and cannabis. With her free hand she took Dahlia's jaw in her hand. Her fingers were long and they scrolled up the sides of Dahlia's mouth and formed her lips into a pucker. "Shane, get out the cigarette."

One-by-one the cousins had been marking the youth in the town with the embered ends of their clove cigarettes, just behind the ear. Dahlia looked out the corners of her eyes, her pupils tremoring. The surf was suffocating in its roar, entombing them in a world apart.

"Oye mamones." It was Ray-Ray. "Where I come from, you keep your hands to yourself."

Dahlia began sobbing, overcome by relief, a deluge of it, a million thank yous in her head dislodged. But Shane acted first. A butterfly knife appeared from his jacket pocket, the blade dull under the marine layer.

Ray-Ray stood on the damp beach, legs apart and grounded, and pulled a snub-nosed pistol from a sweatshirt pocket, a tiny thing in his hand with disproportionate gravity. She remembered the end of its muzzle, that perfect, pearl-sized hole.

Ray-Ray crossed himself with his left hand.

His right arm, he lowered it to five o'clock and fired, the crack numbing, arresting the passage of time, a dime-sized pock opened in the beach mud.

Back at the aqua van Ray-Ray stuffed the handgun in the glovebox next to a Ziploc bag. Dahlia still trembled, her heartbeat in her fingertips, but Ray-Ray was calm, as though whatever he'd felt ended with the expiration of those dangerous moments on the beach. Her attention lingered on the baggie in his glovebox, powder inside it. Her lips parted, then closed. She wondered what mattered anymore.

"Thank you," she said.

"Ain't nothing," he said. "You're my sister, and nobody messes with family."

She nodded. And she envied him, this ability to metamorphosize and change roles like an actor, a terror in one moment, calm the next. She thought of her father on the screen, his surrender to a character's role. She looked around for something interesting to comment on, to make herself relevant.

When her parents fought that night, an end-all-be-all hollering match over the teenage boy in the van; when she wrapped herself in a goat-hair blanket and tossed and turned just to remind herself that she had a place in this world; when she realized her father, addicted to paths of least resistance, would ghost this town with his newfound son and start a new universe elsewhere, leaving her and her mom alone with the villagers and their black-and-white judgments while the town's children sharpened their knives, rendering her a sad victim, that being the sum of her existence — that's when she called the police.

A half-asleep dispatcher in Santa Rosa asked about her emergency and she reported a machine gun in a van. Only then did she feel the billion cells in her chest fall still.

The deputy sheriffs threw the town under a disorientation of flashing blue and red lights. They found a bag of dirt in the glovebox, next to the handgun, and arrested Ray-Ray for illegal possession of a firearm. A half-hour later Dahlia called the sheriff's office a second time.

It was an unlawful search and seizure, she said. The dispatcher transferred her to a detective with a voice like an idling chainsaw. "What?" he barked, and she told him: constitutional error, all theirs, to dare search the glovebox because the reported weapon, a machine gun, couldn't have fit there. Said who? The United States Supreme Court, that's who, and she cited chapter and verse *United States v. Ross*, 456 U.S. 789 and *California v. Acevedo*, 500 U.S. 565. Whatever they'd found was tainted with undue process.

In the morning's bleary light Ray-Ray was free to go anywhere but Skara Brae. And in that same milky light Dahlia reveled in her ability to manipulate the world with invisible strings.

Marty didn't follow the boy out of town, but nor did he stay — he split for Los Angeles — so she and her mom threw themselves into the bewitchments of California divorce law and decided they'd take all his money.

They got half, but it was plenty.

Midway to the Dry Tortugas, Dahlia looked at her own hands, aware the machinations in her head were infinite but bounded by a real world of flesh and blood and hard surfaces, and that the physical universe on the yacht was tiny but organized against Marty Farr's children. The sun's rim touched the horizon and a college-age man with braids strummed an acoustic guitar into a microphone. The memorial service had begun.

Waiters distributed champagne in stemmed glasses and she grabbed two and downed them both. It was a small joy to drink, to feel childless and husbandless, and with whirring consciousness attuned to this moment she noticed Ray-Ray eyeing a table near the opposite gunwale where their father's flask shone copper in the long rays of the sun, centered on an altar and fenced by broad-chested men appointed to stand guard. Ray-Ray glided toward them, his shoulders curled forward, his gait suffused with the mesmerizing certainty of a predator, so she blinked when he veered off course and grabbed Sammie by the elbow.

"El Cheapo," he told her, Dahlia could read his lips. And Ray-Ray walked up alongside the man with the guitar and picked the microphone from the stand and beckoned to Sammie. His eyes were lit.

"You want a eulogy, folks," he said. "I give you the best."

*****

At times like this Sammie was glad her brother was a tough guy. He tossed the microphone, she snatched it from the air.

Sammie blessed the crowd with her gap-toothed, shit-eating grin, sowing the promise of blasphemy. This was her moment, the eulogy her job, though nine-out-of-ten passengers disagreed. The meatheads around the altar had stepped from their posts, eyes zeroed in, shoulders flexed, and Hadassah lorded over her from the upper deck, arms folded, daring her.

"A eulogy, huh?" Sammie said.

She dared.

She paced in front of the guitar player who'd appeared to be thinking quite hard. She winked at him. "Always toughest, that first time." She turned to the crowd. "Eulogies," she said, "are meant to be serious. So look, people, I'm absolutely *not* going to tell you about the time my father crapped in a wheelbarrow in a Flagstaff alley."

But nobody laughed, not even the few allies peppered among the crowd. Not her dad's old agent, who she'd known since she was five, not even Ray-

Ray, who wore a pained look. Sammie blinked. She'd broken the cardinal rule of comedy: stay ahead of the audience.

Her mind spun, scanning a Roledex of bits. The Mormon tabernacle choir. Crisco lard. Elephant sex. All wrong.

It brought her back to her first real stand-up performance in a basement club in downtown Oakland. Her father had come to see, and she was bombing. A man in the audience wearing blocky glasses and a waxed barber's moustache heckled her. "Born on third base," he'd called, "and thinks she hit a triple." His people chuckled their closed-mouth chuckles.

She hated him. Her mind scrambled for something, anything. This stoogy hipster, to think he could hide his entire sad past behind a douchey moustache. Making baseball metaphors and yet just enough coordination to clean dip-spit off a dugout floor. She opened her mouth, but her father was quicker.

Marty stood up from his seat against the back wall and hit the light switch, casting the club in kitchen-bright wattage. The audience blinked. Marty had come late during the first comic's set, quietly, as conspicuous as furniture, and the club murmured with realization.

Her father walked in no hurry to the soundboard with its myriad buttons and pressed one, streaming elevator music through the club's speakers. And then he danced. A slow, sexy dance to a muted saxophone playing a canned melody. Giggles bloomed here and there and Marty hip-twisted his way to the heckler.

"Do you have a dream?" he asked the guy.

The hipster took a healthy sip of craft beer. Motes of dust drifted through the light and Marty caught one with his finger and placed it on the boy's waxy forehead.

"You do," Marty said, looking at the younger man's moustache, then into his eye. "We all do. And this little girl here has big dreams, so let's allow her to have a shot, okay? All of us, please, let's lay back in our gutters and gaze upon the stars and let each other do the same." Marty sat next to the boy and signaled to the waiter. "Two beers, maestro."

Five years later Sammie looked at a hundred imperfect but beautiful people on a boat drifting through the Strait of Anian and realized the answer to every problem was, simply and wonderfully, compassion.

She cleared her throat. She saw her older sister, Dahlia, clutching her baby bag with a strange look in her eyes, sad and determined and lonely all at once. Sammie sought Ray-Ray but couldn't locate him.

Her broken siblings. She understood then, for the first time, what they never had. That sense of belonging, of being protected.

"My father," Sammie said, "was a man whose attention was in great demand, and there wasn't enough for everyone. I was lucky, I get that now. But however much time he gave each of us, he loved us. In his own way, the best he could, he loved everyone." She looked across the crowd, saw hesitant agreement in its faces, and she thought of her father's antics — crashing fortieth birthday parties in major cities, befriending waiters and waitresses in roadside diners and sending them plane tickets to dream destinations. It wasn't right for anyone to have wanted her father for himself or herself, no more than a single person could claim possession of a songbird. "In his heart," Sammie said, "he wanted people to know they were okay, that they'd be okay." Her lips moved without thought, without need for it, for she simply relayed those things her dad would say in his best moments, channeling him, and for some block of spacetime she stood outside herself, behind and just to the right, observing this moment. Neither she nor Ray-Ray nor Dahlia needed the flask or its ashes to feel okay about this.

Commotion, it came from the back. The altar which showcased the flask. "Get your fucking hands off me, I'll punch your goddamn teeth into your colon."

Her brother's voice.

People blinked; they turned to see. Ray-Ray stood by the altar, the flask on the gunwale by his hip, his arms drawn up and fists by his cheeks.

*****

Hadassah's baddies had circled.

Ray-Ray sized them up. Hollywood meatheads, muscles built on Venice Beach with the tensile strength of popcorn. But here they were on the high seas, and here they faced a modern-day rogue, who like his father could touch a sledgehammer to his nose. Here was someone with much, much less to lose, and if they thought he wouldn't use the flask as a weapon, they'd missed a memo.

"Ray!" This, from Sammie behind the microphone. Her eyes, open and hazel too, the fibers of her irises rewoven with a foundering disappointment. He saw this same look that night in the bar when he smashed the nose of that ding-dong comedian. He'd seen this same look in his father's sagged face at the sheriff's office that night when he told the boy he must move on.

But what did she know?

This was not a good world. Not at all, and every tribe needed its warrior, as grotesque and distasteful as he might be, roaming the perimeter at night to keep out the wolves. What did Sammie know of this?

What did she know of the night they stumbled back to her apartment and found the doorknob removed, the bolt lock dismembered and lying on the floor?

While Sammie called the police, Ray-Ray pondered the scene. Nothing had been taken, he thought, which seemed worse. He sat on the couch, surveying the lock on the carpet, then the chessboard where their pieces sat seven moves in. Ray-Ray hadn't memorized the board but knew well enough his black knight on b8 couldn't have jumped clear across the board, to nestle next to Sammie's e2 queen. Whoever had broken into the apartment had sat in this very seat and the inside of Ray-Ray's throat burned, from stomach to mouth. She was the only good thing in his life, a gossamer strand between love and the great big empty. Until they'd connected, he'd spent most of his years adrift on container ships, inhaling diesel particulate matter in engine rooms, passing months in close quarters with strange men, hard men, who like him were unfit for companionship.

He didn't know why but he ran his hands through the cracks between the couch cushions, his fingers abraded by the tweed. But there, a wad of leather, this he fished out. A wallet with the driver's license entombed by a hazy plastic film.

He knew this face.

Ray-Ray had sat through Sammie's routines a dozen times and at some point started watching the audience. At those who laughed, those obsessively fielding texts, those simply present to drink and be around people, even if they were strangers. And this guy in the DMV-grade photo. He inhabited a corner booth a few nights a month eating dinner in the comedy club, sawing through Grade-C steaks with tin flatware. Blue eyes, freckles. Oafish but with a boyish face, the kind one might find pasted on a can of oatmeal.

Ray-Ray noted the address on the driver's license, then folded the wallet and slipped it into his jacket.

Twenty hours later Ray-Ray rolled up on a cottage in the port, the cranes along the quay underlit and transformed into giant hulking monsters against the night sky. His knock on the door yielded no answer so he walked to the garage and extended an unwound coat hanger through a seam at the top of the door and hooked the door release.

Inside the house an oil painting hung above the fireplace. A clown grimaced at him through sloppy brushstrokes but what interested him more was the row of Christmas cards along the mantle.

At the fridge he helped himself to a one-liter bottle of Pepsi. In the den he closed the mauve velveteen curtains — this was a house inherited, he decided, not acquired — and he sat on the couch and laid a .38 special on the cushion. He waited.

The man came home about one o'clock in the dark. He rummaged through the fridge, didn't find what he sought, then crossed through the kitchen into the den and slapped a palm over the light switch. In the dim yellow wash of incandescent bulbs, Ray-Ray saw the world through his eyes: a stranger on the couch, pointing a pistol at him, his feet propped on the coffee table next to the soda bottle.

"I prefer Coca-Cola, just so we're clear," Ray-Ray said.

The man stiffened. "Who the fuck?"

He stepped forward and Ray-Ray shook the pistol at him.

The man took another step forward and Ray-Ray knew another would follow. The countermove was a no-brainer, simple chess. If Sammie opened with a rook on e4 he'd attack c5, no question. The gun went off, the crack hushed by shag carpet and the old-lady curtains.

An iron stain bloomed across the man's plaid shirt. He knelt down, palm cupping his belly.

Ray-Ray picked up the soda bottle and took a swallow. His skin pulsed, his heartbeat drumming through his neck and temples; he couldn't believe what he'd done. "I'll make you a deal," he said. His teeth felt cold in his mouth.

The man paid attention.

"Forget my sister," he said, appraising the kneeling stranger. But the man's eyes were dull little stones, unmoved, and a cold front descended through Ray-Ray's chest. It was a fear, a recognition this man was a special creature, and he knew only a bargain would work. "Forget her, I walk outta here."

The man looked Ray-Ray in the eye. "You shot me."

"Just once."

The stain on the man's shirt had dilated and the blood, syrupy, welled through his fingers and ran along his wrist. A drop fell on the man's boots, and then Ray-Ray noticed: Red Wing 4448s with an aluminum safety toe, the same as his, all four boots in the room stained with machine oil up to the line where the coveralls began. The two looked into one another's eyes and they traded an understanding. Both merchant marines, unwanted and ostracized and banished to existence out at sea, grips in a play that delivered consumer goods to greedy consumers. In different circumstances they might have things to talk about.

Ray-Ray sighed. "I'll drop you at the hospital, then you have amnesia."

He left the man fifty feet from the emergency room doors. In a Wal-Mart parking lot he switched license plates with a moldering RV, then took the eastbound ramp onto Highway 1 and drove until he'd crossed two state lines. Then he contemplated what he'd done.

No hesitation, no hiccups. He'd beaten fear, turn off grief, and quit all those other sticky feelings. It was as if the needle of a record player settled home into a vinyl groove, a bittersweet music released. He thought of his sister's world, filled with gentle people. To live in her world, he had to play by her rules. His mind skipped to the night in the club when he popped her friend in the nose. It was only a stinger, but it didn't matter. She'd disappeared for a few days and canceled him thereafter with a solid week of the silent treatment. Fair? He'd stopped asking that. The world had its shape, people had their shape, and these shapes were die-cast molded and eternally fixed. You had to fit into them. But he did not resent Sammie. If he could keep her in that gentle world, if such a thing could exist with his help, he'd do that for her.

The lines of the interstate highway ticked away under the nose of his van. He pictured his father on the screen, on late-night talk shows, harnessing a best version of himself. Ray-Ray shared that ability with his father but the truth was that he couldn't, especially after this night, maintain a façade. The truth was that feelings were sticky. The truth was that his soul brimmed with resentment and he couldn't pretend anymore and certainly not in front of his sister. It was better not to say goodbye, so he picked a lane and sped east on a planet already revolving into a new dawn.

Sammie looked at him now, the microphone dangling limp in one hand. The sun's long rays slanted across her brow, her eyes, and he could see there her soul and its own sadness, the death of a core belief the world was good, that Ray-Ray was good.

Hadassah's men exchanged nods, it was time, and Ray-Ray held the flask over the edge of the catamaran. Across the boat Sammie closed her eyes on this.

"Ramiro, that's enough." Dahlia pushed through the men, weary, her words pianississimo. She placed a palm on his collarbone and with her other hand took hold of the flask and passed it to one of the men. "Besides," she said, "the third time's a charm."

He didn't understand, he shook his head. "Traitor," he growled. But there was nothing more to muster, nothing left in his heart. He glanced back at Sammie to see if anything had changed and found only unfathomable grief and he knew then, truly knew, that the only time he felt good about himself was when he could see himself through her eyes.

In the narrative of his life he'd arrived at a closing scene, one that'd played out, he imagined, hundreds of times in these lawless seas inhabited by pirates and knaves and those who pursued them. This was the part where the odd man out walked the plank.

Ray-Ray looked at Sammie. He mouthed "I'm sorry" and stepped onto the gunwale of the boat and stepped again into the sea.

The water, purpled under the last touch of the day's light, was warm in its embrace. It cushioned his limbs, lifting him to the surface, and Ray-Ray relaxed into the idea of becoming lost in something much greater than himself. The distant lights of Fort Jefferson appeared and disappeared with the undulation of waves. Behind him people amassed at the gunwale. He could hear their murmurs, feel their gazes, but Ray-Ray refused to look. That was his past, and he let his legs drift up and behind him and began swimming toward the island fort.

But then a splash. Then another.

Ray-Ray turned in the water.

Sammie paddled toward him with one arm, her other arm threaded through a tangle of life preservers. His lips parted. An exhale, something dissolving inside — that otherness. He knew then she loved him, unconditionally, and was only sorry he'd made her prove it.

But Dahlia too. A life preserver folded under an armpit, and there was that stupid fucking breast pump bag, somehow buoyant in the inky sea, and Ray-Ray smiled. "Andalé hermana," he called, and reached for her. "La sacaleche podría salvarnos todavía."

*****

The sand was blue under the lunar glow.

Dahlia sat with her siblings on the shore of an island no larger than a cul-de-sac. It lay smooth and worn, host to neither rock nor tree.

The salt had dried in their hair and on their faces. It was nighttime but the trade winds brought warmth, and the water lapping their toes merely tickled, its temperature the same as their blood. The lights from the island fort twinkled a mile away. To their left and at some distance, a Coast Guard boat steadily moved amongst the shallows, the beam of a spotlight roving over the black surf, failing to notice them.

Dahlia sat in the middle and neither sibling seemed to begrudge this position. She was one of them, finally. Her shoulders fell; she hadn't realized the weight she'd carried.

Sammie put a hand on her knee. "I'm sorry," she said.

"For what?"

"I don't know," her sister said. "For dad."

Dahlia kissed her shoulder. "Everything's okay," she said. And Dahlia knew it would be. The morning would bring boat traffic. They might even swim to Fort Jefferson through the clear tropical waters, in the company of fish and coral. She looked at Ray-Ray but he wasn't of the same mind. His were knees drawn up, his gaze trained on the blued sand. "They got dad," he said.

Dahlia smiled. "Objection," she said. "Lack of foundation." She unsnapped her breast pump bag and folded back its flap and removed a tangle of plastic tubing and suction cups. What remained fell under the dance of moonbeams, playing along a curve of stainless steel and its cambering. She pulled the flask from its nest.

He looked at her; really looked at her.

"No."

"Yes."

"But the one you handed —"

"Another replica. The cheapo kind."

"Ay, chica, you sonufabitch."

Dahlia shrugged.

It was a moment begging for a hug, she knew it, but it wasn't something they'd done, not ever. They could both feel that distance, she knew he felt the same, for in the end they were the same blood, the same heart. She said, "I could lie, Ray, and tell you I like it this way." The tears were just behind her eyes.

"I don't want that," he said, and he opened his arms and took her in and she sobbed an uncontrolled blabber on his shoulder. But he held her there. And then there was Sammie, roping them both into a wonderfully awkward hug, almost on top of them.

Dahlia understood, then, why their father loved this place, its history of piracy, its lawlessness, bathed in the philosophy that one could leave everything behind, those shames and memories jettisoned. Dahlia patted her brother's shoulder and her sister's arm. "Well," she said, "let's destroy the evidence."

The waves, gentle, washed across the shore. They unscrewed the flask and gave their father to the sea.

Shrewd Women

Lynn Hesse

Deloris put two sanitized twenties on the entryway bench for the young man fixing her computer. His real name sounded like the Biblical Barabbas but not precisely. He went by Barr. On his computer fix-it visits, they shared coffee and chatted. People confided in Deloris without prompting, always had, so she wasn't surprised when Barr shared stories about his mother's addiction. The best one described how she stumbled drunk into a revival church meeting, was saved, and later the same night, Barr was born in a rural hospital north of Macon.

One of the hallway overhead lights flickered as Deloris rounded the corner into her office. Seated and hunched over, Barr tapped at the keyboard and bounced, jerking his neck to music coming from his headphone-clad ears.

The computer and the new ergonomic leather chair—not worth the price tag—were compensation Christmas gifts from her son because he had moved to Silicone Valley for an IT job at the beginning of the New Year. Maybe she would fly to see him next Thanksgiving. Atlanta was a long way from the West Coast. It depended on her sciatic pain and COVID.

Behind Barr laid a lumbar pillow Deloris' sister had made with an image of her dog Blue, his ever-present pleading countenance captured. It rested on the cold laminate floor.

She gazed out the window at the leafless Japanese maple Joe had planted after their son's birth. The branches blocked her view of the rest of the overgrown backyard. Everything needed her attention. Deloris picked the pillow up and grunted from the pain in her right knee. Poor Blue. The Beagle-mix mutt's sad eyes had caught her attention at the pound, but not any amount of love had mended that poor animal's spirit. He whined for attention and then cowered for thirteen years until he died days after Joe passed last spring. She didn't blame Blue for leaving her, but she was mad as hell at her husband. Optimistic Joe had promised there was plenty of time left.

Deloris tuned on a lamp behind Barr.

He yanked off his headphones. "Miss Deloris, don't be sneaking up on me.

I have skills I learned in the streets."

"Is that so? Since you're in my home, you might want to tamp down those ninja skills."

Barr offered her a fist bump, and his eyes widened as she hit his knuckles.

"Surprised you, huh? Don't let this withered face fool you. I have a grandson. He keeps me up-to-date." That was a lie. She hadn't heard from Dillion's skinny behind since he won a track scholarship, borrowed money for a down payment on a car, and went off to college.

Barr laughed. "All right then. Your computer is updated, virus-free, and ready to go."

"How much do I owe you?"

"Like I told you before, you're a neighbor so a piece of your delicious pound cake and a cup of coffee."

"Come on then."

He followed her down the hallway into the living room. "Hey, you should let me show you how to invite your family for some screen time. The first forty-five minutes are free."

"Maybe next time. You take the money lying on the table in the entryway on your way out, or else I won't ask you to help again. I'll have to call some geeky stranger into my house. No telling what will happen." She pranced around her modest home like Vanna White, pointing to the forty-eight-inch television and a six-year-old laptop. "They might take all my worldly possessions."

"Okay, I hear you. Did you make my favorite?"

She walked into the galley kitchen with dark wood cabinets and gray granite countertops. "I made my favorite, vanilla with powder sugar sprinkled on top."

Barr rubbed his hands together. "Yes. Cut me a big piece."

She handed him a slab of cake on a saucer and leaned her backside against the counter.

"I'll bake *you* a cake, a big one, if you do me a favor."

"What?" He took a bite standing up.

"I want you to track down the solicitors who keep calling about buying ours, I mean my house. They've been calling multiple times a day for ten years. Both phones and texting. Joe was headed toward his ringing cell when his heart gave out."

"I'll block them for you. No sweat." He inhaled another huge chunk of cake.

"No, my Joe tried that, and they switched numbers. I want their street addresses. Can you do that?" She moved to the cabinet across from the sink, took out two mugs, and poured coffee.

"Yeah, with a special app, but they could be calling from anywhere—not just around Atlanta. Besides, that sounds like you want us to confront somebody. Dangerous business."

"Not us, me. I want to hit them where it hurts, figuratively speaking."

Barr handed her an empty saucer in exchange for a black coffee. "Whoa, you mean payback?"

"It depends on their greed. They'll never see me coming. Don't you know gray-hair women over fifty are invisible unless they're prospective marks?"

*****

Barr had rescheduled the bribe-cake pickup and hadn't shown up.

Finally, Deloris ditched the cake in the trash bin, scrolled through her voicemail, and found the call-back number for the last buy-your-property solicitor. It wasn't showing a company name, but it would do.

The employee's voice was a repeating wave, either too loud or too soft, with a sustained syllable at the end of each phrase. It reminded Deloris of a buzzard circling on an air current, getting closer and closer to its prey. Scavenger. The voice ended his spiel, "We'll buy your house as-is and give you money in the bank for a fresh start."

"Funerals are so expensive nowadays. I'm a widow living alone. Maybe an estimate would be a good idea," Deloris said, adding a quiver in her voice. She wanted them to think she was vulnerable.

*****

Deloris took notes as the *WE BUY AS IS* real estate broker knitted his brow and pointed to the bowed garage ceiling. "That drywall replacement will cost you. Looks like it's an old leak. When was the last time you replaced the roof?"

"After this leak, we had someone come and redo the roof." The roof was fine, but the bowed water-stained panel was one of those repair jobs Joe never got around to fixing.

The salesman shook his head, feigning sympathy. "You'll need to find all the information about the old house repairs before you sell it. Fix everything. It might take months, or my company could make you a fair offer as it is."

"Hum. Out of curiosity, how many elderly homeowners do you talk to in a week?

"It depends. We buy homes from all sorts of people, but maybe five or six a week."

"How do you get most of your leads?"

"Word of mouth, but we hire outside telemarketing companies to advertise for us."

"You mean they call homeowners randomly off a list?"

"Sort of. Many are ready to downsize, or they've lost a spouse. We gather their names and phone numbers from their county's list of property owners. Public records. Some bought their houses in the eighties and nineties, so they're retirement age or older. The upkeep and the yard work are too big for them now. They need a simpler lifestyle."

Deloris suspected they checked the obituaries too.

"You mean a retirement home?"

"Some decide to go that route."

"Would you write down the name of the telemarketing company you use? She smiled her best harmless old-lady smile and handed him her notepad and pencil. "I'd like to call and thank the young woman who gave me your name. Such a sweetheart."

He took her pencil, shifting it several times between his fingers, and printed *Greenhall Marketing* on a notepad. The paunchy middle-aged man probably hadn't used a pencil since elementary school. "I'm not sure you'll be able to track down the woman who helped you. They come and go, but you can leave a message."

She thanked him and tucked the notepad in the pocket of her sweater. "Let's get out of the cold, go back inside, and eat some cake. Cup of coffee?"

He followed her inside. "Coffee would hit the spot, and the smell of your cake would sell any house."

"What do you mean?"

"It's an old trick baking cookies before an open house, so a house smells homey."

"Associates the dream of owning a home with a craving." She gave him a piece of cake.

"Yes, you're a smart cookie." He laughed, took a nibble, and pointed to the cake with his fork. "Wow, you should sell these online."

"Couldn't do that in an old folk's home."

To break the awkward silence, the man asked about a photo hanging on the kitchen wall of a sleepy Dillion with birthday cake icing smeared on his six-year-old face, a cheek propped on one hand.

Two cups of coffee later, a photo album—a delay tactic—she had dug out was open between them on the table. The man yawned. Deloris told the same story twice to make the man antsy. She loved telling how Joe and her first met at an antique car show. She walked to the sink and ran water into the filter pitcher. "I'm still not sure I want to sell. More coffee?"

"No, no. Could I use your restroom? That coffee went right through me." The man stood up.

"Of course. The first door on the right in the hallway." Deloris smirked.

As soon as the bathroom door shut, Deloris took the magnetic tracker from the junk drawer, slipped out the back door, and around to the street. She placed the tracker under the back bumper of the real estate guy's shiny Subaru and returned to the kitchen. She checked her Timex. Exactly three minutes.

Deloris met the man in the living room as he placed a card on the television cart. His pants looked damp. He had washed his hands and, not finding a towel, had wiped his wet hands on the front of his pants.

Her plan to slow him down inside the bathroom had worked.

"Your restroom door sticks, or the lock is haywire. I thought I might need to call for help to get out." He glanced at the living room wall clock. "Shoot, I have another appointment. It was a pleasure meeting you. I hope we can do some business together. I left my card. Remember to ask for Jake." He pointed, an annoying habit of the inarticulate.

Holding the porch banister with one hand to steady herself, Deloris waved goodbye to the salesman. Plan B was in motion. She didn't need Barr's help anyway.

*****

Deloris put on a baseball cap and sunglasses and tracked Jake to a dumpy motel. The app worked like magic. Trash dotted the parking lot, and the faded orange doors and wrought iron railings needed painting. She parked near the man's Subaru and watched. She pretended to be looking down at her cell held against the steering wheel.

Jake knocked on two doors, stayed less than ten minutes at each room, and then proceeded to a third room on the ground floor where a Latino teenager dressed in tight jeans and a tank top came to the door and handed him what appeared to be receipts.

Preparing to follow the smarmy man, Deloris put down her thermos of coffee and egg-salad sandwich, but Jake sat inside his car and made a phone call. The idea for the tracker came from the mystery book's plot on her bedside table. She had bought the tracker at her local electronic store, and the young man behind the counter had installed the app on her phone.

Deloris scribbled the motel's name and the ground-floor room number on a piece of paper. Next time she would bring her binoculars and take photos. She had expected an office of slick sales reps with headsets behind computers, adults, not whatever this was.

Jake drove to the front of the motel, handed an envelope to the clerk, and exited the parking lot. He turned north on North Shallowford Road in heavy traffic. Deloris decided to stay put and returned to her parking spot. Maybe the workers would leave and go home. As she nibbled on a sandwich and drank coffee, two teenagers wearing black and sporting tattoos and piercings came outside for a break and lit up. Still, before they could finish their cigarettes, a young woman, maybe twenty, poked her head out of the doorway and fussed at them in an eastern European language and broken English. They dropped their cigarettes and shuffled back inside. While the door was open, Deloris glimpsed about a dozen young people either cross-legged on a bed or sitting on the carpet using the edges of the bed as their desks, talking into headsets, and typing on computers.

In the late afternoon, the same Latino girl Deloris had spotted earlier left on foot and returned with two bags of burgers. Deloris took a short break and walked to the restroom at a nearby QT. For the next few hours, nothing happened except a couple of adult guests bought junk food from the vending machine.

At dusk, a maintenance man wearing a utility belt strapped around his skinny waist walked by the downstairs units, stared in Deloris' direction, and walked toward her car. He yelled, "Hey, you there with the engine running."

She dropped her coffee in her lap, cussed, and sped away.

The next day Deloris posed as a guest at three other motels that Jake frequented. She ate in their cafes or the adjoining restaurants and took strolls observing the comings and goings. There were three to four rooms in each dumpy motel with young immigrants and probably runaways working long hours and living in the rooms where they worked. Deloris had read about sex traffickers picking up runaways in bus stations but never about exploiting teenagers in this way, like indentured servants.

At the end of the month, a big van drove up, and fifteen or so kids piled in the van, and Deloris followed them to a new casino in Buckhead. Envelopes were handed to each worker as they exited. Two adult overseers smoked cigarettes and talked. They didn't see Deloris' car parked in the shadows with her windows down.

She heard every word.

"I gave them fake I.D.s and just enough cash to get loaded and gamble—enough to feel like winners for one night."

"What if some of them take off?"

"It doesn't matter. We can replace them easily. They know immigration or child protective services will send them back where they came from. That's why most of them stay put." The man in charge turned away from the parking lot and faced his apprentice.

Deloris stuck her head out the window.

"Only had one who wouldn't learn enough English to say his script. We cut him loose. The kids with parents we send them home. Give them a bus ticket if they don't make their quotas."

"That sounds kinda harsh."

"Hey, we give them three squares a day and a roof over their heads. We pay them more than minimum wages. Bonuses. Believe me, this job is safer, better than being out there working as a cook, dishwasher, or prostitute. They age out eventually, but without a GED and or papers, it's tough. Some of them make assistant managers and stick around until they can afford a lawyer and get a work visa."

The youngest white guy threw his cigarette butt on the ground. "I see. What's the story on the Native American kid?"

Deloris felt as if the man asking the questions was staring at her. She ducked back inside the car.

"He ran away…Rez…Doesn't drink. Prefers…herb. These kids need…reinforcement, and we're the proud managers of the highest-producing team around. Jake frick'n loves us." He slapped the other man on the back as Deloris propped her ear on the window's rubber edging.

"The guy who comes around and picks up the maybe-to-yes cards?"

"Yep. We get paid for each lead, but when he closes a deal, we get a cut of his commission. Let's go have some fun." They turned and walked inside the casino, passing a neon sign with an outline of a bikini-clad woman with big breasts holding a cocktail.

*****

Deloris hadn't slept well, and she didn't like texting. She couldn't express her thoughts in clip phrases and silly emojis. She erased her message and started over: "We need to meet. Kids being exploited. This is Deloris."

She hit send, but she couldn't tell if it was delivered. In a couple of minutes, the phone lit up with a message from Barr: "At work. Meet after 5."

Her hand twitched above the phone. She used her index finger to type out: "Tacos on Main Street, Tucker 6 p.m.?"

She received a thumbs-up emoji. Now, she had to convince Barr to help without going to the police.

*****

The taco restaurant was full of loud patrons winding down after their workday. Barr ate his taco without his usual play-by-play banter about whatever side hustle he was into. The last deal Deloris knew about was a computer game he created and was trying to sell.

Deloris read the beer ad on the wall for the third time. "You're quiet. Everything okay?" She scooted around on the cracked booth seat, trying to get comfortable.

"The usual. My sister lost her job. Again. No filter. She spouts off, and they fire her."

"Sorry to hear that."

"Yeah, hard to make rent when I'm feeding her and my little nephew."

"You have a lot on your mind. I understand if you don't want to get mixed up in my plan."

"Just another day in the life of a Black man. Shoot. What you got?"

Deloris told Barr about the setup at the motels, the teenagers being housed, and the conversation she overheard between the manager and his trainee.

"As long as the kids can come and go as they like I'm not sure it's a bad thing. Believe me, there are worse. My sister and I were in and out of the foster-care system. It sucks. I ran away several times myself. The immigrants without green cards would interest ICE, but I wouldn't rat out somebody trying to make a living and survive in a new country." He devoured half of his third taco.

Deloris was glad Barr hadn't suggested going to the police. She wanted to exact her revenge before she called the authorities, but her young friend acted apathetic. "So Jake's not a lowlife?"

"I didn't say that, but maybe he's like everybody else, using the system however he can to make money."

"At the expense of homeless teenagers—runaways and refugees."

"I don't doubt some are illegals, but most probably aren't?"

She must have looked incredulous.

"Hey, some people from other countries are fleeing from genocide, war, and awful poverty, but here, when you're in the projects and if your lucky, your parent works two or three jobs, not a drunk or an addict, you think you know better. You find yourself in the streets," Barr said with conviction. Obviously, he was speaking from experience. She didn't try to argue.

They finished up their meal, and Deloris paid the bill. "I could loan you a few dollars for the rent until your sister goes back to work."

"Naw, eviction isn't knocking on my door yet, but I appreciate the offer."

"Okay, but keep in mind I'd be glad to pay you to do some surveillance work on Jake and his wife."

"How much?"

"What do you make at work per hour?" Deloris asked. Barr worked at a retail sports shoe shop.

"A little more than minimum wage plus commission."

"I'll pay you twenty an hour."

Barr slapped the table. "When and where? I'm off on Thursday and Friday."

*****

On Wednesday, Deloris followed Jake home. In less than an hour, he came out of his two-story brick house with his suburban housewife dressed in name-brand sportswear and three stair-step boys in tow. The youngest was strapped into the latest version of a baby's safety seat. The child fussed and squirmed as his father secured the car seat and his mother railed about the neighbor's garbage can left too long at the curb.

Deloris took photos, wondering if the wife knew how her husband provided for her and her children. Throughout dinner at the pizza restaurant, Jake nodded as the wife talked too loudly about her sister's latest doctor's appointment and kept the children from climbing over the table and grabbing at each other. The youngest boy, maybe eighteen-months-old, turned around in the booth, stuck his bottom in the air, and waved a toy train at Deloris.

She covered her face with her napkin and bumped her helmet-like wig askew.

Jake didn't look up from his cell, and his wife, Heather — Jake called her by name—was asked to control the toddler. She jerked the child into her lap and didn't bother turning around to notice who or what had caught her son's interest.

The married couple never noticed the old lady in the back booth.

*****

Barr called from jail, and Deloris bailed him out. "What happened?" she asked, trying to block out the anxiety she felt standing outside a jail.

"I punched Jake, who had the scared shitless Indian kid backed up against a wall, choking him."

"Did the police arrest Jake too?"

"Are you kidding me? He's white. He told the cops I tried to rob him." A citizen dressed in a suit and an officer walked behind Barr. The cop eyed Deloris and Barr but kept walking up the stairs to the double-glass entrance doors.

"Did you take some photos?"

"Yeah, but Jake told the cops it was his cell phone. They gave my phone to him. By the way, the wife, Heather, was a big-time lawyer. Has an Ivy League education. What she's doing with Jake the snake, I don't know."

"Jeez, let me take you home. I have an idea."

"I'm sitting this one out. I'm done."

*****

The next day after Jake left his house, Deloris knocked on the door. "Mrs. Higley, I'm a client of Jake's."

"You just missed him. Did you try calling him?"

"I would like to talk to you, ask your advice. My friend and your husband had a disagreement, and they fought."

"Men. Jake told me he'd had a nosebleed yesterday. I knew he lied."

Deloris eased herself onto a lower step. She peeked inside the glass-pane panels framing the doorway and spied a foyer large enough to be a sunroom.

"Honestly, I googled you, Ms. Higley, and I know you're a smart, educated woman. A lawyer. I need your help. May I come inside?"

"I can't. I haven't practiced since the birth of Junior, so—"

"Just point me in the right direction. I won't stay five minutes. I promise. I brought some warm pound cake."

"My mother made me pound cake on my birthdays. Before she passed." Heather opened the storm door and invited Deloris inside. She wondered how long it had been since anyone asked Heather's opinion.

Deloris explained why she'd started following Jake and the unexpected results.

"You're describing exploitive behavior towards vulnerable young people. I can't believe…that's not true. I choose not to see. Jake always takes the easiest route. So, you're telling me my husband has this Barr's cell?"

"Yes."

"Hold on. I found an android phone in his coat pocket. Honestly, my youngest was crying, and I hid it away for later. I'm rather good at deciphering Jake's passwords. He has strayed a time or two."

In less than fifteen minutes, Deloris called Barr and entered his password in the andriod cell. Heather saw Barr's photos of her husband choking the Native American teenager and Deloris's surveillance photos of Jake picking up client leads from desperate teenagers housed in cheap motels.

"He actually put his hands on that young man," Heather said.

Deloris sent all the incriminating photos to Heather's email for her to use as leverage.

Heather straightened her shoulders. "Don't you worry. I'll handle this matter. Barr's charges will be dropped, and I'll contact a discreet friend in social services. My family has money, and my husband will be a good boy from now on."

Deloris hugged Heather goodbye. "Thank you. We, women, know how to get things done."

"Yes. Your vigilance pricked and awakened this busy mother's conscience."

Grateful for her years with kind, honest Joe, Deloris waved at Heather, promising to email her the pound cake recipe, and shut the car door.

Who knew a slice of perfect revenge came packaged in a shrewd woman named Heather?

Burnt Tree Hill
Hernán Salvarezza

There's a pulse, a beat to the streets. I can feel it unbound and disjointed tonight. When this happens, good people die. Careers end. Reputations go to hell. Lives are ruined. Far from where I stand, I see a cluster of mirrored-windows buildings rising to the blue sky of Buenos Aires. Close by there's an old, rusted bicycle without wheels, a few burnt candles, some dead flowers, and a lot of pictures of dead people.

This is the way the dead reach out to us.

This is how they mess up our lives.

Every person in this neighborhood is now either afraid or oblivious. They know a bad thing happened last night and something worse is coming. They will avoid the streets for a while. They will avoid Burnt Tree Hill. They will avoid the police. They know that they're on their own and that a detective is but a visiting force that can't change anything. There's no one else here that can help them.

I park my car a few feet from the giant oak that gives this place its name—a massive tree lightning scorched but still stands. It's surrounded by the Riachuelo, a black-water river so polluted nothing survives in it. I suppose the world is like that sometimes, bent but not broken. But how that tree stands, well it defies physics. I stay in the car for a moment, gazing at the picture of my dead wife and kid that I carry with me everywhere I go. They are my rock, my only hope of ever forgiving the man who killed them, and even in death, they bind me to the world of the living.

I get out of my car and see the dead body of a young woman by the tree, and I know in that instant that this case is going to be my last. The air is cold and smells of rot and decay. The temperature must be in the twenties. The body sits with her back to the tree, tied, and with a broken neck. Her eyes are covered with a piece of black cloth. Her mouth is stuffed with brown leaves. Something tells me it was some kind of ritualistic death. Maybe it's the body talking to me—tied to the tree with sections of rope around her neck, wrists, and ankles, as if crucified. I think the murderer took some time to set things up like that. Not only did he break the victim's neck, but he also shot her afterward. That could mean cruelty, fixation, or rage.

I shiver thinking of the damage done here, thinking about the rage that it takes to pull such a crime. Who would play with a body like this? Not a sane person. Not a human being, but a monster. I grab my wife and kid's picture in my coat's pocket and remember they are always close. A resemblance of hope comes back to me.

A solitary squad car arrives. I can see two faces through the white and blue strobe lights. Two cops approach me and I tell them to seal the scene while we wait for the forensic unit. They set up a perimeter. I don't care about sealing the scene, because no one in their right mind is going to come tonight. Not even the crazies dare. It's just us.

Minutes later, the CSU technician arrives. He wears a blue jacket and carries an instrument bag. He takes pictures, picks up dirt samples, and uses Luminol to check for hidden fluids. There's a fine mist settling on the trees, the cars, the houses. In the distance, a dog howls.

"You can pick up the report tomorrow," the CSU tech says. He's a languid, blonde, six- foot-six tower of muscles.

"Okay." I nod but don't care about the report. Right now I don't think he'll find any evidence I can make use of. This is not that kind of case.

"You know about the tree?" he asks.

"Yes. Lightning scorched it," I say.

He sucks his teeth and points his flashlight at the tree. "Lots of innocents died here, Detective Moreno. Lots. Good luck with this case."

I look around it and see at least twenty discernible vertical slashes. Not one case was solved. But this case is different. Everything about this victim screams for justice.

We'll see.

One of the cops tells me they've closed down the scene. He's hinting that I can leave anytime. I agree there's nothing else here for me. There's only a feeling of sadness and waste. It makes me both sad and angry. It must be the brutality of the crime or the loss of a young life, someone's daughter.

It sticks with me.

*****

"Look out for the symbol of decay." Clara says.

In a dream, I see the tree hit by lightning and catching fire. There's a line of people by the tree that walks into the flames. Twenty human beings make a total of twenty victims. And victim twenty-one is Clara. I wake up startled, get out of bed, get dressed, put on a clean white shirt and brown pants, drink a Coke, get my gun, and leave. The streets are empty and silent. Old, decaying two and three story buildings crop up here and there with graying fronts and cracked walls. Some storefronts, pawnshops, hardware stores, and car shops show up in between the buildings and empty, ruined lots around the corners. The outskirts of this sprawling city shows two faces. One is thriving and full of life. The other is so dark it scares people off the streets. This is a place where nobody is enough of a fool to leave home during the dark of night, except myself. I don't mind a bit of danger.

I have to talk to Clara's parents, but first things first. I'm taking a second look at the crime scene. The sun is coming up, and there's enough light to get around. I move beyond the yellow tape. The tree looks the same. The body has been removed and there's nothing left on the ground, nothing I can see. I look around, and I see someone has added yet another knife mark to the tree. Twenty-one vertical slashes, not just twenty like it was yesterday. Someone wasn't afraid to come over and mark the tree, I guess.

I spend a few hours driving around the neighborhood. People start crawling out of their homes by 07:00 am. Traffic picks up and everything looks normal again, it ever will. I find Clara's former home and park the car across the street. The smell of grilled meat and burnt wood comes out of a small barbeque place by the street corner.

Neighbors walk by carrying lit candles. There's a small altar of pictures and burning candles and flowers by the door of Clara's former home. I wait to see if someone shows up, someone doing something a bit different than the rest. I'm looking for aggressive, crazy, grieving, or obsessed people. I look for anything and anyone who might seem…different.

I get out of the car and make it across the street. Homemade signs cover the trees with pictures of missing children. I stand by Clara's door and observe the altar people have built for her, while I rap on the door and wait. A few hushed voices get to me from the inside of the house. The door opens just an inch. A tall man hides behind it. His name is Victor Suarez, Clara's father. He's got dark circles under his eyes, and he looks weary. I can tell he's hurting.

"I'm Detective Moreno."

Clara's father nods and understands. He understands everything is so final and decisive. He understands he'll never see his twenty-one-year-old daughter again. So, I try to be cautious with the words I choose to question him.

"I'd like to ask you a few questions."

"Yes, of course," he says.

The house is spare. The entrance leads to the living room and the kitchen. It's small and packed. Every piece of furniture is cramped into the apartment to make the most of it. I see a table, some chairs, a big TV screen on the wall, and a couch nearby. Clara was an only daughter. So, this couple has lost their only child. I'm careful. They're heartbroken, and they'll always be, but time may make the pain less excruciating.

A woman shows up in the living room. It's Ana Rua, Clara's mother. She sees me and sneers, and I can tell she's angry. Her hair is a mess: long bangs, black as raven wings, but a shock of white on the top. I wonder if the white hair is new, from the pain and stress of losing your only child. Even though I wonder about a lot of things, I don't ask questions right away, I like to wait.

I start easy.

"How are you holding up, Mrs. Suarez?" I say.

Victor Suarez is hurting. He shrugs his shoulders and looks down at the floor, and I see a face of a million wrinkles.

"We're holding up," Victor says.

"A beautiful altar people have built out there," I say.

Ana Rua stifles a tear. "It's okay."

I see a lot of pain every day. And our only tools to treat that pain are out there on the streets. But every day, out there, things are getting worse, making it next to impossible to see the silver lining.

"Do you know of any problems or enemies your daughter had?"

She shakes her head no.

"No, she was lovely," Victor says. "Everybody liked her."

"What about her friends? Any recent fights? Relationship trouble?"

"No, not that I know of." He lights a cigarette and takes a pull—blows smoke that surrounds him like a blue snake about to bite.

"Catalina hated her," Ana says. She's been crying. Her eyes are red.

"They hated each other," Victor says, shaking his head.

"What's her last name?" I ask.

"Addario," Ana says, clearly angry. "That bitch."

"Any problems at home?" I ask, and make a mental note to investigate Catalina Addario. "Anything she could've reacted to?"

"No. We were a happy family." Victor says.

"How about work?"

"Work is fine. I'm a supervisor at the meat factory on Amancio Alcorta Avenue."

"Anyone new in her life? Any new hobbies?"

"She was going to church," Ana says, shaking his head. "What a waste of time."

I nod in silence, biting my tongue. I too understand that hoping that God will protect your children is nothing but a fantasy. I want to tell them that God has forsaken us long ago, but I don't.

"What church?" I ask, and pull out my notepad.

"San Bartolome on Saenz and Tabare."

"What about Burnt Tree Hill?" I jot down a few notes. "Does that place mean anything to you?"

"It's that damn tree," Victor says and starts rubbing his hands nervously. "People are superstitious. Some are crazy. They pray to it. They light candles. It's insane."

"Do you believe any of it?"

Ana nods in agreement as Victor says:

"It's all bullshit."

I spend another twenty minutes talking to them, collecting what I can as they fill me in on the rest of Clara's life. She was in her last year at the local college, majoring in economics. She lived with her parents, had a job at a local bookstore, and did voluntary work around the neighborhood. She was a nice girl, and everybody loved her. It's hard to find fault in a girl like that. But I have to dig anyway. Dig deep this time. And digging deep means questioning Catalina Addario and finding out what was her real relationship with Clara and what they did at the church. What was going on only time will tell.

*****

The next morning, I get a call from Carlos Jimenez, the forensic team leader. The office is busy, everyone is running around. He tells me that the bullet we found in Clara's chest is a 9mm, and it belongs to a police-issued handgun. The lot the bullet belonged to was registered as being issued to the Buenos Aires City Police.

Jimenez says it's going to take a while, but he can pinpoint the precinct the bullet was delivered to. I hang up and call our tech team and ask for Clara's phone call records going two weeks back.

I leave my desk, get out of the station, and get in my car. I drive for about ten minutes and find San Bartolome, the church that doesn't look like a church, more like a community center. Grey and green paint up front, a few windows on the top. People are coming in and out carrying boxes with supplies, food, and clothing. A lonely kid, that must be a twelve-year-old, is selling mate and torta fritas, lost in a sea of people. I park by the Pompeya's bridge—an early twentieth-century concrete monster—and make it across the street thinking of how many unsolved murders have taken place by the bridge. Inside the church, I find a blind man by a desk listening to a tango radio station. I ask for the man in charge and the blind man says "End of the hallway to the right. Deacon Eduardo is waiting for you."

The man in charge isn't a Deacon and he isn't related to any churches I know of. He's short, languid, poorly dressed, and has gray eyes. He sports a three-day beard. He strikes me as a social worker. I don't ask. I let it slide, for now.

"How well did you know Clara Suarez?" I ask.

"She used to help here, once a week." he says, shaking his head.

"Did she have any friends?"

He scratches his goatee. "No friends, just the regulars."

"Regulars?" I shrug.

"The people we help here," Deacon Eduardo says, pointing toward the front of the church, where the pews are.

"Anyone new or different among them?" I ask.

"They all seem harmless to me," Deacon Eduardo shrugs his shoulders.

"Tell me about them. I need to know."

"There's a woman from Venezuela. She used to come here with her six-year-old son."

"Name?"

"Alicia Gutierrez. The kid's name is Antonio. We call him Tonio."

"Anyone else?" I ask while I write the names down.

"Some strange-looking guy. Young. Early twenties."

"What's so strange about him?" I look at Deacon Eduardo's face, fishing for a tell.

"He's always distracted, aloof."

"What else?"

"He is always talking about the tree."

It takes me a moment to connect his words to my investigation, but when I do, my mind opens up and I feel I'm onto something.

"Burnt Tree Hill?"

He snaps his fingers, his eyes light up. "Yes. That damned tree."

"What do you know about it?"

"Not much. Some people believe in God, others in something else,

Here, people believe in the tree."

"What do you mean?"

He looks over both of my shoulders, making sure no one is listening to us. "Word on the street is people pray to it. They ask for favors. They ask for luck or a change. Nothing unusual. People are crazy about beliefs. They hide behind them. Every belief system or ritual is more irrational than the previous one."

"What's this kid's name?" I ask, putting my notepad and my pencil back in my pocket.

"We don't ask for personal data. Clara must've known."

"Did you see Clara talking to this guy the night she died?"

"I couldn't say." Deacon Eduardo shakes his head. "I was in my office."

"Anything going on between them?" I ask.

"Not that I know of. Clara was a sweetheart. She was lovely. She listened to people no matter how crazy they sounded."

"Do you know where I can find this guy?"

"No. We don't ask for personal data."

I don't like the way this case is going. The people I need to talk to are scared and not talking. An odd character and possibly obsessive young man was a friend of Clara's. I can already see how it all went down, and I hate the fact that we couldn't do anything to stop it from happening. These obsessive types are always dangerous. People that had lost their natural restraint to avoid conflict. They'll go to any lengths to justify their thinking. To make themselves feel right and "save face", but it always ends up badly. They're always tagged as crazy people, even though half of them are not crazy or deranged. They're lost and lonely and emotional and take it too far. Now… how do I find this young Casanova?

*****

Back at the precinct, I talk to the station's technical department and ask for Clara's phone records. They patch me through to the phone company and I get a CDR, a call detail record, of the last week of Clara's phone calls. I check the night of the murder and find one phone number belonging to Daniel Figueroa. I look him up in the system and find an address. I could try to call him, but I choose to visit him instead. Again, danger never bothered me.

Figueroa's ashen-yellow building stands between a deli and a shoe repair store. Metallic planks and signs cover the bottom floor windows. Inside, a wooden counter is topped by small packages and cardboard boxes. A man behind the packages talks to his girlfriend on the phone. He's fat and has gray hair and brown eyes. His white shirt looks about to explode.

I show him my badge. He stops talking and puts the phone down.

"I'm looking for Daniel Figueroa," I say. "He's about twenty-two. Looks distracted most of the time."

"Yeah. The kid. He's on 5-A."

The elevator takes about a minute to come down. The hallway is packed with cardboard boxes. Most of it is contraband. I don't mind people being entrepreneurial. I'm looking for a killer, not for contraband.

I rap on the door. It opens an inch or two. Two black eyes stare at me. I can't see much of the face behind the door. I'm careful. I don't want to scare this mouse away.

"I'm Detective Moreno," I say. "I need to speak to Daniel Figueroa."

"I'm Daniel."

He opens the door. I see he's skinny and emaciated. He wears a green hoodie and blue jeans.

"I just need to talk for a bit. Is that alright with you?"

He looks down and frowns. "I guess."

"It'll be a minute. I promise. May I come in?"

"C'mon in," he says and steps back.

Inside, the room is Spartan. I can see a gray couch and a table where a TV used to be. Cardboard boxes go around the couch and into the back. I remind myself that I don't care about the contraband. All I care about is Clara's murder.

"Do you know this girl?" I say and produce a picture of Clara.

He nods.

"Her name was Clara," I say. "She was killed a few nights back."

He sighs and responds,

"Awful."

"How do you know her?"

"Church."

The kid clams up pretty fast. I'm facing a non-talker. I'm not sure what to do next. I need him to share something I can use, but I don't want to antagonize him, not this early in the conversation.

"What do you know about her?"

"She was good. Nice, with people."

I nod while I think about my next move, my next words.

"Do you know any of her friends?"

"No."

"No other girls at the church?"

He takes a moment. He's thinking, remembering. Finally, he says,

"No."

"What about that Addario girl?"

"Catalina?"

"Yes, Catalina. Do you know her?"

"They were good friends. Don't know what happened between them."

"What do you do for a living, son?"

"I sell stuff."

"The stuff in the boxes? Who gets you that stuff?"

"The guy downstairs."

"What about Burnt Tree Hill?" I say, looking straight into his eyes. "What do you know about the legend?"

"The tree is sacred to some. They think it can grant graces. That it solves problems."

"For a price?"

"Yes. There's a price to pay."

"What is that?"

"I don't know. Everyone is different."

"Who can I talk to about the tree?"

"Mother Lucia. 2123, La Plata Avenue. She knows things."

My cell phone rings and I take the call. It's Detective Orellana. He tells me there's been a hit in the DB. Clara came up. She's mentioned in a prostitution case. I tell him I'll be there next and hang up.

"What about your phone call with Clara last night? What did you talk about?"

Daniel stares into my eyes like there's something he wants to say but he can't. "Relationship stuff, nothing serious."

"Was she distressed?"

"No," Daniel shakes his head and sighs. "I mean she seemed normal. I never expected this. How can she be gone? It's not fair."

"Did you talk about anything important?" I press.

"No. She just wanted to know about that damned tree," Daniel says, his eyes brimming with tears. "She called me to talk about the damned tree."

*****

Back at the station, I check the file Orellana gave me. It was Sara Romero's case. She was killed in an apartment in Saavedra Park, up north. The CI informed her that the pimp killed her. The man was condemned for the murder. The CI's name is Catalina Addario. Clara Suarez is mentioned in the case as a witness but was never linked to the legal process.

I take a break from the file to think things through. How was Clara related to this? The file didn't say anything about her. It's just a mention. The rest has been omitted. I wonder how she got herself into this. Maybe she was being a good friend to Catalina Addario. And Catalina was forced to tell. Maybe she mentioned Clara, and the detective in charge of the case dismissed her for some reason. I look him up and find Mateo Garcia. He's retired. There's a phone number and an address. I throw my empty cup of coffee in the trash bin, shut the computer down, and leave. It's around midnight and I realize it's too late for a visit.

*****

My cell phone rings in the middle of the night. I hesitate, but I end up picking it up. Inside, I'm praying it's not another murder.

"Hello?" I say.

"It's a message from Mother Lucia," a man with a deep voice says. "She wants to know when you're going to come to see her."

"I was planning on doing that tomorrow," I say.

"Mother Lucia is waiting for you right now," the man says.

"I'll be there in a half hour."

I wonder how Mother Lucia knows I was about to contact her. Someone must be talking. Someone is trying to push me in the right direction. Mother Lucia is a known spiritual and community leader. I'm the detective in charge. I feel I'm doing something important, after all this time chasing dead ends. I get out of bed and get dressed and leave the house. The streets look lonely and deserted. The silence engulfs me. The wet concrete smell is strong. I reach 2123 La Plata Avenue and park. There's a man, tall and languid, waiting by an open building door. I walk to him and notice he's holding a cane and wearing sunglasses.

"She's waiting for you," he says in a deep, booming voice.

"Let's go see about that."

I walk through a narrow corridor covered in house plants. The walls and the floor are carpeted by green foliage. The scent of jasmine gets to me. I see a few wooden chairs at the other end. A patio opens up at the end of the corridor, and I see more plants, more green, more flowers. A woman is standing by a small water fountain in the middle of the patio. She's small and skinny. Her hair is white, and her eyes are blue. An amber light bulb hangs from a wire, lighting the fountain and leaving the other half of the patio in the dark.

"I'm Detective Marcos Moreno," We shake hands. Her hand is tiny, fragile, and cold "Nice to meet you."

"People tell me there's been another murder." Mother Lucia looks me in the eye, frowning, worried. I can tell there's something beyond the murder bothering her.

"I can't discuss the case, but yes."

"There's power e in Burnt Tree Hill, Detective."

I nod but don't say a word. She says,

"Old magic. It's been around for a long time," she stands, slowly walks toward me, grabs my face, and stares into my eyes "And it's not going anywhere unless we end it."

"Who is supposed to take care of it? Us? The police?"

"Someone will come and fight the evil that this tree represents."

I wonder who that person will be. And under what pretense will he or she operate? Police officer, pacifier, believer?

"The police must find out who the murderer is," I say.

"I just wanted to meet you, Detective. It's your case, I understand. But there are other forces at play here. Once you meet these forces and learn how they relate to each other you'll be in the position to vanquish evil."

"We'll solve the case. I promise we'll find this killer."

"Are you having dreams, Detective?"

"Dre…drea…dreams." I hadn't stuttered since I was in high school.

"Dreams," Mother Lucia says, "about a line of men and women walking into the fire."

*****

The next morning, I drive to Detective Mateo Garcia's place. He lives in Boedo, near San Lorenzo Park. The house has a tiny, but beautiful front yard. I reach the porch and rap on the door. A six-foot-three man steps out. He's wearing a San Lorenzo football jersey and drinking a Quilmes beer. He needs a decent shaving, and his hair looks greasy and unkempt.

He nods but doesn't say a word. It's my turn.

"I'm Detective Moreno." I show him my shield. "I'm working on the Clara Suarez case. I need to ask you a few questions if you don't mind."

I shut up and wait. He knows exactly what I'm doing. And I know most of his responses will be deflective at best. Still, I have to press him for answers.

"What can I do for you, Detective?" he asks.

I choose to be direct. Not to beat around the bush.

"I was looking into one of your cases and I found a mention of Clara."

"What case?"

"The death of Sara Romero."

"The hooker," Detective Garcia says, and his face clouds over like a coming storm.

I take it slow. I don't want to rush things.

"Yes. Your CI reported that she was killed by her pimp."

"Yes. Sara was a good girl. Young and good-hearted. Her pimp was a vicious animal. He killed her for no reason. It was a slam dunk trial. Don't have a clue where he is now."

"You mentioned Clara in your file. What was that about?"

"Well. The girl was the first on the scene alongside my CI."

I take notes and nod. I'm thinking about what to ask next.

"Why wasn't she mentioned in the trial?"

"Well, she was a minor."

"A witness."

"Sure but, she was so young and had nothing to do with it. When I arrived on the scene I saw her with the neighbors and asked a few questions, and that was all. But my CI mentioned her and I had to include her in the case. Then the DA decided not to present her testimony."

"So, the DA ruled her out."

"Sort of."

"What do you mean?"

"I mean by the time he got involved it was obvious she had nothing to do with the murder."

"But that wasn't the case."

"Clara and your CI Catalina Addario were close friends. They had met at the community center, probably where Catalina went for help. Clara was more than just a bystander."

He nods.

"I did my best to keep her safe," he says. "It cost me my badge."

"Who else was involved?"

"That's all I'm going to say."

I look at him and wonder why this man would go through such shit to hide a teenage girl's testimony.

"Thanks for your help," I say.

He nods and waves me out.

"One more question, Mateo. What do you know about Burnt Tree Hill?"

"I know people are crazy about that damn tree. It's just folklore."

I nod at him, thank him, and leave. My car smells of cigarette smoke and beer. There were a couple of hamburger boxes and a can of Red Bull on the passenger seat. On my way back to the station, I realized I had to get in touch with the DA to clarify a few things about Clara's involvement in Sara's case. So, Catalina was a prostitute and not Clara's friend, but someone she knew from the community center. Catalina needed help and went to Clara for it. That's how Clara got involved with the wrong people in Sara's case. And did they have anything to do with her death? An old grudge maybe? Clara's mother said Catalina hated her. The next logical step would be Catalina, but I need to talk to the DA and clear a few things first.

Back at the station, I find Clara's mother, Ana Rua, waiting by my desk. I know she has something to say. Something she had kept from me. I sit and give her a curt nod.

"How are you doing, Ana?" I ask.

"Better," She looks up and runs a hand through her hair. "I think."

I have to find the DA before he leaves the office so I don't have much time on my hands. But this is important, so I take a cautious step.

"What can I do for you?" I ask.

"There's something I have to tell you."

"What about?"

"It's about Victor. My husband."

"Is he alright?"

"Yes, he's fine. But it's about him and Clara. They had a hard time lately. They were always fighting."

"It's common with teenagers," I say, nodding.

"Yes, but…" she hesitates. "It's something else."

I nod and look at her. She has a face of regret.

"He was arrested recently."

"I see. Is he in the system?"

"I don't think so. It was all dropped. I don't think it was even a formal arrest."

"What was it about?"

"She had a girlfriend. A prostitute."

I lean back, nodding. I'm beginning to understand.

"And the cops arrested her?"

"She died."

"What was her name?"

"Sara Romero."

I jot down her name for emphasis, but I can't believe my ears.

"Are you sure that was her name?"

"Yes, that was her name."

"How did she die?"

"It was an overdose."

"What about your husband? What was he arrested for?"

"He found her. They arrested him on the spot."

"I understand. What about Clara? Why was she having trouble with him?"

"Well, Victor tried to steer her away from Catalina. And she found out recently about Sara. So, he called him a hypocrite and then they stopped talking to each other."

"Why didn't you mention any of these before?"

"I can't talk when he's around."

I check my wristwatch and see I have a half hour before the DA leaves the office for the day.

"Anything else you can think of?" I say, worrying.

"No. That's it."

"So your husband was never convicted? He was cleared of all charges?"

"Yes."

"Then I don't think we have to worry about this," I say, smiling. "Go home. If something else comes up, let me know."

*****

Victor Suarez, Clara's father, was involved in the murder of Sara Romero and was finally cleared of all charges. At the same time, his daughter Clara was mentioned in the case and then released from the judiciary process, even before it started. But how is this all related to Clara's death?

I phone the DA hoping for an interesting conversation.

"Clara was spared of any participation in the trial because at the time she wasn't necessary for the process," DA Rodriguez says. "And it was a court ruling."

"What about Victor Suarez?"

"Who?"

"Sara's boyfriend."

"He was cleared of all charges," Rodriguez says.

"I understand he beat up the pimp."

"Yes, there was some of that."

"And Sara died of an overdose?"

"Yes."

"But she was brutally beaten up before."

"Yes."

"So, she was forced to take the heroin that killed her by her pimp."

"Correct."

"And the pimp?"

"He died a few weeks later. The whole trial was dismissed by the judge."

"Another overdose?" I ask.

"No. It was suicide."

"Was he suicide watch? Mentally ill?" I switch from the phone receiver to the speaker.

"No."

"Did you have any hints about his choice?"

"He wrote a letter, short and hard to follow, incoherent."

"What was it about?" I ask, curious.

"About a tree," DA Rodriguez says. "About the tree at Burnt Tree Hill."

*****

While driving, I try Catalina Addario's phone and get a disconnected tone. The only address I have for her is an apartment on Colombres 4754. The building looks decayed and ashen, with a rough-soil front yard, and a lot of missing windows. People on the street come and go. A young man, with his face scared by smallpox, stands by the door smoking. I walk across the street and make it inside. The lobby is empty. I get to the third floor, apartment C and rap on the door. After a minute or so, a small person, about four-feet tall that looks kind of lost opens the door. He's got a pot belly, brown eyes, and a receding hairline. The man steps back and Catalina stands by the door. She's got blue eyes and blonde hair, and her skin looks parched.

"I'm detective, Moreno," I say and already dislike this girl. She's everything opposite to Clara.

"What do you want?" Catalina asks, clearly annoyed.

"I need to talk about Clara."

"What about her?"

"How come you hated her?"

"She was a hypocrite," she says, both her hands up in midair, reinforcing her words. She seems to talk with her hands a lot "Her whole family is."

"Why do you say that?"

She looks at me with the eyes of a predatory creature. I'm not sure if she wants to get rid of me or torture me to death. I wait, in silence.

Catalina blows her bangs out of her eyes and sighs. "She was always acting like a saint, but she was a whore."

"How come?"

"Nothing, never mind."

"What about her father, Victor?" I ask. "What is he like?"

"He's worse than Clara was."

"What do you mean?"

"He used to be a pimp. He was involved in a crime."

"A pimp?"

"Yes, he was Sara's lover and pimp."

I finally get a clearer picture of the Suarez family. Victor used to be or wanted to be, Sara's pimp. Then Sara Romero died after getting beat up by her pimp, and a couple of weeks later he killed himself. But what happened to Victor meanwhile?

"You were involved in the trial," I say.

"Yes. It went nowhere."

"What do you mean?"

"Sara deserved better. She deserved to live. But everyone around her wanted to take advantage of her."

"Do you know who killed Clara, Catalina?"

She shakes her head; angry tears roll down her face.

"Was Clara a prostitute?"

"Whenever she needed the money, she found the clients."

"Where?"

"With Daniel Figueroa," she says and pulls out from her pocket a picture of Clara with him.

*****

I drive to Daniel Figueroa's place and park across the street from his building. There's a small plaza where kids gather and compete in Cumbia and Trap battles. When I get out of the car, I see Daniel walking out of the building, carrying a gym bag, and looking sketchy as usual. I walk across the street, and when he sees me, he drops the bag and runs.

I run behind him yelling, "I just want to talk to you!", but he doesn't stop.

He runs through the yard behind the building and makes it through a high wooden fence into the next lot. I climb the fence, jump and land in mud and fall on one knee. I get up and look around. Daniel is nowhere to be found. I run to the other end of the lot and see the street across is empty.

Daniel was in love with Clara, obsessed maybe. He saw her every other day at the community center. He was also her pimp. One day those two worlds collided, obsession and profit, and Daniel couldn't take it anymore. He let out his rage and told Clara to stop hooking up. When she said no, he killed her.

I walk back to my car and drive to the station. I need to collect my thoughts. I reach my desk and use the phone to put an APB on Daniel

Figueroa. I sit down and close my eyes and imagine taking a vacation. I open my eyes when I hear a voice calling my name.

"Detective." Daniel Figueroa says.

I look up.

"Daniel."

"I'm ready to talk."

"Sit down."

I grab my phone and cancel the APB. Then I turn to Daniel. I ponder my options. Daniel Figueroa is giving himself up. He says he wants to talk. I could take him to one of the rooms we use for questioning, but I would rather talk to him here, by my desk. Detective Orellana is around, so I ask him to sit in and listen to Daniel. He takes a seat beside him.

"I'm going to record this conversation if you don't mind," I say, and turn on my voice recording app.

"Sure," Daniel says,

"Why were you running?"

"I thought you were going to arrest me?"

"Why would you think that?"

"Because I was Clara's boyfriend."

"And pimp."

"No. I never needed money," Daniel says, rubbing his chest, anxious "I did well with the contraband stuff you saw at my place. But I never hurt her. I loved her."

I wondered how a man can love a woman and be his pimp. "Did you kill her?"

"No!"

"Who did?" I ask and wait.

"Tell me about the night Clara died. Where were you?"

"I was at the community center, man." He stands up, walks in circles around my desk, then he sits again "I went looking for her."

"Why?"

"I was going to propose to her."

"Marriage?"

"Yes."

"And then what?"

"I had my things ready. We were going to move in together."

"Did anybody see you?"

"Deacon Eduardo. I talked to him."

I nod at Orellana. He grabs the phone and calls the community center. Meanwhile, I wait and ask Daniel if he wants a cup of coffee. He shakes his head, and we wait for a little while, not saying a word. Orellana looks at me and nods. He says the alibi checks out.

"Well, Daniel. What happened after you saw Deacon Eduardo?"

"I called Clara."

"What did you talk about?"

"She told me she was with her dad at Burnt Tree Hill. She was scared."

"Her dad… and Burnt Tree Hill?"

"Did I stutter? Are you going to arrest that son-of-a-bitch or what? We were going to have kids, ya' know?"

"Okay, Daniel, look… Thank you. We appreciate it. We're letting you go—"

"Wait! Aren't you going to find—"

"You can go. Let me do my job, and before the sun comes up, I think we can put this case to bed."

Daniel stood and held out his hand. I shook it.

We let Daniel go and focus on Clara's family. Either Victor or Ana is keeping something from me. I need to find out what it is. I leave the precinct and drive toward their home. I get a phone call while on my way to the Suarez family house.

"We didn't mean to kill her." Detective Garcia says.

"What in the hell are you talking about?" I ask.

"We took her to the tree to scare her. I'm sure he didn't mean to kill her."

"Who did, Mateo? Who?"

"Victor."

"Stay home. I'm on my way."

Garcia' place is darkened. A deep shadow covers the front yard and the steps to the house. The door is open. I pull my gun out and walk in. There's a bottle of whiskey on the floor. Ahead, I find former Detective Garcia, in the living room, sitting in front of the TV with a bullet hole in his head; his .38 Smith & Wesson lies on the carpet nearby.

My cell phone rings. It's Carlos Jimenez. He tells me that the fingerprint found on the bullet casing belongs to Mateo Garcia. I call it in as I leave the house. With Garcia dead, Victor Suarez is the only person left to pay for Clara's death. I drive through a busy street, put on the siren, and cut through traffic without care. I reach Victor Suarez's place and see his wife, Ana, standing by the door. I stop the car and she points south.

"He's waiting by the tree," she says.

*****

I reach Burnt Tree Hill. From afar, I see Victor standing by the tree, beside the shrine that the community built for Clara. I tread lightly.

"I know everything," I say, pointing my gun at him.

"She was becoming a whore," Victor says "Hanging around with so many of them at the community center. She finally became like them. Can you believe that? My daughter… a whore. That weird guy Daniel Figueroa was her pimp. I just wanted to talk to her. I didn't mean to kill her. I hit her and she fell and broke her neck on the fall. I didn't do it! The tree did!" He wipes away snot and tears, and points at the tree." I tied her to the tree to make it look like a ritual… She wouldn't listen to me. She wouldn't stop!"

A sob wells up in his body. "I hate myself. I. Hate. Myself."

"Put the gun down," I say.

He aims the gun at his head. He is crying, trembling with fear. I've seen this before. The man who killed my wife and daughter did the same thing before putting a bullet in his cranium.

"I never tried to hurt her," Victor says. "But a whore?"

"I'm sure you didn't," I say and put my gun in my holster. "You're a good man."

"I just wanted her to learn!" he screams and hits his chest with his fist. "I wanted her to be a decent young woman!"

He's on his knees now.

"I just wanted to be better," he says. "I didn't abuse her. I never hurt her. It was that damn tree. It turns people into monsters! It was always the tree!"

I think he's ready. I wait for the worst to happen. I run toward him, and risk my own life to stop him from taking his own. Time halts, comes to a stop, and everything happens in slow motion. The speckles of his blood reach my face before I realize a shot has been fired. I grab him as he falls into my arms. The sound of gunfire echoes in my ears. I put him down on the ground and think about loss and regret and all the lives ruined already.

I stand under storm clouds. The winter season is upon us. People gather around me. "I'm a police officer," I say. From the distance, I can hear my car's radio. It's a homicide call. It must be another murder case I've been assigned to.

The howling wind blows out the candles around the tree and the pictures of Clara fly in midair and the mystery is finally over.

But not the pain her death caused. That pain gets added to my photo album of darkness. That pain remains.

The Usual Unusual Suspects

Scott Talbot Evans won the 2021 Script Studio & RAFAS present Scriptitude competition, the 2021 GEVA Theater/Writers & Books 2 Pages/2 Voices competition, and second place in the New Yorker caption contest #839. His short story appears in *Shoreline of Infinity 28*. His poems are published in *Poetry Salzburg Review 39*, *Straight On Till Morning #5*, and *Samjoko Magazine Fall 2022*. He is working on his fifth book, *Super Special Dogs in Rio*. For more info visit: https://scotttalbotevans.wixsite.com/scott-talbot-evans
https://www.amazon.com/Love-Police-Scott-Talbot-Evans-ebook/dp/B0B6QD48CW
https://scotttalbotevans.wixsite.com/scott-talbot-evans
https://scotttalbotevans.wixsite.com/super-special-dogs
Twitter @FunnyTidalWave

Edward Sheehy has had various pieces of short fiction published in *The Boston Literary Magazine*, *The Write Launch*, and *Lake Street Stories* (Flexible Press). A selection of his poetry was featured in *Jerry Jazz Musician* magazine celebrating the music of Miles Davis. He was baptized in the Delaware River before the eyes of the Lord and several catfish. He lives in Minneapolis.

Robb T. White is a Midwest USA writer of genre fiction, especially crime and noir. *Betray Me Not*, a collection of revenge tales, was selected by the Independent Fiction Alliance as a Truly Best Independent Book of 2022. Besides the *Haftmann and Jarvi* private-eye novels, he has four collections of short stories. *When You Run with Wolves* and *Perfect Killer* were named finalists by *Murder Mayhem & More* for Best Crime

Books of 2018, 2019. His short *Inside Man* was selected for *Best American Mystery Stories 2019*.

Further details can be found at:

https://tomhaftmann.wixsite.com/robbtwhite.

He appeared in *Crimeucopia – As In Funny Ha-Ha, Or Just Peculiar* with *Danny Deluca's Bridge*.

Robert Petyo is a Derringer award finalist whose stories have appeared in small press magazines and anthologies, most recently in *The Black Beacon Book of Mystery, Asinine Assassins, Now There Was a Story, Whodunit, Mickey Finn 21st Century Noir,* and *Stonewall Detectives.* He has also appeared in the following Crimeucopias – *We're All Animals Under the Skin, Careless Love,* and most recently in *Strictly Off The Record.*

He writes primarily mysteries, but also SF, fantasy and horror and an occasional mainstream piece. He lives in Northeastern Pennsylvania, is happily married, and is recently retired from the Postal Service, which allows him more time to read and write. Unfortunately, there never seems to be enough time to read and write.

Brian R Quinn is an Emmy Award winning TV news journalist living in Manhattan who has spent the last thirty years covering news in New York City and overseas. Much of his work is rooted in those experiences. His publication credits include: *The Rabbit Hole, Figwort, The Chamber, Tender Fury,* and *Adelaide.*

Brian can be found at https://www.brianrquinn.com and on Twitter @BrianRQuinn_

Orca Green is a young writer from Hong Kong. Since 2014, she has been successfully writing in such diverse genres as Science Fiction, Fantasy, Romance, and Campus Life. Her work has received recognition from various groups, including the *Future Summer Popularity Award*. She is also the founder of *SFPNS*, a writing community that aims to provide support and resources to emerging writers. Her ability to write in both

English and Chinese has allowed her to reach a wider audience and showcase her versatility as a writer.

For more information go to https://my01lifestyle.wordpress.com/ — or follow Orca via Instagram *@mad01freak* — and on Twitter *@starfeather1234*

Robert Parker has turned to writing mystery novels and stories after years of publishing nonfiction. *The Zoom Room* is his first mystery short story. You can find him at:

https://rparker9999.wixsite.com/robertparkerwriter.

Brandon Barrows is the author of several novels, most recently 3rd LAW: MIXED MAGICAL ARTS, a YA urban fantasy, and over one-hundred published stories, mostly crime, mystery, and westerns. He is a two-time Mustang Award finalist and a 2022 Derringer Award nominee. He is also the editor and driving force behind *Guilty Crime Magazine* (https://www.guiltycrimemag.com/) – also find out more at http://www.brandonbarrowscomics.com and on Twitter @Brandon Barrows

S.E Bailey's stories have appeared in the American magazines *Thuglit*, *Switchblade* and *Mystery Tribune* as well as the *Noirville* anthology from *Fahrenheit Press*. He's currently working on a historical crime fiction novel when he isn't toiling at the day job.

He also appears in *Crimeucopia – Say What Now?* with his piece, *Sureshot*.

Edward St. Boniface lives and works in London UK and writes across various genres including crime, Science Fiction & Fantasy and contemporary literary fiction. He's always interested in exploring an unusual angle to a story, and is keen to build up a readership. In addition to work freely available on his WATTPAD account he has also self-published several novels and surreal humour pieces available on Kindle.

He believes literature like all the arts should start from being Fun, and hopes you enjoyed his story.

Ed has recently had short stories published on the *Mystery Tribune* and *HalfHourToKill* websites, and hopes you will read his madness-inflected forays into Andy Warhol's bizarre counter-cultural milieu in *Factory Settings* https://mysterytribune.com/factory-settings-neo-noir-short-fiction-by-edward-st-boniface/ and the diminishing universe of a small and hollow man in *Penner Viscount-Alexander* https://halfhourtokill.com/home/penner-viscount-alexander-by-edward-st-boniface respectively! For Ed's works available on the Amazon websites, go to:

https://www.amazon.co.uk/Edward-St.-Boniface/e/B00JBCZMDS

Dan Cardoza's most recent darkness has been featured in *BlazeVOX, Black Petals, Blood Moon Rising, Bull, Cleaver, Close to the Bone, Dark City Books, Dark Dossier, Dissections, Door=Jar, Dream Noir, Horror Sleaze Trash, The Horror Zine, Mystery Tribune, Suspense Magazine, Schlock, The Yard Crime Blog, Variant,* and *The Five-2.*

Anthology appearances include: *Coffin Bell Two, Running Wild Press, Anthology of Stories, Vita Brevis Poetry, Pain & Renewal, Chilling Tales for Dark Nights, Audio Horror Anthology (13 stories).*

Dan has been nominated for *Best of the Net* and *Best Micro-Fiction.*

Sean Marciniak is a well-respected former crime and investigative reporter, originally based around the Texas borderlands. He has had various articles in *The Wall Street Journal, Dallas Morning News* and the *Houston Chronicle* – winning awards from both *The Associated Press,* along with *Bloomberg News.* His fiction has appeared in the *Best Mystery Stories of the Year, Shooter Literary Magazine, the Mystery Tribune,* and elsewhere. #HEIST is part of a novel that Sean is working on, which is close to completion.

Lynn Hesse is an award-winning author of the novels: *Well of Rage* (Murder in Mobile book 1), and *A Matter of Respect* (Murder in Mobile book 2), *Another Kind of Hero*, and *The Forty Knots Burn.*

Lynn's *Bitter Love* — a humorous view of a homicide detective having a lousy day, appeared in *Crimeucopia — The I's Have It.*

Jewel's Hell appears in the *Me Too Short Stories Anthology* (Level Best 2019)

Lynn left law enforcement to concentrate on her writing and lives with her husband and his six rescue cats near Atlanta, Georgia, USA, where she performs in several dance troupes.

Hernan Salvarezza is a blog post and article writer by day. He writes stories and reads the slush pile for a small press and an online magazine by night. He's been published by Altair Publishers Australia in The Worlds of Science Fiction, Fantasy, and Horror Volume 2 and 38 Caliber/Plentzia.

Follow him on Twitter: @Hsalvarezza — and on Facebook at https://www.facebook.com/hernan.salvarezza/

Investigators and investigations are the mainstay of most Crime fiction sub-genres. Everything from the original *Golden Age* of country houses and the amateur sleuth, through to the high tech ultra-modern 21st Century – a place where the cyber investigators sometimes appear to be baffled by old-fashioned motivations of power and greed, and human foibles such as love and revenge.

So is there any real difference between the Private and the Public Sector investigators? Not much, if writers are to be believed, and the two can often be found straddling both sides of the 'what's legal procedure?' fence.

Of the twelve authors contained within, eleven are voices new to the world of Crimeucopia - and although the theme is *Investigators*, the material ranges from Cosy, through to not too Hardboiled - and most are touched with a vein of humour, be it light or dark. Rather like a box of chocolates…

Paperback ISBN: 9781909498327   eBook ISBN: 9781909498334

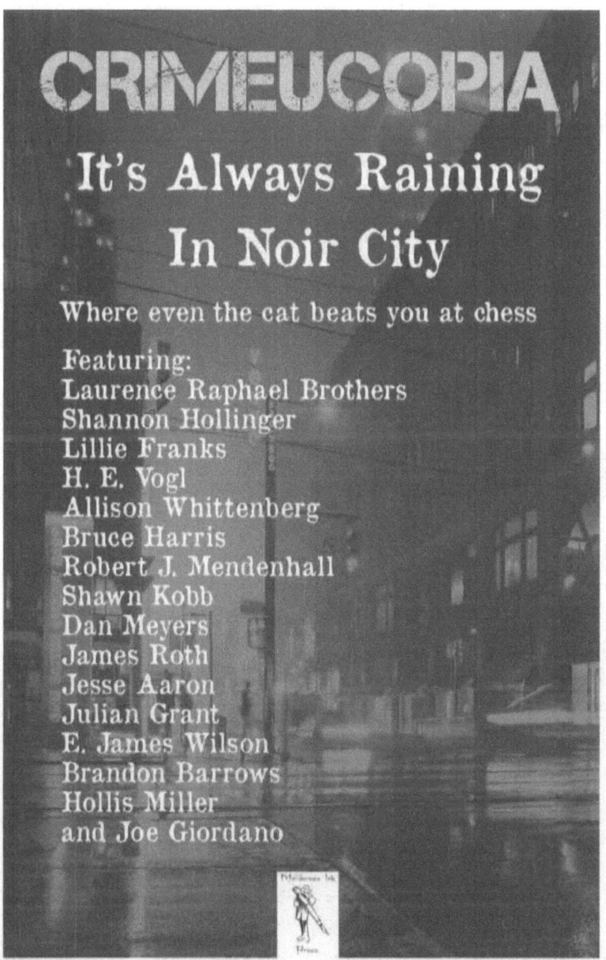

Is the Noir Crime sub-genre always dark and downbeat? Is there a time when Bad has a change of conscience, flips sides and takes on the Good role?

Noir is almost always a dish served up raw and bloody - Fiction bleu if you will. So maybe this is a chance to see if Noir can be served sunny side up - with the aid of these fifteen short order authors.

All fifteen give us dark tales from the stormy side of life - which is probably why it's *always* raining in Noir City....

Paperback Edition ISBN: 9781909498341
eBook Edition ISBN: 9781909498358

Small town, big city, watercooler or the back of that 1950s beat-up Chevy Bel Air with the leather back seat that your parents told you never to get familiar with. It doesn't matter where you hear it, gossip is 100% pure ear addiction – and knowledge is, after all, power when all's said and done.

So why don't you settle down, get yourself comfy, and pour yourself a drink – long and tall, or just short and nasty, the choice is yours – and let these 16 story tellers spin their tales as only they know how.

Paperback Edition ISBN: 9781909498365
eBook Edition ISBN: 9781909498372

CRIMEUCOPIA

When the theme is no theme at all, you've just got to ask the question

Say What Now?

Featuring:
Peter Ullian,
S. E. Bailey,
N. M. Cedeño,
Edward St Boniface,
Jan Glaz,
Eleanor Luke,
Momodou Bah,
Eve Fisher,
John M. Floyd,
Joan Leotta,
Glen Bush
and DL Shirey

Sometimes editors are forced to reject submissions through no fault of the author. It could be a wonderfully written manuscript, but if the editor cannot place it, then what do they do?

MIP has been lucky in its flexibility and its "Can we start a new project with this?" attitude. Some of the dozen authors contained within are seasoned professionals, having been published in the likes of Alfred Hitchcock's, Ellery Queen's, or other notable publications, while some are making their publishing debuts as Crimeucopians. And while the quality throughout remains exceedingly high, the subject spectrum is the widest we've published so far. But that's only fitting when you consider that the theme of this Crimeucopa is that of No Theme At All.

And in true Murderous Ink fashion, with a dozen authors to choose from, you're bound to find something you'll like, and something you didn't know you'd like until you've read it.

Paperback Edition ISBN: 9781909498389
eBook Edition ISBN: 9781909498396

This is the first of several 'Free 4 All' collections that was supposed to be themeless. However, with the number of submissions that came in, it seems that this could be called an *Angels & Devils* collection, mixing PI & Police alongside tales from the Devil's dining table. Mind you, that's not to say that all the PIs & Police are on the side of the Angels....

Also this time around has not only seen a move to a larger paperback format size, but also in regard to the length of the fiction as well. Followers of the somewhat bent and twisted Crimeucopia path will know that although we don't deal with Flash fiction as a rule, it is a rule that we have sometimes broken. And let's face it, if you cannot break your own rules now and again, whose rules can you break?

Oh, wait, isn't breaking the rules the foundation of the crime fiction genre?

Oh dear....

New Crimeucopians *Aran Myracle, Alexei J. Slater, Gerald Elias, Terry Wijesuriya, Issy Jinarmo, Larry Lefkowitz,* and *Vinnie Hansen* smoothly rub literary shoulders with a fine collection of familiar Crimeucopia old hands: *Bob Ritchie, Michele Bazan Reed, Nikki Knight, N. M. Cedeño, Wendy Harrison, Andrew Darlington, Madeleine McDonald, Joan Leotta, H. E. Vogl* and *Jesse Aaron.*

All 17 tell tales that will make you realise there's always going to be One More Thing To Worry About....

With 16 vibrant authors, a wraparound paperback cover, and pages full of crime fiction in some of its many guises, what's not to like?
So if you enjoy tales spun by
Anthony Diesso, Brandon Barrows, E. James Wilson, James Roth,
Jesse Aaron, Jim Guigli, John M. Floyd, Kevin R. Tipple, Maddi Davidson,
Michael Grimala, Robert Petyo, Shannon Hollinger, Tom Sheehan,
Wil A. Emerson, Peter Trelay, and Philip Pak
then you'd better get
CRIMEUCOPIA - Strictly Off The record
by the sound of it!